Dear Reader,

Thirty years ago I began my career by writing romances under several pseudonyms. These were stories of women and men who meet, fall in love despite the odds against them and endure the heartache and joy that is unique to that experience.

These stories reflect those classic themes, which have engaged and entertained audiences since storytelling first became a popular pastime. They have been reissued at your request and for your enjoyment. I hope you have as much fun reading them as I did writing them.

As in all romance novels, expect a happy ending....

Sandra Brown

D0451386

SANDRA BROWN

Honor Bound & Two Alone

Previously published under the pseudonym Erin St. Claire

ISBN-13: 978-0-7783-1515-5

HONOR BOUND & TWO ALONE

Copyright © 2010 by Harlequin Books S.A.

The publisher acknowledges the copyright holder of the individual works as follows:

HONOR BOUND
Copyright © 1986 by Sandra Brown

TWO ALONE
Copyright © 1987 by Erin St. Claire

Recycling programs
for this product may
not exist in your area.

For questions and comments about the quality of this book, please contact us at CustomerService@Harlequin.com.

HARLEQUIN®
www.Harlequin.com

Printed in U.S.A.

CONTENTS

HONOR BOUND

One

The refrigerator door was open, projecting a pale, blue-white wedge of light into the dark kitchen. A carton of milk was standing on the countertop. Beside it was a loaf of bread, gaping open, two slices lying half in, half out.

But even without those peculiarities, she instinctively knew the moment she came through her back door that something was amiss. She sensed another presence, dangerous and motionless, waiting.

Automatically she reached for the light switch.

Before her hand made contact, it was manacled by iron-hard fingers, twisted behind her and painfully shoved up between her shoulder blades. She opened her mouth to scream, but another hand, callused and tasting slightly of salt, clamped over her mouth, so that her scream came out only as a frantic, guttural sound, that of an animal entrapped.

She had always wondered how she would react in such a situation. If assaulted, would she faint? If her life were imperiled by an attacker, would she plead to be spared?

It came as a mild surprise, now, that besides being frightened she was angry. She began to struggle, trying to twist her head away from the unyielding hand over her mouth. She wanted to see her assailant's face. Get a description. Wasn't that what the rape-prevention centers advised? Look at his face.

Easier said than done, she realized. Struggling proved to be futile because of her attacker's strength. He was tall. That much she knew. She could feel his breath, ragged and hot, against the crown of her head. Occasionally her head bumped into his chin. So he must be well over six feet tall, she reasoned, and filed that bit of information away.

The body she was being held against was hard, but she wouldn't use "bulky" or "muscle-bound" in her description to the police. Indeed, it seemed to her that he was whipcord lean. From the corner of her eye, his biceps looked as firm and round as a green apple.

Her struggles were only succeeding in wearing her out. Rationalizing that she should conserve her energy and strength, she suddenly ceased her efforts to escape his inescapable hold and became still. Her breasts rose and fell with every insufficient breath she tried to draw through her nostrils. Gradually the arms restraining her relaxed, but only a trifle.

"My name is Lucas Greywolf."

A raspy voice, as soft and sandy as the wind that blew across the desert, spoke directly into her ear. It was a gentle sound, but Aislinn wasn't deceived. Like the winds it reminded her of, she thought, it could be whipped into a fury with the slightest provocation.

And considering the source of that whispery voice, such a whimsical shift was probable. Frightfully so.

The name Lucas Greywolf had been repeated over television signals and radio frequencies throughout the day. Last night the Indian activist had escaped from the federal prison camp in Florence, about fifty miles away. Law-enforcement agencies were combing the state in search of the escaped convict.

. And he was in her kitchen!

"I need food. Rest. I won't hurt you if you cooperate," he growled close to her ear. "If you even try to scream I'll be forced to gag you. Do we have a bargain?"

She nodded once in agreement and the hand came away from her mouth cautiously. As soon as it was removed, she gasped for air. "How did you get here?"

"On foot, mostly," he replied, without elaboration or apparent concern. "You know who I am?"

"Yes. They're looking all over for you."

"I know."

Her initial anger had dissipated. She wasn't a coward, but she wasn't a fool either. Heroics had their place, but now wasn't the time to start playing Wonder Woman. This intruder was no petty thief. Lucas Greywolf should be considered dangerous. All the news reports said so.

What was she to do? Overpowering him was unthinkable. He'd have no difficulty subduing her, and in the process she would probably get hurt. No, the only way she could possibly hope to outmaneuver him was by using her wits, while waiting for an opportunity to escape.

"Sit down." He nudged her shoulder roughly.

Without argument, she went to the table in the center of the kitchen, laid her purse on it and pulled out a chair. She lowered herself into the seat carefully.

He moved as silently as smoke and as nimbly as a shadow. She hadn't heard him cross the floor, and only knew that he had when his shadow stretched across the tabletop. Timorously lifting her eyes, she saw his silhouette looming in the eerie light of the open refrigerator door. Like a panther, he looked dark and lean and lethal when he crouched down and took a summer sausage from the meat drawer.

Apparently believing that she had capitulated, he negligently closed the refrigerator door. The kitchen went dark. She lunged from her chair, aiming for the back door. He caught up with her before she had taken two steps, bisecting her middle with a steely arm to anchor her against him.

"Where do you think you're going?"

"To...to turn on the light."

"Sit down."

"The neighbors will know—"

"I told you to sit down. And until I tell you otherwise, that's what you're going to do." He hauled her across the kitchen and pushed her into the chair. It was so dark that she didn't quite make the seat's center and nearly toppled out of it before regaining her balance.

"I'm only trying to help you," she said. "The neighbors will know something is wrong if they saw me come in and I don't turn on any lights."

Her threat was an empty one, and she rather imagined he knew it. She lived in a new condominium complex on the outskirts of Scottsdale. Fewer than half the units had been sold. No doubt he had selected her house for pilfering because of its remote location.

She heard a metallic whispering noise coming out of the darkness. The sinister sound filled her with dread. She knew the terror of a small jungle animal when rustling leaves alert it that an unseen predator is nearby. Lucas Greywolf had spotted the rack of butcher knives on the countertop near the sink and had slipped one from the wooden scabbard.

Expecting any moment to feel its cold metal edge slicing across her throat, she was stunned but at least grateful that she was still alive when the kitchen light came on, momentarily blinding her. She adjusted her eyes to the sudden brightness. He was still holding the long, gleaming silver blade of the knife to the light switch.

From that intimidating sight, her eyes tracked the length of a brown, sinewy arm up to a curved shoulder, over to a determined, square chin, along a straight, narrow nose, and into the most chilling pair of eyes she'd ever seen.

All her life she'd heard the expression "heart-stopping." Countless times she had casually used the adjective herself, describing any number of inconsequential things. But she'd never actually experienced that graphically descriptive sensation. Until now.

Never had a pair of eyes conveyed such unmitigated contempt, such uncompromising hatred and undiluted bitterness.

Unlike the rest of his features, which were clearly American Indian, his eyes belonged to an Anglo. They were gray, so light a gray they were almost transparent, which only made the pupils in their centers look even deeper and blacker. They seemed to have no necessity to blink, because they stared at her without movement. Set in that dark, brooding face, those steadfast, gray eyes were a startling contrast that held her attention far too long.

She lowered her eyes, but when she saw the knife flash, she fearfully jerked them back up to him. He had merely sliced off a disk of summer sausage. As he raised it to his lips, the hard, set line lifted at one corner to form a smirking smile before straight, white teeth bit into the meat. He was enjoying her fear and that made her furious. By an act of will, she rid her face of any telltale expression and surveyed him coolly.

Which might have been a mistake.

Before tonight, if she had been asked to conjure up a picture of an escaped convict, it would never have resembled Lucas Greywolf. She vaguely remembered reading about his trial when it was making the news, but that had been several years ago. She recalled the prosecutors making him out to be a chronic troublemaker and rabble-rouser, a dissident who went around spreading malcontent among the Indians. But had the reports ever mentioned him being so handsome? If they had, she hadn't been paying attention.

He was dressed in a blue chambray shirt that was no doubt prison issue. The sleeves had been ripped out, leaving ragged, stringy armholes. One of the sleeves had been fashioned into a headband, tied Apache-style around his head to hold back hair so unrelievedly black that it barely reflected the light shining directly on it. But then the dust clinging to it might have been partly responsible for that dull finish; his jeans and boots were covered with it.

Around his waist he wore a belt made of intricately worked silver set with chunks of turquoise. Dangling from a chain worn around his neck was a silver Christian cross. The charm nestled in a thatch of dark hair on his chest. He wasn't pure Indian.

Again she let her eyes fall away. Under the circumstances, it disturbed her deeply that the sweat-stained shirt was open almost to his narrow waist. It was equally disturbing that the earring in his right ear didn't repel her.

The tiny silver kachina mask represented a spirit of another religion and was incongruent with the cross worn around his neck. Yet if Greywolf had been born with that earring pierced into his earlobe, it couldn't have looked more in keeping with the total aspect of the man he was.

"Won't you join me?" he asked in a taunting voice, holding out a slice of sausage on the blade of the knife.

She lifted her head and thrust her chin out defiantly. "No thank you. I'll wait to eat dinner with my husband."

"Your husband?"

"Yes."

"Where is he?"

"At work, but he'll be home at any moment."

He tore off a bite of bread from the slice he raised to his mouth and chewed it with an unconcerned leisure that made her want to slap him. "You're a terrible liar."

"I'm not lying."

He swallowed. "I searched the house before you came home, Miss Aislinn Andrews. There's no man living here."

Now it was her turn to swallow, and she did so with great difficulty. She willed her heart to settle down and stop drumming against her ribs with mounting anxiety. Her palms were perspiring. She pressed them together beneath the table. "How did you know my name?"

"Your mail."

"You went through my mail?"

"You sound alarmed. Do you have something to hide, Miss Andrews?" She refused to be baited and kept her lips firmly closed over the vituperative rejoinder that pressed against them from the inside. "You got a telephone bill today."

His sly grin set off her temper again. "They'll catch you and send you back."

"Yes, I know."

His calm response rendered her mute and made the threatening, argumentative speech she was about to voice unnecessary. Instead she watched him raise the carton of milk to his mouth, tilt his head back and drink thirstily.

His neck was deeply tanned. The sliding action of his Adam's apple intrigued her as a hypnotist's pendulum would. He drank until there was no more, then set the empty carton down and wiped his mouth with the back of the hand that still held the knife.

"If you know they'll catch you, why make it harder on yourself?" She asked out of a sincere curiosity to know. "Why not just turn yourself in?"

"Because there is something I have to do first," he said grimly. "Before it's too late."

She didn't pursue her question further, because she thought it might jeopardize her well-being to know what criminal acts he was contemplating. However, if she could get him to talk, maybe he would relax his guard and she could make a dash for the back door. Then once in the garage, she would hit the button that raised the automatic door and...

"How did you get in?" she asked abruptly, realizing for the first time that there had been no visible signs of forced entry.

"Through a bedroom window."

"And how did you escape from the prison camp?"

"I deceived someone who trusted me." His hard mouth curled derisively. "Of course he was a fool to trust an Indian. Everybody knows Indians are untrustworthy. Right, Miss Andrews?"

"I don't know any Indians," she answered softly, not wanting to provoke him. She disliked the way his taut body seemed about to snap with tension.

But by trying not to aggravate him, she only seemed to have aroused his temper. His eyes pored over her slowly, spilling heat on everything they touched. She was made painfully aware of her blondness, her blue eyes and fair skin. His sneer deepened into a scowl. "No, I don't suppose you do." Faster than her eyes could monitor the motion, he crammed the knife into his waistband and reached for her. "Get up."

"Why?" She gasped with fright as he roughly pulled her to her feet. Holding her back against his chest, with his hands on her shoulders, he propelled her out of the kitchen. On their way through the door, he switched off the light. The hallway was dark. She stumbled ahead of him. He was going toward the bedroom and her mouth went dry with fear. "You got what you came for."

"Not all of it."

"You said you wanted food," she countered frantically, digging her heels into the carpet. "If you leave now, I promise not to call the police."

"Now why don't I believe you, Miss Andrews?" he asked in a voice as smooth as melting ice cream.

"I swear it!" she cried, despising her weakness and the panicked sound of her voice.

"Promises have been made to me before by white men...and white women. I've learned to be skeptical."

"But *I* had nothing to do with that. I—oh, God, what are you going to do?"

He shoved her into the bedroom. As soon as he had cleared the door, he closed it behind them. "Take a wild guess, Miss Andrews." He spun her around and pinned her between the door and his unyielding body. He closed his hand around her throat just under her chin and bent his head down low over hers. "What do you think I'm going to do?"

"I...I...don't know."

"You're not one of these sexually repressed ladies who entertain rape fantasies, are you? Hmm?"

"No!" she gasped.

"You've never fantasized about being taken by a savage?"

"Let me go, please."

She turned her head away and he let her, but he didn't release her. If anything, he moved nearer, lewdly pressing himself against her, holding her against the door with his hardness and strength.

Aislinn squeezed her eyes shut and bit her lower lip in fear and humiliation. His long, tapering fingers strummed her throat, moving up and down in an evocative rhythm.

"Well I *have* been in prison for a long, long time." His fingers slid down her chest. He hooked his index finger on the top button of her blouse, then fiddled with it until it popped open. She whimpered. His face was so close to hers that she could feel his breath falling warmly on her skin. It struck her cheeks, her nose, her mouth. She inhaled it by necessity, hating the forced intimacy of breathing the air he expelled.

"So if you're real smart," he warned silkily, "you won't give me any ideas."

When she realized what he was telling her, her eyes sprang up to meet his. They clashed, a meeting of wills and a battle of tempers. For a long moment they seemed suspended, taking each other's measure, analyzing the strengths and weaknesses.

Then gradually he pulled back. When his body was no longer making contact with hers, she almost sank to the floor with relief.

"I told you I needed food and *rest*." There was a strange new quality to his voice now. A gruffness.

"You've rested."

"Sleep, Miss Andrews. I need sleep."

"You mean...you intend to stay? Here?" she asked, aghast. "For how long?"

"Until I decide to leave," he answered obliquely. He crossed the room and turned on the lamp beside her bed.

"You can't!"

He returned to where she still stood by the door and took her hand. This time he pulled her along behind him. "You're hardly in a position to argue. Just because I haven't harmed you yet doesn't mean that I won't if I'm desperate enough."

"I'm not afraid of you."

"Yes you are." He dragged her into the adjoining bathroom with him and slammed the door. "Or you should be. Look, get this straight," he said through clenched teeth, "I have something to do, and nothing, especially not an Anglo princess like you, is going to stop me from doing it. I knocked a guard unconscious to escape prison and I made it this far on foot; I have nothing to lose but my life, and it ain't worth a damn where I've been. So don't press your luck, lady. You've got me as a houseguest for as long as I want to stay." To punctuate his threat, he yanked the knife out of his waistband.

She sucked in a sharp breath as though he had pricked her belly button with the tip of the blade. "That's more like it," he said, gauging her fear. "Now sit down." He hitched his chin toward the commode. Aislinn, keeping her eyes trained on the knife, backed up until she bumped into the bathroom fixture and then collapsed onto its lid.

Greywolf laid the knife on the edge of the bathtub, well out of her reach. He pulled off his boots and socks, then began tugging the tail of his tattered shirt from the waistband of his jeans. Aislinn, sitting as motionless as a statue, said nothing as he peeled it off his shoulders and shrugged out of it.

The center of his chest was smattered with dark hair. The brown skin was stretched tightly over curved muscles that looked incredibly hard. His nipples were small and dark. The skin of his belly was stretched as taut as a trampoline, and the shallow part of it around his navel was dusted with black hair. The crinkly fan narrowed into a sleek stripe that disappeared into his jeans.

He began unbuckling the silver belt at his waist. "What are you doing?" Aislinn asked in alarm.

"I'm going to take a shower." He undid the belt, letting it hang open as he bent toward the taps in the bathtub. He turned them until water was gushing from the faucet full blast. Even over that roaring sound, Aislinn heard the rasp of his jeans' zipper as he lowered it.

"Where I can *see* you?" she cried.

"Where I can see *you*." He calmly pushed the jeans down past his hips and buttocks and stepped out of them.

Aislinn's eyes closed. She was overcome by a wave of vertigo and gripped the lid of the commode beneath her to keep from swaying. Never in her life had she been so outraged, so insulted, so assaulted.

Because to look at his nakedness was to be assaulted by masculinity incarnate. He was perfectly proportioned. His shoulders were broad, his chest deep. His limbs were long and leanly muscled, testimonies to agility and strength. Where his skin was smooth, it looked like polished bronze, yet alive and supple. Where it was hair-dusted, it looked warm and touch-inviting.

He raised the lever of the shower and stepped beneath its powerful spray. He didn't draw the curtain. Keeping her head averted, Aislinn drew in several restorative breaths.

"What's wrong, Miss Andrews? Haven't you ever seen

a naked man before? Or is it seeing a naked Indian that has you so visibly upset?"

She whipped her head around, stung by his mocking tone. She wouldn't have him thinking she was either a prudish old maid or a racial bigot. But her verbal barb died unspoken on her tongue. She was unable to utter a sound, paralyzed by the sight of his lathered hands as they slid over his sleek nakedness. The water must have been hot, for the mirrors were fogging up and the atmosphere was as steamy as an Erskine Caldwell novel. The mist settled on her own skin. She could barely draw the heavy, sultry air into her lungs.

"As you can see," he taunted as his soapy hands slid to the lower part of his body, "we're equipped just like any other man."

Well, not quite, Aislinn thought with a secret part of her mind, as her eyes took one forbidden glance down his torso to where that beautiful body hair provided a dense, lush base for his impressive manhood.

"You're crude," she said scathingly, "as well as being criminal."

He smiled cynically and whipped off the makeshift headband, tossing it out of the tub and down on top of his other clothes. He ducked his head under the shower's spray just long enough to moisten it, then picked up a bottle of shampoo. He sniffed the top of it before pouring a dollop of the creamy stuff into his hand, slapping it to the top of his head and lathering it into a white foam that soon coated the ebony strands of his hair. He scrubbed mercilessly.

"This smells better than prison shampoo," he remarked as he ran his fingers through the luxuriant lather.

Aislinn said nothing because a plan was formulating in her mind. If he had put his head under the shower nozzle to wet his hair, he'd have to put it under there longer to rinse all the shampoo off, wouldn't he? She didn't have long to think her plan through. Already he was squeezing the suds out of his hair and slinging them off his fingers into the water that swirled around his feet.

There was a telephone on the nightstand beside her bed. If she could dash through the bathroom door and manage to dial the emergency number before—

He plunged his head beneath the shower's nozzle. There was no more time to ruminate.

Aislinn hurled herself toward the door, pulled it open, almost wrenching her arm from its socket in the process, and flew into the bedroom. She reached the nightstand in less than a second, grabbed up the telephone receiver and began frantically punching out the sequence of numbers she had memorized.

She pressed the receiver against her ear and waited for the ring. Nothing happened. *Damn!*

In her haste, had she punched a wrong number?

She clicked the disconnect button and tried again, her hands shaking so badly she could barely hold the receiver. Risking one frenzied glance over her shoulder, she was dismayed to see Lucas Greywolf framed in the doorway between the bedroom and bathroom, his shoulder propped against it in a stance of lazy indifference.

A towel was draped around his neck. Other than that, he was naked. Water dripped from his wet hair and funnelled down his coppery body. Beads of it clung to places she wished she didn't notice. He held the wicked knife in his right hand, idly tapping the flat side of the blade against his bare thigh.

Aislinn realized that the second telephone call hadn't

gone through either and that no other calls were going to go through. "You did something to my phone." It wasn't a question.

"As soon as I entered the house."

Rapidly, her hands moving end over end, she reeled the telephone cord up from behind the nightstand. The connector that normally fit into the wall outlet had been ruined, ground by a boot heel as best as she could tell.

Frustration overcame her then. And fury. It enraged her that he could appear so composed when she felt ineffectual and idiotic. She cursed and threw the telephone toward him, then launched herself toward the door, seeking escape at all costs. It was hopeless, of course, but she had to do *something*.

She managed to reach the door; she even managed to get it open a crack before his wide hand splayed over it directly in front of her face and shoved it closed again. She turned, her fingers curled into claws, bent on attacking him.

"Stop it!" he commanded and grabbed for her flailing arms. The knife nicked her on the forearm. She screamed softly in pain. "You little fool."

He grunted with surprise when she drove her knee up toward his crotch. She missed her mark, but succeeded in unbalancing him as he made a dodging movement. They fell to the floor, struggling. His skin was still wet, slippery, and he easily deflected the blows and slaps she frantically delivered. In seconds, he had her pinned beneath him, her wrists stapled to the floor by his widespread fingers.

"What the hell was that for? You could have gotten hurt," he barked. His face was a scant few inches above hers. His chest was heaving in and out from exertion. The anger in his eyes struck terror in Aislinn, but she didn't let it show. Instead, she glared up at him.

"If you're going to kill me, get it over with," she ground out.

She had no time to prepare herself before he jerked her to her feet. Her teeth clicked together. She was still trying to regain her equilibrium when she saw the knife arcing down toward the side of her face. She felt a rush of wind as it passed. She tried to scream, but the sound became a faint little whimper when she saw the lock of her hair dangling from his hand. The wavy blond strand of hair being squeezed between those hard brown fingers symbolized her frailty and emphasized how easily his strength could overpower it.

"I meant what I said, lady," he said, still breathing heavily. "I have nothing else to lose. You pull one more stunt like that and it'll be more than your hair I'll use this knife on. Understand?"

Eyes round and gaping at the strand of curling blond hair still clasped between his fingers, Aislinn nodded dumbly. He opened his fingers and let the light-catching strands of hair filter to the floor.

Accepting her acquiescence, he stepped away from her and retrieved the towel. He dried the remaining moisture from his skin and made a pass over his chin-length hair. He tossed the towel to her. "Your arm is bleeding."

She hadn't noticed. Looking down, she was surprised to see a thin trickle of blood oozing from the nick just above her wrist. "Are you hurt anywhere else?" She shook her head no. "Get over there by the bed."

Fear tamped her resentment at being ordered around in her own house by a fugitive from justice. Without a murmur of protest, she obeyed him. The bleeding on her arm had stopped. She laid the towel aside and turned to face her captor.

"Take off your clothes."

She had thought he couldn't frighten her any more than he already had. She was gravely mistaken. "What?" she wheezed.

"You heard me."

"No."

"Unless you do as I say, that cut on your arm is only a beginning." The naked steel blade of the knife glinted in the lamplight as he waved it back and forth in front of her face.

"I don't think you'd hurt me."

"Don't bet on it."

Cold, unfeeling eyes glittered back at her defiant stare, and she admitted that the odds for her to remain untouched and unscathed through this night didn't look good.

"Why…why do I have to take off my…my…?"

"Do you really want to know?"

No, she didn't think she wanted it spelled out for her because she had a pretty good idea why, and somehow hearing his intent from his own lips only made the prospect more frightening.

"But if you were going to rape me," she said, speaking aloud the question her musings raised, "why didn't you—"

"Take off your clothes."

He pronounced each word carefully. They fell from his stern lips like chips of ice.

She considered her options and decided that she had none. At least if she went along with him, she was granting herself time. Perhaps someone would try to call and find that her phone was out of order. The telephone company would send someone to check, wouldn't they? Someone might come to her door. The paperboy for instance. Anything was possible if she could just keep stalling him. For all she knew the police could have the house surrounded right now, having tracked Greywolf there.

Slowly she raised her hands to the second button of her blouse, the first already having been opened by him. She cast one last, pleading glance toward him. His face could have been carved from stone, his eyes formed from hardest crystal for all the humanity they conveyed. Pride kept her from begging, though she didn't think any amount of pleading would budge this emotionless man.

She pushed the button through its hole and reluctantly lowered her hand to the next.

"Hurry up."

She looked up at him where he stood naked and sinister only a few feet from her. He remained impassive under her seething gaze. She took her time with every single button, testing the perimeters of his patience, until all were undone.

"Now take it off." He made a brusque gesture with the knife. Lowering her head, Aislinn slipped the blouse from her shoulders, but held it up against her chest. "Drop it." Still not looking at him, she let the garment slide away from her body and onto the floor.

After a long silence, he said, "Now the rest of it."

It was summertime in Arizona. She had closed her studio early that afternoon because she had no appointments scheduled. After a workout at the health club, she had slipped on a skirt, blouse and barefoot sandals, not wanting to put on stockings.

"The skirt, Aislinn," he said with tense emphasis.

His use of her first name was the supreme insult under the circumstances and it fueled her anger. Reaching behind her, she virtually ripped the hook on her skirt open, and let it fall from her hips in a show of defiance.

At his strangled sound, she raised her eyes. The skin over his high cheekbones seemed to be stretched so tight she thought it might split. His eyes were moving over her like flickering torches.

She wished her lingerie was plainer, less alluring. The silk bra and panty set was the color of lemon sherbet and was trimmed in dove-gray lace. While they weren't sheer, they were designed for brevity and prettiness, not functionality. They left nothing to the imagination, and a man who had been in prison would have a well-developed imagination.

"The bra."

Trying to stem hot tears she was too proud to shed, Aislinn slipped down the lacy straps, drawing her arms through them and holding the fragile cups over her breasts before unfastening the front clasp. Greywolf extended his hand. Aislinn jumped reflexively.

"Hand it to me," he said hoarsely.

Her hand was trembling as she passed the flimsy piece of silk and lace to him. The garment seemed even less substantial when his fist closed around it and, held in that patently masculine hand, far more feminine. He fingered the soft fabric. Knowing that it would still hold the heat of her body, Aislinn experienced a funny feeling deep inside her as she watched his fingers rubbing the soft cloth.

"Silk," he murmured in a low, growling sound. He lifted the bra to his face and crushed it against his nose. He groaned, closing his eyes, briefly making a fierce grimace of his face. "That smell. That wonderful, woman smell."

Aislinn realized then that he wasn't talking to her. He was talking to himself. He wasn't even talking about her. Particularly. Any woman would have done. She didn't know whether to be terrified or comforted by that thought.

The poignant moment lasted only a few seconds before he tossed the bra down with an angry flourish of his hand. "Come on. Finish."

"No. You'll have to kill me."

He looked at her for an agonizingly long time. Aislinn couldn't bear to watch his eyes moving over her, so she closed hers.

"You're very beautiful." She braced herself for his touch. It never came. Instead, he spun away from her, apparently vexed, either over her stubborn resistance or the vulnerability he had inadvertently expressed.

Whatever it was had made him exceedingly angry. He pulled several drawers in her dresser from their moorings before he found what he was short-temperedly searching for. He came toward her with two pairs of panty hose.

"Lie down." Reaching around Aislinn, who stood rooted to the spot in terror, he flung back the covers on her bed.

She lay down, her body stiff with fright, her eyes wide as he knelt over her. But he wasn't even looking at her. His face was set in tense, remote lines as he reached for her arm and pulled it back toward the rails of her brass headboard.

"You're tying me up?" she asked tremulously.

"Yes," he answered curtly, pulling the nylon tight around her wrist and securing it to the rail.

"My God." A hundred hideous nightmares flitted through her brain. Every deviate practice she'd ever heard about, she was reminded of now.

His mouth tilted into another of those sardonic smiles, as though he had read her mind and seen her fears.

"Relax, Miss Andrews. I told you I wanted food and rest and that's what I intend to get."

Still frozen with shock and fear, Aislinn lay docile as he bound her other wrist to his, using the second pair of panty hose. When they were tied to each other, the backs of their hands pressing together, she stared up at him with incredulity. He merely snapped off the lamp and lay down beside her, his back to her.

"You bastard." She tugged hard on the fetter that tied her to him. "Untie me."

"Go to sleep."

"I said to untie me," she shouted, trying to sit up. He rolled over and yanked her back down. Though she couldn't see him in the darkness, the body lying so close to hers communicated a terrible menace that was more repressive than sheer force.

"I had no choice but to tie you up."

"Why did you have me undress?"

"To make it more difficult for you to escape. I seriously doubt you'd go chasing out into the night as you are. And—"

"And what?" she asked angrily.

After a slight pause his reply came through the darkness like a stealthy, sensuous, black cat—anticipated, but unseen until it's there. "And because I wanted to look at you."

Two

"**G**et up."

She pried her eyes open reluctantly, unable to remember why she dreaded waking up. Then her shoulder was roughly shaken and she was reminded. Her eyes popped open. Coming to a half-sitting position, holding the blanket over her naked body, she shoved the disheveled hair out of her eyes and looked up into Lucas Greywolf's remote features.

It had taken her hours to fall asleep, hours in which she had lain there beside him listening to his rhythmic breathing, knowing that he was fast asleep. She had struggled to release her arm from the headboard until her entire body ached with the futile effort. Cursing him, she had finally surrendered and relaxed enough to get her eyes to close. After that, her body had taken over and she had fallen asleep.

"Get up," he repeated tersely. "And get dressed. We're leaving."

Both pairs of stockings, the one that had bound her to the headboard and the one that had bound her to the man, were lying across the foot of the bed. Sometime earlier he had freed her. Why hadn't she awakened then? Was his touch that deft and light? And now, too, she vaguely remembered being uncomfortably cold in the early morning hours. Had he covered her? It made her insides tremble to think so.

She was relieved to see that he was already dressed in the dusty clothes he had shed the previous night, before availing himself of her shower. The ripped-out sleeve of his shirt had been replaced by one of her own cotton bandannas to serve as his headband. His earring and neck chain were still there, gleaming against his bronzed skin. She could smell her shampoo in his raven-black hair.

No, she hadn't imagined him. Lucas Greywolf was very real and embodied everything that women had nightmares about...or dreamed of.

She snapped her mind back to attention. "Leaving? Where? I'm not going anywhere with you."

His dismissive air indicated just how much credence he placed in her protest. He opened her closet and began riffling through the hangers. Designer dresses and silk blouses were bypassed in favor of a pair of old jeans and a casual shirt. He tossed them across the bed toward her.

Bending at the waist, he examined several pairs of shoes before selecting a pair of low-heeled boots. He carried them toward the bed and dropped them on the floor. "You can either dress yourself or—" he paused while his light gray eyes traveled over her form beneath the covers "—I can dress you. Either way, we leave here in five minutes."

His stance was bold: thighs widespread, chest out, chin high. Arrogance was stamped all over his classic American face. Self-confidence emanated from him like the musky scent of his skin.

Meekly yielding to such raw audacity was untenable to Aislinn Andrews.

"Why can't you just leave me here?"

"Stupid question, Aislinn, and unworthy of you."

She conceded that. As soon as he was out of sight, she'd run screaming down the street until somebody heard her. The authorities would be on his trail before he got to the city limits.

"You're my insurance policy. Every jailbreaker worth his salt takes a hostage." He took a step closer to her. "And my patience with my hostage is wearing thin. Get your butt out of that damn bed!" he thundered.

Though it galled, she prudently obeyed, dragging the covers with her. "At least have the decency to turn your back while I dress."

One of his brows, sleek and black and shaped like an inverted V, arched slightly. "You're asking a noble gesture from an Indian?"

"I have no racial prejudices."

He looked at her tumbled blond hair and smirked with derision. "No, I don't suppose you do, because I doubt if you even knew we were out there." Then he turned on his heel and left the room.

She took umbrage at the insult and angrily pulled on the clothes he had selected. She had found a bra and a pair of panties in the piles of clothes he had left on the floor after vandalizing her drawers the night before.

As soon as she had snapped the jeans on, she rushed toward the window and opened the shutters. She reached for the lock and twisted it open, but a hard brown arm came around from behind her. Strong fingers formed a vise around her wrist.

"I'm getting tired of these little games, Aislinn."

"And I'm getting tired of you manhandling me," she

cried, trying to wrest her arm free. He let go of her only after he had relocked the window and closed the shutters. Resentfully, she massaged the circulation back into her wrist as she glared up at him. She had always despised bullies.

"Listen, lady, if I didn't need you as protection to get where I'm going, I wouldn't give you the time of day. So don't flatter yourself." He spun her around and, placing his hand in the small of her back, gave her a hefty shove. "Get going."

He led her into the kitchen where he picked up a Thermos and a grocery sack.

"I see you made yourself right at home," she said snidely. Inwardly she was cursing herself for sleeping so soundly. She might have made good her escape through the bedroom window while he was brewing coffee and looting her pantry.

"Where we're going, you'll be glad to have the provisions."

"And where is that?"

"Where the other half lives."

He didn't expand on that, but, with his hand securely around her upper arm, he led Aislinn into the garage. After opening the passenger door of her car, he shoved her inside, then went around and slid behind the steering wheel. He placed the Thermos and grocery sack on the seat between them. Reaching beneath the seat for the lever, he adjusted the seat back as far as it would go to accommodate his long legs. Using the electronic transmitter that always lay on her dashboard, he raised the garage door. Once he had backed the car out, he closed the door the same way. At the end of her street, he skillfully maneuvered her car into the flow of traffic on the boulevard.

"How long will I be gone?" she asked. Her question was casual and out of keeping with her busy eyes.

He didn't stay close to another car long enough for her to make eye contact with either the driver or passengers. There were no police cars in sight. Greywolf was driving carefully and well within the speed limit. He was no fool.

Nor was he talkative. He offered no answer to her question. "I'll be missed, you know. I have a business to run. When I don't show up for work, people will start looking for me."

"Pour me a cup of coffee."

Her mouth fell open at the imperious way he issued orders, as though he were the big bad brave and she his squaw. "Go to hell."

"Pour me a cup of coffee."

Had he shouted at her, flown into a fit of temper, she might have met him nose to nose. But the words left his mouth quietly, like serpents slithering from a cave. They sent chills down her spine. He hadn't hurt her so far, but he was a dangerous man. The kitchen knife was still tucked into his waistband. One look into the hard gray eyes that left the road long enough to nail her to the car seat convinced her that he was an enemy to be reckoned with.

She found two foam cups in the sack he had brought with them. Carefully she poured him half a cup of steaming, fragrant coffee from the Thermos and passed it to him. He didn't thank her, but sipped from the cup, squinting his eyes against the vapor that rose out of it.

Without asking his permission, she poured another cup for herself before recapping the Thermos. She stared down into the coffee as she rolled the cup between her palms and tried to imagine what his plans for her were.

She was concentrating so hard that she jumped when he suddenly spoke.

"What kind of business?"

"What?"

"You said you have a business to run."

"Oh, a photography studio."

"You take pictures?"

"Yes, portraits basically. Brides. Babies. Graduates. That kind of thing."

If he understood, approved, or disapproved, he kept it a secret. His chiseled profile revealed nothing. Granted, her work was nothing to get excited about, she thought with an inward sigh.

When she had graduated from college with a journalism degree, she had had aspirations to set the world on fire with her provocative photojournalism, to travel the globe capturing flame, famine and flood on film. She had wanted to evoke intense emotions such as anger, love and pity with each photograph.

But her parents had had vastly different plans for their only child. Willard Andrews was a prominent businessman in Scottsdale. His wife, Eleanor, was a society queen bee. Their daughter was expected to do the "suitable" thing, that being to amuse herself with suitable projects until she decided to marry a suitable young man. There were any number of clubs she could join, any number of committees she could chair. Charity work was permissible, so long as it didn't entail getting personally involved.

A career, especially one as gritty as traveling to remote parts of the world to take pictures of things too horrid to discuss at dinner parties, certainly didn't fit into her parents' plans for her. After months of endless argument, they finally wore her down and she bowed to their will.

As a concession, her father bankrolled a photography

studio where Aislinn could take vapid portraits of her parents' friends and their offspring. It wasn't a bad occupation; it was just a far cry from the meaningful work she had always wanted to do.

She wondered what her parents would say now if they could see her in the company of Lucas Greywolf and she was unable to withhold a laugh that bubbled up from her throat.

"Do you find the situation amusing?" he asked.

"Not at all amusing," she replied, becoming serious again. "Why don't you let me go?"

"I didn't intend to take a hostage. I intended to eat your food, avail myself of your house for a few hours' rest, and then leave. But you came in and caught me plundering your kitchen. Now I have no choice but to take you with me." He glanced at her before adding, "Actually I *do* have a choice, but I'm no murderer. At least not yet."

She suddenly lost her desire for the coffee. Instead the acrid taste of fear filled her mouth. "Do you plan to kill me?"

"Not unless you give me no choice."

"I'll fight you every step of the way."

"In that case we might have difficulties."

"Then I wish you'd go ahead and do it. The anticipation you're putting me through is cruel."

"So is prison."

"What did you expect?"

"I've learned to expect little."

"It's certainly not my fault you went to prison. You commit a crime, you pay for it."

"And just what was my 'crime'?"

"I…I don't recall. Something to do with—"

"I organized a demonstration at the courthouse in Phoenix. It resulted in violence, injury to police officers and damages to federal property." He said it in a way that made her think he wasn't confessing, but only quoting verbatim what he'd heard repeated numerous times. "But I think my real crime was being born an Indian."

"That's ridiculous. You have no one to blame for your misfortune but yourself, Mr. Greywolf."

His tight grin was mirthless. "I believe the judge said something to that effect when he sentenced me."

They lapsed into a silence that lasted until she ventured to ask, "How long have you been in prison?"

"Thirty-four months."

"And how long did you have to go?"

"Three months."

"Three months!" She was dismayed. "You escaped when you only had three months left on your sentence?"

His eyes sliced across the front seat of the car toward her. "I told you there is something I have to do and nothing is going to stop me."

"But if they catch you—"

"They'll catch me."

"Then why are you doing this?"

"I told you I had to."

"Nothing could be this important."

"It is."

"They'll tack months, possibly years, onto your sentence."

"Yes."

"Doesn't that mean anything to you?"

"No."

"But you're throwing away years of your life. Think of all the things you're giving up."

"Like a woman."

The three words were spoken shortly and, like tiny bullets, put her sermon to death. She closed her mouth quickly, wise enough to keep silent on this particular subject.

Neither spoke, yet their thoughts were running along the same channels. From different perspectives each was remembering the events of the night before. Aislinn didn't want to acknowledge her disturbing memories—Greywolf standing in the doorway of the bathroom, naked and wet, his very indolence a threat. Or pressing her bra to his face, inhaling her scent with such carnal greed. Or untying her and covering her when she wasn't aware of it. The thoughts were stifling; she felt suffocated by them, by his nearness.

Finally she shut him out in the only way she could. She closed her eyes and rested her head on the back of the seat.

"Dammit!"

She must have been dozing. Aislinn awoke abruptly with Greywolf's curse. He pounded the steering wheel with his right fist.

"What is it?" she asked, sitting up straight and blinking her eyes against the afternoon sunlight.

"Roadblock," Greywolf said, his lips barely moving.

Through the heat waves shimmering above the stretch of highway, Aislinn saw that state patrol cars had blocked off the highway. Officers were stopping each vehicle before letting it pass.

Before she could even register what a welcome sight that was, Greywolf pulled her car onto the shoulder of the highway and shoved the gear shift into Park. In one lithe movement, he straddled the console, crouched over her, and unbuttoned her blouse, working the cups of her bra down over the mounds of her breasts.

"What are you doing?" she gasped, swatting at his

hands. At first she'd been groggy from her nap, then too astounded to fight him off. By the time she realized what he was doing, he had her blouse unbuttoned halfway to her waist and her breasts bulging up between the deep V.

"I'm relying on human nature, that's what." Objectively checking his handiwork, and apparently finding it satisfactory, he vaulted over the seat. "Your turn to drive. Get us through that roadblock."

"But... No!" she protested vehemently. "I'll be only too glad to have you captured, Mr. Greywolf!"

"Get this damn car moving or they'll notice us pulled over and get suspicious. Put your tush in that driver's seat and pull the car back onto the highway. Now!"

The look she shot him over the back of the seat was fiercely hostile, but she obeyed him when he whipped the butcher knife from the waistband of his jeans and waved it at her menacingly.

"Don't even think of honking the horn," he warned, just as she thought of that very thing.

Butcher knife or not, she had every intention of pulling into that roadblock screaming bloody murder. As soon as she braked, she would burst out of the car door and let the authorities handle the savage.

"If you're entertaining any notions of turning me in, forget them," he said.

"You don't stand a chance."

"Neither do you. I'll say you were in collusion, that you harbored me last night and helped me get this far."

"They'll know you're lying," she scoffed.

"Not when they investigate the sheets on your bed."

Shocked by his words, she quickly glanced back at him. He was lying down on the back seat as though asleep. In his hand he was holding a photography magazine, which she assumed he intended to use as a tent over his face. "What do you mean?" she asked shakily, not liking the self-assurance in his gray eyes. "What do the sheets on my bed have to do with anything?"

"The police will find the evidence of sex on them." Her face went pale and her hands gripped the steering wheel so hard her knuckles turned white. She swallowed dryly from profound embarrassment. "Now, if you want an explicit explanation," he said softly, "I'll be happy to provide it. But you're a grown-up, so I think you can figure it out. I hadn't seen an unclothed woman in a long time, much less lain in bed with one, close enough to smell her, hear her breathing." His voice lowered. "Think about it, Aislinn."

She didn't want to think about it. Not at all. Her palms were already slick with perspiration and her stomach was roiling. When? How? He could be lying, making it up. He could also be telling the truth.

Before they arrested her, would the police give any credence to her side of the story? What proof could she show them to substantiate it? There would be no signs of forced entry at her condo. She wouldn't be implicated for long, of course. Eventually it would be proved that he was lying. But in the meantime he could sure make life difficult. And embarrassing. The incident would be something she would never live down, especially with her parents, who would be mortified.

"And I won't surrender without a fight," he whispered as she applied the brake to slow down, taking her place in line with the other cars.

"They won't take me alive." His voice was muffled by the magazine. There was only one car ahead of her now. The patrolman was bending down to speak with the driver.

"Unless you want my blood on your conscience, not

to mention that of any innocents I might take with me, you'd better do your damnedest to get us through this roadblock."

Time for making a decision had run out. The patrolman waved the car ahead of her on and signaled for her to move forward. *Lord, how did I get into this situation and what am I going to do?*

It was strange, but when the time came, she didn't have to think about it. Nor did she weigh her decision in the delicate balance between common sense and conscience. She merely reacted spontaneously.

She rolled down the window and before the state patrolman could utter a word, she blurted out, "Oh, officer, I'm *so* glad you stopped me. I think there's something wrong with my car. This little red light keeps blinking on and off. What do you think that means? Nothing bad I hope."

The ruse worked. Aislinn looked up at the patrolman wide-eyed and short-winded. At least the shallow, anxious breaths she was taking made her appear short-winded.

Her hair, which Greywolf hadn't given her time to comb properly that morning, was even more tousled from her nap in the car. It fell over her shoulders in a disarray that was most appealing, particularly to an underpaid state-highway patrolman who had drawn the thankless task of stopping cars on a lonely stretch of highway in the midday August heat to look for some renegade Indian who, in his opinion, was probably well into Mexico by now.

"Well, now, little lady," he said expansively, pushing his hat back from his sweating forehead, "let's see what the problem is here."

He leaned into the open window, ostensibly to check

on which "little red light" was blinking on and off, but Aislinn knew his eyes were trained on her breasts. His expression changed, however, when he glanced into the back seat.

"Who's that?"

"Oh, that's my husband," she said with distaste, giving a negligent shrug. She twirled a lock of hair round and round her finger and suddenly wondered if the strand Greywolf had cut off would be noticed. "He gets as cranky as an old bear if I wake him up while we're traveling. He always makes me drive. Today, I'm glad he did." She batted her eyelashes over her big baby blues, and the officer smiled again.

Greywolf was a fair judge of human nature. Why she was going to such extremes to protect him at that moment, he couldn't say and didn't have time to analyze. The patrolman was speaking to her again.

"I don't see any red light right now." Ridiculously, he was whispering, apparently not wanting to wake up the sleeping husband who might prove to be a little more than cranky toward anyone who ogled his wife.

"Oh, well, thank you." Her bravery was in short supply. Now that she *had* aided and abetted a criminal, she was anxious to get away from the roadblock without being detected. "I guess it was nothing, then."

"It could mean that your motor's overheated," the patrolman said, leering. "I know mine is," he whispered in an even lower voice. Aislinn smiled weakly even as her skin crawled with repulsion.

Greywolf stirred and mumbled something. The officer's smug smile collapsed.

"I'll be seein' you," she said, easing her foot off the brake and gently applying it to the accelerator. She didn't want to appear too eager to be off, though the driver behind her was honking impatiently.

The patrolman shot him an intimidating look. "Better have that light checked if it comes back on. I could radio ahead and—"

"No, no, don't bother about me," she called back through her window. "I'll wake up my husband if it comes on again. Bye."

She cranked up the window and stamped on the accelerator. Looking through the rearview mirror, she saw that the patrolman was now engaged in explaining the situation to the irate motorist who had been detained longer than necessary.

Only when the roadblock was out of sight did she let her muscles relax. She had a death grip on the steering wheel and forcibly unclenched her fingers. Her nails had gouged crescent-shaped wounds into her palms. Letting out a long, shuddering breath, her body sagged within the confines of the driver's seat.

Greywolf climbed over the seat with a lithe agility surprising for a man as tall as he. "You did just fine. No one would ever guess that you're new to a life of crime."

"Shut up!" Aislinn shouted at him. With the same carelessness he had shown earlier, she wheeled the car onto the shoulder of the highway. Gravel sprayed from beneath the tires when she applied the brakes. As soon as the car came to a skidding stop she laid her head on the steering wheel and began to sob.

"I hate you. Please let me go. Why did I do that? *Why?* I should have turned you in. I'm scared and tired and hungry and thirsty. You're a criminal and I've never deceived anyone in my life. A law officer! I could go to jail now, too, couldn't I? Why am I helping you when you'll probably kill me anyway?"

Greywolf sat unmoving at her side. When she had at last cried herself out, she dried her wet cheeks on the backs of her hands and looked up at him with tear-swollen eyes.

"I'd like to tell you to cheer up, that the worst is behind us, but it seems our troubles have only started, Aislinn."

He was gazing down at her breasts, which she immediately remembered were indecently displayed. Her hands trembled as she pulled the cloth of her blouse over them. "What do you mean?"

"I mean the damn roadblocks. I hadn't counted on them. We need to find a television set."

"A television set?" she parroted in a thin voice.

His eyes scanned the stretch of highway behind and ahead of them. "Yes. I'm sure there will be a news story about the dragnet. Hopefully it will give us a thoroughly detailed account of how the authorities plan to apprehend me. Let's get going."

He hitched his chin forward. Wearily she steered the car back onto the highway. "What about the car radio? We can hear the news on that."

"Not as detailed," he said, shaking his head. "And haven't you ever heard that a picture is worth a thousand words?"

"I suppose you'll tell me where to go and when to stop."

"That's right. You just drive."

For almost an hour they rode in silence, though he passed her cheese and crackers he took from the sack. He peeled an orange and divided the sections between them. She didn't like eating from his hand, but opened her lips obediently each time he pressed a section of the orange against them.

As they approached the outskirts of a dreary-looking

town, Greywolf instructed her to slow down. They were driving past the beer taverns that lined the highway like sad old whores in desperate need of customers.

"There," he said shortly, pointing with his finger. "Pull into the Tumbleweed."

Disgust registered on Aislinn's face. The Tumbleweed was the sleaziest-looking of all the honky-tonks. "I hope we're in time for happy hour," she remarked sarcastically.

"They have a television," Greywolf said, having spotted the antenna sticking out of the tin roof. "Get out."

"Yes, sir," she mumbled, tiredly shoving open her door. It felt good to stand. She placed her hands at the small of her back and stretched, then stamped circulation back into her feet.

There were only a few other vehicles parked in the dusty gravel parking lot in front of the tavern. Greywolf took her arm and dragged her along with him to the door. A good portion of the rusty screen had been ripped from its frame. The jagged edge, which curled outward, looked as intimidating as the rest of the place. Aislinn's plan was to appear resigned, but the moment they cleared the doorway, to scream for help.

"Forget what you're thinking."

"What am I thinking?"

"That you're going to escape me and run into the safe arms of a rescuer. Believe me, I'm the safest companion you could have in a joint like this." That wasn't saying much, considering that she had seen him slide the knife down into his boot before he left the car. "No," he said, slinging his arm across her shoulders, "look like you're having a good, sexy time."

"What!"

"That's right. We're having an illicit afternoon affair."

"You're insane if you think— And stop that!" she exclaimed when he slipped his arm around her waist and his hand came up her side alarmingly close to her breast. His hard fingers pressed into the tender flesh, securing her in a hold there would be no escaping from.

"Why, honey, is that any way to talk to your lover?" he whined.

Assuming an ambling, none-too-steady swagger, he pulled open the screen door, pushed open the rickety door and stumbled into the murky, smoky interior. To maintain her balance, Aislinn gripped the front of his shirt, pressing her hand against his stomach. He glanced down at her and winked, as though she had won his approval. She wanted to shout at him that she wouldn't have touched him had it not been a choice between that or falling down.

However, she said nothing. She was disheartened into speechlessness by her seedy surroundings. Such places as the Tumbleweed were portrayed in movies, but she had certainly never been inside one. The low ceiling was all but obscured by a pall of tobacco smoke. It took her eyes a moment to adjust to the darkness, but seeing the place clearly only distressed her more.

In front of the bar was a row of stationary stools with red vinyl seat pads. At least they had been red once. Now they were all aged to a greasy, dirty maroon. Only three of them were occupied. As the door slapped shut behind Greywolf and her, three pairs of mean eyes turned toward them and gave them a suspicious once-over.

One pair, laden with crusty make-up, belonged to a blowsy blonde who had her bare foot propped up on the stool next to her. She was painting her toenails. "Hey, Ray, we got customers," she hollered.

Ray, Aislinn assumed, was the obese man behind the bar. He was leaning forward with his massive forearms braced on a refrigerator, his eyes glued to the television set that was mounted high in the corner. He was engrossed in a soap opera. "So wait on 'em," he bellowed back. He hadn't taken his eyes off the screen.

"My nails ain't dry."

Ray let go a string of obscenities that Aislinn thought were reserved only for public rest room walls in seaports. He pushed his fat bulk off the refrigerator and shot Greywolf and her a sour look. She was the only one who saw it. Her escort had his face buried in her hair and his tongue in her ear.

But apparently he hadn't missed anything. "Two cold beers," he said loud enough for Ray to hear. Then he gave Aislinn a slight push and maneuvered her toward one of the ratty-looking booths along the wall. It would provide them with a clear view of both the TV set and the door. "Sit down and scoot over," he whispered for her benefit.

Since he all but shoved her down, she had no choice. She didn't have a chance to inspect the cleanliness of the seat, but it was probably just as well. Greywolf slid into the booth after her and crammed her against the wall. "You're squashing me," she complained beneath her breath.

"That's the general idea."

He was gnawing on her neck when Ray waddled over carrying two beers in his hands, which looked like hams with dirty fingernails. The bottles of beer made solid thumps on the chipped Formica table when he set them down. "Three bucks. You pay as you go here."

"Pay the man, will ya, hon?" Lucas wheedled, sliding his hand over her shoulder in a circular, caressing motion. "I'm busy."

She ground her teeth together in an effort not to scream at him to take his hands off her, or to take her out of there, or to go to hell. But right then, she was glad he was there. He had known what he was talking about. Even if she could coax some sympathy out of Ray and the others, she doubted she would want to entrust herself into their care. At least Greywolf was a familiar villain.

She dug into her purse for three one-dollar bills and laid them on the table. Ray, still looking over his shoulder so he wouldn't miss a second of his soap opera, scooped them up and shuffled away.

"Good girl," Lucas spoke softly into her ear.

She wished Greywolf wouldn't be so earnest in his playacting now that Ray no longer posed a threat to him. He could at least remove his hand from inside her blouse, where his fingers were fiddling with her bra strap. "Now what?" she asked.

"Now we neck."

"You go—"

"Shh!" he hissed angrily. "You don't want to attract Ray's attention, do you? Or maybe those two cowboys are more to your liking. They'd just love rescuing a damsel in distress."

"Oh, stop," she said, when his lips slid down her neck. "I thought you came here to watch television."

"I did. But I don't want them to know that."

"So I'm supposed to sit here and let you paw me?" He made a humming sound of affirmation. "For how long?"

"For as long as it takes. Every half hour or so we'll order fresh beers so Ray won't get mad at us for taking up his valuable space."

How a man could talk so rationally while nibbling so dedicatedly, she didn't know. She squirmed away from his seeking lips. "I can't drink that much."

"When no one is looking, pour the beer on the floor. I doubt it will ever be noticed."

"So do I," she said with a shiver, lifting her foot off the

floor. It was sticky with substances she thought it best not to identify. "Are you sure this is going to be worth it?"

"What's the matter, sweetheart? Ain't you having a good time?" His hand found the placket of her blouse and plucked at the buttons.

"No."

"Do you want to go through another roadblock? Or did you enjoy driving that poor cop a little crazy?"

"You're despicable." She leaned back against the hard, lumpy upholstery of the booth and tried to be passive under the gropings of his hands and mouth.

"I'm not convinced you're hot for it, sugar, and neither will they be. Put a little more into it," he growled, his lips very near her mouth.

"No. This is disgusting."

His head snapped up and he stared down at her coldly. "Why?"

He had taken offense. Why? Because he thought her comment was a racial slur, or because he thought she was maligning his lovemaking expertise? And either way, what the hell did she care if he was offended or not? "I'm not accustomed to making out in public places, Mr.—"

She never said his name. She never had a chance. He mashed his lips over hers and sealed his name inside. It was a functional kiss, impersonal, delivered only to keep her quiet. He kept his lips closed. Still, Aislinn's insides somersaulted and she couldn't utter a sound.

Which was the point, after all. When he finally lifted his mouth off hers he whispered, "Careful."

She merely nodded her head, wishing that her heart would cool. One thing she knew, she wouldn't provoke him with any more questions or conversation. She didn't want him to kiss her again.

She was ambivalent as to why, but she did *not* want him to kiss her again.

Thankfully no one took much notice of them. It seemed to be an unwritten rule that the patrons of the Tumbleweed minded their own business unless invited to do otherwise.

Though he gave every semblance of being absorbed in his lovemaking, Greywolf was fully aware of what went on. His eyes were never still, though he made them appear slumberous with arousal by keeping his eyelids at half-mast. From beneath the hood of his brows, he watched each face for signs of recognition, but no one paid them any attention. Ray—or his waitress when her nails had dried—carried beer to the booth when Greywolf drunkenly called out an order for it. Beyond that, no one paid them the slightest heed.

Customers drifted in and out. Most stayed only for a couple of drinks before leaving. Some drank alone. Others entered in groups of two or three. One played on the pinball machine until the pinging bells and flashing lights nearly drove Aislinn crazy. When he finally left, the television provided the only distraction. Situation comedy reruns now held Ray enthralled.

For Aislinn the time dragged by. Not because she was bored. Her nerve endings were sizzling. She kept telling herself it was because she was waiting for a potential savior to walk through the door. But honestly she thought her skittishness had more to do with Greywolf's foreplay.

And what else could it be called? What other term applied to the way he slid his fingers up through her hair, holding her head still while his lips nibbled their way down her throat. Or the way he squeezed her upper thigh when the waitress delivered their beer. Or the way his lips were wont to play around her ears.

"Don't," she moaned once, when that particular caress caused goose bumps to break out over her arms.

"The moaning is good. Keep it up," he whispered as a pair of truckers moseyed past the booth on their way to the pinball machine.

He took her hand and slipped it inside his shirt, holding it palm down, against his skin. Aislinn made a feeble attempt to withdraw her hand, but Greywolf wouldn't let her. As long as she was forced to touch him, she submitted to her own curiosity. As unobtrusively as possible, she curled her fingertips into the hard flesh. Her thumb moved a fraction. It encountered his nipple. It was erect.

He sucked in his breath sharply. "Godalmighty," he cursed. "Don't do that." His body had been tense all afternoon, but nothing compared to the rigid, still way it pressed against her now.

She snatched her hand back. "I'm just doing what you—"

"Shh!"

"Don't say—"

"*Shh!* Look. On the screen."

She glanced toward the TV. A Phoenix newscaster was reading a story about the search for the elusive prison escapee, Indian activist Lucas Greywolf. A picture of Lucas was flashed onto the screen. Aislinn stared at it, barely recognizing him. His hair was cropped short, almost shaved.

"Not a very flattering picture," she said dryly.

The corner of his mouth twitched with the hint of a smile, but his attention was riveted to the map of Arizona that was now being shown. As he had guessed, the media weren't doing the law-enforcement agencies any favors; they were pinpointing where roadblocks had been set up. Even though leaked news stories like this sabotaged police work, each television station's main goal was to scoop its competitors.

As soon as the announcer switched to other newsworthy events of the day, Lucas scooted to the edge of the booth. "Okay, let's go. And remember to weave. You've supposedly drunk several beers."

He offered her his hand, but his attention was diverted to the door as it was opened to admit another customer. Greywolf's curse was soft, but no less scorching, as a uniformed man came strolling in.

Three

Casually taking off his hat, the uniformed man ran his sleeve over his sweating brow. Aislinn sat up and took notice. His uniform was that of a sheriff, at the very least a deputy.

"Stella, get me a beer," he called out as soon as the door slammed closed behind him.

The blond waitress turned and gave him a wide, welcoming smile that indicated their level of familiarity. "Well, look what the cat just drug in." Leaning back against the bar, she propped her elbows on it. The posture displayed her huge bosom to its full potential. The sheriff showed his appreciation by giving her a lecherous smile.

"Missed me, didja?"

"Hell no," she drawled, curling her arm around his sunburned neck as he squatted on the stool next to where she was standing. "You know how it is with me. Outa sight, outa mind."

"For two days I've been chasing some damn Indian nobody's seen hide nor hair of. What I need is a coupla cold ones and some tender loving care."

"In that order?" The blonde leaned down and purred

the question near his mouth. He kissed her, but then swatted her ample hip.

"Get me that beer."

Stella went to do the hunter's bidding while the hunted
sat seething next to Aislinn in the booth. "Damn," Greywolf said beneath his breath, pounding his fist against
his thigh under the table. "Just a few more minutes and
we would have been gone. Damn."

He kept up the frustrated litany, all the while leaning
over Aislinn in the corner of the booth as though they
were petting. "Don't you dare do anything to attract his
attention. Because to rescue you, sweetheart, he'll have
to go through me."

"What do you plan to do?"

"For the time being, more of the same," he said, kissing her neck. "Maybe he'll leave."

But apparently the officer intended to make a night
of it. His "coupla cold ones" turned into three, then four.
Stella didn't move far from his side, unless forced to wait
on other customers. They flirted outrageously, exchang-
ing sexual innuendos, until their provocative banterings
mellowed to soft, private whispers punctuated occasionally by Stella's low, sexy laugh. The sheriff's hands were
never idle, but caressed her unceasingly. Stella never de-
murred.

Aislinn's hopes had flared with the unexpected appearance of the sheriff, but now she doubted that the
law officer even cared whether the escaped convict was
captured or not. There were a lot of people, Indian and
Anglo alike, who had felt that Lucas Greywolf got a bum
rap and had been in sympathy with his cause. This over-
worked sheriff might be one of them. He might look the
other way if Greywolf crossed his path.

Still, the sheriff represented Aislinn's only hope of

getting away from her kidnapper. She planned to use him, though she was sure he wouldn't thank her for ruining the evening he planned to spend in Stella's company.

"When the time is right, we're going to get up and walk out, got it?"

"Yes," she agreed. Perhaps a little too quickly.

Greywolf raised his head slightly and, staring down into her eyes, reached beneath the table. Even before she saw the blade of the knife reflecting the dim lights, she realized he had drawn it from his boot. "Don't make me use this, Aislinn. Particularly on you."

"Why not on me?"

His eyes slid down her body suggestively. "Because after spending such a pleasurable afternoon feeling you up, I'd hate to hurt you."

"I hope you burn in hell," she said, pushing each word of the harsh condemnation through her teeth.

"And I'm sure your wish will be granted." He said no more, but turned his attention back to the couple at the bar. He watched them like a hawk, his gray eyes unwavering. When the sheriff's hand made an exploratory pass across Stella's breast, then paused to investigate, Greywolf said, "Now."

Aislinn had expected him to slink out of the booth and through the door. Instead, he jerked her to her feet suddenly, giving him the element of surprise. It worked to his benefit beautifully. She slumped against him to regain her balance. His arm wrapped around her waist, securing her to his side. She pressed her fists against his chest, angling her body away from his, and opened her mouth. All that came out, however, was a short gasp. He slipped the knife up between their bodies.

"Don't." His raspy voice was dangerously calm, cool,

and collected. It effectively changed her mind about trying to escape him now.

They made their staggering progress toward the door, his head bent low over hers as though he was drunk.

"Hey, mister."

Aislinn's footsteps faltered, but Greywolf's didn't. He kept going.

"Hey, mister! I'm talking to you, Chief."

Against her cheek, she felt Greywolf's aggravated expulsion of breath before he halted and lifted his head. "Yeah?" he asked of Ray, who had addressed him.

"We got rooms in the back," he said, hitching his thumb over his shoulder. "You and your lady want one for the evenin'?"

"No thanks," Lucas said. "Gotta get her home before her ol' man gets back."

Ray chuckled lewdly and went back to watching the detective series that was now blaring forth from the television. The sheriff, pouring all his romantic passions into the kiss he was grinding onto Stella's receptive mouth, never even looked up. Once she was outside, Aislinn's lungs drank in the pure air. She didn't think she'd ever filter the dank smell of beer and stale tobacco smoke out of her nasal passages. Greywolf wasted no time on luxuries like deep, cleansing breathing, but hustled her into the car.

Within minutes they had put several miles between them and the Tumbleweed. Only then did he breathe deeply. He rolled down the window and seemed to relish the wind beating against his face. "You're becoming very good at eluding the law," he remarked.

"I didn't like having that knife against my ribs," she shot back.

"You weren't supposed to."

He seemed to know where he was going, though Aislinn knew this wasn't a well-traveled highway they were on now. The lanes were narrow. There were few signs. No lights. Shoulders were nonexistent. Other cars were few and far between. When they met them, she held her breath out of fear of crashing head-on.

Greywolf drove fast, but safely. Before long, staring at the white stripes chasing each other down the center of the highway became hypnotic and she nodded off. But only moments later, Greywolf's blistering curse rent the silence.

"Dammit all to hell!"

"Is somebody following us?" she asked hopefully, sitting up and glancing behind them.

"The heat light just came on."

Her spirits sank as low as her weary shoulders. For a moment she had entertained the hope that the sheriff or somebody in the Tumbleweed had recognized Greywolf, but had played it safe and not tried to apprehend him until reinforcements could be called in. "It was doing that this afternoon," she said, slumping back against the seat.

He swiveled his head around and glared at her. His face was illuminated only by the lights on the dashboard. They lent it a greenish cast, making it look even more fearsome. His eyes were pale, silver, furious. "You mean the engine was actually overheating this afternoon?"

"Didn't you hear me tell that to the highway patrolman at the roadblock?"

"I thought that was just part of your act," he shouted.

"Well it wasn't."

"So why didn't you say something before I pulled onto this abandoned highway?"

"You didn't ask!"

He ended the shouting match with a curse she couldn't

possibly champion for fear of being struck by lightning. Her lower teeth almost went through the roof of her mouth when he suddenly steered the car off the highway. "Where are you going?" she asked fearfully.

"I have to let the car cool off or the engine will burn up completely. I can't do anything to repair it in the dark anyway." He drove the car several hundred yards off the highway. The terrain was so rough that Aislinn had to brace her hands against the dash to keep from getting jostled onto the floorboard. When they finally came to a standstill the motor was hissing like a boiling teakettle. Greywolf pushed his door open and got out. He leaned his back against the car and bowed his head.

"Damn! I've wasted so much time today. First in that godforsaken tavern. Now this." He appeared to be extremely upset over the forced delay. He walked toward the hood of the car and viciously kicked one of the tires, cursing expansively.

Aislinn got out on her side and stretched her cramped muscles. "Are we under some kind of deadline?"

"Yes. We're under a deadline." His grim tone advised her to hold her peace and not pursue the subject. After a while, he shook his head and heaved a sigh of resignation. "As long as we're stuck here, we might just as well make use of the time and get some sleep. Get in the back seat."

"I'm not sleepy," she said sullenly.

"Get in the back seat anyway."

His voice rolled over the desert like ominous, distant thunder. Aislinn gave him a murderous look, but she obeyed him. Leaving all the car doors open save one in the back seat, he got in behind her. Settling himself into the corner against the door, he spread his thighs wide and, before she knew what he was going to do, pulled her between them.

"Let me go," she demanded, outraged. She squirmed against him, but since that only served to better acquaint her bottom with the fly of his jeans, she stopped.

"I'm going to sleep. And so are you." He situated her back against his chest and wrapped his arms around her. They felt like bands of steel crisscrossing just beneath her breasts. It was an extremely unnerving position, though not painful. Not even uncomfortable, if she would let herself relax against him. Which she wouldn't.

"I can't go roaming off in the desert, Greywolf. Let me go."

"Not a chance. Unless you'd rather be tied to the steering wheel."

"Where would I go if I escaped?"

"If I've learned one thing about you, it is that you are a resourceful lady."

"We're in the middle of nowhere. It's dark."

"There's a moon."

Yes, she had noticed. And there were stars, the likes of which she'd never seen. They were huge and bright and close, not city stars at all. At any other time, she could have admired this night, savored it, let its magnificence embrace her, and enjoyed her smallness when compared to it.

But she wanted nothing about this night to be beautiful. She wanted to remember only the horror of it later. "I'd be a fool to strike out on my own, even if I knew where I was and could get away from you."

"Which I'm making certain you won't do. Now, for your own good, be still."

The tenseness underlying his warning alerted her to other things as well. Like the tremors vibrating through the arms that supported her breasts. Like the pressure at the small of her back. She swallowed, denying to herself what that could mean.

"Please don't do this." She was willing to swallow her pride and plead with him, because she didn't think she could stand to be this close to him all through the night. Not because she disliked it so much, but because she didn't dislike it nearly enough. "Let me go."

"No."

Knowing that it was useless, she stopped trying to change his mind. But she refused to relax. Her back was as stiff as a board against his chest. Before long her neck began to ache from the tension of maintaining the small distance between them. Not until she thought he was asleep, did she let her head fall back onto his shoulder.

"You're very stubborn, Aislinn Andrews."

Aislinn closed her eyes and gnashed her teeth, knowing that he'd been privy to her stubbornness and her final surrender. He'd probably waited her out deliberately. "If you'd loosen your arms I could breathe easier."

"Or reach for the knife." They lay in silence, then he said, "You are one of few."

"Few what?"

"Women that I've spent more than one night with."

"Don't expect me to be flattered."

"I don't. I'm sure an Anglo virgin like you can't imagine anything worse than having an Indian between her lily-white thighs."

"You're unspeakably vulgar. And I'm not a virgin."

"Have you been married?"

"No."

"Then you lived with a man?"

"No."

"Affairs?"

"None of your business."

She would rather die than have him know that there had been only one. Hardly worth mentioning. It had been a terribly disappointing experience that she had engaged in mainly to satisfy her curiosity.

Between her and the man, there had been only mild affection, little communication, no warmth or closeness, nor even much passion. Afterward, she had been disillusioned and disappointed and imagined that her partner had been as well.

She had never risked that kind of awkward encounter again and recently had begun to think that she simply wasn't sexually inclined. The men she went out with tried, but none stirred even enough interest for her to pursue the relationship beyond dinner dates and an occasional good-night kiss.

Rather than talk about her love life, or lack thereof, she asked him, "What about you? How many affairs of the heart have you had?"

But either he had dropped off to sleep or he ignored her. In any event, no answer was forthcoming.

She snuggled closer to the warmth.

A soft growl, like the purr of a great cat, echoed through the waking chambers of her mind. She stirred and when her brain began to piece together the information her senses were sending she came suddenly awake and her eyes popped open.

"Oh my God," she cried.

"No, that's my line," he groaned.

She was sprawled atop Lucas Greywolf.

Sometime during the night she had turned over, so that now her cheek was resting on his bare chest where his shirt had fallen open. Her breasts were flattened against his stomach and her hips... "Oh, Lord." She repeated her plea to heaven because the cleft of her thighs was cuddling his manhood.

And it was very hard.

Cheeks flaming, she pushed herself up and scrambled to the other side of the back seat. "I'm sorry," she stammered, keeping her face averted.

"So am I," he grated, as he opened the door on his side and practically fell out. For a long while, he just stood there by the side of the car. Aislinn didn't dare ask what the matter was. She knew.

After several minutes, he walked to the front of the car and raised the hood. He fiddled with something beneath it, then came back to crouch down inside the open car door. "Take off your bra."

If he had said, "Sprout wings and fly," she couldn't have been more astounded. "I beg your pardon?"

"You heard me. Either that or your blouse. But hurry up. We've lost enough time."

It was well past dawn, and her blush deepened when she realized how soundly they had both slept. Of course yesterday had been an exhausting day and—

"Either you take it off or I do," he interrupted her thoughts brusquely.

"Turn around."

"Oh for…" He turned around. Hastily she peeled off her shirt, took off her bra, then pulled the shirt back on, buttoning it quickly.

"Here." She thrust the garment at him. He took it without a word and carried it back with him to the front of the car. After several minutes of sweat-breaking work and elaborate cursing, he slammed the hood and got into the driver's seat, wiping his hands on the legs of his jeans.

All he said by way of explanation was, "That might hold it for a while."

But not nearly long enough. They had driven only twenty miles or so when threads of white smoke began ghosting from beneath the hood. Then it began to billow.

"You'd better stop before the car blows up," Aislinn suggested tentatively. They hadn't spoken a word since starting out. If he was as shaken as she by the position in which they had found themselves upon waking, then she could understand his reticence.

She kept remembering things she wished she could physically blot from her mind, like how his chest hair had felt warm and fuzzy and fine against her lips. And how his hands had been cupping and caressing her derriere before she was fully awake. And how good she had felt moments before realization stunned her into consciousness.

His remote features gave away none of what he was thinking as he pulled the car off the road again. It wheezed to a stop. "Well, that bra did no more good there than it did keeping your nipples from showing."

She gaped at him in shock, but he merely opened his door and stepped out. "Come on."

"Come on where?"

"To the nearest town."

"You mean we're going to *walk?*" she asked incredulously. They were in the middle of nowhere, surrounded by rugged terrain on all sides. In the distance was the purple silhouette of mountains. Between here and there was nothing but rock-strewn ground, the callused palm of Mother Nature, unrelieved except for the gray swath of the highway.

"Until someone stops to pick us up," he said in answer to her question. He struck off. Aislinn had no choice but to leave the car and trot along behind him until she caught up.

She wasn't about to stay there alone. He might not

come back for her, and it looked as though it could be days before another car came along. She was already thirsty and hadn't helped that by eating a few cookies out of the provisions Greywolf had taken from her kitchen.

They walked for what seemed like hours. She had to virtually jog to keep pace with him. The sun beat down unmercifully on her uncovered head. The terrain was fit only for Gila monsters and other reptilian creatures that occasionally slithered across their path.

Finally they heard the chugging sound of an approaching vehicle and turned to see a pickup truck coming from behind them. It looked like a faded red specter materializing out of the shimmering heat waves. Before Greywolf even raised his arms and waved, the driver was downshifting. Three stoic Navaho men sat shoulder to shoulder in the cab of the ancient pickup. After conversing with them briefly, Greywolf hauled Aislinn into the back of it with him.

"Did they recognize you?"

"Probably."

"Aren't you afraid they'll turn you in?"

His head swung around and, despite the heat, she shivered against the cold glance he sent her. "No."

"Oh, I see. They're honor bound to keep their silence."

He didn't even bother to reply, but turned his eyes toward the northeastern horizon, where she had already deduced they were headed.

They maintained a hostile silence for the length of the ride into a small, dusty town. Conversation would have been difficult anyway. The hot wind pounded her and sucked the breath out of her lungs.

While they were still on the outskirts of the town, Greywolf knocked on the rear windshield of the pickup and the driver downshifted to a halt in front of a service station. Greywolf jumped to the ground and assisted Aislinn down. "Much obliged," he called to the driver, who doffed his straw cowboy hat to them before reengaging the gears of the truck and driving off.

"Now what?" Aislinn asked, tiredly. She had known instinctively that the Navaho men would be in sympathy with Greywolf, but hope had briefly glimmered at the prospect of stopping in a town.

Hope died the moment she saw the community. The streets were deserted. Except for chickens pecking on the barren ground in a yard across the highway, there were no signs of life anywhere. The town looked as unwelcoming and inhospitable as the desert that surrounded it.

Greywolf walked toward the tin building which housed the service station. Aislinn forced herself to follow him, dragging her feet. She had never been so uncomfortable in her life. The perspiration that had soaked her clothes and body while they were walking on the highway had dried now and left a gritty, salty residue on her skin that itched like mad. She was hot, sticky and sunburned. Her lips were parched, her hair a tangled mess.

She groaned when she read the sign posted on the grimy window of the service station. "Siesta!" she exclaimed mournfully.

"They're closed until four o'clock," Greywolf said, turning his head to consult the sun.

Aislinn discovered a meager sliver of shade near the wall of the building and pressed herself against it. Leaning her head back, she closed her eyes. They came open instantly when she heard the crash of breaking glass.

Greywolf had smashed out a window in the door with a rock. Without so much as a blink of his eyes, he reached inside and unlocked the door. It swung open with a protesting squeak and he went inside. Aislinn, who would never have considered deliberately breaking a window, much less trespassing onto anyone else's property, followed him into the marginally cooler interior.

Once her eyes had adjusted to the dimness, she saw that the place was not just a gas station, but a small grocery store as well. Wooden shelves were stocked with potato chips and canned goods, paper products and household cleansers.

There was one dusty glass counter filled with even dustier Arizona souvenirs. On top there were boxes of candy bars, cigarettes and chewing gum. Behind it, the pegboard wall was covered with an inventory of small automotive parts.

Greywolf crossed the aged wooden floor, which protested each of his footsteps with a groan, to an old-fashioned cold-drink vending chest. Lifting the lid, he jimmied the lock that was supposed to prevent thefts, took out two bottled Cokes, opened them and passed one to Aislinn even as he raised the other to his mouth and drank thirstily.

"I intend to pay for mine, " she said sanctimoniously.

He lowered the bottle from his mouth. "I intend for you to pay for mine, too. Also for the broken pane of glass. And for the water hose."

She drank the cold cola, thinking that it was the best-tasting thing she'd ever had. "What water hose?"

He was scanning the various implements behind the counter. "To replace the one that busted. Like this," he said, lifting one off its peg and holding it up to her.

With his other hand, he was opening drawers behind the counter and examining the contents. Metal tools clanked and rattled as he moved them about in the drawers. The sound emphasized to Aislinn how deserted the place was.

She felt alien, consumed by the feeling of desolation that lurked around the place. Greywolf suffered from no such unease. When he found the tools he was looking for, he took them out. Just when she was about to succumb to abject despair, she spotted the pay telephone.

She was sure Greywolf hadn't noticed it. He was still pilfering the tool drawers and hadn't looked in the direction of the corner where the phone was attached to the wall. It was partially hidden by a rack of outdated magazines.

If she could keep him talking, maybe she could get to that phone and place a call without his knowing. But where was she? What was the name of this godforsaken town? What highway had they been on? She didn't recall seeing any signs. Had it even been a highway? For all she knew they could have crossed a state line and were no longer in Arizona.

"Finished?"

She jumped guiltily at the sound of Greywolf's voice. "Yes," she said and passed him her empty bottle. Where only moments before she had felt laggardly, her mind was now alert, whirring with plans for ways to distract him.

"Give me some money," he said, holding out his hand, palm up.

Eager to please him for the moment, she fished in her purse and came up with a twenty-dollar bill. "That should cover it."

He folded the money and tucked it under an ashtray on the counter. "There are facilities in the back," he said. "Do you need them?"

Yes, she did, but she deliberated on her next course of action. She could lie and say she didn't need the rest room, encouraging him to go ahead while she waited for him. But that would seem unlikely and would arouse his suspicions. Better to go along, get him to think that she no longer sought to escape.

"Yes, please," she said meekly. Without a word, he led her out the door and around the corner of the building to the two doors appropriately marked. She dreaded what awaited her inside as Greywolf pushed open the door of the women's rest room. The odor was overpowering, but she stepped inside and switched on the feeble light.

It was better than she had expected, though still bad. Now that she was reminded of how long it had been, she needed very badly to use the facility no matter how offensive it was. When she was finished, she rinsed her face and hands in the rusty sink. Even the tepid water felt cool against her sun-and-wind-chafed skin.

Opting to let it air-dry, she went to the door, unlatched it, and tried to push it open. It wouldn't budge.

At first she thought she was pushing the wrong way and tried drawing it toward her, but to no avail. She pushed on it with all her might. It didn't move. Panic welling inside her, she threw herself against it.

"Greywolf!" she cried frantically. "Greywolf!"

"What is it, Aislinn?"

"I can't get the door open."

"That's right."

Her mouth dropped open in dismay. He had locked her in!

"Open this door," she screamed, banging on it with her fists.

"I will as soon as I return."

"Return? *Return?* Where are you going? Don't you dare leave me locked up in here."

"I have to. I don't want you using that telephone you made such a point of not noticing. I'll let you out as soon as I get back."

"Where are you going?" she repeated, desperate over the thought of being cooped up in the rest room for an unspecified period of time.

"Back to the car. As soon as I get that busted water hose replaced, I'll be back to pick you up."

"The *car?* You're going back to the car? How will you get there?"

"I'll run."

"Run." She mouthed the word, but little sound came out. Then a thought occurred to her and she wanted to flaunt her cleverness in his face. "As soon as the owners of this dump reopen at four, they'll find me. I'll scream the place down."

"I'll be back well before four."

"You bastard. Let me out of here." She pushed against the door with her full weight behind her, and still it wouldn't give. "It's stifling. I'll die cooped up in here."

"You'll sweat, but you won't die. I suggest you rest."

"Go to hell!"

He made no reply. Her words echoed off the walls of the public rest room. Pressing her ear to the door, she listened but could hear nothing. "Greywolf?" she called tentatively. Then loudly, "Greywolf!"

Nothing. She was alone.

Slumping against the door, she covered her face with her hands and submitted to the luxury of tears again. A woman like herself wasn't prepared to cope with adversity of this sort. Life-and-death situations were beyond the realm of her sheltered environment. She had grown up in a gilded ghetto guarded by parents who wanted "the best" for their child.

She had never even attended a public school because of the "undesirable elements of society" she would encounter there. She hadn't been trained in survival tactics at the exclusive women's college she had attended. Situations like this made great movie scripts, but no one really believed that they actually *happened.* But this was happening—to her.

For the first time in her twenty-six years, Aislinn Andrews was confronted with real fear. It was tangible. She could breathe it. She could taste it.

What if Greywolf never came back for her? What guarantee did she have that the service station would reopen at four o'clock? That sign could have been posted on the door months ago and forgotten when the owners decided that keeping the business open wasn't worth their effort.

She could die of thirst.

No, the rest room had water. Not the purest, she was certain, but it was wet.

She could die of starvation.

Actually that would take a long time, and surely someone would drive into the place before then. She'd have to keep alert for the sound of a motor and start pounding on the door and shouting when she heard one.

She could die of suffocation.

But there was a window, a small one, located high on the wall just under the ceiling. It was open several inches. The air might be arid and hot, but there was plenty of it.

She could die of rage.

Now that was a very real possibility, Aislinn thought. How dare Greywolf desert her in this disgusting place? Calling him every vile name she could think of, she paced the small rest room.

Finally it was that very anger which fueled her mind and sparked her imagination. Even he had said she was resourceful. She could get out of this rest room if only she would put her mind to it. She knew it! But how?

Again and again, she threw herself against the door, but it wouldn't budge. Whatever he had used to brace it shut wasn't going to give, and she was only wasting her strength trying to move it. Sweat ran down her body in steady streams. She could feel it trickling along her scalp beneath her hair, which was heavy and hot.

Despairing over her futility and weakness, she raised her eyes imploringly toward heaven. And therein lay the answer to her dilemma. *The window!* If she had some way to—

There was a metal barrel standing in one corner of the rest room. Apparently it had served as a trash can for as long as the rest room had been in use. Steeling herself against thinking of its stinking contents, she struggled to upend it. The thing was monstrously heavy and bulky, but she finally succeeded in turning it bottom side up and scooted it beneath the window.

By standing on the barrel, she was able to grasp the bottom of the windowsill. For several minutes she labored, pulling herself up with the strength of her arms alone, searching for nonexistent footholds in the concrete block walls, until finally she levered herself up over the sill. Poking her head through the open window, she hauled in great gulps of air and welcomed the wind against her face. She hung there for several minutes, giving her arms, which trembled with fatigue, a much-needed rest.

Then she used her shoulders to raise the window as high as it would go. The opening was narrow, but she thought that with some effort and good luck, she could get through it. Pulling one knee up and bracing it against the sill, she tried turning herself so she could go feet first out the window.

It was when she raised her other knee to the sill that

she lost her balance. Deliberately, she propelled herself toward the outside. With that much momentum behind it, her body slipped through the open window. As she fell, her arm caught on a nail on the sill. It ripped a seam in her flesh from wrist to armpit.

Miraculously, she landed on her feet below, but the ground was uneven. Grasping her arm in pain, she reeled backward and went toppling down a slope, rolling, somersaulting, only to bump her head on a rock at the bottom.

For a few blinding seconds, she stared up at the fiery orb of the sun, which seemed to be mocking her. Then all went black.

Four

He was anxious to get back. His eyes, missing nothing, had memorized the landmarks. He knew he had only a few miles left to go. Three at most. He pushed the accelerator to the floorboard.

Thankfully, the car responded. It was back in prime working condition. Switching out the hoses hadn't been a problem. The difficulty had been running all the way back to the car with heavy tools in his pockets and carrying a gallon jug of water to replace what had leaked out. He was accustomed to running distance. Even in midsummer heat that wasn't a challenge. But carrying the unevenly distributed extra poundage had been.

Greywolf was grateful for the opportunity to think as the car ate up the remaining miles. The hot wind whipped against his cheeks and through his hair. He preferred driving with the windows down; disdaining artificial air conditioning when he could glory in the elements of the desert. Only because of the woman had he left the car windows rolled up in the first place.

The woman.

His conscience pricked him to think of her locked

up in that hot, filthy rest room. But what else could he
have done? Left her to phone the nearest sheriff's office?
Taken her with him? She would never have been able
to walk back to the car, and even if she had, she would
have added hours to the time it had taken him. Hours he
couldn't afford.

How soon before they caught up with him? How soon?
Would he make it there in time? He had to.

He had known what the prison escape would cost him,
but he was willing to pay any price. He only regretted
that it had cost others as well. He hadn't enjoyed knocking unconscious the trustee who had considered him a
friend. He hadn't enjoyed frightening the woman either.
She represented everything he despised: Anglos in general and affluent Anglos in particular. Still, he wished
he hadn't been forced to involve her.

Forced to?

With an aggravated motion, he switched on the radio
and turned it up full volume, telling himself he wanted
to catch any forthcoming news bulletins. Actually, he
hoped the blaring music would block out thoughts of *her.*

Why had he saddled himself with this responsibility? Why hadn't he just clipped her on the chin and left
her house as quickly and quietly as he had come? By the
time she regained consciousness and alerted the police,
he would have had time to elude them again.

Instead, *stupidly,* he had stayed and heckled the Anglo
woman. He had needed a shower, yes, but that was a luxury he could have done without. He had needed sleep,
yes, but he could have found a place less comfortable
than her bed with its scented sheets and fluffy pillows.

Even granting himself that much luxury, why hadn't
he left before dawn the moment he had awakened? Sure,
she would have notified the authorities when she woke

up, but that could have been hours later. By then his trail would have been cold.

Instead of doing what he knew he should, he had lain there gazing at her blond beauty. She was too easy to look at, and he had never entertained the thought of resisting the temptation. Eyes starved for the sight of a woman had feasted on her. He had breathed deeply of her scent, treating his nostrils, too long deprived, to the perfume of a woman's body.

Rather than sneaking out as he knew he should, he had foolishly decided that he would take her with him. It was never his intention to harm her.

All right, so why did you threaten her with a knife?

Safety precaution.

Did you have to make her strip?

That was unnecessary, I admit. But I just wanted to look at her.

Like hell.

It's true. I wouldn't have forced her. Besides, she's an Anglo. I don't even like Anglo women. I sure don't desire them.

You desire this one.

I've been in prison for God's sake! Any woman would be desirable!

You wouldn't like to make love to her?

No.

You're a damn liar.

Well I didn't and I won't.

He would maintain rigid control over his lust if it killed him. He just wanted the woman near him. That's all. To keep that taunting voice of his conscience at bay, he thought of all the reasons he didn't like his blond hostage.

She was rich and spoiled, no doubt. She had about her

that Do-Not-Touch look that Indian boys like him had come to recognize on Anglo coeds. That was one of the first things he had learned when he left the reservation to attend college. Girls like Aislinn Andrews might flirt with you, but they sure as hell didn't want to make it with you. Or if they did let it go that far, it was for kicks, for the novelty of it, to brag to their sorority sisters that they'd had an Indian. "No!" "Yes!" "Just how savage was it?" The next day they acted like they didn't know you and the social barriers were up again.

This Anglo woman had spunk, though; he'd give her that. She could have been a real pain in the ass, whining and crying all the time, but she hadn't been. She'd kept a stiff upper lip no matter what he put her through.

His grim face relaxed into a facsimile of a smile when he recalled the way she had handled the highway patrolman. Why had she done it?

He owed her for that, he supposed.

And after last night, he was no longer sure he could keep to his resolve not to touch her. The hours spent in the Tumbleweed had been pure heaven and pure hell. There had been times, far too many for his peace of mind, when he had wanted the kisses to be real, when he had wanted to part her lips with his tongue and taste her, when he had wanted to open her clothes and touch her.

God, she had felt good lying against him this morning, her breath lightly fanning his chest, her breasts so soft and sweet, her thighs...

Damn! he thought, *I've got to let her go.*

When he got to the gas station, he would fill up the car, check with her to see that she was all right, then leave a note telling the owners where she could be found. When the police were notified, she would be able to tell them where he had been, but not where he was going. Or rather, not specifically where. They already knew his approximate destination and would be searching anyway. It was only a matter of time.

He only hoped he would accomplish what he had to do before that time ran out.

Sighting the town, he sped forward. Now that the decision to leave the woman behind had been made, Greywolf was eager to see it done and be on his way. He would have to take her car, of course, but for a woman like her, cars were probably easy to come by.

He pulled up to the gas pump and got out to put the nozzle into the tank. While it was filling, he added more water to the radiator. Keeping a careful eye on the time, he even washed the windshield and checked the tires. To avoid another sticky situation like the roadblock, he wanted to be well away when the owners of the service station returned.

Finally he went around the corner of the building to the rest room. Reaching over the salvaged steel girder he had pulled in front of the door, he knocked loudly. When there was no response, he called her name.

"Answer me. I know you're in there, Aislinn. This is childish."

He waited, pressing his ear to the door. After several seconds of intent listening, he knew that the room beyond the door was empty.

Apprehension squeezed his vitals like a cold fist. Before he could account for his actions, he shoved the girder out of the way and pulled the door open. He rushed inside, almost hoping that this was a ruse and that she was planning to launch some sort of amateur attack on him.

But he was met with nothing but an empty heat and a revolting stench. He rapidly deduced the meaning of the overturned barrel beneath the open window. When he did, his apprehension turned to black rage.

The little hellcat had gotten out!

Spinning on his heel, he went tearing out the rest room door and around the corner of the building. He dashed into the main room where they had been before, but there was no trace of Aislinn and no evidence that either she or anyone else had been there.

The broken glass of the window still lay undisturbed on the floor. The twenty-dollar bill was still tucked beneath the ashtray. He checked, but the dust on the telephone's receiver hadn't been smudged.

Puzzled, Greywolf crammed his hands into the back pockets of his jeans. Where could she have gone? And how? Had someone picked her up? He gnawed the inside of his cheek as he paced. Wouldn't she have telephoned someone right away? Wouldn't the authorities have made this their temporary command post while they questioned her and searched for him? It didn't make any sense.

He retraced his steps back to the rest room.

"Easy, easy, drink slowly or you'll choke."

Aislinn's parched throat thirstily welcomed the trickle of cola being poured into her mouth. She angled herself up, but moaned when a pain went rocketing through her head.

"Lie back," the gentle voice said. "That's enough for now anyway."

Her eyes flickered open. Greywolf was bending over her. His face was dark and inscrutable. Then she realized that the sun must have gone down because everything was dark. Moving her eyes caused her head to throb, but she let them wander far enough afield to determine that she was lying in the back seat of her car. The windows were all opened to let in the desert breeze. Greywolf was hunkered down beside her, wedged between the seats, his hip propped on the seat beside hers.

"Where—"

"About thirty miles from the service station. I've got bandages."

"Bandages?"

"You were moaning in your sleep," he said tersely, as though that explained everything.

Garnering all her strength, she reached up and gripped a handful of his shirt. "Talk to me, damn you. I'm sick of your Indian stoicism. Where am I and why do I need bandages? Did you finally use that knife on me?"

The rebellion had cost her every ounce of reserve energy, and she collapsed back onto the seat. But she didn't release Greywolf from her hostile stare. It was like looking into mirrors, but she kept staring into his eyes until he answered.

"Don't you remember climbing out the window and falling?" he asked.

Her eyes slid closed then. Now she remembered. The fear, the despair, and the hatred for the man who had caused it. Everything came rushing back to her in a tide of bad memories.

"I brought some aspirin for your headache."

She opened her eyes. He was shaking the tablets out of the bottle into the palm of his hand. "Where did you get them?"

"From the store. Can you take them with Coke?" She nodded. He passed her the aspirins and when she had laid them on her tongue, he slid his arm beneath her shoulders and supported her while she drank from the bottle he pressed to her lips.

When she was finished, he eased her back down. "The

sun blistered your lips." As he informed her of that, he opened a tiny jar of lip salve and gouged into it with the tip of his index finger. He touched it to her lip, smoothing the cool salve over the dried, sunburned skin.

The touch of his finger on her mouth elicited sensations in her middle, sensations she was ashamed of since they strongly resembled curls of arousal. His finger slid from one corner of her lower lip to the other, quickly and businesslike at first, then more slowly. When he traced the shape of her upper lip with his fingertip, she could barely hold still. Her body was restless with an ache that had nothing to do with the injuries she had sustained.

When he withdrew his finger, she tentatively touched her lips with her tongue. The ointment tasted slightly of banana and coconut. "Don't lick it off," Greywolf instructed brusquely, staring down at her mouth. "Let the salve work."

"Thank you."

"Don't thank me. You almost got me caught."

His cruel tone was so vastly different from his tender ministrations that she flinched. She should have known better than to expect tenderness from a man of stone like him. Her eyes flashed up at him angrily. "Well you *should* be caught, Mr. Greywolf. If there was no reason before, then because of the way you've mistreated me."

"You've never been mistreated in your life, Miss Andrews," he said scornfully. "You can't even begin to grasp the meaning of the word."

"How would you know? You know nothing about me."

"I know enough. You were reared with all the privileges that go with being rich and white."

"I'm not at fault for the way the Indians have been mistreated." She knew that all his anger and bitterness stemmed from that. "Do you indict every Anglo?"

"Yes," he hissed, his teeth bared.

"And what about yourself?" she shot back. "You're not a full-blood Indian. What about the part of you that's Anglo? Is it rotten to the core?"

He retaliated, grabbing her shoulders in his hard hands and pressing her back into the seat. His razor-sharp eyes were as cold as naked steel. "I am Indian," he whispered, emphasizing his words by shaking her slightly. "Don't ever forget that."

Aislinn knew she never would. Not now. The fierceness of his gaze dispelled any hopes that he was softening toward her. He was dangerous. Fully aware of his brute strength as he leaned over her, she shuddered with trepidation.

In the sleeveless shirt, the muscles of his arms looked as hard as granite. Most of the buttons on the soiled shirt were undone and his exposed chest sawed in and out with each angry breath he took. His corded throat was a perfect pedestal for a face that could have been hewn out of native rock.

The silver earring fastened in his lobe winked at her like a menacing eye in the darkness. The silver cross hanging from his neck mocked her because of the benevolence it symbolized. He exuded a scent that was part sun, part sweat, and all male.

Any woman with an ounce of common sense wouldn't dare to provoke such a potentially dangerous animal. Aislinn was smarter than average. She didn't even blink.

During that tense silence, he kept his muscles coiled as though ready to spring. Now, he visibly relaxed them and loosened his hold on her. "I should bandage your arm before it gets infected." He spoke with a notable lack of emotion, as though their heated argument had never taken place.

"My arm?" Only when she tried to move it did she realize that her left arm was hurting almost as badly as her head. She remembered tearing open the skin as she fell out the window.

"Here," he said, noticing her grimace when she tried to raise it, "let me." He levered her up and settled her into a half-reclining position in the corner of the back seat. His hands moved to the front of her blouse. Reflexively her right hand flew up and clutched the material to her body. He didn't move, but continued to stare back at her levelly, then said, "It has to come off, Aislinn."

She looked down and was shocked to see that her sleeve was soaked with blood. "I...I didn't know," she stammered, suppressing a wave of nausea and dizziness.

"I needed to get away from there in a hurry, so I bundled you into the back seat. I put some distance between us and that place, but now your arm has to be seen to."

Seconds ticked by. Minutes? They stared deeply into each other's eyes. His took a detour down to her mouth, glossy now with the emollient. Hers looked at the grim line of his lips and wondered how they could be both stern and sensual. Then Greywolf shook his head impatiently and muttered, "As I said before, you are my insurance policy."

Once again his hands reached toward the front of her blouse, and this time she didn't forestall him. He unbuttoned it quickly, emotionlessly. Embarrassment rose inside Aislinn like a warm, red tide as her bare breasts were revealed to him button by button. But if he noticed them, his face gave nothing away.

Only when he settled his hands on her shoulders and began to peel the cloth back, did his movements become slow and tender, almost caring. He eased the sleeve off her uninjured arm first, then gradually began lowering the other one. She winced when the cloth tugged on places where the blood had dried.

"I'm sorry." Before she could prepare herself, he ripped the remaining sleeve away. "That's the best way. I'm sorry," he repeated.

"It's all right. I know you had to." Her eyes filled with tears, but she didn't let them fall. He seemed momentarily entranced by her eyes, or was he merely watching to see if an Anglo woman would surrender to pain and cry?

Then, abruptly, and with the same kind of detachment he had shown as he unbuttoned her blouse, he angled her forward in order to remove it. For an infinitesimal second, Aislinn leaned against him, her breasts grazing his chest.

Myriad sensations flocked to her mind like fluttering birds. How fragile her nipples felt against the solid wall of muscle. How his chest hair felt both crisp and soft as it tickled her skin. How warm he was.

They pretended not to notice the brief contact, though his jaw was clenched tighter than ever when he eased her back into the corner of the seat.

The reopened scratch, which ran the entire length of her arm, oozed blood. Greywolf tossed her blouse aside and reached into a paper sack. He took a box of sterilized cotton and a bottle of antiseptic from it. "This is going to burn like hell," he said, uncapping the bottle and pouring some of the liquid onto a wad of cotton. "Ready?" he asked.

She nodded. He lifted her arm and applied the cotton to the wounded skin on the underside. Her knees jackknifed; she gasped; tears spurted out of her eyes. Quickly he dabbed the entire scratch from wrist to armpit, then went back to press the soaked cotton to the places where the nail had plowed deeper.

"Oh, please," Aislinn moaned, squeezing her eyes shut against the fiery pain.

He hurriedly recapped the antiseptic and set it aside. Lifting her arm again, he began to blow gently on the scratch.

Aislinn opened her eyes and was dismayed to find his dark head bending so low over her. One brown hand was wrapped loosely around her wrist, holding her arm up. The other was splayed open just behind her head bracing him above her.

She watched his cheeks beneath the blade-sharp ridge of his cheekbones. They ballooned in and out as he cooled her skin with his gentle breath. His lips hovered scant inches above her arm. His head moved higher as he worked his way up her arm until his mouth was even with her breast.

His breath touched her there. Warm and balmy and soft. Responsively, her nipples reacted. They beaded to the size of small, perfect, pink pearls.

When he saw what had happened, his head made a jerking motion, as though he was going to raise it. But he paused. Lowered his head. Blew on her again. More gently this time, but directly over the tip of her breasts.

Then he became perfectly still. Raw hunger made his eyes look bleak as his gaze became fixed on her. He swallowed. He strained toward her, but, as though an invisible leash were around his neck, he refrained from touching her.

Aislinn was afraid to move, though she was tempted to. She fell victim to an almost irresistible urge to thread her fingers up through his hair and draw his head down to her. A forbidden and unaccountable tenderness for him overwhelmed her. It was unlike any emotion she had ever experienced before. She longed to grant him the use of her body. She wanted to use his. She should hate him and yet…

Why hadn't he deserted her at the service station? Why had he wasted his precious time getting aspirin and medicine for her scratch? Was there more to this man than met the eye? Did he have a capacity for human kindness after all? Was his austerity only a reaction to the injustices he had suffered?

Her expression conveyed her bafflement and made her appear extremely receptive and vulnerable. When Greywolf looked up into her face, the fire in his eyes went out instantly and he growled a warning. "Don't look at me like that."

She shook her head uncomprehendingly. "Like what?"

"Like you've forgotten that I've been in prison. Do you want to know if I desire you?" he asked harshly. "Well I do." The fingers encircling her arm became a manacle. "Yes, I want you. I want to touch you all over. I want to feel your breasts. I want to take one in my mouth and hold it there for a long, long time. I want to be so deep inside you I can feel your heartbeat. So unless you're ready to take an Indian between your thighs, I suggest you don't give me that come-on look again, Miss Andrews."

Outraged that he could so grossly misinterpret her expression, and furious with herself for giving him the benefit of the doubt only seconds before, she shielded her breasts with her free arm. "Don't flatter yourself," she hissed. "I'd die first."

He laughed shortly. "I'm sure you would. At least you'd *want* to die before having your pure Anglo body tainted by an Indian. But at least you won't bleed to death. Not if I have anything to do with it," he said bitterly.

She averted her head and didn't deign to look at him while he bound her arm with gauze he had taken from the sack. Once that was done, he gathered together the first-aid supplies and stuffed them back into the paper bag.

Her eyes widened with alarm when he picked up the knife, but he used it only to cut the sleeves from her shirt, much as he must have his own. He wielded the sharp blade viciously, making jagged cuts in the material until the job was done, then tossed the ravaged garment to her.

"Put this back on. We've wasted enough time here."

He got out and went around to the driver's seat. In broody silence, Aislinn stared at the back of his head. While the car made the best of the pockmarked highway, she devised a dozen ways to overpower him. Each one was eliminated before she could even think it through. She thought of making a garrote out of one of her sleeves and strangling him from behind. But then where would she be? Out in the middle of nowhere without a map or water. The gasoline in the car wouldn't last forever. Should she succeed in physically besting Greywolf, her chances of surviving in the wilderness were remote.

So she rode in stony silence until exhaustion overcame her and once again she fell asleep.

She woke up when the car was brought to a slow, gradual halt. Struggling to pull her aching, tired, sore and bruised body into a sitting position, she blinked the sleep out of her eyes and adjusted them to the dark.

Greywolf gave her no more than a cursory glance over his shoulder before opening the car door and getting out. He strode up an incline that led to a structure. She could barely distinguish its outline against the darkness, but she recognized it as a Navaho hogan. Aislinn doubted that the six-sided log dwelling would have been visible at all had it not been for the faint light coming through the rectangular doorway.

The hogan was nestled against the side of the mountain and was cloaked by its dark shadow. The slightly rounded, conical roof was left untouched by the silvery moonlight, which spilled down the mountain like mercury.

Curiosity, as much as the profound desire not to be left alone in such primitive, almost mystical, surroundings, motivated her to leave the car and follow him. She scrambled up the rocky path, trying to keep her eyes both on where she was going and on Greywolf's lean silhouette.

Before he reached the hogan, another silhouette, much smaller than his, was outlined in the patch of light in the doorway. It was that of a woman.

"Lucas!"

His name was uttered in a soft, glad cry before the petite figure left the doorway, ran down the path and launched herself against him. His arms locked around her, hugging her tight. His head and shoulders bent low, protectively, over her diminutive frame.

"Lucas, Lucas, why did you do it? We heard about your escape on the radio and saw your picture on TV."

"You know why I did it. How is he?"

He held the small woman away from him and peered down into her upturned face. She shook her head sadly. Without another word Greywolf took her arm and guided her back up the path and through the doorway.

Intrigued, Aislinn followed them. Never having been in a hogan before, she tentatively stepped inside. The single-room house was stifling hot. A low fire burned in the center. Smoke, seeming to lack the energy to make the climb, was emitted through a hole in the roof. Kerosene lamps provided the only other lighting. In the foreground was a rough square table with four crude chairs. A dented enamel coffeepot and several battered tin cups were on the table. There was a dry sink in the corner with a hand-crank water pump.

The floor was hard-packed dirt. On the floor, not far from where Aislinn was standing, someone had done a beautiful sand painting. The design was intricate and meticulously executed. She had no idea what it symbolized, but she knew that such sand paintings were used in ancient curing ceremonies.

Against the wall opposite the door was a low cot draped with Navaho blankets. Greywolf was kneeling beside it. Lying on the cot, beneath a blanket, was an elderly Indian man. Long, gray braids framed gaunt, jaundiced cheeks. Gnarled, callused hands fitfully plucked at the blanket. His eyes shone feverishly as they gazed up at the much younger man bending over him, speaking softly in a language Aislinn couldn't understand but knew was of the Na-Dene group.

There were two other people in the room—the woman who had greeted Greywolf so intimately, and another man, surprisingly, an Anglo. He stood at the foot of the cot on which the old Indian lay. He was of average height and had thinning brown hair streaked attractively at the temples with gray. Aislinn placed his age at around fifty. He stared meditatively down at Greywolf and the old man.

For a multitude of unnamed and unacknowledged reasons, Aislinn had avoided looking at the woman. She did so now. She was very pretty. Indian. She had high cheekbones, raven-black hair styled in a soft, straight pageboy to just above her shoulders, and liquid dark eyes. Dressed like an Anglo, she wore a simple cotton dress, low-heeled shoes and inexpensive jewelry. The way she held her small head lent her an air of elegance. She was slender, but her figure was feminine and perfectly proportioned.

Greywolf pressed his forehead against the work-worn hands of the old man, then turned to speak to the man standing at the foot of the cot. "Hi, Doc."

"Lucas, you crazy fool."

A ghost of a smile flickered across Greywolf's austere features. "Some greeting."

"Some damned stunt. Escaping prison."

Greywolf shrugged and glanced back down at the old man. "He says he isn't in any pain."

"I've made him as comfortable as I can here," the man addressed as "Doc" said. "I urged him to go to the hospital—"

Greywolf was already shaking his head and interrupted the other man. "He wants to die here. It's important to him. How long?" he asked hoarsely.

"Morning. Maybe."

The woman shuddered, but didn't make a sound. Greywolf took the steps necessary to enfold her in an embrace. "Mother."

His mother! Aislinn thought, aghast. The woman looked so young, far too young to have a son as old as Lucas Greywolf.

He put his lips close to her ear and murmured words that Aislinn imagined to be consoling. She was awed that the cold, remote man she had been with for almost two days could show such compassion. His eyes were pinched shut. The stark contrast of light and shadow playing over his face made his anguished expression even more pronounced and testified to the depth of his emotion. When he finally opened the light-gray eyes, they happened to fall on her where she still hovered in the doorway.

He eased away from his mother, and bobbed his chin toward Aislinn. "I brought a hostage with me."

The blunt statement brought his mother around and

she saw Aislinn for the first time. She raised a dainty hand to her chest. "A *hostage?* Lucas!"

"Have you lost your mind?" Doc asked angrily. "Hell, man, they're looking all over the state for you."

"So I've noticed," Greywolf said with casual disregard.

"They'll slam you back in prison so fast it'll make your head spin. And this time they might throw away the key."

"That's a risk I was willing to take," Lucas said, matching the other man's anger. "I asked permission to leave the prison in order to see my grandfather before he died. The formal request was denied. I played by their rules, but it did me no good. It never has. This time I've learned my lesson. Don't ask, just do."

"Oh, Lucas," his mother sighed, slumping down into a chair. "Father understood why you couldn't be here."

"But *I* didn't," Greywolf said fiercely, baring his teeth and spitting the words out. "What difference would it have made to let me out for a few days?"

The three fell silent because there seemed to be no answer to that question. Finally Doc stepped forward and kindly said to Aislinn, "I'm Dr. Gene Dexter."

She liked him immediately. His looks were unremarkable, but his demeanor was soothing and reassuring...or did it just seem so because she had spent the past forty-eight hours in the volatile company of Lucas Greywolf? "Aislinn Andrews."

"You're from...?"

"Scottsdale."

"You look tired. Won't you sit down?"

Gene Dexter offered her a chair and she accepted it gladly. "Thank you."

"This is Alice Greywolf," Dexter said, laying a hand on the woman's shoulder.

"I'm Lucas's mother," she said, leaning forward in her chair. Her dark eyes were filled with sincerity. "Will you ever forgive us for what's happened?"

"He's your father?" Aislinn asked softly, pointing to the still figure on the cot.

"Yes, Joseph Greywolf," Alice answered.

"I'm sorry."

"Thank you."

"Can I get you something?" the Anglo doctor asked Aislinn.

She sighed tiredly and gave him a wry smile. "You can get me home."

Greywolf made a scoffing sound. "I was an unpleasant surprise to Miss Andrews when she came home the night before last and found me scavenging food out of her refrigerator."

"You broke into her house!" Alice exclaimed in disbelief.

"I'm a criminal, Mother. Remember? An escaped convict." He poured himself a cup of coffee from the enamel pot on the table. "Excuse me." He gave Aislinn a smirking smile before he returned to the bedside of the dying man.

"He escaped prison, broke into my house, and took me hostage just so he could come here to see his grandfather before he died?" All the perplexity Aislinn felt went into the question she hardly realized she had spoken aloud.

When she recalled how Greywolf had frightened her, how he had threatened her with the knife, how he had taunted and tormented her, she wanted to get up, walk across the dirt floor, jerk him up by his long hair and slap him as hard as she could.

She had submitted to his threats because she had thought him capable of violence. Looking at him now as he leaned over the old man, whispering tender words, stroking the creased forehead with a loving hand, she doubted Lucas Greywolf would harm a fly.

Aislinn drew her eyes back to the two people who were quietly watching her as though she were an object of curiosity. "I don't understand."

Alice Greywolf smiled gently. "My son isn't easy to understand. He's impulsive. He has a short temper. But his bark is worse than his bite."

"Personally I'd like to whip his butt for involving this young woman," Dr. Dexter said. "Why would he make things more difficult for himself by kidnapping Miss Andrews?"

"You know how determined he is, Gene," Alice said with resignation. "If he made up his mind to get here before Father died, nothing could have stopped him." She looked at Aislinn with concern. "He didn't hurt you, did he?"

Aislinn hestitated before answering. She could tell them he had humiliated her by forcing her to watch him strip off his clothes and take a shower. Then he had made her strip and had tied her to him while they slept. He had mauled and pawed her, but never for recreation. He had verbally abused her, subjected her to embarrassment many times, but she couldn't honestly say that he had *hurt* her.

"No," she answered quietly. Confused, she shook her head as she glanced down at her clenched hands. She was protecting him again. Why?

"Your arm is bandaged," Gene observed.

"I hurt it trying to get out of a rest room."

"A rest room?"

"Yes. He, uh, locked me in."

"What?"

Aislinn backtracked and told them everything that had happened, leaving out the more personal aspects of her encounter with Greywolf and glossing over the incident at the roadblock. "Lucas bandaged my arm just an hour or so ago."

"Well, I'd better check it," Gene said, going to the basin in the dry sink and pumping water into it. He began to wash his hands with a cake of yellow soap. "Alice, get my bag, please. She probably ought to have a tetanus shot."

A half hour later, Aislinn felt better. Her arm had been examined and diagnosed as having nothing more than a painful scratch. She had washed at the sink and had used a borrowed hairbrush to untangle her hair. To replace her tattered blouse and dirty jeans, Alice lent her a traditional tunic blouse and long skirt of a Navaho woman, having taken them from a storage trunk against the wall. "It's very kind of you to agree to wait here until…until Father dies."

Aislinn buttoned the blouse. "I expected to be taken to an outlaws's hideout." She glanced toward the bed where both Gene and Greywolf were attending the elderly Indian. "I don't understand why he didn't just tell me why he had escaped."

"My son is often defensive."

"And mistrustful."

Alice briefly laid her hand on Aislinn's arm. "We have some soup that's still hot. Would you like some?"

"Please." Only then did she realize that she was starving. Alice sat at the table with her while she ate. Aislinn used that opportunity to ask questions about Greywolf, questions that had previously piqued her curiosity.

"Am I to understand that he was serving a three-year sentence for a crime he didn't actually commit?"

"Yes," Alice replied. "Lucas was guilty of only one thing—of organizing that demonstration on the steps of the courthouse in Phoenix. He had gone through all the legal channels. He had secured a permit to march. It wasn't supposed to get violent."

"What happened?"

"Some of the marchers, much more militant-minded than Lucas, got rowdy. Before Lucas could regain control, public property was being vandalized and fights had broken out. It resulted in a brawl. Several people, including policemen, were injured."

"Seriously?"

"Yes. Because he had already won a reputation as a dissident, Lucas was the first one arrested."

"Why didn't he tell them he was trying to put a stop to the violence?"

"He refused to name the men who were actually responsible. He represented himself at his trial and wouldn't allow anyone else to speak in his defense. But I think that the judge and jury had already made up their minds before the case ever came to trial. There was a lot of media publicity about it. He was found guilty. The sentence was disproportionately severe."

"Wouldn't he have been better off to hire a lawyer to defend him?" Aislinn asked.

Alice smiled. "My son didn't tell you much about himself, did he?" Aislinn shook her head. "He *is* a lawyer."

Speechlessly Aislinn stared at the other woman. "A lawyer?"

"A disbarred one now," she said sadly. "That's one reason he's so bitter. He wanted to help our people through the legal system. Now he won't be able to."

Aislinn could hardly assimilate everything Alice had told her. It seemed that Mr. Greywolf was more complex than even she had imagined. She glanced at the cot just as he stood and turned toward the table where she was sitting with Alice. Gene Dexter laid a comforting hand on his shoulder.

"You said 'our people,'" Aislinn remarked to Alice. "Your Indian heritage is extremely important to you. Is that why you and Lucas use the name Greywolf?"

"What name *should* we use?" Alice asked, apparently bewildered by the question.

"Why, Dexter," Aislinn said, equally bewildered. "Isn't Gene Lucas's father?"

Aislinn was met with three stunned stares. Alice's velvety brown eyes were the first to look away. A becoming blush stained her dusky cheeks. Gene Dexter cleared his throat uncomfortably. Greywolf's response was somewhat more abrupt and to the point.

"No, he isn't."

Five

"Alice, Joseph is asking for you," Gene said diplomatically. They withdrew, Gene with his arm around Alice's shoulders.

Aislinn wished the proverbial hole would open up and swallow her. "I th-thought since you're only half Indian... I mean..."

"Well you thought wrong." Greywolf dropped into one of the chairs at the table. "What are you still doing here anyway? I thought that by now you would have wheedled Gene into taking you back to civilization."

"He's got better things to do, like taking care of your grandfather."

Balancing his chair on its two back legs, he looked up at her tauntingly. "Or maybe this life of crime has proven to be exciting. Maybe you don't want to go home."

She gave him a fulminating look. "Of course I do. It's just that I'm not as shallow and unfeeling as you seem to think."

"Meaning?"

"Meaning that I sympathize with you and your mother. Instead of terrorizing me, holding a knife on me and tying me up, you could have told me why you escaped prison. I would have helped you."

He uttered a sound that could have passed for a laugh. It wasn't a jovial sound, but one laden with skepticism and rebuke.

"A nice, respectable, law-abiding WASP like you, giving aid to an escaped convict, an escaped *Indian* convict?" His tone was derisive. "I seriously doubt that. Anyway, I couldn't gamble on your kindheartedness. I've learned to be distrustful." The front legs of the chair hit the floor hard, as though punctuating his statement. "Is there any more of that soup?"

As she dished up a bowl of soup from the pan that simmered over the smoky fire, she realized that the identity of his father was still a mystery. Apparently his Anglo blood wasn't a topic open to discussion, which only made her more curious about it.

He wolfed down the steaming soup. Without his asking, she poured him a fresh cup of coffee. While hours ago her sole desire had been to put distance between herself and this dangerous man, she now sat down in a chair across the table from him. He looked up at her with an inquiring tilt to his eyebrows, but went back to eating without offering a comment.

He no longer seemed so ferocious. Was it the hushed atmosphere or the limited confines of the hogan that had mellowed him? It was difficult to feel terror for a man who would kneel at the bedside of his ancient, dying grandfather and speak with such gentleness.

Greywolf hadn't changed physically. His hair was just as jet black, just as rebelliously long. His eyes were still as cold as a pond glazed with morning frost. The muscles in his arms still rippled with latent violence beneath the sinuous, coppery skin. His expression remained just as aloof.

And yet he was different.

He wasn't so much frightening now as he was intriguing, and so very different from the men her parents often paired her with. They were cookie-cutter replicas of each other. They wore conservatively tailored suits that only varied in their shades of gray. All were upwardly mobile executive types who conversed at length on subjects like market analyses and growth indexes. Their idea of spicing up a conversation was to talk about their tennis game and the expense of maintaining a foreign sports car. So-and-so's recent divorce and so-and-so's hassles with the IRS could always be counted on as good cocktail-party topics.

How boring they all seemed compared to this man, who wore one silver earring and gulped down canned soup as if it might be his last decent meal for a long time, who wasn't embarrassed by sweat and dirt and the fundamentals of life, like dying.

Quite frankly, she was fascinated by Lucas Greywolf.

"You didn't tell me you were a lawyer." He wasn't given to chitchat. Aislinn knew no other way of commencing a conversation with him than to jump in feetfirst.

"It wasn't relevant."

"You might have mentioned it."

"Why? Would you have felt better knowing that the man holding a knife on you was a lawyer?"

"I suppose not," she said wearily. He went back to eating his soup. Conversation closed. Information would have to be pulled out of him like a deeply rooted bicuspid. She tried again. "Your mother told me you went to college on a track scholarship."

"That must have been some conversation you two had." He finished the soup and pushed the empty bowl away.

"Well, did you?" she demanded impatiently.

"Why the sudden interest?"

She shrugged. "I just… I don't know. I'm interested."

"You want to know how a poor Indian boy bettered himself in the Anglo world, is that it?"

"I should have known you'd take umbrage. Forget it." Angrily she scraped her chair back and stood up, but when she reached for his soup bowl to carry it to the sink, his hand shot out and captured hers.

"Sit down and I'll tell you all about it, since you're so curious to know."

She couldn't possibly win an arm-wrestling match with him, not the way his fingers were biting into her flesh, so she sat back down. He stared across the table at her for several moments before he finally released her hand. His eyes smoldered with contempt. The degree of it made her squirm uneasily.

"I graduated from a school here on the reservation," he began. His lips were held in a firm, grim line which barely moved as he formed words with them. "I got the scholarship because an alumnus who scouted for the coach had seen me run in a track meet. So I went to Tucson and enrolled in the university. The athletics was easy. But I was woefully ignorant compared to the other freshmen. Dedicated as the teachers on the reservation had been, I wasn't prepared for college by any stretch of the imagination."

"Don't look at me like that."

"How's that?"

"Like I should feel guilty over having blond hair and blue eyes."

"I know someone like you will find this hard to understand, but when you're the outcast to begin with, you'd better be damned good at *something*. That's the only way you even come close to being accepted. While you and your crowd were enjoying the fraternity and sorority parties, I was studying."

"You wanted to excel."

He scoffed. "I wanted to stay even. When I wasn't in class or in the library or on the track, I was working. I held two jobs on campus because I didn't want it said that I had gotten a free ride just because I was an Indian and could run fast."

He folded his hands on the table and stared down at them. "Do you know what a half-breed is?"

"I've heard the word, yes. It's an ugly word."

"Do you know what it's like to straddle a line like that? That's a rhetorical question. Of course you don't. Oh, I earned a certain celebrity from track. I could run," he said reflectively, as though he could still hear the cheering from the stadium fans. "By the time I graduated with honors—"

"So you *did* excel."

He ignored her. "My name was so well-known that they even wrote an article in the newspaper about me. The slant of it was how commendable my accomplishments were...for an Indian." His eyes speared into hers. "You see, there's always that qualification: 'For an Indian.'"

Aislinn knew that he was right, so she said nothing.

"I went straight into law school. I was eager to set up practice, to help keep the Indians from being exploited by mining companies and such. And I did win a few cases, but not nearly enough. I became disillusioned with the legal system, which I found out is as political as anything else in the world. Justice is *not* blind.

"So I began playing dirty ball, too. I became much more outspoken and critical. I organized the Indian protesters so they would have a louder voice. I staged peaceful demonstrations. My activities only served to win me a reputation as a troublemaker who bore watching. When they had the opportunity to arrest me and lock me up for a long time, they did."

He sat back in his chair and eyed Aislinn stonily. "So there. Are you satisfied now? Did you learn what you wanted to know?"

It was a lengthier speech than she could ever have imagined him making. The missing pieces were easy to fit in. He belonged in neither society, being neither wholly Indian nor wholly Anglo. She knew the slurs he must have been subjected to. Words like "breed" would have been intolerable for a headstrong, proud young man.

He was smart and physically superior. No doubt other Indian discontents looked up to him as their leader and rallied to his side. He became someone the Anglo community feared. Still, she thought, most of Lucas Greywolf's hardships stemmed from his own deep-seated bitterness and stubbornness.

He could have saved himself years in prison by naming the guilty parties. Aislinn could just imagine the granite hardness of his jaw when he refused to answer the authorities' questions.

"You've got a chip on your shoulder," she said candidly.

Surprisingly he smiled, though it was a chilling grin. "You're damned right I do. Now. Not always. When I left the reservation to go to college, I was full of naiveté and high ideals."

"But society did a number on you."

"Go ahead, mock me. I'm used to it."

"Did you ever stop to think that the reason you weren't included wasn't because you are Indian, but because of your less-than-charming personality?"

Again his hand lashed out and caught her wrist. "What do you know about it? *Nothing,*" he growled. "Even your name reeks of your pure Anglo-Saxon blood. Have you ever been invited to a party and plied with liquor just so the others can see how much alcohol an Indian can really tolerate? 'How drunk will he get?' 'Maybe he'll put on a war bonnet and do a dance for us.' 'Where's your bow and arrow, Chief?'"

"Stop it!" She tried to pull her arm free but she couldn't.

Both had stood, though neither noticed. He had her bent at an awkward angle over the table. His teeth were clenched, and though his voice was as smooth as honey, it carried with it a terrible malice. "After you're subjected to that kind of ridicule, you come back and tell me all about that chip on my shoulder, Miss Andrews. You—"

"Lucas!"

His mother's sharp reprimand ended Greywolf's tirade abruptly. He stared deep into Aislinn's eyes for another heartbeat before he dropped her hand and spun around. "He's calling for you," Alice said. Her beautiful eyes sawed back and forth between her son and his captive, as though wary of the sparks she sensed crackling between them. She took Lucas's arm and led him back to the cot.

Aislinn watched them. The top of Alice's head barely reached his shoulder. The arm he settled across her narrow shoulders as they approached the sickbed conveyed affection and tenderness. She couldn't imagine him experiencing those natural human emotions.

"You have to forgive Lucas." Gene Dexter's quiet voice coaxed Aislinn out of her musings.

"Why should I? He's a grown man, accountable for his actions. Bad behavior is inexcusable, no matter the cause of it."

The doctor sighed and poured himself a cup of coffee. "You're right, of course." As he sipped his coffee, he, too, watched the mother and son kneeling at the bedside of the dying man. "I've known Lucas since he was a boy. He's always been angry. Bitter. Alice's mother was Navaho, but Joseph is Apache. Lucas inherited that warrior spirit."

"You've known them that long?"

He nodded. "I came to the reservation fresh out of my year of residency."

"Why?" She blushed when the doctor looked down at her, a smile curving his lips. Good Lord! Was Greywolf's rudeness rubbing off on her? "I'm sorry. It's none of my business."

"That's all right. I'm happy to answer." He drew his brows together, collecting his thoughts, carefully choosing his words. "I felt a 'calling,' I guess you might say. I was young and idealistic. I wanted to make a *difference,* not a lot of money."

"I'm sure you have." She paused before adding, "At least in the lives of Alice and Lucas Greywolf." When she dared to glance at him from the corner of her eye, she saw that he wasn't fooled by her subtle probing.

"I met Alice when she brought Lucas to the clinic with a broken arm. Over the next several weeks we became friends, and I asked if she would be willing to lend me a hand at the clinic. I trained her in nursing skills. We've been working together ever since."

His feelings for Alice Greywolf ran much deeper than those of a doctor for his dedicated nurse, but Aislinn didn't have the opportunity to press him on the issue. Just then Alice turned toward Gene, her lovely face stricken with alarm.

"Gene, come quickly! He's—"

The doctor rushed toward the cot and shouldered Lucas and Alice aside. He placed his stethoscope against Joseph Greywolf's bony chest. Even from where she stood near the table, Aislinn could hear his rattling, struggling respiration. It sounded like two pieces of sandpaper rubbing together. The abrasive sound didn't cease until daybreak.

When it did, the sudden silence was louder than the racket had been. Aislinn covered her trembling lips with her hand and turned her back to the three keeping vigil at the cot, affording them a modicum of privacy. She, being the outsider, didn't want to intrude on their grief. She sat down in one of the chairs and bowed her head.

She heard the shuffle of feet on the packed-dirt floor, the quiet sound of Alice's weeping, whispered murmurs of consolation. Then her ears were met with the heavy thud of boot heels. The front door squeaked as it was shoved open. Aislinn raised her head and, through the door, saw Lucas stalk off down the rocky path.

His powerful body was as fluid and graceful as ever, but the sinewy muscles were stretching his skin, straining it. He seemed able to hold himself together only by sheer willpower. Since his back was to her, she couldn't see his face, but she could imagine it—tense, hard, unrelentingly stern.

Aislinn watched him stamp past her car and the four-wheel-drive truck she assumed belonged to Dr. Dexter. With that same determined stride, he crossed the floor of the canyon, then took a rocky, uneven path up the side of the hill.

She never remembered moving. She didn't consciously make up her mind. She simply stood up and rushed toward the door, some subconscious area of her brain directing her. She quickly glanced at Alice. Gene Dexter was holding her in his arms, crooning words of comfort into her midnight-black hair.

Aislinn ran through the door and out into the still morning. Dawn light was just peeping over the ridge of the mountains that ringed the hogan. The air was considerably cooler up there in the mountains, particularly at that time of day, when the sun hadn't had time to bake the rocks to a grilling heat.

Aislinn noticed nothing, not even the gorgeous, ever-changing violet hues of the eastern sky as the sun rose higher. Her eyes were trained on the man who was no more than a rapidly shrinking speck against the rocky terrain as he climbed, seemingly without effort, higher.

Her progress wasn't as rapid. The boots he had chosen for her came in handy now, but the borrowed skirt kept getting snagged on brush and wrapped around her legs, impeding her efforts. Innumerable times she skinned her knees; her palms bled from stinging scrapes.

Before she even reached the halfway point to the summit, she was winded and laboring for every breath. But she kept climbing, driven by an emotion she didn't stop to contemplate. It was something she simply had to do. She had to get to Greywolf.

At last the plateau, which formed a tabletop crest to the rocky incline, no longer seemed unreachable. She took heart and began climbing faster. Looking up, she could see Lucas standing at the summit, his body a dark, lean silhouette against the cloudless lavender sky.

When she finally reached the top, she virtually crawled the remaining distance. Once there, she slumped down on the level rock and hung her head in exhaustion. Her breath soughed in and out of her body. Her heart was beating so fast that it actually hurt. She stared down at her hands in disbelief. Rocks had been cruel to her palms. Her nails were broken.

Ordinarily, she would have been horrified by such injuries. Now, the pain meant nothing. She didn't even feel it. Its significance was reduced to nothingness when measured against that of the man.

Greywolf remained motionless, his back to her, staring out over the opposite cliff. His feet were braced a shoulders' width apart. His hands, balled into fists, were held rigidly at his sides.

As she watched, he threw his head back, squeezed his eyes shut, and released a howl that echoed eerily off the walls of the surrounding mountains. The animal wail came straight from his soul. It was an outpouring of grief, despair and frustration, so profound that Aislinn felt his pain as her own. Tears coursed down her cheeks. Leaning forward, she stretched out a hand as though to touch him, but he was standing several yards away. Her offer of solace went unseen.

She didn't know why she wasn't repulsed by his soul-rending display of emotion. In her family such exhibitions were forbidden. If one felt sadness, rage, even joy, demonstrations of the emotion were kept restrained and refined. Self-expression, just as everything else, was governed by rules. One kept one's feelings bridled. To do otherwise was considered bad taste and vulgar in the extreme.

Never in her life had Aislinn witnessed such an honest, boundless expression of emotion. Greywolf's raw cry opened up a secret pocket of her heart and left a wide and gaping wound. A spear couldn't have pierced her more thoroughly. The impact was that jarring, that sharp, that deep.

He sank to his knees, bowed his back and hung his head low, covering it with his arms. He rocked back and forth, keening and chanting words she didn't comprehend. She understood only that he was a man totally disconsolate, made alien and alone by the measure of his grief.

Still sitting, she inched her way over to him and touched his shoulder. He reacted like an injured animal. His head snapped around and he made a snarling sound. His eyes were tearless and icy on the surface, but the black centers burned from within like the fathomless pits of hell.

"What are you doing here?" he asked disdainfully. "You have no place here."

Not only was he implying that she didn't belong on this wild plateau with him, but also that she couldn't begin to understand the depth of his grief and that he resented her thinking she could.

"I'm sorry about your grandfather."

His eyes narrowed dangerously. "What could you possibly care about the death of an old, useless Indian?"

Tears smarted in her eyes at his harsh words. "Why do you do that?"

"Do what?"

"Cruelly shut other people out, people who are trying to help you."

"I don't need anybody's help." He looked at her with open scorn. "Especially yours."

"Do you think you're the only person on earth who has ever been disillusioned, or hurt, or betrayed?"

"*You* have? In your ivory palace?"

The contemptuous question didn't merit an answer.

She could have told him there were endless varieties of abuse but swapping tales of woe would have been ridiculous. Besides, she was too angry at him for spurning her sympathy. "You carry your bitterness like a shield to protect yourself. You hide behind your anger like a coward who is afraid to get caught experiencing some human warmth. Someone offers you tenderness, and you misread it as pity. Anyway, we all need to be pitied at times."

"Well then," he said silkily, "pity me."

He moved with the speed of summer lightning and his touch was just as electrifying. His hand shot out and sank into her hair, winding the long strands around his fist and yanking her head forward. He tilted it back so far she feared her neck would snap.

"You're feeling benevolent toward the Indians, hmm? Well let's see just how much."

His mouth came crashing down on hers. The contact was brutal and punishing. She made an outraged sound deep in her throat, but it had no effect on him. If anything, his fist wound tighter in her hair and his lips pressed harder upon hers.

Moving her head was out of the question, so she gripped his biceps and tried to push him away. The skin beneath her grasp was warm and smooth. The muscles felt like braided cables of steel. Her efforts were to no avail.

Raising his lips only inches above hers, he smiled sardonically. "Ever been kissed by an Indian, Miss Andrews? It'll be something you can tell your friends about the next time you have a tea party."

He ground his lips against hers again. This time, she experienced a sense of falling and realized only when she felt rocks digging into her back that he had lowered her to the ground. He stretched above her, covering one side of her body with his.

"No!" she gasped when he released her mouth to press hot kisses into her neck just below her jaw. She tried to kick, but he threw his long leg over hers, imprisoning them beneath his thigh.

"What's the matter? Lost your taste for pity so soon?" he mocked. "Taste this."

He kissed her again. She felt the probing of his tongue against her lips and stubbornly kept them sealed together. His hand released her hair and caught her just under the jaw. Hard fingers squeezed until she had no choice but to open her mouth or risk her jawbone being shattered.

His tongue thrust its way into her mouth. It was an angry, plundering, ravishing, hurtful intruder. Silently she screamed in mortification and fury, struggling against him, arching her back above the hard ground in an effort to throw him off.

All she accomplished was to get his knee wedged between her thighs and his hips intimately pressing upon hers. Desperate to end the savage embrace, she curled both hands into claws and reached for his face.

But the moment her fingertips came into contact with his face, she felt the wet patches on his cheekbones. Immediately, her wrath was banished and replaced by wonder. Her fingers relaxed their curled tension, and she used them to blindly explore the chiseled ridges of his cheekbones and the almost gaunt planes beneath them.

Her lack of resistance squelched his brutal intent as well, and he lifted his mouth from hers. Silently they stared into each other's eyes—his so beautifully incongruous with the rest of his face; hers blue, awash with her own tears.

She saw her hand move of its own accord and touch

the damp streaks on his face. She traced the salty track of one of his tears all the way down to his chin. To think of the absolute grief it had taken to make a man of stone like him cry caused Aislinn's heart to pound.

Lucas stared down into her face and instantly regretted what he saw. Her lips were discolored and swollen from the anger behind his kiss. Never in his life had he physically mistreated a woman. The thought of it made him ill.

He moved slightly, intending to lift himself off her. But Aislinn's hands were still resting on his cheeks. She was studying his mouth. He paused.

"I warned you not to look at me like that again," he said roughly.

She didn't move.

"I told you what would happen if you did."

She didn't alter her expression either.

It lasted for only a heartbeat, but his hesitation seemed to stretch out for an eternity before he made a hungry, mating sound and lowered his lips once again to hers.

This kiss was vastly different. His mouth was changed. It settled over hers gently, despite the yearning sounds that it emitted. He rubbed his lips over hers, a comfort-giving, forgiveness-asking gesture.

She responded by letting her lips part. But slightly. Slightly. So that when his tongue touched the seam of her lips, it had to probe them gently to gain the sweet inside.

He groaned low and long as his tongue delved into the warm interior of her mouth, reaching far, swirling deep. He angled his head; she tilted hers in a corresponding movement. Their mouths were sealed.

Aislinn had never received such a blatantly sexual kiss. He brazenly imitated lovemaking, stroking the inside of her mouth with his tongue until she gasped breathlessly. She wanted more.

Her hands moved up from his face. She touched the silver earring in his right ear. He made a catchy, breathy little sound as she fondled it. Her other hand sank into the long, straight strands of his hair. She slipped the headband from around his head and let his hair fall over her fingers. Black silk.

His hand moved between their bodies and fiddled with the buttons on her unattractive, borrowed blouse. She felt them falling open and did nothing to stop it.

Don't think about this. Don't think, she commanded herself. For to think would be to end it. And at all costs she didn't want it to end.

Since she had walked in on him in her kitchen, she had been assaulted by emotions and sensations. Almost without stop, they had come hurling toward her like bullets from an automatic weapon. Sometimes she hadn't dodged them quickly enough and had known their full impact, in her head, her heart, her body. Until three nights ago, her life had seemed as wasteful and barren as the desert compared to the abundance of emotions she had experienced since meeting Greywolf. Now she longed to experience the ultimate emotion. With him.

His breath fell hotly on her neck as his mouth moved over it greedily. He spread kisses across her chest. His hand, without permission or apology, fondled her breast. Just thinking of his strong, brown fingers moving against her pale flesh sent tongues of desire licking through her belly.

She bit her lower lip to stifle a moan when his fingertip located her taut nipple. He dallied with it, circling and fanning it with gentle strokes. When she felt his open mouth closing around it, she released a shuddering cry and clasped his head with both hands, holding it against her.

He exercised no discipline. He used his tongue, his teeth, the suckling ability of his mouth. She couldn't give enough and he couldn't get enough. Each caress brought her higher, further, than she'd ever gone before.

She peeled his shirt open, shoved the cloth aside and spread her hands over his chest. Her fingers engaged in an orgy of discovery. They pressed shallow dents in the curves of his muscles, combed through the pelt of hair, made brief, shy contact with his hard nipples.

Lucas buried his face between her breasts and groaned his pleasure. He gathered a handful of her skirt and lifted it, then laid his hand against the inside of her thigh.

Drums pounded in his head. Heat collected in his sex and spread through his thighs. He had needed a woman, but his desires had focused on this one. This woman. This blond, blue-eyed symbol of everything he hated had become what he wanted most.

Ever since he had seen her standing before him, her body golden in the lamplight of her bedroom, his senses had been humming with desire. He had wanted to seek out every tantalizing inch of her flesh and, once discovered, to know it thoroughly by sight, feel, smell and taste.

Her small, beautifully rounded breasts with their dainty pink crests appealed to him mightily. She was slim, but delectably shaped. He had dreamed of running his hands up and down her slender form, molding it to fit the palms of his hands.

Vividly he could recall how she had looked unclothed. Tremulous, but proud. Vulnerable, but brave. To him her skin had looked as smooth and rich as cream. What he hadn't seen but what his imagination had visualized until he ached.

And now he was touching. That sweet delta was as warm and as soft as he had dreamed it would be. Working his hand deeper inside her panties, he sifted through that silky nest until he found the heart of her womanhood. Impatience overcame him then and he pushed her panties down until she was free of them.

Spontaneously they both fell still, save for their rapid breathing. He braced himself above her and stared down into her face. It was calm. He could appreciate her expression. It held a challenge.

Her breasts were exposed to the new sun and the limitless sky. She didn't flinch as he raked them with his eyes. Her skirt was bunched up around her waist. He lowered his gaze to her womanhood. She was beautiful. He closed his eyes against the immense pleasure that surged through him.

He opened his jeans and positioned himself between her raised thighs. Then, bending his head down to cover her mouth with his, he penetrated her. He entered by slow degrees, savoring every creamy inch of femininity that sheathed him. Only when there was no more of himself to give, did he let his weight settle over her. His face burrowed in the fragrant hollow between her shoulder and throat.

He prayed for death.

Because nothing would ever be this good.

Aislinn, her eyes closed, reached beneath his shirt and ran her hands up and down the supple expanse of his back. His waist was neat and narrow. She loved scooping out the small of his back with her palm. She barely investigated the flare of his hips before she lost her nerve and pulled her hands back. She wanted to slip them into his jeans and cup the hard curves of his buttocks. She wanted to draw him deeper inside her. Not that that was possible. He more than filled her, and yet her body had delighted in accommodating him.

Turning her head, she kissed his ear where the silver earring was secured. He moaned deeply, more vibration than sound. He lowered his head to the tender tip of her breast. He rubbed his open mouth over it until it was quite wet. His tongue was capricious.

Their middles convulsed, reflexively, and then he began to move. Pumping slowly, he entered and withdrew repeatedly. He was smooth and hard and warm. He was animal. He was man. He was wonderful. Aislinn wondered how she had survived all these years without knowing this, without having him.

He whispered something in his native language, then suddenly braced himself above her with stiff arms. "My name is Lucas," he rasped.

"Lucas," she repeated on a breath. Then more loudly, "Lucas."

"I want to…oh, God…I want to see this…us…" He looked down at the place where their bodies were joined, where dark met fair, where male met female. He made a circular, grinding motion with his hips. It robbed Aislinn of breath. Her throat arched. But she couldn't close her eyes, even though the sublime ecstasy of it commanded her to.

She stared into his face and recorded it for memory. It was dark, beautiful, savage. Sweat beaded on his forehead as his movements gained momentum.

"I want to remember I want to remember I want to remember," he chanted as he thrust into her. "When they take me back…oh, God…"

He reared his head back. His gray eyes bore down into hers for only a second before they closed. He grimaced, locked in the throes of exquisite sexual climax. He slid his hands beneath her hips, palmed her derriere and held her tightly as the tremors claimed him.

Aislinn wrapped her arms around his neck, pressed her face into the mat of hair on his chest, and trembled with her own fulfillment.

Endless moments later, he collapsed on top of her. His lips moved against her ear, but if he was actually speaking words, they were indistinguishable. She stroked the back of his head, loving the feel of his hair against her cheek.

How long they lay there, their bodies damp with perspiration, she never remembered. Nor could she ever recall exactly what it was that roused them from that blissful lassitude.

All she could ever remember was the expression on his face when he lifted his head and gazed down at her. For an instant, he looked infinitely sad, resigned, somewhat grateful, before his face closed again and became remote.

He left her. Standing, he zipped his jeans, but made no effort to rebutton his shirt. He walked to the edge of the cliff and looked down toward Joseph Greywolf's hogan.

"You'd better get dressed. They've come for me."

The words struck her chest like heavy stones. She wanted to cry out in protest, but to what avail? Where could she hide him? How could she protect him? Besides, Lucas looked as though he was supremely indifferent to either his immediate or long-range future, much less to hers.

Feeling chilled to the bone despite the rising temperature, Aislinn hurriedly adjusted her clothing. Shakily she stood and dusted off her back as best she could. She reeled with the enormity of what they had done. Her cheeks were hot with shame even as her body continued to pulse with aftershocks.

She wasn't finished yet. It was over too soon. Incomplete. She wanted a tender aftermath. She wanted the closeness that was supposed to follow what they had just shared.

What had she expected, a profession of love, a hearty thank-you, a tension-easing joke? Lucas gave her nothing more than a casual glance with empty, emotionless eyes before he started down the rocky path toward the floor of the canyon.

She covered her face with her hands in a vain attempt to get a grip on herself. Her knees could barely support her as she walked to the edge of the plateau. The sight that greeted her did nothing to restore her composure.

Official cars, each with its red and blue lights flashing, clustered around the hogan. The small dwelling was swarming with men in uniforms, like bees around a honeycomb. One officer was poking around in her car.

"Put your hands over your head, Greywolf," a voice barked at him through a bullhorn.

Lucas complied, though it made his descent down the mountainside hazardous.

Feeling helpless, Aislinn watched from above. An ambulance roared up to the front door of the hogan. Moments later Joseph Greywolf's draped body was carried out on a collapsible gurney. Alice, supported by Gene Dexter's arm, followed close behind.

Two officers came scrambling up the slope toward Lucas. When they reached him, each grabbed an arm and roughly drew it behind him. One clamped on a pair of handcuffs before they started down again.

Lucas walked tall. His bearing was haughty, almost condescending. He seemed impervious to what was going on around him. Only when he saw the ambulance doors closing on his grandfather's body did Aislinn notice a tension in his shoulders. Alice ran toward her son and threw her arms around his waist. Lucas bent his head and kissed her cheek before a deputy sheriff rudely jerked him toward a waiting car.

Seconds before they pushed him inside, he raised his head and looked directly at Aislinn where she still stood on the precipice. Except for that, she might not have existed for Lucas Greywolf.

Six

"When are you going to marry me?"

"When are you going to give up and stop asking?"

"When you say yes."

Alice Greywolf folded the dishtowel she'd been using and carefully laid it on the drainboard. Sighing, she turned and faced Gene Dexter. "You're either steadfast or stubborn. I can't decide which. Why haven't you given up on me?"

He slid his arms around her slender waist and drew her close, laying his cheek against the sleek crown of her head. "Because I love you. Always have. Ever since the first time I saw you in the clinic."

And that was true. The doctor had fallen in love with her that very day. She had been awfully young, incredibly beautiful, and frantic over her rowdy little boy with the broken arm. Within an hour, Gene had set the arm… and set his heart on Alice Greywolf. In the years since then, his love hadn't diminished.

It hadn't always been easy to love her. There had been times when, out of sheer frustration, he would issue ultimatums that either she marry him or he'd never see her again. No amount of ranting and raving ever did any good. She still refused his marriage proposals.

Several times he had stayed away from her and deliberately cultivated other romances. They never lasted for long. He hadn't bothered to use that jealousy tactic in years, partially because it wasn't fair to the other women. Alice was the single love of his life, whether she ever married him or not. He had resigned himself to that fact.

Alice rested her cheek against his chest and smiled sadly at the bittersweet memory of the day they had met. Gene Dexter had been a friend to her in every sense of the word for so long she couldn't imagine a life without his solid presence in it. She treasured the first time she had seen him and heard his gentle voice. But at the same time, she had been anxious over her son.

"Lucas had been in a fight," she said reminiscently. "Some of the older boys at school had been aggravating him. One called him an ugly name." Even now it was painful for her to think of the double stigma her son had had to grow up with.

"Knowing Lucas, I guess he threw himself right into the thick of it."

"Yes," she said with a laugh. "I was worried about his arm, of course, but I remember being angry with him as well for not ignoring their name-calling."

Gene thought Lucas probably would have if they had slurred only him. His guess was that Alice had been maligned, too. Defending his mother had kept Lucas in fights during his childhood and adolescence. Gene refrained from mentioning that.

"I never liked for him to cause trouble at school because that only drew attention to him," Alice continued. "Then, too, I was worried about how I was going to pay the new Anglo doctor for his services."

She tilted her head back to look up into Gene's face. He was no longer as young as when she had first met him, but he was just as handsome in his kind, quiet way. "You knew I didn't have the money to pay you. Why did you extend me credit?"

"Because I wanted your body," he said, nudging his nose beneath her chin and making playfully ferocious growling sounds. "I thought that treating your kid on credit might give me some bargaining room."

Laughing, she pushed him away. "I don't believe that for a minute. You're far too nice. On the other hand, you insured payment. Right after you set Lucas's arm, you offered me a job."

He framed her face between his hands and stared down into it lovingly. "All I knew then and know now is that I couldn't let you walk out that day if there was the slightest chance I'd never see you again. All I ensured myself was that you had to come back." He kissed her, his mouth both tender and passionate as it moved over hers. "Marry me, Alice." There was a desperate edge to his voice and she knew that his yearning was sincere.

"My father—"

"Is dead now." Gene dropped his arms to his sides and agitatedly raked back his hair. "I know it's only been several weeks since he died. I know you're still feeling the pain of losing him. But you used him as an excuse not to marry me for years. I understood. You had to take care of him. But now that he's gone, are you going to use his death in the same way you used his life?"

She walked around him, leaving the kitchen and moving into the living room of her small but tidy house. "Please don't badger me about marriage now, Gene. I have Lucas to consider, too."

"Lucas is a grown man."

"He still needs the support of his family, and I'm all he's got left."

"He has me, too, dammit!"

She looked up at him then, apologetically, and reached for his hand. Angry as he was, he let her pull him down onto the sofa beside her. "I know that. I didn't mean to exclude you."

Gene's tone softened considerably. "Alice, Lucas isn't a child any longer, but he's still getting into fights. He's hellbent on making life as tough on himself as he possibly can. With only a few months to go, he escaped prison. He took a young woman hostage."

"She's still a mystery to me," Alice interjected at the mention of Aislinn Andrews. "It was unlike Lucas to involve anyone else."

"Exactly my point. He didn't consult you, or ask my counsel on whether he should escape prison and become a fugitive. Why should you feel it's necessary to involve him in your decision to marry me? He knows how I feel about you. Maybe if you had married me when I first asked you, he wouldn't be as wild as he is." She looked hurt. Gene sighed. "That was a low blow. Sorry."

"Lucas had enough to live down when he was growing up. Having an Anglo stepfather, who was rich by reservation standards, would have been another."

"I know," he conceded. "But you used Lucas as an excuse for years. Then once he was grown and away at school, you said your father was the reason you couldn't marry me." He pressed her hands between his. "Neither of them was a viable reason. They were flimsy excuses, and they just ran out."

"Can't we just go on as we have been?"

He shook his head. "No, Alice. I'll love you till the moment I draw my last breath, but I'm a man. I want and need a total loving relationship." He leaned forward. His voice was low and earnest. "I know why you're afraid to marry me."

Her head dropped forward and she drew a deep breath as though preparing herself to face a firing squad. Gene brushed the raven-black hair away from her face, his eyes compassionate. "You associate sex with being victimized. I swear to you, I won't hurt you as you were hurt before."

Her eyes were glossy with tears when she raised them to look at him. "What do you mean?"

"We've been needing to have this conversation for years, Alice, but I didn't want to antagonize you by bringing it up." He paused momentarily before plunging ahead. "You're afraid to love a man again, especially an Anglo." She clamped her teeth over her lower lip, and he knew he had hit the target squarely. "You think that as long as you maintain your distance you can't get hurt again."

He carried her hands up to his mouth. His lips moved against her knuckles as he said, "I swear I'd never, never, hurt you. Don't you know me well enough by now to know that you are the center of my life? I love you. Let me and I'll cherish your body. Why would I hurt someone who is a vital part of myself?"

"Gene." She whispered his name through her tears and leaned against him. His arms went around her and held her with the fervent passion reserved for something most dear. He kissed her long and thoroughly.

When at last the kiss ended, he asked, "When are you going to marry me?"

"As soon as Lucas gets out of prison."

He frowned. "God knows when that will be."

"Please, Gene, give me until then. He'd never forgive us if we married without him. And we don't want him to break out again," she added on a soft laugh.

He smiled, allowing her that rationalization. Actually, Gene thought that Lucas would feel better knowing his mother was happily married. Now, however, after getting that much of a commitment from her, was not the time to argue. "All right. But I'm going to hold you to that. As soon as Lucas gets out. And in the meantime…" he murmured as his eyes gazed deeply into hers.

"In the meantime…?"

"In the meantime, I'll keep doing what I've always done. I'll impatiently wait for you, Alice Greywolf."

"Come in, Mr. Greywolf." Lucas stepped through the door of the office. "Please close the door and sit down." Warden Dixon didn't extend the prisoner the courtesy of rising from his chair behind the wide desk, but he exhibited no condescension toward him either. He studied the man with interest.

Lucas walked across the office and dropped into the chair the warden of the prison camp had indicated. Dixon was surprised that there was no meekness in the man's attitude. Far from being cowed, the prisoner had the bearing of a proud, undaunted man. His cool, gray eyes made no furtive movements, dead giveaways of guilt. They met those of the warden without a trace of repentance or remorse. Humility and deference were noticeably absent.

"Apparently the ordeal of the past several weeks hasn't cost you physically," the warden observed out loud. Since his return to the prison, the prisoner had been kept in a cell away from the others and disallowed any privileges.

"I'm fine," Lucas said laconically.

"A bit thinner, I think. A few days of cafeteria food should remedy that."

Lucas crossed one ankle over the opposite knee. "If

you're going to spank my hands, get it over with, please. I'd like to return to my cell."

Warden Dixon curbed his temper. Years of dealing with recalcitrant prisoners had taught him to withstand the strongest provocation. He got out of his chair behind the desk and went to stand at the window, deliberately putting his back to Greywolf. He hoped the man would interpret that as a sign of trust. "The disciplinary action we've decided to take isn't nearly as severe as your escape warranted."

"Thanks," Lucas said sarcastically.

"Up to the time of your breakout, you were a model prisoner."

"I always try to do my best."

Again the warden exercised extreme self-restraint. "The board and I, after carefully reviewing your records, have voted to extend your sentence by six months in addition to the weeks you've already cost yourself. Our decision met with the approval of the penal-system officials."

Dixon turned quickly, in time to see Greywolf's astonishment before he abruptly masked it. Turning back to face the window, the warden hid his smile. Mr. Greywolf might try to remain indifferent, but he was as human as the next. Perhaps even more so. Dixon hadn't run across too many men who would risk spending more time behind bars to attend the death of their grandfather.

Lucas Greywolf sparked an admiration in the warden that was rare and unsettling. Given the same set of circumstances, would he have done what Greywolf had? It was a question that bothered him.

"Was it worth six more months in prison to see your grandfather before he died?"

"Yes."

The warden returned to his desk. "Why?"

Lucas lowered his leg back to the floor and assumed a

more respectful posture. "Joseph Greywolf was a proud man. He clung stubbornly to tradition, often to his detriment. My being in prison bothered him more than it did me. He couldn't stand the thought that the grandson of a chief had to live behind bars."

"He was a chief?"

Greywolf nodded. "Little good that it did him. He died poor, disillusioned, defeated, as many men of my race do."

The warden studied the dossier in front of him. "It says here he was a landowner."

"But he had been swindled out of three-fourths of his land. He gave up. Stopped fighting. Before he got too sick, he was reduced to performing Indian ceremonial dances for tourists. Religious ceremonies that had at one time been solemn rites to him had become spectator sports to others."

Suddenly he lunged out of his chair. The warden jumped and reached beneath his desk for the panic button that would set off an alarm. But when he saw that the prisoner posed no physical threat to him, he placed his hand back on the desktop. He gave his full attention to Greywolf, who was pacing angrily, his body taut.

"Grandfather's only hope lay in me. He forgave me my white blood and loved me in spite of it. He raised me more as his son than grandson. The idea of my being in prison was intolerable to him. He had to see me out of it, he had to know that I had conquered it, before he could die peacefully. That's why I had to do it."

He faced the warden and Dixon thought that if this man couldn't sway jurors, no one could. His physical presence was dynamic. He was eloquent. He was a man of conviction and passion. What a waste that he wouldn't be allowed to practise law.

"I didn't want to escape, Warden Dixon. I'm not a fool. I asked for permission to leave for two days to see my grandfather. *Two goddamn days*. Permission was denied."

"It was against the rules," the warden countered calmly.

"To hell with the rules," he spat. "That is a stupid rule. Don't you people running this place realize how rehabilitative it would be to grant a prisoner some favors, give him back some dignity?" He was leaning over the desk now, full of threat.

"Sit down, Mr. Greywolf." Dixon spoke with just enough firmness to let the prisoner know he was getting out of line. After a considerable time had passed while they stared each other down, Lucas threw himself back into the chair. His handsome face was sullen.

"You're a lawyer," the warden said. "I think you realize how light you're getting off this time." Putting on a pair of silver-rimmed reading glasses, he scanned the report lying on his desk. "There was a young woman, a Miss Aislinn Andrews." He peered at Lucas over the rims of his glasses. The inflection at the end of the statement indicated that it was actually an inquiry.

Lucas said nothing, merely stared back at the warden with implacable eyes that revealed nothing of what he was thinking. The warden returned to the report. "Curious that she didn't press any charges against you." Still Lucas held his silence, though a muscle in his cheek jumped. Finally the warden closed the folder and took off his glasses. "You may return to your regular cell, Mr. Greywolf. That's all for now."

Lucas stood and headed for the door. He had already turned the knob before the warden halted him. "Mr. Greywolf, were you personally responsible for the assault on those policemen during that riot? Did you order the destruction of those government offices?"

"I organized the protest. The judge and jury found me guilty," he said succinctly before opening the door and making his exit.

Warden Dixon stared at the door for a long time after Lucas had closed it. He knew when a guilty man was lying. He also sensed when a man was innocent. Consulting the file on Lucas Greywolf again, he made a decision and reached for the telephone.

As Lucas was being escorted back to his cell, his heart was thudding, though on the outside he gave no indication of his inner turmoil.

He had expected to be told that he was being charged with breaking and entering, assault, kidnapping, and God knows how many other state and federal crimes. He had dreaded the ordeal of another trial, a trial that would further embarrass his mother and add to her heartache.

To learn that his escape had cost him only six more months in prison was a tremendous surprise. He would be busy during that time. By now the small table in his cell would be stacked with letters from people seeking legal advice. He couldn't charge them for it. He could never officially practise law again. But he could offer free legal advice. Among the Indians the name Lucas Greywolf represented a ray of hope. He wouldn't turn down anyone asking his help.

But why hadn't Aislinn Andrews pressed charges? Surely the state and federal authorities had tried to build a case against him. But without her testimony they couldn't prove he'd done anything but break out of prison. Why hadn't she cooperated with them?

Lucas Greywolf hated being indebted to anyone, but he owed Aislinn Andrews his gratitude.

Aislinn slipped through the bedroom door and closed it quietly behind her. The doorbell rang for the second time. She rushed down the hallway to answer it, hurriedly tucking loose strands of hair up into her casual ponytail. She checked her appearance in the hall mirror and saw that she was at least decent. Her face was expectant and wearing a half-smile when she pulled the door open.

The smile never made it to a full-fledged one. Indeed, it froze in place when she saw who her caller was. Her eyes glazed; she slumped against the door for support. For a moment she thought she would very likely faint.

"What are you doing here?"

"Did I frighten you again?"

"Are you...out?"

"Yes."

"When?"

"Today. Released this time. I walked out a free man."

"Congratulations."

"Thank you."

The conversation was ridiculous, of course, but for someone having just received the shock of her life, Aislinn thought she was doing fairly well. She hadn't fainted at the sight of Lucas Greywolf. She was maintaining her equilibrium with the help of the door, though her palms had become so slick with perspiration that she might slide down its smooth surface at any moment. Her mouth was dry, but she hadn't completely lost her capacity for speech. If the world had suddenly turned upside down, she couldn't have been more astounded. Taking all that into consideration, her behavior was remarkable.

"May I come in?"

One hand fluttered up to her throat. "I...I don't think that's a very good idea." My God! Lucas Greywolf in her house? No!

He stared down at the toes of his boots for a moment,

then raised those unforgettable gray eyes up to hers. "It's important or I wouldn't trouble you."

"I—"

"I won't stay but for a minute. Please."

She looked everywhere but directly into his face, knowing that it would exude the determination of the Rock of Gibraltar to remain standing where it was. There was a hint of humility in his tone, but it was backed by generations of Indian resolve.

Finally she nodded briefly and moved aside. He came in and she shut the door behind him. The entrance hall seemed to shrink around them. She had been under the same roof with him for fewer than ten seconds, but already she was having difficulty breathing.

"Would you like something to drink?" she asked hoarsely. *Say no, say no.*

"Yes, please. This is my first stop."

She almost tripped on her way into the kitchen. Why here? Why had he made her house his first stop? Her hands were shaking as she reached into the cabinet for a glass. "A soft drink?" she asked.

"Fine."

She took a can of soda out of the refrigerator and opened it. It spewed over her hand. She yanked up a towel and clumsily blotted the sticky mess off her hand and the countertop. She was all thumbs as she opened the freezer and took out ice cubes, thunking them into the glass. Only when she had poured the soda over the ice did she turn around. Disconcertingly, her eyes were on a level with his chest. She was surprised to find him still standing.

"I'm sorry. Please sit down." She nodded toward the table.

He pulled out a chair and sat down, accepting the cold drink with a terse thank-you. His eyes roamed around the kitchen. They stopped on the rack of knives, then slowly moved to her. "I wouldn't have used the knife on you."

"I know." Before her knees gave way, she sank into the chair across the table from his. "I mean I know that now. Then, I was scared to death."

"You demonstrated remarkable courage."

"I did?"

"I thought so. But then you were my first hostage."

"You were my first abductor."

They should have smiled then. Neither of them did.

"Has your hair grown back out?"

"What?"

"Your hair. Remember that hank of it I chopped off?"

"Oh, yes," she said distractedly. Unconsciously she reached for that shorter strand. "It's tucked in there somewhere. Barely noticeable now."

"Good."

He sipped his drink. She pressed her hands together and slid them between her thighs, keeping her arms stiff. The tension squeezing her chest felt very much as she imagined a heart attack would. She feared suffocation.

From moment to moment she didn't know if she could stand the anxiety any longer without losing control. However, the silence was more unbearable than the stilted conversation, so she asked, "Have you been home yet, seen your mother?"

He shook his head. "I meant it when I said this is my first stop."

He hadn't even seen his mother before coming here? *Don't panic yet, Aislinn.* "How did you get here?"

"Mother and Gene came to the prison last week. Gene left my truck there."

"Oh." She rubbed her palms up and down her thighs, wiping the sweat on her jeans. But her hands were cold and her bare toes felt bloodless. "Why did you come here?"

"To thank you."

Startled, she looked straight at him. His steady stare caused her tummy to do a flip-flop. "Thank me?"

"Why didn't you press charges against me?"

She let go of her pent-up breath on a rushing gust. If that's all he wanted to know, she could live with that. "The sheriff and all those policemen who came to pick you up didn't even know about me." She recounted for him the events that followed his capture. "They had taken you away before anyone even noticed me coming down off that mountain."

Their eyes met fleetingly, each remembering what had taken place on that mountaintop.

Quickly she started speaking again. "They, uh, they questioned me about who I was and what I was doing there with you." She blushed, recalling how awkward she had felt, wondering if the men who interrogated her could tell that she had recently been made love to. Her hair had been a mess. Her lips had still felt swollen from ardent kisses. Her breasts still tingled. Her thighs— "What did you say?"

"I lied to them. I told them I had met you on the road and given you a ride. I denied knowing that you were an escaped convict. I said that I had agreed to drive you to your grandfather's house because he was gravely ill and I felt sorry for you."

"They believed you?"

"I suppose so."

"You could have been implicated."

"But I wasn't."

"You could have had me charged with any number of crimes, Aislinn." The sound of her name startled both of them. They glanced at each other. Their eyes locked and held for a moment before falling away. "Why didn't you tell them the truth?"

"What would have been the point?" she asked, coming out of her chair and moving restlessly around the kitchen. "I was safe. You were going back to prison anyway."

"But you had been…hurt."

The euphemism fooled neither of them. They both realized that had she wanted to accuse him of rape she could have, and probably got him convicted of it. It would have been his word against hers, and who would have believed him?

"The scratch on my arm was superficial. Besides, that wasn't your fault." Both knew that he hadn't been referring to the scratch, but it seemed prudent to pretend that he had been. "I think it was wrong of the prison officials not to let you go see your grandfather. In my eyes your escape was justified. No harm had been done. Not really."

"No one missed you?"

It cost her a great deal of pride to answer, but she told him the truth. "No." She had returned home as soon as the officials had released her. There hadn't been any media present in the canyon when Greywolf was arrested, so no one knew she had been involved.

"What about the people at your business?" he asked.

"What people?"

"You told me you would be missed."

"Of course I told you that."

"Oh," he said, shaking his head with chagrin, "there weren't any people."

"Not then. But I have two employees now."

He actually grinned. "Don't worry. I don't intend to pull a knife on you this time."

Aislinn smiled back, struck by how handsome he was.

Now that the shock of seeing him had subsided, she was able to truly look at him for the first time. His hair was a trifle shorter in front, though it was still collar-length at the back. No prison pallor lightened his bronzed skin. Had she asked why, he could have told her that he ran every day around the prison yard, encircling it numerous times until he got in his quota of miles, which also accounted for his superb physical condition.

The silver earring still pierced his right lobe. The cross still rested in the soft black hair on his chest which she could see through the open collar of his shirt. His mother and Gene must have brought him new clothes for his release. His shirt and jeans looked new. Only the cowboy boots and the turquoise-studded belt around his trim waist were familiar to her.

"Well," he said, coming to his feet, "I promised you I wouldn't stay long. I just wanted to thank you for not making things rougher on me."

"You didn't have to bother."

"I started to write, but I wanted to thank you in person."

Lord, it would have been much easier on her nerves if he had mailed her a thank-you note! "I'm just glad you're out."

"I don't like being in anyone's debt, but—"

"You're not in my debt. I did what I thought was right, just as you did."

"Thanks all the same."

"You're welcome," she said, hoping that would end it. She led him through the living room and into the entrance hall.

Lucas had dreaded this meeting, not certain of how she was going to react to seeing him. The second she opened the door, she could have run screaming in terror and been justified in doing so.

He had been desperate the night he randomly chose her house to break into seeking food and shelter for a few hours. Desperate men did things they wouldn't ordinarily do. Like take a blameless Anglo woman hostage. It was still incomprehensible to him that she hadn't made him pay for that.

But now that he had accomplished his mission and thanked her, he was reluctant to leave. Odd. He had thought that once he had said what he had come to say, he would be more than ready to leave Aislinn Andrews for good and close that page of his life's history.

He hated to admit, even to himself, that he had thought about her while he was in prison. It had been months since that morning on the mountaintop, when she had given herself to him. He still found it hard to believe that it had really happened. Before his escape, his desire had been for a woman, period. Any and all.

But after his escape, his desire had had a face, a name, a tone of voice, a scent. And all of them belonged to Aislinn. Many nights, lying alone in his narrow prison bed, he had convinced himself that she wasn't real and that he had imagined the whole thing.

His body told him otherwise. Especially now, while his eyes were taking in the snug fit of her casual slacks over her bottom and thighs. She was shorter than he remembered, but maybe that was because she was barefoot. Her shirttail was out. It was an old shirt, a trifle too small for her. Oh, yes, while he had been sitting there sipping her soda, he had been thinking about sipping her breasts. He couldn't help but notice how amply they filled the front of the old shirt.

As she led him toward the front door, he was hypnotized by the swaying motion of her youthful ponytail. Was her hair as silky as he remembered? Had that rich blondness, such a flagrant trademark of her Anglo background, actually known his pillaging, Indian hands? And did her mouth, the one giving him a vapid, vacant smile now, remember the hard, searching strokes of his tongue inside it? He did.

"Good luck to you, Lucas. I hope all goes well for you now." She stuck out her hand.

"Thanks." He clasped her hand. Their eyes met. Held. Then the sound.

It came from the back of the house. It was so out of context that at first he thought his ears were playing tricks on him. But then he heard it again. He glanced in that direction, his brows drawn into a puzzled frown.

"That sounds like a—"

Aislinn jerked her hand out of his. Surprised, his head snapped around. The instant he saw her face, he knew his ears hadn't been deceiving him. She looked as pale as a ghost and as guilty as sin. He went perfectly still. He stared at her with eyes razor sharp enough to flay her skin away, much less any deceit.

"What is that?"

"Nothing."

He moved her aside and stalked across her fashionable living room.

"Where are you going?" she cried, chasing after him.

"Guess."

"No!" She grabbed his shirt and held on with the tenacity of a bulldog. "You can't just come waltzing in here and—"

He spun around, knocking her hands away. "I did before."

"You can't."

"The hell I can't. Watch me."

He was intent on finding the source of that sound. Sobbing, Aislinn trailed after him, clutching at him ineffectually. He swatted her off like a pesky fly.

He glanced into her bedroom. It was exactly as he remembered it. Feminine, neatly arranged. He passed it. At the end of the hallway he came to a closed door. With no hesitation, certainly no apology, he turned the knob and pushed it open.

Then even he, the man with the heart and blood of an Apache warrior, was brought up short.

Three of the walls in the room were painted a soft yellow. The other was papered with a pastel Mother Goose print. A Boston rocker with thick cushions stood in one corner. A chest of drawers was topped by a quilted pad. It was lined with jars of cotton swabs and tubes of ointment. White shutters had been closed against the afternoon sun, but enough light seeped through the slats to silhouette the crib in front of the window.

Lucas closed his eyes, thinking that this must all be a bizarre dream from which he would awaken and have a much-needed laugh. But when he reopened his eyes, everything was unchanged. Especially that unmistakable sound.

He crept forward, illogically making as little noise as he could, until he reached the crib. It was rimmed with a padded border. A teddy bear smiled at him from the corner. The sheet was yellow to match the room. As was the downy blanket.

And beneath the blanket—squirming, squalling, flailing its tiny fists in rage—was a baby.

Seven

The baby continued to cry, unimpressed by the havoc he had caused in the heart and mind of the tall dark man standing beside the crib. The face that was usually so remote was working with emotion.

Aislinn, standing slightly behind and to one side of Lucas, pressed her fingertips to her lips in an effort to stem her own emotions. They ranged from anxiety to abject terror.

Her first impulse was to tell him that she was babysitting, that the infant belonged to a friend or relative. But the uselessness of that was clear. The baby had been fathered by Lucas Greywolf. One had only to look at the child to dispel any doubts.

The beautifully rounded head, which hadn't been marred during the easy birth, was covered with midnight-black hair that hugged the soft scalp. The shape of the brow, the angle of chin, the slant of cheekbones, all were miniature replicas of Lucas Greywolf's features.

She watched in growing dread as Lucas stretched out a slender brown finger and touched the baby's cheek. Reverence and awe filled the light-gray eyes. His lips twitched slightly. Aislinn recognized the symptoms of keenly felt emotions. The same slight facial spasms seized her every time she held her baby. The kind of love that welled up inside her when she touched the child couldn't help but be registered on her face.

It terrified her that Lucas was experiencing the same kind of emotional tumult.

She jumped when he flicked the baby's blanket away with a swift motion of his hand. Her maternal instincts went into play when he tore open the tapes securing the disposable diaper. Lunging forward, she clutched his arm, but he negligently shook her hand off and pulled the diaper down.

"A son."

His rusty tone of voice sounded like a death knell to Aislinn. She was almost crazed with panic and wanted to cover her ears and shout denial. Frantically she prayed this wasn't really happening.

But it was. Helplessly she stood there and watched Lucas remove the one-snap sacque. Sliding his hands beneath the baby, he lifted him from the crib. All she could do was watch in mute despair as Lucas took the infant in his arms. The moment Lucas lay the baby against his chest, the child stopped crying.

The instant rapport between man and child gave Aislinn no peace. For once she would have preferred that her baby scream. He did nothing but make those sweet baby sounds against his father's shoulder.

Lucas carried the naked infant to the rocking chair. He folded his long legs low enough to sit in the rocker, awkwardly balancing himself while holding the baby. Under other circumstances, Aislinn might have thought that was a funny sight. As it was, her features were stark. All her worst nightmares were unfolding.

Had the situation not spelled such doom, Lucas's tender exploration of the baby would have touched Aislinn deeply. To see the dark, manly hands moving over the baby with such delicate curiosity was indeed poignant, and she would have had to be a pillar of salt not to be moved to tears by such instant adoration on the part of the father for the child.

Lucas gently turned the baby this way and that in loving inspection. He rolled him over and supported him in one large palm while he smoothed his other hand down the infant's back and over the tiny buttocks. He touched each toe, each transparent fingernail, and examined the baby's ears.

Finally he laid the child on his thighs and looked up at her. "What is his name?"

She wanted to tell him it was none of his business, but unfortunately it was. "Anthony Joseph." She saw an immediate reaction to the name in his gray eyes. "I had a grandfather named Joseph, too," she said defensively. "I call the baby Tony."

Lucas glanced down at the child who was beginning to wave his fists fretfully. "When was he born?"

She hesitated, giving thought to fudging on the dates and thereby negating Lucas's paternity. But his stare demanded the truth. "May seventh."

"You were never going to tell me, were you?"

"There was no reason to."

"He's my son."

"He has nothing to do with you."

He barked a short laugh. "From now on, he has everything to do with me."

Tony was crying in earnest now, the novelty of hearing a new, deeper voice having given way to hunger. Lucas lifted the baby to his shoulder, and immediately

the wet little mouth went blindly searching. The most unexpected sound Aislinn had ever heard was Greywolf's
soft chuckle. "That's one thing I can't do for you, Anthony Joseph." Holding the baby in his arms, he stood up
and extended Tony toward his mother. "He needs you."

She took the child and laid him back in his crib, hurriedly replacing the diaper Lucas had taken off. She was
made clumsy by the baby's strenuous protests, his churning arms and legs, and by Lucas's watchfulness. When
Tony was once again dressed and diapered, she lifted
him to her shoulder and carried him to the rocker. Sitting there, she rocked him, patting his back and crooning softly. All ineffectually.

"He's hungry," Lucas said.

"I know that," she snapped, taking offense at his implication that she didn't know her own baby's needs.

"Well then? Feed him."

She looked up at Lucas, the baby acting as a fragile
shield she held in front of her. "Will you excuse me?"

"You mean will I leave the room?"

"Yes."

"No."

They continued to stare each other down. Miraculously, Lucas was the first to relent. He turned his back
and went to stand looking out the window after adjusting
the shutters to allow him a view. Aislinn knew then that
if this hard man were ever vulnerable about anything,
it would be this son. An unbreakable bond had already
been established between them, though Lucas hadn't even
known the child existed until minutes ago. Would that he
didn't know now. He could make her life hell.

"Why didn't you tell me?"

Aislinn, ignoring his question, unbuttoned her blouse
and pulled down the cup of her nursing bra. Tony lustily

latched on to her nipple and began to suck noisily. She draped a light flannel blanket over her shoulder to cover herself and the baby's head.

"I asked you a question." This time Lucas's tone was imperative.

"Because Tony is my baby."

"He's mine, too."

"You're not sure of that."

He swiveled his head around abruptly. Had modesty not made her flinch, the incisive gray eyes would have. "I'm sure." He was so positive there was no sense in arguing the point. So what if she beat him in a contest on semantics? The facts would remain the same. Tony was his.

"Tony was a biological…accident," she said by way of concession.

"Then why didn't you just get rid of him?"

A shudder ran through her body. "Why didn't you just get rid of it?" her mother had screamed at her when Aislinn informed her parents of her pregnancy. Purposefully she had waited to tell them until it was too late for an abortion, knowing that termination would have been their solution to "the dilemma."

Why *hadn't* she terminated the pregnancy? Before she went to the doctor, she had had a niggling suspicion in the back of her mind as to the cause of her afternoon malaise. Then there had been the morning bouts with nausea, the sudden bursts of appetite and the sour indigestion after satisfying it. All unusual.

She hadn't consciously entertained the idea that she might be pregnant. She hadn't allowed herself to. But when the doctor told her his laboratory-verified diagnosis, she hadn't been shocked or even surprised. In fact, her first reaction had been a stupendous rush of joy.

After that initial reaction, when reality had set in, she

gave considerable thought to the negative ramifications of rearing a child as a single woman. She recognized the grave repercussions, but never did she consider having the pregnancy terminated.

From the moment she had learned of his existence, she loved the child fiercely. Her life suddenly had purpose and meaning. Now she had something to look forward to. There were goals to be met, horizons to move toward.

So now she could answer Lucas's question without hesitation or qualification. "I desperately wanted the baby." Reaching beneath the blanket, she laid her hand on Tony's soft head, lightly rubbing it while he avidly sucked at her breast. "I have loved him from the beginning."

"Didn't you think I was entitled to know about him?"

"I didn't think you'd care."

"Well, make no mistake; I do."

"What…what do you intend to do?" she asked fearfully, despising the tremulous quality of her voice.

"I intend to be his father."

Tony impatiently thumped her breast with his tiny fist. Only that could have distracted her from Lucas's hard stare. "I need to turn him," she said huskily.

Lucas looked down at her chest. Aislinn saw him swallow reflexively before he diverted his eyes.

She switched Tony from one breast to the other. Once he was resettled and nursing again, she said, "I ask nothing from you, Mr. Greywolf. I carried Tony for nine months. I went through the entire pregnancy and delivery without any assistance from you, from anyone. Financially I'm able to provide—"

He came around so suddenly, she fell silent out of fear that he might reach across the room and strike her.

"Do you think a checkbook can supply him with everything he needs?"

"I didn't mean that," she flared. "I love him."

"So do I!" He roared so loudly that Tony's mouth fell still for several seconds before he resumed nursing.

"Be quiet! You scared Tony."

Lucas lowered his volume but not his intensity. "If you think I'm going to abandon my son and let him grow up in your sterile, Anglo world, think again."

She clutched the baby tighter. "What do you mean?"

"I mean that when I return to the reservation tomorrow, he goes with me."

She paled drastically. Even her lips looked chalky. The only color in her face was the deep blue of her eyes, which looked abnormally large as she stared up at the man who was once again her enemy.

"You can't take him."

"I can. I will."

"No!"

"There will be no stopping me."

"I'll have you hunted down like the criminal you are," she threatened.

His lips quirked into a cynical smile. "If I didn't want to be found, I wouldn't be, Miss Andrews. But even if by some remote chance I *were,* I'd fight you to the Supreme Court if necessary to win my son away from you. I know how. I'm a lawyer, remember? I think he's finished."

His threats had frozen her with fear. By the time she assimilated his last sentence, he was already across the room and crouching down in front of her. Before she could stop him, Lucas removed the blanket from her shoulder.

Tony was lying in her arms, satiated. His plump cheek rested against her breast. His small mouth, pearlized with milk, lay close to her nipple. He was asleep, looking as full and contented as a despot after a three-day bacchanal.

Lucas caressed his sleeping baby's cheek. He touched the soft lips with the tip of his finger. His dark head moved closer. He kissed the top of Tony's head.

Aislinn sat petrified. Too stunned to move. Hardly able to breathe. Lucas slid his hands up over her stomach, wedging them between her and Tony, and lifted the child away from her. He stood and carried the baby to the crib. Tony burped and Lucas released another of those surprising chuckles.

Aislinn forced herself out of the trance that astonishment had imposed. Lucas's nearness had immobilized her. Feeling his breath on her skin had stupefied her. Now she hastily replaced the cups of her bra and buttoned her blouse. She swayed slightly when she stood up. "He's ready to go to sleep now," she said, shouldering Lucas aside as she joined him beside the crib. She turned Tony over onto his tummy.

"He sleeps on his stomach?"

"Yes."

The baby drew his knees up and poked his bottom into the air. He made a few sucking motions with his mouth, then lay still, fast asleep.

"He looks satisfied," Lucas said.

"For now," Aislinn said gently, drawing the light blanket over the baby.

"Well I'm not."

She looked up at Lucas and was startled to see the uncompromising expression on his face. "You wouldn't really try to take him away from me, would you?" she asked, willing herself not to beg.

She didn't think a father could ever win custody over

a mother who was loving, caring and affluent, no matter what legal machinations he tried. But in the meantime, Tony would be a subject of litigation. He might even become a ward of the state and be placed in a foster home until the matter could be settled. That might take years. "Think of Tony."

"I am." He took her by the shoulders. "Do you think your society will accept him?" Not giving her time to answer, he said, "Never, Aislinn." His hands were hard on her shoulders. Hard and warm. She recalled other times he had touched her and dearly wished she didn't. "Believe me, I know. In an Anglo's opinion, being part Indian is tantamount to being all Indian. And he has so much white blood, he'll be an outcast in Indian society, too. He won't be accepted in either world."

"I'll see to it that he is."

The corner of his mouth tilted into a smile that was both scoffing and pitying. "You're naive and deluding yourself if you think that. I know what it's like to straddle the cultures, for christsake! I've had to live with the ambiguity every day of my life. I will protect my son from that."

"By doing what? What's your solution? Taking him to some remote part of the reservation where he'll never come into contact with other people?"

"If that's what it takes," he answered grimly.

She looked at him incredulously. "And you think that would be fair?"

"The circumstances of his birth weren't fair. Life isn't fair. I gave up on it ever being fair a long time ago."

"Yes, and you wear your bitterness where all the world can see it," she accused, angrily shrugging off his hands. "I won't let Tony grow up so steeped in hatred that he's made a prisoner of it as you are, Lucas Greywolf. And in the long run, who do you think he'd hate the most? *You!* He wouldn't thank you for separating him from the world."

Apparently he realized there was some merit to that because he gnawed the inside of his cheek in indecision. But he wasn't about to let her win the argument. "What did you plan to do, tell him that his Indian features were a fluke? Did you intend to keep my identity a complete secret from him?"

"I...I hadn't planned that far ahead."

"Well, you'd better be giving it some thought, lady. Because one of these days he'll ask about his father. I did."

For the beat of several seconds Aislinn let a tense silence reign, then she asked in a low voice, "And what were you told?"

He stared down at her for so long she thought he was going to refuse to tell her. But then he took up his stance at the window again, his broad shoulders almost spanning it. Unseeingly, he stared at the mountains on the horizon as he began to speak.

"The man who fathered me was an Anglo soldier stationed at Fort Huachuca. My mother was sixteen. She had graduated early from the reservation school and moved to Tucson where Joseph had friends who gave her room and board. She took a job waiting tables in a diner."

"Is that where she met your father?"

He nodded. "He flirted with her and asked her to go out with him after she got off work. She refused. But he kept coming back to the diner. She told me that he was very handsome, dashing, charming."

Turning his hands palms out, he slid them into the rear pockets of his snug jeans. If the father had looked anything like the son, if he had had that same long, lean physique, Aislinn could understand how easily Alice Greywolf's head might have been turned.

"Finally she consented to go out with him. To put it bluntly, Miss Andrews, he seduced her. I'm not sure how many dates it took. Mother was understandably not specific. Only weeks after she met him, he was shipped out to parts unknown. He didn't say goodbye. He just stopped coming by to see her. When she worked up her nerve to call the base to tell him that she was pregnant, she was informed that he was gone."

He turned around. His features were closed tighter than she had ever seen them. Intuitively she knew that meant he was hurting. It was an unbearable hurt that he kept tightly bottled up inside him.

"She never saw or heard from him again, nor did she try to contact him. She returned to the reservation in disgrace, pregnant with a white man's baby. She delivered me a month before her seventeenth birthday. She got a job making souvenir kachina dolls because she could work at home while taking care of me. Grandfather earned enough money selling horses to feed and house us in an old trailer. Mother and I lived with him until she met Gene Dexter. He offered her a job in town that vastly improved her standard of living. Thank God," he added softly.

He turned back to Aislinn. "So you see, I grew up knowing what a burden I was to my mother."

"She didn't think so, Lucas." Her throat was tight with emotion. "She loves you very much."

"I know that. She never became bitter because of what happened to her."

"You more than compensate."

"You can't know bitterness until you grow up a half-breed bastard," he said with an angry hiss. "So don't give me any lectures about it. And I'll see you in hell before I'll let my son be subjected to that kind of stigma. Do you think I'd do to him what my father did to me?"

"But your father didn't know. Maybe if he—"

"Don't even suggest anything so ridiculous," he interrupted sharply. "To him, Alice Greywolf, the beautiful Indian girl, was an easy roll in the hay. A novelty, no doubt. Even if he had known about the pregnancy, he probably would have deserted her. At best he would have driven her across the border for a cheap, speedy abortion." He shook his head. "No, the Anglo soldier would have wanted no part of his little Indian baby. But by God I want my son. He is going to know his father."

Reading his face, Aislinn knew that trying to deter him would be futile. He meant what he said. He would know his son and vice versa. And in so doing Lucas could make her life unbearable.

She had thought she would never see Lucas Greywolf again. She had imagined that he would view their morning on the mountaintop the way he supposed his father viewed his encounter with Alice. A roll in the hay. An *easy* roll in the hay.

Well, surprising as it was, he hadn't. Or if he had before, he had changed his mind about it when he saw Tony. Simply put, she had been found out. She had wanted to keep Tony's existence a secret from him forever. Such was not to be. The only choice she had now was to make the best of a bad situation.

"What do you suggest, Lucas? That we divide Tony's life between us? Don't you think that will only compound the confusion? It will be years before he's old enough to understand. Life here six months, life with you six months." It pained her to even verbalize the possibility that an arrangement like that might have to be made. "What kind of life would that be for a little boy?"

"I have no such arrangement in mind."

"Then what?"

"We'll get married. You'll both live with me."

It wasn't a suggestion. It wasn't even an alternative offered up for discussion. It was an edict.

When the words finally sank in, she splayed her hand over her chest and said on a soft laugh, "You can't be serious." But his unmoving features and unblinking eyes told her he was deadly serious. "Are you crazy? That's impossible!"

"It's essential. My child will not grow up branded a bastard."

"Don't say that word."

"It's ugly, isn't it? I want to guarantee that Tony will never hear it."

"But we can't get married."

"I didn't count on that either," he said, somewhat chagrined. "But we are, as soon as arrangements can be made. I'll be back tomorrow."

He leaned down and patted Tony on the behind, smiling down at him fondly and speaking something in his native tongue. Then, as though everything had been settled, he turned and left the nursery.

Aislinn ran after him, catching him by the sleeve as he reached for the knob on the front door. "I can't marry you."

"Are you already married?"

He fired the question at her and it stunned her for a moment. "No. Of course not."

"Then there's no reason why we can't marry."

"Except that I don't want to."

"Well, neither do I," he grated, bending down and

putting his face close to hers for emphasis. "But we'll just have to put aside our own feelings for the sake of our son. If I can tolerate having an Anglo wife, you can damn sure tolerate having an Indian husband."

"Oh, for Pete's sake," she cried angrily. "This has nothing to do with my being Anglo and your being Indian. Don't you ever think of anything else?"

"Rarely."

"Well, make an exception this time. Considering the way we met, don't you think the idea of marriage is just a little ridiculous?"

"Meaning that a kidnapping is hardly a courtship."

"Exactly."

"What to you want from me? To go down on bended knees?"

She gave him a withering look. "I only meant to point out that we don't even know each other. We made a baby, but—" She broke off, alarmed by her own words. She didn't want to be reminded of that morning. She certainly didn't want to remind him of it.

She had been facing him squarely, her fists planted on her hips. Now, she quickly lowered her arms, suddenly aware of how her militant posture was stretching her blouse across her breasts. Nervously, she wet her lips with her tongue and looked someplace else besides Lucas's face.

"Yes, we made a baby," he said quietly. "That's really the point, isn't it? Tony had nothing to do with what happened between us, so he damn sure isn't going to go through his life paying for it. *We*," he said, waving his hand between his chest and hers, "we shared that lust. There's not a damn thing we can do about it now but share the responsibility for the life we created."

He placed a finger beneath her chin and yanked her

head up, forcing her to look at him. "As surely as I planted my seed in you, Tony will know me." He released her and stepped back. "I'll be back tomorrow. Whether you consent to marry me or not, I'm taking my son with me when I leave."

"Under the threat of a knife?" she asked snidely.

"If necessary."

His eyes drove the words home. She believed him and was frightened into speechlessness. Nothing more was said before he left by the front door.

She was nervous. Chastising herself for acting like a ninny, she still jumped at every sound. She nearly came out of her skin when the doorbell rang. It turned out to be the postman hand-delivering a catalog that was too large for her mailbox. She felt foolish, but she couldn't curb her jitters.

She tried reassuring herself that her nervousness might all be for naught. Lucas Greywolf might never return. Seeing Tony might have made him think he wanted to take on the responsibilities of child-rearing. But upon thinking about it last night, he might very well have changed his mind.

She didn't think so, however. Lucas—strange how her mind formed his name so easily—wasn't a man given to outbursts of emotion that were quickly spent. Nor was he likely to make promises he didn't intend to keep. Sometime today he would show up on her doorstep. When that happened, what would she do?

Exercise all the powers of persuasion at her disposal.

Throughout the long night, the problem had clattered around and around in her head like the ball in a roulette wheel. Lucas Greywolf was a fact of her life now, and she would have to cope with him.

She outlined what she thought would be a fair arrangement for Lucas to see Tony. Surely he would recognize the sound reasoning behind that. A baby needed his mother, especially for the first few years. Unless Lucas was totally unreasonable, he would admit that. And she knew that he didn't really want to get married, any more than she did.

She was enjoying the stability of her life now. In her fifth month of pregnancy, she had hired another photographer to take over her duties at the portrait studio. Then, since she had been busy converting the spare bedroom in her condo into a nursery, she hired a receptionist/bookkeeper. Both young women were doing well in their jobs, and the studio was prospering as it never had before.

She made periodic visits to check on things. Beyond that, her primary responsibility was to care for and love Tony. That was no chore at all. He was only a month old, yet he was such a vital part of her life that she couldn't imagine not having him.

Only one thing could have made her happier—that her parents would leave her alone. Resigned to the fact that their daughter had an illegitimate baby, they had turned their energies toward finding her a husband who would accept her and the child. Marriage to a respectable man would remove the blight on the family name.

Aislinn wasn't fooled by the tolerance of these prospective husbands, who were introduced to her under the most embarrassingly contrived circumstances. They overlooked Tony's illegitimacy and her indiscretion with amazing benevolence. However, she knew that each was keeping in mind her father's bank account and depending on his generosity. They expected recompense for their charitable attitude toward a wayward girl.

But stubborn as they were in wanting to dictate her future, her parents would be easier to dissuade than Lucas Greywolf. Of that Aislinn was certain.

When the doorbell rang for a second time shortly before noon, she knew who it was. For a moment, she clasped her hands together, squeezed her eyes closed, and drew a deep breath. The bell rang again and she didn't imagine the impatience behind that imperious ring. She moved toward the door with leaden footsteps.

Suddenly she wished she hadn't surrendered to vanity and dressed in "civilian" clothes. She had been wearing maternity clothes, giving her body time to slim down. Today, she had tried on last summer's skirt and found to her delight that it would go around her waist.

The full, calf-length skirt had always been one of her favorites. The soft blue fabric brushed against her legs when she walked. With it she had put on a white blouse with a white-on-white embroidered yoke. It buttoned down the front to facilitate nursing Tony. She had washed her hair in the shower and left it to dry in its natural waves. Now the sides were looped behind her ears, into which she had secured small gold rings.

Maybe applying makeup had been going too far. And fragrance. Why had she put on perfume today when she hadn't worn any for months? But it was too late to do anything about it now, because the doorbell was ringing for a third time.

She pulled open the door. She and Greywolf stared across the threshold at each other. Both wanted to feel antagonism. Instead each was experiencing a pleasurable jolt at the other's appearance.

Aislinn was never quite prepared for those light-gray eyes set in that dark, lean face. His shirt was different. Otherwise he was dressed the same as the day before, in jeans, which rode low on his narrow hips, and boots, which had seen better days. The silver cross lay against his chest in the open V of his shirt. The earring in his ear seemed to punctuate the pronounced intersection of his cheekbone and jaw.

Moving aside, she let him come in and closed the door behind him. Lucas looked down upon the crown of her head, then let his glance slide down her slender neck to her breasts. He could see the swelling mounds beneath her neckline.

His gut twisted with desire, remembering the shape of her breasts and the color of her nipples bedewed with milk. He shouldn't have looked at her yesterday. Then he wouldn't know what a lovely sight she was when nursing his baby, and he wouldn't be remembering it now. But he had had to look, or die.

Her breasts were noticeably fuller than they had been ten months ago. That only made the rest of her figure appear trimmer. Her feet looked incredibly childlike in the barefoot sandals.

He cleared his throat of congestion. "Where's Tony?"

"Asleep in his room."

With an economy of movement and an absence of sound, he turned and went toward the nursery. Aislinn marveled over how agilely and silently he could move.

By the time she had followed him into the nursery he was bending low over Tony's crib. The tenderness with which he gazed at his sleeping son coaxed an emotion from her that she didn't want to acknowledge. To deny it, she asked him, "Did you think I was lying? Did you have to see for yourself that he was still here? Did you think I had hidden him from you?"

With that same animallike grace, he turned around to face her. "You wouldn't dare."

For several beats, their eyes held. He glanced back

at the child once more before crossing the room, taking her by the arm, and leading her back into the hallway.

"Get me something to drink," he said.

She started to snap something sarcastic like, "This isn't a tavern, you know." But she decided that sitting in the kitchen with the table between them was better than sharing the living-room sofa.

"All right. If you'll let go of me," she answered, working her arm out of his grasp. She didn't want to know the warm, strong pressure of his fingers, which seeped through the cloth of her sleeve. His touch evoked too many memories she had spent months eradicating from her mind. She wanted to yell at him to keep his hands off her, but she didn't want to provoke his temper unnecessarily. Now wasn't the time to gamble with his moods, not when she must appeal to his reason.

"None of Tony's things are packed," he observed, sitting down in the same chair as the day before.

"What would you like? Juice or a soft drink?"

"A soft drink." She took one out of the refrigerator and went through the same ritual as yesterday, finally handing the icy glass to him.

"None of Tony's things are packed," he repeated before taking a single sip of the drink.

She sat down across from him, willing her hands not to shake. "That's right."

"Then I take that to mean we're getting married."

"Then you take it wrong, Mr. Greywolf. I'm not marrying you or anybody."

He drank from the glass; then with careful thoroughness, scooted it away from him. "I will have my son."

Aislinn licked her lips. "I think Tony should know you. That's only fair to both of you. I won't keep you from seeing him. You may come here whenever you like. All

I ask is that you give me several hours' notice to prevent any conflicts in schedules. I'll try to cooperate— Where are you going?" Lucas had suddenly left his chair and headed for the door.

"To get my son."

"Wait!" She bounded out of her chair and caught his arm. "Please. Let's be reasonable about this. You can't believe that I'll stand by and let you cart my son off with you."

"He's my son, too."

"He needs his mother."

"And a father."

"But not like he needs me. Not now, anyway. Yesterday you said yourself that you couldn't feed him."

His eyes dropped to her breasts. She held her ground. "There are other ways," he said tersely and tried to move away.

She gripped his arm harder. "Please. Maybe when he gets older."

"I told you my alternative. Apparently you've chosen not to accept it."

"You mean marriage?" She let go of his arm, realizing how close they were standing and how tenaciously her fingers were curled around his forearm. She turned her back and went to stand at the sink. As she tried to think of a graceful way to broach this subject, she nervously crossed her arms over her middle and ran her hands up and down her opposite biceps. "Marriage between us is out of the question."

"I fail to see why."

His obtuseness made her grind her teeth in frustration. He was forcing her to spell it out for him and she hated him for it. "I can't marry you because of all it entails."

"Leaving the city, this house?"

"That's part of it."

"What's the other part?"

"My studio."

"Your studio is being capably operated by two employees. Try again."

"All right then," she cried, spinning around to confront him. "Living with you. And…and…"

"Sleeping with me." He finished her sentence for her. The low, sandy sound of his voice was so intimate she could all but feel it brushing against her skin.

For answer, she turned her back to him again and bowed her head low. "Yes."

"Then we're not talking about marriage, are we? We're talking about sex. I used the term 'marriage' in a strictly legal context. Apparently you read more into my proposal."

"I—"

"No, no. Since you brought it up, let's explore all the possibilities."

He moved up behind her. She could sense he was there even before she felt his warm breath drifting over her neck as he bent his head down. It was a taunting movement, as though he had trapped her, but before devouring her, wanted to play with her.

"You can't stand the thought of having sex with me, is that it?" He slid his hand around her, pressing it flat against her midriff, drawing her closer. "You didn't seem to have any objections that morning on top of the mountain."

"Don't." Her breathy command carried little weight. It didn't stop him from nuzzling her hair with his nose until his mouth touched her ear.

"Did I miss something that morning? Or do white society girls say no differently from others?"

"Stop, stop this," she moaned. His fingertips lightly brushed her nipple, coaxing a drop of moisture from it.

"It sure as hell sounded like you were saying yes."

"It should never have happened."

"What's the matter, Miss Andrews? After all this time are you getting squeamish about screwing an Indian?"

She threw off his arms, spun around and smacked his hard cheek with the flat of her palm. The sound cracked through the room like a slashing whip. Both were as stunned by the sound as they were by her flare of violence and the crude words that had precipitated it.

She withdrew her hand quickly. "Don't ever talk to me like that," she said breathlessly, her breasts rapidly rising and falling with anger.

"All right," he growled, taking the few steps necessary to pin her against the countertop. "Then let's talk about why you're all dolled up today. Did you want to make sure I'd notice your blond beauty? Did you think you would intimidate the Indian boy with it? How dare I ask such a golden goddess to marry me? Is that what you wanted me to think?"

"No!"

"Then why do you smell so damn good? And why did you make yourself look good enough to eat?" he asked through clenched teeth. "And why do I want to?"

He couldn't resist the groan that rumbled from his throat, anymore than he could resist crushing her against him. He buried his face in the hollow of her throat and held her tight. He rubbed his chest against her breasts. His hips pantomimed lovemaking against hers.

The embrace lasted only a few seconds before he shoved himself away from her. His chest was heaving. A few buttons on his shirt had come loose. The color in his dark cheeks had deepened. To Aislinn's startled eyes he looked undisciplined and dangerous, and wildly sexy.

"You see, Miss Aislinn, I can control my lust. Don't flatter yourself into thinking that I want you any more than you want me. You're just excess baggage that has to come along with my son because I don't have mammary glands. But I'm willing to pay the price of living with you in order to make a home for Tony." He ran his hand through his hair and took several more restorative breaths. "Now I'm going to ask you one last time. Do you come along or not?"

Before she could collect herself enough to form an answer, the doorbell rang.

Eight

"Who is that?"

"I don't know," Aislinn said.

"Were you expecting somebody?"

"No."

Always polite and adhering to the rules of etiquette, she asked him to excuse her. In light of what had just transpired, her courtesy was rather ludicrous. She left the kitchen and went to answer the front door bell, but she was distracted. Her mind had stayed in the other room with Greywolf. What was she going to do?

She swung the front door open and for several seconds didn't move. She just stood there wondering what else would happen to make this day one of the most disastrous of her life.

"Aren't you going to invite us in?" Eleanor Andrews asked her daughter.

"I…I'm sorry," Aislinn stuttered. She moved aside and her parents stepped into the living room.

"Is something wrong?" her father asked.

"No—I, uh, just wasn't expecting you." As usual, they intimidated her. Her parents could always make her feel like a child on the verge of being reprimanded. It wasn't something she liked to admit, but it happened every time she saw them. Today was no exception.

"We just left the club," Eleanor said, propping her tennis racquet against the wall, "and thought that as long as we had to come this way, we'd stop by."

Not very likely, Aislinn thought. If her parents had stopped by, there was a reason behind the impromptu visit. They didn't keep her in suspense long. "You remember Ted Utley," her father said for openers. "You met him at a symphony ball several years ago."

"He was married then," her mother supplied.

As Eleanor expounded upon Mr. Utley's unfortunate divorce and fortunate real-estate investments, Aislinn tried to view her parents objectively. They were both tanned and handsome and fit. They personified the American dream come true. They lived what most people would consider the good life. Yet Aislinn wondered if either of them had ever experienced any passion for living.

Oh, they smiled for the camera on Christmas mornings. Her mother cried daintily at funerals. Her father got emotionally involved when he discussed the national debt. But she had never once heard them either laughing lustily together or shouting in anger. She'd seen them kiss, formally, and pat each other affectionately, but she'd never intercepted a smoldering glance between them. They had produced her, yet she thought them to be the two most sterile people she had ever met.

"So we want you to come to dinner next Tuesday night," her mother was saying. "We'll eat on the patio, but wear something nice. And make arrangements with a sitter for...the...the child."

"The child's name is Tony," Aislinn said. "And I won't

need to make arrangements with a sitter because I won't be coming to your dinner party."

"Why not?" her father asked, scowling. "Just because you've had an illegitimate baby doesn't mean you have to hide yourself away."

Aislinn laughed. "Why, thank you, Father, for your broadmindedness." Her sarcasm escaped them. "I don't want to go through an embarrassing evening where you and Mother try to match me up with some man who has a tolerant attitude toward fallen women."

"That's enough," he said sharply.

"We're only doing what we feel is best for you," Eleanor said. "You've made a mess of your life. We're trying to rectify your mistakes as best we can. I think the least you could do is—"

Eleanor ended her lecture with a soft indrawn breath. She even raised a fearful hand to her chest as though to ward off an attacker. Willard Andrews followed his wife's startled gaze and he, too, was visibly taken aback. Without even turning around, Aislinn knew what had ruffled her usually unflappable parents.

Indeed, when she turned and looked at Greywolf, she felt that tingling in her system that was a combination of fear and anticipation. Every time she saw Lucas, she experienced that initial reaction.

He stood straight and tall in the doorway between the living room and kitchen. His unwavering gray eyes were fixed on her parents. His mouth was set in a hard, thin line. His shirt was open almost to his waist, and his torso barely moved as he breathed. He was so still he could have been a statue had it not been for the latent energy he emanated.

"Mother, Father, this is Mr. Greywolf," Aislinn said, her voice cutting through the heavy silence.

No one said a word. Lucas gave the Andrews a curt nod of his head in acknowledgement of the introduction, but Aislinn thought that was because Alice Greywolf had probably grilled her son in proper manners and not because Lucas felt any deference or respect for her parents.

Lucas could have been an uncaged tiger for the fearful stare Eleanor gave him. Willard was almost as dumbfounded, but he finally asked, "*Lucas* Greywolf?"

"Yes," Lucas answered in a clipped tone.

"I read about your release from prison in this morning's paper."

"My God." Eleanor swayed and gripped the back of a chair for support. She had the white-faced look of a victim about to be massacred and scalped, who was calling on a deity for mercy.

Willard subjected his daughter to a hard look. Out of habit, Aislinn lowered her eyes. He said, "What I can't understand, Mr. Greywolf, is what you're doing in my daughter's house, apparently with her consent."

Aislinn kept her head lowered. She had thought her encounters with Lucas were bad, but nothing could be worse than this. From the corner of her eye, she saw Lucas leave the doorway and silently move into the room. He came directly toward her. Eleanor recoiled and uttered another gasp when he reached out and jerked Aislinn's chin up, forcing her to look at him.

"Well?"

He was giving her a choice, albeit not much of one. Either she was to tell them what he was doing in her house or he would. She lifted her chin off his index finger and turned her head slightly to meet her parents' incredulous stares. Taking a deep breath and feeling like she was about to step off a gangplank, she said, "Lucas is…is…Tony's father."

The following silence was so thick it could have been cut with a knife. Aislinn could hear the thudding of her own heart as she met the glazed expressions on the faces of her mother and father. Never at a loss for words in any social situation, they now stared at her as wide-eyed and gape-mouthed as dead fish on the beach.

"That's impossible," Eleanor wheezed at last.

"Lucas and I, uh, met when he escaped from prison ten months ago," Aislinn said.

"I don't believe it," Eleanor said.

"Yes you do," Lucas said scornfully, "or you wouldn't be so horrified. I'm sure it comes as an unpleasant shock to you to learn that your grandson is also the grandson of an Indian chief."

"Don't you dare speak to my wife in that tone of voice!" Willard ordered stridently and took a belligerent step forward. "I could have you arrested for—"

"Spare me your threats, Mr. Andrews. I've heard them all. And from men richer and more powerful than you. I'm not afraid of you."

"What is it you want?" Willard demanded. "Money?"

Greywolf's face went hard and cold with contempt. He pulled himself up straighter. "I want my son."

Eleanor turned to Aislinn. "Let him have him."

"What?" Aislinn fell back a step. "What did you say?"

"Give him the baby. That would be best for everyone."

Aghast, Aislinn stared first at her mother, then at her father, who, by his silence, had endorsed Eleanor's suggestion. "You expect me to give my child away?" It was a rhetorical question. She could tell by their expectant faces that her mother was sincere.

"For once in your life, listen to us, Aislinn," her father said. He reached out and clasped her hand. "You've always gone against our wishes, bucked the system, done what you knew we would disapprove of. But this time you've gone too far and made a ghastly mistake. I don't know how you could have…"

Unable to bring himself to say it, he merely cast a scathing glance at Lucas, a glance that said it all. He turned back to his daughter. "But it happened. You'll regret this mistake the rest of your life if you don't give the child up now. Apparently Mr. Greywolf sees the wisdom in it even if you don't. Give him the child to raise. If you like, I'll send money occasionally to—"

Aislinn wrested her hand from her father's and backed away from him as though he were diseased. At the moment, she thought he was—diseased in the heart. How could either of her parents even suggest that she give Tony away? Never to see him again. To dispose of him as though he were the incriminating debris of a wild party.

She looked at them and realized they were strangers. How little she really knew them. Even more, how little they knew her. "I love my son. I won't give him up for anything in the world."

"Aislinn, be reasonable," Eleanor said testily. "I can admire your attachment to the child, but—"

"I think you'd better leave."

Even if Greywolf's voice hadn't been so raspily commandeering, his stance was. He seemed to tower over the three of them when, as one, they turned at the soft dangerous sound.

Willard snorted scoffingly. "I sure as hell won't be ordered from my own daughter's house by an…by *you*. Besides, this discussion doesn't involve you."

"It involves him very much," Aislinn contradicted. "He's Tony's father. Whatever my decision is, it concerns him."

"He's a criminal!" her father exclaimed.

"He was unjustly accused. He took the blame for something others did." She noted that Lucas swung around toward her, revealing his surprise at the way she defended him.

"The courts didn't think so. According to the record, he's an ex-con. And, as if that isn't enough," Willard said, "he's an Indian."

"So is Tony," Aislinn said courageously. "That doesn't mean I love him any less."

"Well, don't expect us ever to accept him," Eleanor said coldly.

"Then I guess you'd better do as Lucas suggested and leave."

Willard came as close as Aislinn had ever seen him to losing his temper, but he held it in check and said tightly, "If you have anything, *anything,* to do with this man, you'll get nothing more from me."

"I never asked anything of you, Father." Tears were stinging her eyes, but she held her head up proudly. "I paid back your investment in the photography studio, which I didn't want in the first place. I don't owe you for anything, not even for a happy childhood. You said a moment ago that I had always bucked the system, but that isn't true. I always *wanted* to, but you always dissuaded me. I bowed to your wishes in every major decision of my life. Until now. If you and Mother can't accept the fact that Tony is your grandson, then I can't hold a place in your lives either."

They weathered her ultimatum with the same cool control they had every sad crisis and joyous occasion of their lives. Without a word, Willard took his wife's arm and steered her toward the door. Eleanor paused only long enough to pick up her tennis racquet before they left. They never looked back.

Aislinn's head dropped forward. The tears, which had been threatening for the past several heart-wrenching minutes, slowly slid from under her eyelids and rolled down her cheeks. Her parents wanted to dominate her life completely or have no part in it at all. She couldn't believe that they could be so resolute in their prejudice as to refuse to acknowledge their own grandson. She bitterly regretted their decision.

On the other hand, if they were that narrow-minded and unbending, she and Tony were better off without them. She wanted her son to be unashamed of the emotions he experienced. She wanted him to grow up having the freedom to express himself in a way she had never been allowed to. She wanted him to feel things intensely, as she had with...

Aislinn spun around and looked at the man standing so still and silent behind her. Her thoughts had inevitably brought her to those days she had spent as a captive of Lucas Greywolf. Then for the first time, life had been unpredictable. She clearly recalled the rushes of excitement, of joy and sadness. That brief period of time hadn't been romanticized in her mind, as she had later thought it had been. It hadn't all been wonderful. Far from it. But it had been *real.* She had never felt so alive as during those turbulent hours.

"What are you going to do?" Lucas asked her.

"Do you still want me to marry you?"

"For our son's sake, yes."

"Will you be a good, loving father to Tony?"

"I swear it."

It was the hardest thing she had ever had to ask another person, but she met his pale gray eyes steadily. "And to me? What kind of husband can I expect you to be?"

"You are the mother of my son. I'll treat you with the respect that deserves."

"You have frightened me on numerous occasions. I don't want to live in fear of you."

"I would never harm you. I swear it on the body of my grandfather, Joseph Greywolf."

What a bizarre proposal, Aislinn thought. Like most women, she had imagined candlelight and roses, wine and soft music, a full moon and professions of undying love. She smiled weakly and with self-derision. Oh, well, one couldn't have it all.

She had just closed the door on everything that was safe and familiar. There would be no going back. And besides, Lucas wasn't going to give up his son. He had made that perfectly clear.

It would be a loveless marriage, save for their common love for Tony. There was no love in her life now anyway, so it wouldn't be missed. Life with Lucas and Tony wouldn't be just an endless series of days, made monotonous by their sameness. It would at least hold some surprises.

Her eyes were steadfast as she looked up at him. Without further hesitation she said, "All right, Lucas Greywolf. I'll marry you."

She did, two days later at nine o'clock in the morning in a civil ceremony in the same courthouse where Lucas Greywolf had been found guilty of his alleged crimes almost four years before.

The bride held her baby on her shoulder as she recited the vows that legally bound her to a man who was little more than a stranger. She hadn't known what would be suitable to wear, but had finally decided on a peach-colored linen suit with a pleated skirt and unstructured jacket. Beneath the jacket was an ivory lawn shell so sheer that her lacy camisole showed through. The outfit was soft and feminine without being flagrantly bridal.

She held one side of her hair back with an ivory comb, an antique bequeathed her by her paternal grandmother. That was her "something old." She had chosen blue panties, not wanting to thumb her nose at tradition altogether.

Lucas had surprised her by wearing dark slacks and a sport coat over a pale-blue dress shirt and a sedate necktie. He looked incredibly handsome with his long, dark hair brushed away from his face and lying against his collar. Side by side, she knew they made a striking couple. Heads had turned to look at them when they entered the courthouse.

Before she even realized that the vows had been solemnized, the ceremony was over and they were leaving the building. Lucas had given her a light, perfunctory kiss when the judge had pronounced them man and wife. Now his hand rode loosely beneath her elbow as he guided her toward his parked pickup truck. It was at least a decade old. "We'll go load up the things you've packed, then get on our way."

He had told her the day before that he wanted to have the ceremony—though the few minutes they had spent in the judge's chambers hardly qualified as such—early, so they could reach their destination before nightfall. He wanted to waste no more time getting back to the reservation.

At her condo, while she changed Tony and herself into more comfortable traveling clothes, Lucas loaded the things she had set aside to take with them into the bed of the pickup. As she went through the rooms of the condo one last time, she couldn't conjure up an iota of regret for leaving it.

It had been a residence, not a home. No sentiment had been attached to anything. The only thing she hated to leave was the nursery she had prepared for Tony. Love had been poured into that room.

"Got everything?" Lucas asked her as she entered the living room from the back of the house after making sure all the lights had been turned out.

"I think so."

He had changed clothes, too. He was wearing the same shirt, but the sleeves had been rolled to his elbows. His slacks had been replaced with jeans, his dress shoes with boots, and there was a bandanna tied around his forehead. He hadn't worn the earring that morning, but he had it on now.

They locked the doors behind them, having agreed that for the time being they would leave her furniture there until they decided on the best way to dispose of it and the property. Knowing her husband might be sensitive about such things, she offered to leave her car in the garage. How much of a sacrifice that was soon became apparent.

"This damn thing isn't air conditioned," Lucas said of the truck. They were on the highway and the wind was wreaking havoc on Aislinn's hair. Tony rode in his carrier, which they had secured between them on the seat. He was protected by a light blanket. It was too hot to keep the windows rolled up. But it was a constant battle for Aislinn to keep her hair out of her face. She hadn't complained, but Lucas had noticed.

"It's not so bad," she lied.

"Open the glove compartment," he said. She did. Inside she found a variety of items. "Get that extra bandanna and tie it around your hair. That will keep it from blowing so much."

She removed the bandanna from the glove compartment and neatly folded it into a triangle, then into a narrow band. She twisted it before securing it around her head. Leaning forward, she checked her reflection in the rearview mirror. "Does this officially make me a squaw?"

She looked at him and smiled. At first he didn't know what to make of her question, but when he saw the teasing light in her blue eyes, he answered her smile with one of his own. It was slow in coming, almost as if his lips didn't remember how to form a smile. But at last it broke across his handsome face, relieving it of its foreboding austerity. He even gave a short laugh.

After that, the tension between them eased somewhat. Little by little, she drew him out. They exchanged stories about their childhoods, some funny, some painful. "In a way, I was as lonely as you," Aislinn said.

"After meeting your parents I can believe that."

"They don't have near the capacity to love that your mother does."

He only glanced at her and nodded.

As anxious as he was to get home, he consulted her frequently about stopping to rest, eat or drink. "We'll have to stop soon," she said shortly after noon. "Tony is waking up and he'll want to be fed."

He had been a perfect angel, sleeping in his carrier. But he woke up hungry and impatient for his lunch. By the time they reached the next town, his strenuous wails were echoing in the cab of the pickup.

"Where should I stop?" Lucas asked her.

"We can keep driving. I'll manage."

"No, you'd be more comfortable if we stop. Just say where."

"I don't know," she replied, gnawing her lip anxiously. She didn't want Tony's crying to aggravate Lucas. He might yet change his mind about wanting to be a parent. What if he quickly got tired of the everyday hassles?

"A rest room?" he suggested, his eyes scanning the buildings on the main street.

"I hate to take him into a public place when he's putting up such a fuss."

Lucas finally wheeled the truck into a municipal park. He found a private spot beneath a shade tree and parked. "How's this?"

"Fine." Aislinn hastily unbuttoned her blouse, adjusted her bra and positioned Tony against her breast. His cries ceased abruptly. "Whew," she said, laughing, "I don't know if we could have gone…"

Her sentence trailed off to nothingness because she had innocently lifted her gaze from her son's flushed face and looked at his father. Lucas was staring down at his nursing son. The intensity on his face stopped whatever Aislinn was about to say. When he saw that she was watching him, his eyes flickered away to stare through the windshield.

"Are you hungry?" he asked.

"Sort of."

"How about a hamburger from a drive-through window?"

"That's fine. Anything."

"As soon as Tony is, uh, taken care of, we'll find a place."

"Okay."

"Did I hurt you?"

She raised her head and looked at him. He was still staring through the windshield. "When, Lucas?"

"You know when. That morning."

"No." Her denial was so soft even her own ears could barely detect it.

He tapped the steering wheel with his fist. He wagged

one knee back and forth in a steady rhythm. His eyes darted over the landscape. In any other man these symptoms would have indicated nervousness. But that was unthinkable. Lucas Greywolf didn't get nervous. Did he?

"I had been in prison—"

"I know."

"And without a woman."

"I understand."

"I was rough."

"Not too—"

"And later I got to worrying about it. That maybe I had hurt you…your breasts…or your…"

"No, you didn't."

"You were so damn small—"

"It had been a while."

"And…and tight…and I—"

"It wasn't rape, Lucas."

His head snapped around. "You could have claimed that it was."

"But it wasn't."

The messages their eyes telegraphed to each other were laden with things better left unsaid. Aislinn bowed her head and closed her eyes as waves of heat, having nothing to do with the still, summer day, surged through her. Even now she could feel the driving thrusts of his body into hers.

And Lucas shut his ears to the delicious sound of his son nursing at her breast. He remembered his own lips tugging at her nipples, hard and peaked with arousal. His tongue had circled them, nudged them, stroked…

God, don't think about it or you'll get hard.

"When did you first know you were pregnant?" he asked gruffly after a long moment.

"About two months later."

"Were you sick?"

"A little. Tired more than anything. I didn't have any energy. And I had stopped having…"

"Oh. Yeah."

From the corner of his eye, he saw her gently lift Tony from one breast and transfer him to the other. She was modest. He knew what this enforced intimacy must be costing her. Yet, he wanted to reach across the seat, spread her blouse open and gaze at this marvel of nature. He wanted to look at her breasts. He yearned to touch them. To taste. Her femininity filled him—his nose, his throat, his loins. He was inundated with the scent and sight and sound of woman and he wanted to stay immersed in it for a long time.

"Was it an easy pregnancy?"

"As far as pregnancies go," she said with a smile.

"Did he kick a lot?"

"Like a soccer player."

"I prefer to think of him as a marathon runner."

Their eyes met across the narrow distance. The look they exchanged was mellow. What passed between them was the shared dream of parents for their child. "Yes. Like a marathoner," she agreed softly. "Like you."

His heart swelled with pride. Emotion welled so high inside his chest that for several seconds he could barely breathe. "Thank you." She looked at him inquiringly. "For carrying my son."

Then it was Aislinn's turn to become embarrassingly emotional. Thanks didn't come easily to a man with Greywolf's pride. To have made an issue of it would ruin the moment, so she merely nodded her head.

She gave Tony her attention until he was finished, then she passed the baby to Lucas. He held him while

Aislinn readjusted her clothing. He even assisted as she changed Tony's diaper.

They said nothing more. Enough had been said.

"Gene's here," Lucas remarked as he pulled the pickup to a stop in front of a tiny, neat, white stucco house. Its fenced front yard was well manicured. A porch light burned in welcome. Zinnias bloomed in flower beds on either side of the front sidewalk.

It was well after dark. They had been driving on the reservation for hours, though this time they hadn't had to use back roads as they had when Lucas was a fugitive. Still, their trip had been long and tiring. Aislinn was exhausted. "Are we staying here tonight?" she asked hopefully.

"No, we'll stop and say hello. But I'm anxious to get to my own land."

His own land? She didn't know he had any land. Until then, she hadn't even thought to ask how he intended to support Tony and her since he couldn't practice law anymore. Somehow she wasn't worried about it. Greywolf had proven to be resourceful, intuitive, and capable. She had no doubts that he would make life as comfortable for his son as possible.

Lucas came around and helped her out of the truck. For the first time, she felt a twinge of apprehension. What if Alice Greywolf and Dr. Dexter reacted to the baby the same way her parents had? She was more an outsider here than Lucas was in her world. How would she be received?

Lucas seemed to have no such qualms. He jogged up the sidewalk and jumped onto the porch. He rapped on the front door twice before Gene Dexter pulled it open.

"Well, it's about time. Alice has been—"

When the doctor saw Aislinn coming up the sidewalk, his welcoming speech was cut short.

"Gene, is it Lucas?" Alice called from inside the house. "Lucas?" She stepped around Gene, her face wreathed in smiles. "Oh, you're here! We've been worried. Why didn't you come straight home? Did you decide to stay a few days in Phoenix?"

Lucas stepped aside. When Alice's eyes fell on Aislinn, they widened as prettily as a doe's. When she saw the baby nestled in Aislinn's arms, her mouth formed a small O. "I think you'd better come in out of the night air."

Aislinn knew then that she would come to love Alice Greywolf. No questions. No recriminations. No censure. Just gracious, unqualified acceptance.

Lucas held the screen door open for Aislinn and Tony. She stepped into a living room that was simply but tastefully furnished.

"Mother, Gene, you remember Aislinn."

"Of course," Gene said.

"Hello."

Alice smiled at her and asked shyly, "May I see the baby?"

Aislinn turned Tony so that he could be seen easily. Alice gasped softly. Tears filled her eyes as she reached out and touched the dark down on his head. "Lucas," she breathed.

"Anthony Joseph," Lucas proudly corrected her. "My son."

"Oh, yes, I know he's your son." Alice clamped her small, white teeth over her lower lip to keep from laughing and crying at the same time. "He looks just like you. Gene, did you see him? Isn't he wonderful? Anthony Joseph. After father." She looked at Aislinn with tear-spar-kled eyes. "Thank you."

"I...*we*...call him Tony. Would you like to hold him?"

Alice hesitated for only a moment before opening her arms to receive the child. For years she had been tak-ing care of newborns at the clinic, but she handled Tony so carefully he might have been made of porcelain. Her eyes never left him as she carried him to the sofa and sat down, crooning a Navaho lullaby.

"Guess that leaves me to take over as host," Gene said, finally thinking to shut the front door to preserve the air conditioning. "Aislinn, come in and have a seat," he said, sweeping his arm wide to indicate the living room.

"We got married today," Lucas said bluntly, almost as though he expected to be challenged.

"Well that's...that's great," Gene said dubiously.

Again the situation could have been awkward if Alice hadn't intervened. "Please sit down, all of you," she urged. "I'll get you something to eat and drink shortly. But I want just a few minutes with Tony."

"Don't go to any trouble, Mother. We can't stay long."

"You're leaving? But you just got here."

"I want to get out to the place before it gets any later."

Alice looked at her son with disbelief. "Out to the place? You mean to that *trailer?*"

"Yes."

"With Aislinn and Tony?"

"Of course."

"But you can't move them into that trailer. It's too small. It hasn't even been cleaned, and—"

"Alice," Gene said with gentle reproach.

She fell silent immediately. She glanced at Lucas and Aislinn uneasily. "It's none of my business, I realize, but I hoped you'd spend a few days here with me before moving out there."

Lucas looked down at Aislinn. She hadn't offered an opinion and he knew she wouldn't. God, she was courageous. When the occasion called for it, she was as steady as a rock. He had admired that in her from the beginning. But he could see the rings of fatigue beneath her eyes and the weary stoop of her shoulders. "All right. One night," he conceded, surprising himself.

"Oh, I'm so glad," Alice said. "Here, Aislinn, take the baby. I've been keeping some food warm on the outside chance that Lucas would show up tonight."

"I'll help you," Aislinn offered.

"You don't have to."

"But I want to."

Gene and Lucas followed them from the room. At the door, Lucas caught Gene's arm. "We're not putting you out of a bed tonight, are we?" he asked beneath his breath.

"Unfortunately no," Gene said ruefully.

"Still?"

The doctor shook his head sadly. "Still. Your mother is a rare woman, Lucas. I don't intend to give up on her until she is my wife."

Lucas slapped him on the back. "Good. She needs you."

As they entered the kitchen, he was thinking how rare a woman he was married to. That's why his eyes sought out Aislinn immediately.

She caught his glance and looked back at him shyly. This was a family scene, and yet it wasn't. Her new married status would take some getting used to. Yet she was inordinately pleased when Lucas sat down next to her.

"Lucas, why didn't you tell me about the baby?" Alice

asked a half-hour later as she carried their supper dishes to the sink.

The significant pause broadened into a lengthy, uncomfortable silence. Aislinn finally broke it with her confession. "He didn't know about the baby. Not until he came to my house three days ago to thank me for not pressing any charges against him." She tried to meet the startled gazes of Lucas's mother and friend, but found that she didn't have the courage and lowered her eyes.

"I forced her to marry me," Lucas said with characteristic candor. "I threatened to take Tony away from her if she didn't."

Gene shifted uncomfortably in his chair. Alice raised her hand to her lips, hoping her shock wasn't too evident. At last she said, "I'm very glad to have you as my daughter-in-law, Aislinn."

"Thank you," Aislinn said, smiling at the older woman. She knew that Alice and the doctor must be burning with curiosity, so she appreciated their restraint from asking further questions.

"You must be tired after the long drive," Alice said kindly. "Why don't you let me get you settled for the night? You can sleep in my room."

"No." Before anyone could move, Lucas paralyzed them all with that single word. "Aislinn is my wife. She sleeps with me."

Nine

The resulting silence was terrible. Gene stared into his coffee cup and fidgeted in his chair. Alice studied her hands, composed but embarrassed. Aislinn's eyes were riveted to the top of Tony's head while color rose high in her cheeks. Only Lucas seemed unaffected by his bold declaration.

"Do you need anything out of the truck?" he asked, scraping his chair away from the table and standing.

"The small suitcase and Tony's bag," Aislinn replied in a low voice.

"Mother, can you fashion Tony a crib out of a drawer or something?"

"Yes of course. Come on, Aislinn," Alice said, laying a hand on the girl's shoulder. "Let's get Tony settled for the night."

"I'll help Lucas." Gene seemed grateful for something to do. He followed Lucas from the kitchen.

The bedroom into which Alice led Aislinn was small, having room for only an old-fashioned vanity table with a padded stool, a chest of drawers, a nightstand, and a double bed.

"These drawers are empty," Alice said, taking one out of the chest of drawers. "I cleaned everything out after Father died."

"I didn't have time...before...to tell you how sorry I was," Aislinn said.

"Thank you. It was inevitable. He was old. He didn't want to linger for years in a hospital or nursing home. It happened just as he wanted it to. There, do you think that will work?"

While they were talking, she had lined the bottom of the drawer with a quilt, folding it several times in order to make it fit and to form soft bedding for the baby.

"That will be fine. For now. In another month or two he'll be kicking the sides out." Aislinn hugged Tony affectionately and kissed his temple.

"Oh, by then I'll have bought a crib. I'm counting on you to bring him to see me often."

"You don't mind about Lucas and me?" Her eyes shyly sought Alice's.

"Maybe I should be asking *you* that. Do *you* mind about Lucas and you?"

"At first, yes, very much. Now, I don't know," she said honestly. "We hardly know each other, but we both love Tony. The quality of his life is extremely important to us. On that basis, we might make the marriage work."

"Life out there on the ranch will be far different from what you're accustomed to."

"I was sick to death of the life I was accustomed to, even before I met Lucas."

"It won't be easy for you, Aislinn."

"Nothing worthwhile is."

The two women stared at each other, the younger with determination, the other with skepticism. "Let's make up the bed," Alice suggested quietly.

Once the clean sheets had been smoothed over the bed, Aislinn realized how narrow it was. How would she get through the night sleeping there with Lucas? He had come into the bedroom to deposit the bags she had requested from the truck, but had immediately gone out again. She could hear him conversing with Gene in the living room.

"I'd better leave so you can get some rest," Alice said. "Besides, if I don't say a special good-night to Gene, he might think I've deserted him in favor of Tony." She leaned down to kiss the baby who was lying contentedly in the makeshift crib. Before she left, she took Aislinn's hand. "I'm very glad to have you in the family."

"Even though I'm an Anglo?"

"Unlike my son, I don't harbor a grudge against a race for what a few have done."

Without thinking about it, Aislinn kissed her new mother-in-law on the cheek. "Good night, Alice. Thank you for your kindness to Tony and me."

When she was alone, Aislinn fed the baby, hoping he would sleep straight through till morning and not disturb Lucas. She rushed him along, hoping she could get done with the nursing before Lucas came in. She wanted to spare herself another scene like the one earlier in the pickup.

There was only one bathroom in the house. It was located in the hallway between the two bedrooms. Aislinn took her turn as soon as she put Tony to bed. When she came back into the bedroom, there was nothing left to do but get undressed.

Officially this was her wedding night, yet the nightgown she took from her suitcase wasn't exactly bridal. This was its second summer season, and though it was soft and the fabric sheer against the light, its modest, scooped, elasticized neckline wasn't sexually enticing. In fact it looked rather dowdy and plain.

She was sitting at the vanity table, smoothing lotion on her arms when Lucas came in and closed the door behind him. Aislinn fumbled with the bottle of lotion. She told herself that her clumsiness was due to the fact that her hands were slippery and not because she was facing a night alone in a bedroom with Lucas Greywolf.

Had she been looking at herself in the mirror rather than at her husband, she would have seen that her eyes were wide and apprehensive. They made her appear very young and innocent. In contrast, her hair fell around her shoulders seductively. Her lips were soft and dewy and naturally rosy. The nightgown looked maidenly. The total package, especially seen through the eyes of a bridegroom, was sexy.

The lamp on the nightstand was turned down low. The shadow that Lucas cast onto the walls and ceiling was long and ominous in the small, square room.

"Is Tony asleep yet?" he asked, his hands going to the buttons of his shirt.

"Yes. I don't think he minds sleeping in a bureau drawer at all."

In the mirror, Aislinn saw Lucas smile as he bent over the drawer, which she had placed on the floor near the side of the bed. Her heart fluttered at the way his face softened when he looked at his son. It would be very easy to fall in love with a man who could feel that kind of tenderness for a woman.

Mentally she jerked herself erect. Tender emotions like that would be foreign to most of the men she knew. For Greywolf, they would be impossible. As though to sweep the ridiculous musings from her mind, she picked up her hairbrush and began pulling it through her hair, though it already crackled with life.

Lucas sat down on the edge of the bed and tugged off his boots, dropping them to the floor. "Gene told me tonight that he's glad we got married."

It was so unlike him to initiate a seemingly innocuous conversation that her arms fell still and she looked at his reflection in the mirror. "Why?"

He chuckled. Another phenomenon. "He's been trying to get my mother to marry him for years. He made her promise she would when I got out of prison." He stood up and unbuckled his belt. "Our getting married was his ace in the hole. Now she really doesn't have any excuses left."

"He seems like such a dear, kind man. How can she help but want to marry a man like him?"

"A man so unlike *your* husband."

She was laying the hairbrush aside, but at his words, her eyes swung up to meet his in the mirror. "I didn't mean it that way."

"It doesn't matter what you meant. I'm the husband you've got."

She swallowed a knot of apprehension as he came toward her with a stalking, sauntering gait. He epitomized a confident male animal on the scent of a female. He had stripped down to his jeans. The fly was unbuttoned. Aislinn's eyes unerringly went to that narrow V that yawned open just below his navel. Her heart leaped with a mixture of desire and trepidation.

In the dim lighting, his skin took on a deep copper hue. His dark body hair was limned with golden light, especially that which spun around his navel. His cheeks were shaded by the drastic projection of his cheekbones, which were striped now with the long shadows of his eyelashes.

His gray eyes were trained on her like an eagle's on

weakened prey. They seemed to penetrate the layers of her skin and see straight inside her. His look was hot. It seared her, but she shivered.

"Lucas?"

"You have beautiful hair."

He came to stand directly behind her, putting her shoulders on a level with his hips. Against the brown expanse of his hard stomach, her hair looked incredibly fair. It rippled like golden threads in his hands when he lifted bunches of it off her shoulders. Idly he let the heavy strands sift through his fingers.

Aislinn was entranced by the sensuous sight. And even though it was happening to her, she forced herself to become strictly an observer, to pretend that it was happening to someone else. That was the only way she could survive it.

Otherwise, when he spread a handful of her hair over his belly and rubbed it around and around like lather, her heart would have drummed its way out of her body.

If she let herself admit that she was actually participating in such a visually erotic act, she might turn around and kiss that taut stomach. She might treat her lips to a journey around the thin slit of his navel and down that strip of jet-black hair that fanned wide in the opening of his jeans. She might dampen that hair with soft, kittenish licks.

He let her hair fall back to her shoulders and closed his hands loosely around her neck. His fingers strummed it lightly. "Why does your white skin appeal to me so much?" he asked raspily. "I want to hate it."

He touched her earlobes, feathered them with the pads of his fingers, softly pinched them between his thumbs and index fingers. She made a whimpering sound. Against her will, her neck gave way and her head landed against the hard plane of his stomach behind her. Mindlessly, she rolled her head from one side to the other. She watched her hair swish across his dark skin and thought that, together, they were very beautiful.

His hands coasted over her shoulders and slipped beneath the lacy elastic top of her gown. Her eyes, which had been half-closed, opened and met his in the mirror.

"I want to see my hands on you," he said.

She watched, hypnotized, as his strong, tapering, wide-spread fingers slid down her chest. No protest broke across her lips when they moved lower, taking the gown down with them. Her breath rushed into her lungs when his palms slid down over her breasts. He pressed. He massaged. He rubbed.

Her body responded.

He cupped the undersides of her fully aroused breasts and lifted them, lightly whisking the crests with his thumbs. She moaned, grinding the back of her head into his belly, which was rising and falling with each of his rapid breaths.

Their eyes never wavered from the mirror. They were mesmerized by the contrast of his large hands, such testimonies to his masculinity, moving over the soft, velvety mounds of her breasts. He knew just how much pressure to apply to give her optimum sensation. His fingers played delicately with the dusky tips until they throbbed with a pleasurable pain.

Deep inside her, another ache was becoming unbearable. Her womanhood felt feverish and heavy as it flowered to readiness. Only one thing could ease that special kind of ache.

And that was impossible.

The realization struck Aislinn suddenly and she threw off his hands. Springing off the stool, she pulled her nightgown up over her breasts and, turning to face him, said "I can't."

The sound that emanated from his throat was that of an attacking mountain cat. He gripped the upper part of her arms and yanked her hard against him. "You're my wife."

"But not your possession," she flared. "Let me go."

"I'm entitled."

He tunneled his fingers through her hair, pressed them against her scalp and drew her face beneath his. Reflexively she reached up to ward him off. Her hands landed on either side of his torso, just under his arms. His skin was smooth and warm. The muscles were so hard they begged to be explored and admired. She wanted to sink her teeth into them. Her determination wavered.

But this wasn't right. They were married, yes. With that marriage license came certain privileges, yes. But shouldn't love be involved? And if not love, at least mutual respect? She knew that Lucas had only contempt for what she was and where she had come from. She refused to be merely a vessel for his lust.

And even if the wrongness of it weren't enough of a reason to discourage him, there was the other. Since it was the most expedient, that's the reason she would use.

A heartbeat before his mouth ravished hers, she said, "Think, Lucas! Tony is barely a month old." He paused. She saw his gray eyes blink with misapprehension, so she hurriedly clarified her point. "You asked me today if you had hurt me before, and I said you hadn't. That was the truth. But if you...if we...do this, you could hurt me. I haven't had time to completely heal."

He stared down into her face, his hot breath striking her in steady pants. When he had finally digested what she was telling him, he glanced down toward her middle.

Gradually his grip on her arms relaxed and he set her away from him. Nervously she wet her lips with her tongue. "For christsake don't do that," he growled. He ran his fingers through his hair, then covered his face with both hands. He pressed his fingers deep into his eyesockets before slowly dragging his hands down his cheeks. "Get into bed."

She didn't argue. After quickly checking on Tony to make certain he was sleeping soundly, she slid between Alice Greywolf's sunshine-smelling sheets and pulled the top one over her. The air conditioning even required the light blanket.

She closed her eyes, but knew when Lucas peeled down his jeans and stepped out of them. Through the screen of her lashes, she saw his nakedness. Long limbs. Wide chest. A shadowy triangle between powerful thighs. And an aroused virility. Then the room was pitched into darkness when he switched out the lamp.

All she could think about as he lay down beside her was that he was naked and that he was hard. Though they didn't touch at any point, she could feel his body heat. It scorched her skin. The rhythm of his breathing both electrified and soothed. She held her body rigid until his weight shifted and she knew that he had turned away from her.

Only then did she relax enough to eventually fall asleep.

Her eyes drifted open to meet the pinkish-gray, pre-dawn light. Her breasts were full. Tony had slept through the night without a feeding, but he would be waking up soon. She hoped so. Her discomfort had awakened her from a sound sleep.

She lifted her eyelids a fraction more and was alarmed

to see how close to her Lucas was lying. His chest was scant inches from her nose. She could count each crinkly hair. Secretly she thanked his father for giving Lucas enough Anglo blood to have a beard and chest hair.

The bed covers were folded back to his waist. His smooth, dark skin looked touchable beneath the rumpled white sheet. She longed to lay her hand in the valley of his waist. But, of course, she didn't.

Lying perfectly still, she let her eyes wander up his tanned throat to the proud chin. His lips were beautifully shaped, if a bit stern. His nose was long and straight, not flat and wide like many Apaches'. Again she blessed his father's seed.

She gasped softly when her eyes lifted to his and found them steadily watching her. His hair looked very black against the snowy pillowcase. "What are you doing awake?" she whispered.

"Habit." Only an act of will kept her from flinching when he raised one of his hands and picked a wavy strand of hair from her cheek. Looking at it analytically, he rubbed it between his fingers. At length, he laid it with unwarranted care on her pillow. "However, it has not been my habit of recent years to wake up with a woman lying beside me. You smell good."

"Thank you."

Another man might have asked, "What perfume are you wearing?" or said, "I like your fragrance." But her husband was a man of few words. His compliments weren't lavish, but they expressed exactly what he wanted to say. "You smell good." She cherished the simple compliment.

He touched her. His fingers explored lightly, with the inhibited curiosity of a child allowed in the formal living room for the first time. Eyebrows. Nose. Mouth. He gazed at what he touched.

He glided his fingers back and forth across her throat and chest. "So soft," he said, as though marveling over the texture of her skin.

With one fluid movement of his arm he threw the covers off. She willed herself to lie still when he pulled her gown down. This was her husband. She couldn't withhold herself from him. And she discovered that she didn't want to.

He wouldn't hurt her. She knew that. If he were a truly violent man he could have hurt her so many times in the past. She remembered his gentleness when he tended the scratch on her arm. Besides, he had sworn he would never harm her, and she believed him. So she lay perfectly still while his eyes devoured her breasts and his finger traced a vein that rivered toward her nipple.

She saw his jaw bunch with tension. For a brief second, he looked directly into her eyes before he leaned forward and pressed his open mouth to her neck. Moaning low, he inched closer, until her breasts were touching his chest.

His lips sipped at her skin, nipping at it lightly with his teeth. She felt the brush of his tongue, soft and wet and warm. It took every ounce of willpower at her disposal not to dig her hands into his hair and hold his head against her. He was exercising such self-restraint that she dared not move. It would be cruel to instigate something that couldn't be satisfactorily finished.

His mouth moved lower, touching her damply, taking exquisitely gentle love-bites. He raised his head slightly and looked down at her laden breasts. "If I...? Would your milk come?" He looked at her. She nodded.

A spasm of regret flickered across his mouth. He

leaned away from her and paused for a moment before easing the gown down farther. He looked at her. At everything.

His eyes fastened on her womanhood. He touched the golden cloud of hair. He started breathing heavily, rapidly. Indeed, since the covers had been thrown back, the strength of his desire was no secret.

Suddenly his hand clamped her wrist. Alarmed by the abrupt movement, she raised questioning eyes to his. "You're my wife," he grated. "I won't be denied."

Before she realized his intent, he dragged her hand down, below his waist, and opened it over himself. Pressing. Her lips parted in an effort to protest, but his were there to seal hers closed and the words were left unspoken. His tongue plunged deep, filling her mouth.

He rolled her to her back and straddled her thighs. Their hands were trapped between their bodies, locked in the cove of her femininity and grinding against his manhood. He used his hand to maneuver hers, keeping her fingers tightly closed around him. Her palm provided the friction.

What happened then was so personal, so heart- and soul- and gut-wrenching that they both quaked under the tumult of it.

It lasted forever.

Finally, he rested his head on her breasts. His breathing was labored. She could feel his fingers moving mindlessly through her hair, as though reaching for something greatly desired, but elusive and just beyond his grasp.

Then abruptly, he rolled off the bed and came to his feet. He picked up the articles of his clothing with jerky movements and pulled them on haphazardly and angrily. He shoved his feet into his boots and, without so much as a backward glance, flung open the door and walked out.

Aislinn was dismayed and heartsick. She lay there staring at the door through which he had passed, grieved that he couldn't even look at her after what had happened. To her it had been beautiful. When his mouth had softened, when his tongue had ceased to be aggressive, he needn't have forced her to caress him. Though she doubted he realized that.

The immensity of the act had left her weak and trembling. It had left him angry. Had he been ashamed? Embarrassed? Disgusted? With himself or with her?

Or had he been as shattered by the impact of it as she? And, like her, was he bewildered as to how to deal with his feelings about it?

Both of them had survived childhood by keeping their emotions hidden. She had been taught by her parents to do so. Because of the scorn he had suffered as a child, Lucas kept his emotions carefully guarded to protect himself from hurt. He didn't know how to demonstrate affection and tenderness. He was even less adept at accepting them.

Aislinn knew then. She loved Lucas Greywolf.

And if it took her from now until her dying day, she would make him accept her love.

It wasn't going to be easy. She realized that the moment she entered the kitchen a half-hour later. Lucas was sitting at the table talking with Alice, sipping coffee and eating a stack of pancakes. He ignored Aislinn completely.

It was ironic that her penchant to stare at him coincided with his avoidance of her at all costs. While Aislinn's heart was stormy with awakened love, his eyes were as turbulent as a thundercloud. Through breakfast, their departure from Alice, and their drive to Lucas's ranch, he remained practically mute.

He provided monosyllabic answers to the questions she posed. Each inroad she made toward conversation met with a dead end. While her eyes wanted to gobble up the sight of him, he wouldn't make direct eye contact with her. She was amiable; he was querulous.

Once, after they had driven miles with Tony sleeping in his carrier between them, Lucas whipped his head around and demanded, "What the hell are you staring at?"

"You."

"Well, don't."

"Because it makes you nervous?"

"Because I don't like it."

"There's nothing else to look at."

"Give the scenery a try."

"When did you get your ear pierced?"

"Years ago."

"Why?"

"I wanted to."

"On you I like it."

His eyes left the road for another brief moment. "On me?" he sneered. "Meaning that it's okay for a man to have a pierced ear if he happens to be an Indian."

Aislinn bit back a retort. Instead she responded with a softly spoken, "No, meaning that on you I find it very attractive." His stern expression faltered for a split second before he returned his concentration to the two-lane highway that was taking them into the higher elevations of the White Mountains. "I have pierced ears, too. Maybe we can swap earrings."

Her attempt at humor fell flat. If he heard her, he gave no evidence of it. She thought he was going to ignore her entirely. But after a minute or two he said, "I only wear this one earring."

"Does it have special significance?"

"My grandfather made it."

"Joseph Greywolf was a silversmith?"

"That was just one of his talents." There was a defensive edge to his voice as sharp as a double-edged sword. It couldn't have held more challenge if he had said *"En garde."* "Do you find it hard to believe that an Indian could have several skills?"

Again, she held back a rejoinder. Curbing her temper this time was more difficult, but she forced herself to control it. She understood that he was only being nasty because he was mortified over what had happened in bed that morning.

He had revealed a weakness to her, and he found that untenable. Underneath that implacable facade, Lucas Greywolf was an extremely sensitive man. He had the same needs and desires for love as any human being. Only he didn't want anyone to know it.

His hostility was a defense mechanism. He was punishing himself for being a bastard, for being a hardship on his teenaged mother, even for being Indian. He was so hard on himself he had served a prison sentence for a crime he didn't commit. Aislinn wouldn't be satisfied until she uncovered each injury in his soul and healed it with her love.

"You didn't tell me you had some land. I know, I know," she rushed to add, holding up both palms, "I didn't ask. Will I always have to ask to get information out of you?"

"I'll tell you what I think you need to know."

Her mouth fell open in dismay over such outrageous chauvinism. "You think a woman should be seen and not heard, is that it?" she cried. "Well, think again, Mr. Greywolf, because Mrs. Greywolf intends to be an equal partner in this marriage, and if you didn't want it like that, then maybe you shouldn't have been so hasty to force Ms. Andrews into marrying you."

He flexed his fingers around the steering wheel. "What do you want to know?" he asked tightly.

Somewhat mollified, she settled back against the seat of the pickup truck. "Did you inherit the land from your grandfather?"

"Yes."

"Were we there...before?"

"You mean at the hogan? Yes. It was just over that ridge," he said, hitching his chin in that direction.

"Was?"

"I had it burned."

That stunned her, and for several minutes she said nothing. Then she asked, "How large is your ranch?"

"We're not rich if that's what you're asking," he said with injured scorn.

"That wasn't what I asked at all. I asked how much land you own."

He told her and she was surprised and impressed. "That's what was left after the swindlers got to my grandfather. Uranium was found on his property, but grandfather never profited from it."

To save them a heated discussion on the exploitation of Indians, especially when she was already on his side of that argument, she asked, "What kind of ranch is it? Cattle?"

"Horses."

She pondered that for a moment. "I don't understand, Lucas. Why did your grandfather die in poverty if he had that much land and a herd of horses?"

Apparently she struck a chord. Lucas glanced at her uneasily. "Joseph was very proud. He thought things should be done according to tradition."

"In other words," she paraphrased, "he didn't advance to modern ranching techniques."

"Something like that," he mumbled.

It was endearing to her that Lucas defended his late grandfather, even though he apparently hadn't agreed with him on how the ranch should be run.

The rest of the trip was spent in silence. She knew they were getting close to their destination when he turned off the highway, drove through a gate and onto a dirt road.

"Will we be there soon?" she asked.

He nodded. "Don't expect much."

As it turned out, what they saw when they arrived surprised Lucas more than it did Aislinn. "What the hell?" he muttered as the pickup chugged up the last hill.

Aislinn's eyes darted around the clearing, trying to take in everything at once. Admonishing herself for behaving like a kid at her first circus, she slowed her eyes down and tried to digest everything she saw.

The compound was set between two low hills that formed a horseshoe. On one side of the open area there was a large corral. Two men on horseback were leading a small herd of horses through the gate. A barn, obviously old and weathered, was nestled against the mountainside.

On the other side of the semicircle, stood a house trailer. Its paint was chipped and faded, and it looked about ready to collapse upon itself.

Right in the center of this land harbor was a stucco house. Because of its color, it blended into the rock wall that rose almost perpendicular behind it. The house was well suited to its environment.

It was also a beehive of activity. Men were shouting

to one another. The ring of a hammer echoed off the surrounding rock walls. From somewhere as yet undetermined, Aislinn could hear the high, shrill whirring of a buzz saw.

Lucas braked the pickup and got out. A man, dressed in cowboy garb, separated himself from the others who were working on the house. He waved and came jogging toward them. He was shorter and much stockier than Lucas and had the bowlegged, rolling walk of a man who spends a lot of time on horseback.

"Johnny, what the hell is going on?" Lucas said in lieu of a proper hello.

"We're getting your house finished for you."

"I was going to live in the trailer until I could get enough money together to finish the house."

"So now you won't have to," Johnny said, his black eyes twinkling jovially. "Hello, by the way. It's good to have you back." He shook Lucas's hand. But Lucas, still staring over his friend's shoulder up toward the house, barely noticed.

"I can't pay for any of this."

"You've already paid."

"What the hell does that mean? Does my mother know about this?"

"Yeah, but she was sworn to secrecy. We've been working on the house since we found out the date of your release, trying to get it finished before you got here. Thanks for giving us the few extra days."

Johnny was distracted as he spoke. Now he gazed openly at the blond woman who had gotten out of the pickup. She moved to stand at Lucas's side, holding a baby against her shoulder. The child's head was covered with a light blanket to protect it from the glaring sun. "Hi."

Lucas turned, noticing Aislinn for the first time. "Oh, Johnny Deerinwater, this is my, uh, wife."

"I'm Aislinn," she said, sticking out her hand.

In friendly fashion, Johnny Deerinwater shook her hand and swept off his straw cowboy hat. "Pleased to meet you. Alice told us Lucas had gotten married. The sonofa…gun was going to keep you a secret from his friends, I guess."

"Mother must have called you this morning."

"Yeah. She said you'd just left on your way here. As I said, we've been working on the house for several weeks, but we had to get our…uh, rears in gear when we heard this morning that you were bringing a wife and baby with you. Speaking of which, why don't we get them out of the sun?"

Johnny stepped aside, indicating to Aislinn that she should precede him up the path toward the house. She was conscious of the workmen's eyes as they followed her progress. When she ventured to smile at several of them, they returned her smiles with varying degrees of shyness and suspicion.

As Lucas and Johnny fell into step behind her, Johnny said, "Since Joseph died, we've all pitched in to keep the herd fed, but that's about all. The horses were scattered to kingdom come. We've been rounding them up for weeks. Not all of them are accounted for yet."

"I'll find them," Lucas said.

Aislinn stepped onto the low, wide front porch of the house and, because she didn't know what else to do, entered the front door. The smell of fresh paint and raw lumber was almost overpowering, but not unpleasant. She pivoted, taking in the white walls that added to the spacious feel of the house. There were windows on every available wall, naked beams in the ceilings, and quarry tile floors that gave the rooms unity. In the main room there was a huge fireplace. She could imagine a glowing, cheery, crackling fire on a cold evening.

She gazed at Lucas in wonderment, but he seemed as surprised by the house as she. "When I left, there was nothing here but bare walls," he remarked. "Who's responsible for this, Johnny?"

"Well, Alice and I got to talking over a cup of coffee one day," he said, wiping his perspiring forehead with a bandanna. "We decided that we'd call in a few of your debts from people who owed you for legal services. Instead of collecting money, we collected favors. For instance, Walter Kincaid did the tile work. Pete Deleon did the plumbing." He went through a list of names, enumerating what each of Lucas's debtors had contributed to the house.

"Some of the fixtures and appliances are secondhand, Mrs. Greywolf," he said apologetically, "but they've been cleaned up good as new."

"Everything looks marvelous," Aislinn said, looking down at the beautiful, handwoven Navaho rug someone's grandmother had made for Lucas. "Thank you for everything, and please call me Aislinn."

He nodded, smiling. "The only furniture we could round up was a dinette set for the kitchen. This morning we got busy and found a, uh, bed." His dark cheeks flushed hotly with embarrassment.

"I have some furniture we can move up here," Aislinn said quickly, to relieve Johnny's bashfulness. Lucas gave her a sharp look, but said nothing. For that she was grateful. She didn't want to get in a row with him in front of his friends. Their marriage might not be conventional, but she didn't want that fact advertised.

"Linda, that's my wife, will be up later this afternoon to bring some groceries."

"I'll look forward to meeting her."

A truck rumbled to a halt outside. Johnny went to the door and looked out. "Here are the light fixtures we ordered."

"I can't pay for any of this," Lucas repeated stubbornly, his face set.

"You've got good credit." Johnny gave Aislinn a smile and left, bounding off the front porch, already calling orders.

"Maybe you'd better show me where the bedroom is," Aislinn ventured, "so I can lay Tony down."

"I'm not sure I know myself," Lucas said crossly. "This house was just a shell when I left it."

"Where were you living?" Aislinn asked, following him down the hallway. "In the trailer?"

"Yes. I'd been building this house for several years, taking it one step at a time whenever I could get some money together."

"I like it," she said, stepping into the room that was obviously the largest bedroom. It had a wide window that provided a view of the mountains.

"You don't have to say that."

"I mean it."

"Compared to that fancy condo you were living in, this is a slum."

"It is not! I'll decorate it and—"

"You can forget moving any of your furniture up here," he said, pointing his index finger at her.

She slapped it aside. "Why? Because you're too damn proud to use anything belonging to your wife? Didn't Indians barter with their prospective fathers-in-law for their wives?"

"Only in John Wayne movies."

"Consider this my dowry, which, whether you want to admit it or not, I know was a matter of pride to Indian women."

"I can provide for my family."

"I don't doubt that, Lucas. I never have."

"I'll buy furniture as soon as I sell some horses."

"But in the meantime, would you have your son sleeping on the floor?"

At the mention of Tony, Lucas glanced down at the baby. Aislinn had laid him on the wide bed the moment they entered the room. He was awake and looking around curiously, as though sensing he was in new surroundings.

Lucas bent over him and stroked his face with his index finger. Tony opened one of his waving fists and grabbed his father's finger, instinctively pulling it toward his mouth. Lucas laughed softly.

"You see, Lucas," Aislinn whispered, "whether you want to accept it or not, there are people who love you."

He gave her one of his most chilling stares before he swung around and stamped from the room.

Ten

The next few weeks brought about miraculous changes
in their lives. Lucas's friends, under Johnny Deerinwater's friendly supervision, finished the inside of the
house. It wasn't fancy by any stretch of the imagination,
but it was comfortable. Aislinn used her good taste and
decorating skills, elbow grease and paint, until the stucco
house looked like a magazine model home.

As soon as the telephone was installed, she called
Scottsdale and made arrangements for her furniture to
be moved to her new house. She itemized the pieces she
wanted, including her washing machine and dryer, and
double-checked the list with the moving company.

The van arrived several days later. As the furniture
was being unloaded, Lucas rode up on horseback and
deftly slid from the saddle. The first time Aislinn had
seen him sitting astride a horse, he had taken her breath
away he was so handsome. She liked him in his faded
denim jeans, Western shirts, boots, hat and leather work-
gloves. Often she paused from a household chore to watch
him from a window as he went about his work outside.

Now, however, when he rode his horse right up to the

porch before dismounting, she was made breathless by the angry expression on his face.

His spurs jingled as he crossed the porch, patently furious. "I told you not to send for this stuff," he said in a threateningly low voice.

"No you didn't." Despite his glower, she faced him squarely.

"We're not going to argue about this, Aislinn. Tell them to load it back up and return it to Scottsdale where it belongs, I don't need your charity."

"I'm not doing this for you. Or even for me."

"Well, Tony can't sit on a sofa yet," he said snidely, thinking she was going to use their baby as a lever to get her way.

"I'm doing it for Alice."

His face went comically blank. "My mother?"

"Yes, she's consented to hold her wedding reception here. Would you embarrass her by having her guests sit on the floor after all the sacrifices she's made for you?"

A vein ticked in his temple. She had him cornered. Worse, he knew she knew she had him cornered. And while he wanted to admire her cunning and congratulate her for being a worthy adversary, she was still his wife and he was so angry he could throttle her.

He glared at her for a count of ten, then turned on his spurred boot-heels, stamped off the porch and remounted his horse. He kicked up quite a cloud of dust as he rode out of the yard.

Aislinn worked all afternoon arranging the furniture, moving the pieces herself, no matter how heavy. Amazingly, the furniture looked custom-made for the house. She had always liked a Southwestern motif. When she had decorated her condo, that's what she had selected. But the furniture looked even better in this house, its desert tones accented by the native accessories that Lucas's friends had sent as housewarming gifts.

By late afternoon she was exhausted, but as consolation for their argument that morning, she cooked an especially good meal. Her kitchen lacked some of the amenities she was accustomed to, but made up for its deficiencies with space.

Tony was no help on this day when she particularly wanted to please her husband. The baby was cranky and cried fitfully, though she couldn't find any reason for it. While she was keeping dinner warm in the oven, she took a quick bath and made herself as attractive as possible for Lucas's return.

She didn't chastise him for being hours late when he finally came in well after dark. "Would you like a beer, Lucas?"

"Sounds good," he said sullenly, taking off his boots at the back door. "I'm going to take a shower." Without a word of thanks, he took the opened can of beer from her hand and carried it with him to the back of the house. Had he turned around, even he might have laughed at the ogre's face she made at his back.

When he returned to the kitchen, she had dinner set on the table, which was covered now with one of her tablecloths and set with her dishes and cutlery.

He didn't say a word either about that or any of the other furnishings as he sat down and began to eat, virtually shoveling the food into his mouth. "What's that noise?" he asked after a moment.

"The washing machine."

"Washing machine?"

"Uh-huh. And the dryer," she said breezily. "Tony goes through so many clothes. It will be such a relief not to have to drive into town every few days to the Laundromat. I was dreading those trips this winter, carrying Tony out in the cold."

Just as she had expected, Lucas glanced at Tony. She had set the baby's carrier on the table where he could hear their voices and be a part of the mealtime activity. Lucas seemed to weigh the advantages of having a washing machine and dryer under his roof and said nothing more.

One of the knots in Aislinn's chest eased considerably. "Having the nursery set up again is going to be wonderful," she ventured as she spooned another helping of potatoes onto Lucas's plate. "I won't have to worry about him rolling off the edge of something. Have you noticed how active he's getting?" She blotted her mouth with her napkin and coyly lowered her lashes over her eyes. "And he won't have to sleep between us anymore."

She saw Lucas hesitate as he raised his fork to his mouth. He chewed and swallowed that bite, then pushed his plate away. "I've got work to do." He left the table abruptly.

"But I made a pie for dessert."

"Maybe later."

Crestfallen, she watched his broad shoulders disappear through the doorway. She supposed she should be glad that they hadn't engaged in a battle royal over the furniture, but she was disappointed that he was so anxious to leave the table and her company, especially when she had just broached the subject of their sleeping arrangements.

Since they had moved into the house, Tony had, out of necessity, been sleeping in the bed with them. But Aislinn doubted that his tiny presence was the reason Lucas hadn't touched her since that morning at Alice's house. If they weren't in open dispute over something, he treated her with indifference. Rarely, if ever, did he look at her. When he did, it certainly wasn't with smoldering desire.

Not that she wanted him, she averred, as she readied Tony for bed. Still, the house was miles from their nearest neighbor. The nights were lonely. Lucas usually left right after a hurried breakfast. Often she wouldn't see him again until he came in for dinner. With only Tony for company all day, she looked forward to conversation with another adult. But Lucas remained taciturn.

She had grown up in a house where she had been discouraged from voicing an opinion or expressing herself. She didn't intend to live the rest of her life shrouded in silence. Stubbornly she decided to take the bull by the horns and not let Mr. Greywolf get away with his sulking.

She left Tony to sleep in his crib for the first time in weeks. A half-hour later, she carried a tray into the living room. Lucas was sitting on the sofa with papers spread out around him and spilling over onto the coffee table. He was making notes in a black notebook.

Aislinn went unnoticed until she switched on a lamp at his elbow. He raised his head and looked up at her. "Thanks."

"That should help you see better. How can you read without a light?"

"I didn't notice."

She thought he probably didn't want to use "her" lamp even though he was sitting on "her" sofa, but she refrained from commenting. "I brought your pie and fresh coffee," she said. She had set the tray on the end table.

"What kind?"

"Kind?"

"Of pie."

"Apple. Do you like apple?"

"I learned not to be too choosy in prison."

"Then why did you ask?" she snapped.

Ignoring her, he scarfed down the slice of pie in record time. She chided herself for not being more conscientious about his sweet tooth. Apparently it hadn't been satisfied in a long time. From now on she would see to it that every meal included dessert.

When he finished with his pie, he set the plate aside and bent back over his paperwork. "Is that ranching business?" she asked.

"No, a court record. My client…" he paused on the term, because he actually couldn't have clients any longer, "he, uh, wants to know if he should appeal the outcome of a lawsuit."

"Should he?"

"I think so."

She watched him make another brief notation in his tablet, then said, "Lucas, I want to talk to you."

He laid his tablet and pen aside and reached for his cooling coffee. "What about?"

She sat in the corner of the sofa and tucked her feet underneath her hips. "I had my camera equipment sent up with the furniture. I'm anxious to start using it again."

Fiddling with the fringe on a throw pillow, she drew a deep breath. "And I was wondering what you would think of my converting the old trailer into a darkroom."

His eyes swiveled toward her and she rushed on before he could say anything. "It wouldn't take much redoing. The sink is already there, in the kitchen area. I could do most of the work myself. Think how convenient it would be to take pictures of Tony and have them developed right away, as many prints as we wanted. And I could make enlargements and—"

"I'm not a fool, Aislinn." That was the first time he had addressed her by name in days and both were aware of it. Before they had time to reflect on it, however, he went on. "Making that trailer into a darkroom is hardly worth the effort just to have pictures of Tony readily available. What else did you have in mind?"

"I want to work, Lucas. Running the house doesn't keep me busy enough."

"You have a child."

"A very good one, whom I love and adore and enjoy taking care of and playing with. But he doesn't require my every waking moment. I need something to do."

"So you want to take pictures."

"Yes."

"Of what?"

This was the tricky part. The tallest hurdle. The one she had most dreaded. "Of the reservation and the people who live on it."

"No."

"Listen. Please. Before I saw it for myself, I had no idea of the—"

"Poverty," he said harshly.

"Yes and the—"

"Squalor."

"That, too, but the—"

"Prevalence of alcoholism. And despair. And the sense of utter hopelessness." He had surged to his feet and was now angrily pacing the area in front of the sofa.

"I guess that's it," she said softly. "The hopelessness. But maybe if I captured some of that on film, and my work got published—"

"It wouldn't help," he said curtly.

"It wouldn't hurt either." She sprang up, angry that he had squelched her idea without even hearing her out. "I want to do this, Lucas."

"And dirty your Anglo hands?"

"You're an Anglo, too!"

"I didn't ask to be," he shouted.

"All the rest of us are monsters, is that it? Why is it you never ridicule Gene's work on the reservation?"

"Because he's not some grandstanding, bleeding-heart liberal doing us all a big favor."

"And you think I am?"

"Don't you think your charity would be a trifle hypocritical?"

"How?"

"Living like this," he said, waving his arms to include their house, made so much prettier and more comfortable by her contributions to it. "I have always despised Indians who profited off other Indians. Their skin is brown, but they forget that and live like Anglos. And now you've made me one of them."

"That's not true, Lucas. No one would ever mistake you for anything but what you are." He had turned his back on her. Now she caught his arm and spun him around. "You work damn hard at being Indian. Short of painting your face and going on the warpath, you do everything you can to let everyone know you're a big, bad Indian brave right through to the marrow of your bones, despite your Anglo blood. Or maybe because of it."

She paused for breath, but continued, warmed now to the subject. "You've taught me how mistaken I was. Until now, I thought Indian braves had hearts and souls and compassion as well as courage and daring." She poked him in the chest with her index finger. "Those you will never have, Lucas Greywolf. You have no compassion because to you that's a sign of weakness. Well I think bullheadedness is more of a weakness than tenderness. I doubt you even know what it is."

"I can feel tenderness," he said defensively.

"Oh really? Well I'm your *wife* and I've never seen any evidence of it."

She landed against him before she even realized that he had moved and drawn her forward. His arm curved around her waist while his other hand cupped the side of her face. He tilted it until her other cheek almost touched his shoulder.

Then he bent his head low and impressed a soft kiss on her lips. His mouth moved. Her lips parted. The intrusion of his tongue into her mouth was so gentle and sweet, so deliciously sexy, that she shivered. Where before his kisses had been characterized by violence, this one was exquisitely tender.

The kiss lengthened and became an outright act of love. He used his tongue to stroke the roof of her mouth. He explored and enticed until she was weakly clutching handfuls of his shirt in her hands.

When he finally lifted his mouth from hers, he buried his face in the fragrant hollow between her shoulder and neck. "I don't want you," he groaned. "I don't."

She rubbed against him. The lower part of his body unequivocally denied his words. "Yes, you do, Lucas. Yes, you do!"

She imbedded her fingers in his hair and lifted his head. She ran one finger over his sleek eyebrow, along the ridge of his cheekbone, and down his nose. She outlined his mouth. "You could never be a traitor to your people, Lucas."

The touch of her fingertip on his lips made him weak. The scent of her body filled his head and made him forget the stench of despair that permeated certain areas of the reservation. The sight of ill-dressed children was replaced by the desire he saw in her slumberous blue eyes. He could no longer taste the bitterness that kept him strong and resolute. All he could taste was Aislinn, the honey of her mouth.

She was the most dangerous of enemies because her ammunition was her allure. Her softness seduced him. What he felt deep in his gut at that moment terrified him. He used the weapon most readily at his disposal. It was also the most hurtful. His scorn.

"I'm already a traitor. I have an Anglo wife."

Aislinn recoiled as though he had struck her. She stepped away from him, her eyes glazed now with pain. To prevent him from seeing her tears, she turned and ran into the bedroom, slamming the door behind her.

When Lucas came in almost an hour later, she pretended to be asleep. They no longer had Tony serving as a buffer between them. But hostility was there, as sturdy as a brick wall, to keep them separated.

Antagonism continued to seethe between them. On the day Dr. Gene Dexter married Alice Greywolf, Aislinn did her best to put on a good front, pretending that her relationship with Lucas was nothing short of blissful. The wedding decorations weren't extravagant, but there was a distinct party atmosphere in the house. All the guests had a good time. Aislinn had been trained to give good parties. She was a gay, gracious hostess and seemingly enjoyed herself.

The bride wasn't fooled.

"I can't believe you're finally my wife."

Gene and Alice had driven to Santa Fe for their honeymoon. Now, as he held her tenderly, stroking her straight black hair, he couldn't quite believe that his dreams had finally become a reality.

"The church looked beautiful, didn't it?" she asked him.

"*You* looked beautiful. But then you always do."

"Aislinn went to too much trouble over the reception. I wasn't expecting anything so lavish."

"She's a lovely girl," Gene murmured absently as he kissed Alice's velvety cheek.

"Tony seemed fretful."

"Aislinn told me he'd been crying more than usual. I recommended that she bring him in for a checkup when we get back."

"They're unhappy, Gene."

His arms fell to his sides and he sighed heavily. "I didn't know that we had brought Lucas and Aislinn along on our honeymoon."

"Oh, Gene," Alice said, wrapping her arms around his waist and hugging him tight. She laid her cheek against his chest. He had removed his suit coat as soon as the hotel bellman left the room, but they were both still fully clothed. "Forgive me. I'm sorry. I know I shouldn't be worrying about them, but I can't just shut my mind off. Aislinn looks like she's walking a tightrope and Lucas looks—"

"Like a keg of dynamite about to explode," Gene finished for her. "He's more truculent than ever. I've never seen him so brooding and angry." He laughed softly into her hair. "Personally, I think it's a good sign."

"How?" she lifted her head to ask.

He ran a finger along her jaw. "If she didn't disturb him so much, he wouldn't be so touchy and defensive. I think the lady is getting to him in a way no one else ever has. That scares the hell out of the fearless Lucas Greywolf."

"Do you think Aislinn loves him?"

"Yes. Undoubtedly. I've done some checking on her father. Willard Andrews is on about every board of governors and chairs about every committee in Scottsdale.

A woman of her means, whose father holds that kind of position in the community, could have fought one lone Indian and won hands down. I don't care what he threatened her with, she didn't have to marry your son. Yes, I think she loves him."

"And what about Lucas. Does he love her?"

Gene's brow furrowed as he thought back on the reception brunch held in honor of Alice and him. Every time he had looked at Lucas, Lucas had been looking at Aislinn. And not just casually looking, but watching her with total concentration, oblivious to what was going on around him.

Now that he thought about it, Gene remembered Aislinn carrying a heavy bowl of punch to the buffet table she had set up in the living room. He had seen Lucas rush forward, as though to relieve her of it. But Lucas had stopped short of reaching her, suddenly changing his mind.

And while they had been saying their goodbyes, Gene would bet Lucas's mind hadn't been on his mother and her new husband. The young man had seemed captivated by his wife. His whole body had looked stiff, as though he was physically restraining himself from touching her as she waved goodbye, laughing and calling out good wishes, her blond hair blowing against Lucas's shoulder.

"In my professional opinion, he's got a touch of lovesickness," Gene said now, in answer to Alice's question. "He might not know he loves her yet. Or if he does, he doesn't want to admit it, especially to himself."

"I want them to be happy."

"I want *us* to be happy. Do you know what would make me deliriously happy right now?" He tipped her head back with his knuckle beneath her chin and kissed her, tenderly at first, then with mounting passion. His arms slid around her waist and drew her up against him. "Alice, Alice," he moaned when he finally lifted his lips from hers. "I've waited so long for this. I can't remember when I didn't want you, when I didn't ache for Alice Greywolf."

"Alice Dexter," she whispered shyly.

He took that as her way of saying that she shared his love and desire. He reached for the back buttons of her simple, apricot linen dress. Ruffles and lace would have swallowed a woman as petite as Alice. For adornment she wore only a pair of gold earrings, the gold chain he had given her last Christmas, and the slender gold wedding band that now encircled her finger.

When all the buttons were undone, he eased the dress forward. "I'm not young anymore, Gene," she said tremulously. "I'm a grandmother."

He only smiled and pulled the dress off her shoulders. His gasp and the shudder that ran through him testified to his delight in her body. She was small, trim, perfect. Her ecru lingerie was alluring without being overtly sexy. It suited the woman who was wearing it. She was modest but had a latent sensuality waiting to be kindled.

He adored his bride.

Holding her gently and kissing away her nervous shyness, he removed the rest of her clothing. Lifting her in his arms, he carried her to the bed and laid her down. She kept her eyes closed while he undressed.

Then he came to her, gathered her in his arms, and held her body close to his while sheer ecstasy, as sweet and thick as honey, rivered through him. She was trembling.

"Alice," he whispered, "don't be afraid. For as long as you want, I'm content to just hold you. I know you're frightened and I know why. But I swear to you and to God that I would never do anything to hurt you."

"I know that, Gene. I do. It's just that it's been so long and—"

"I know. You don't have to say any more. Nothing will happen until you want it to." He held her protectively, commanding his body to hold itself in check. He knew he must practise infinite patience with this woman who was worthy of being cherished.

Eventually she relaxed and he felt encouraged enough to stroke her caressingly. Her skin was satiny smooth, yet vibrant. She had the body of a woman twenty years younger. He worshipped the breasts that were still high and round and firm. When he touched her there, she moaned, but after one quick glance at her face, he knew it was out of pleasure and not out of fear. The lips that kissed the dusky crests were as soft as a spring rain.

He wooed her that way, alternately arousing and soothing, until he knew she was ready. And then the loving was achingly sweet, exquisitely tender, and in the end, wildly passionate.

Later, holding her against him, he sighed into her hair. "If I had had to wait another twenty years for you, Alice Greywolf Dexter, you would have been worth it."

"And you, Gene," she said, kissing his chest. "And you, my love."

Lucas closed the barn door and latched it. This might be his mother's wedding day, but on a ranch the work never ended. As soon as all the guests had departed, he had changed clothes and put in a full day's work. He was tired, having had to get up early that morning and drive into town for the wedding.

Tomorrow a buyer was coming to look at some of his

horses. He'd spent all day grooming them. If they brought a good price, which he planned on demanding, maybe he would have enough money to hire a ranch hand.

Perhaps his being disbarred had worked out for the best after all. He doubted that he could run a ranch and a law office at the same time. He loved the land and the herd because they had belonged to his grandfather. He liked working outdoors. He didn't even mind the long hours.

But he missed practicing law. He had always enjoyed a good fight. When he had matured to the point of knowing that brawling never solved anything, the courtroom provided him an arena. He had been an excellent courtroom gladiator. He missed the legal skirmishes and the satisfaction of having done his best whether he won the case or not.

He peeled off his shirt and went to the outdoor faucet on the foundation of the house. He sluiced water over his head, his neck, shoulders, arms and chest, rinsing off the top layer of dust and sweat.

Every time he thought about the kindness of friends like Johnny Deerinwater, he got a lump in his throat. Without them he wouldn't have the house. It would have taken him years to finish it in his spare time, not to mention the money it would have cost. He and Aislinn—

Damn! He hated it when his mind automatically paired them together. Aislinn and I. Aislinn and me. We. Us. He didn't ever like thinking of them as a unit, yet his brain stubbornly continued to.

Fuming over the mental slip, he rounded the corner of the house. If he had walked into a wall, he couldn't have come to a more abrupt standstill. He was standing only a few yards from their open bedroom window. Aislinn walked past it. He could hear her humming and see her shadow gliding across the walls as she moved about the room.

That rectangular patch of light looked inviting in the darkness that surrounded the house. It beckoned him as a lighthouse does a sailor. It represented all things warm and cozy and comfortable. Home. He was hypnotized by that open window. He couldn't force himself to move away from it, even though he supposed that this was an invasion of Aislinn's privacy. *Would you stop thinking like a damn fool? The woman is your wife.*

Still, he felt just a little ashamed of his window-peeping. Especially when she stepped into full view again. Especially when she began to undress.

He stood stock-still in the deep shadows, not moving so much as an eyelash.

Lucas watched her unbutton the cuff on the sleeve of her sheer blouse. Much as he hadn't wanted to notice, he had to admit that she had looked beautiful that day. The blouse she had worn was cut like a man's shirt, except that the sleeves were much fuller and the cuffs much wider. The tips of the collar reached far down on her chest.

The blouse had small pearl buttons. As she bent over the ones on her cuff, her hair fell forward in a golden cascade. He wanted nothing more than to bury his face in the stuff, to feel its cool silken movement against his skin. He already knew what it felt like against his belly. What about his thighs? His—

Sonofabitch! Don't even think about that.

When she pulled her blouse off, which she did with a provocative lack of haste, he had an unrestricted view of the lingerie that had teased him all day. Held up by spaghetti-thin straps, it was lacy and feminine and cupped her full breasts as if it adored them. They swelled over the top of it, creamy and enticing in the lamplight. God, he wanted to taste her there. The camisole wasn't sheer enough to see through, since it had obviously been designed to show beneath the blouse. But even from this distance, Lucas imagined he could see the dark centers of her breasts through it. He imagined his mouth there, too.

The skirt she had worn was the color of the eastern sky just before daybreak. It was made of a rustling fabric that had driven him into a fine madness all day as it moved against her body. He held his breath as she reached behind her to unbutton it. It seemed to take forever. Then the skirt slithered past her hips, over her thighs, and down her legs, which were encased in pale stockings.

He cursed beneath his breath and ran his damp palms up and down his thighs. The camisole was a one-piece affair. Lacy suspenders held up her stockings, which he had supposed were panty hose. Between the top of the stockings and the teddy, her thighs looked as soft and warm as velvet. He imagined himself—

Damn! What was he doing out here lusting after his own wife like some pervert? If he wanted her so badly, and his body was insisting that "badly" didn't even come close to describing how much he wanted her, why didn't he just go in there and take her? She belonged to him, didn't she? They were legally bound and he was entitled to conjugal rights, wasn't he?

So move, damn you. Go in there and take what is yours for the taking.

But he didn't, because he knew it would be too risky. If he could take her dispassionately, then he would use her body to rid his of this raging fever. It would be over and done with and he wouldn't even think about it until the next time he got in this condition.

No, it wouldn't be like that at all. She had bewitched

him, that's what she had done. Somehow she had wormed her way into his mind and heart, and what he was thinking and feeling somehow interfered with what his body wanted. His sex couldn't participate without his head getting involved.

He kept remembering that morning on the mountaintop. She had climbed up there to offer him comfort when she sure as hell had had every reason to be fleeing from him. He remembered what her face had looked like as his body moved inside hers.

And at the most inopportune times, when he wanted to feel his bitterest toward her, he thought about her bearing his child and how lovingly she treated Tony. Then, too, there were the generous things she did for him, like keeping the coffee in his cup warm even when he hadn't asked for refills. And the way she was sometimes waiting on the porch for him when he came riding in after working long hours. She always smiled, as though she was glad to see him.

What puzzled him was why she treated him with such consideration and kindness. He couldn't figure out what her motive was. She had every reason to hate him. If she would just demonstrate resentment instead of understanding, then life would be a helluva lot easier. They might even have some rowdy sex every once in a while to let off steam and clear the air. As it was, his blood simmered.

Looking at her through the window now, he felt his blood heating to a full boil. She was no longer standing in full view, but he could tell by watching her shadow on the wall that she was removing her stockings. She lifted one foot to the edge of the bed, unhooked the garter and rolled the stocking over her knee and calf and ankle, peeling it off her foot with studied leisure. She performed the ritual on the other leg.

He stared transfixed when she shrugged the straps of the teddy off her shoulders and shimmied until it slipped down. She stepped out of it gracefully, and when she straightened, her shadow was in profile. Everything was perfectly, painfully silhouetted.

Lucas mouthed a series of scalding obscenities.

Why wouldn't she give him a fight? Huh? Did she feel sorry for him? Was that it? Or did she feel obligated to be an exemplary wife? Well, by God, he didn't need her largess.

He moved then, spinning around on his heels and stalking toward the rear of the house. He slammed through the back door, barely remembering to lock it behind him, before he stamped through the house, viciously turning off lights as he went. By the time he barged through the bedroom door, he was good and mad.

"Just what the hell do you think you're doing?" he roared.

Aislinn looked up at him with innocent, blue-eyed, wide-eyed dismay, which made her look even more guiltless than she already did. She was sitting in the rocking chair. A madonna. Blond hair rippling over her shoulders. One side of her nightgown was open. Tony nursed contentedly at her breast.

"I'm nursing Tony," she answered simply.

Lucas, standing braced in the doorway by his arms, was spoiling for a fight. Shirtless, the recently washed skin on his chest gleamed in the lamplight. The dark hairs were damp and curly. The cross dangling from his neck caught the light and shone almost as brightly as his eyes.

The joke was on him. Feeling like a fool, he dragged his eyes away from his wife and glanced toward the bed. The teddy and stockings lay spread out there like mementos of an indolent afternoon of loving. They enflamed him all over again.

"Next time, you might think twice before parading around half naked in front of an open window with the light on."

"I don't know what you mean, Lucas."

Pointing toward the window with a finger shaking with rage, he blustered, "The window, dammit, the window. Don't undress in front of the window."

"Oh," she said, following the direction of his finger. "I didn't think about it."

"Yeah, well, think about it from now on, okay?"

"But there wasn't anyone out there to see me."

"I was!" he shouted. "I could see you all the way from the barn."

"You could?"

"Hell yes, I could."

"But you're my husband."

There was just a trace of mockery in her voice, but it was so slight that he was afraid to challenge her on it. He was ready for hand-to-hand combat, but he couldn't handle a contest of wits. He had never felt more witless in his life. Nor so out of control. In an entirely different way, she looked just as tempting now as she had a few moments before, doing her guileless striptease in front of the window. Blood pounded in his head and in his sex.

"I'm going to take a shower," he said quickly and left the room before he disgraced himself further.

When he left the bathroom, Aislinn was in the other bedroom, bending over Tony's crib. "Let me hold him a minute," Lucas said. He had calmed down considerably. He was still wet. Drops of water clung to his teak-colored skin. He was naked save for a towel that cut a swath across his loins and looked much like the breechcloths his ancestors had worn. He looked primitive and dangerous except for the lambency in his eyes when he lifted his son and held him close to his face. He murmured Navaho love pledges he remembered from his childhood and kissed Tony's cheek before laying him in the crib. The child fell asleep instantly.

"He looks so peaceful now," Aislinn said with a tired sigh. "I wish he'd sleep till morning. I'm exhausted."

"Why is he waking up so much lately?"

"I don't know. Gene's going to give him a checkup when they get back. Oh, I almost forgot about this," she said as they entered their bedroom. She picked up an envelope that was lying on the dresser and handed it to him. "This came in the mail for you today."

He studied the envelope for several moments before tearing it open. Aislinn feigned disinterest, though she was consumed by curiosity. The return address was the warden's office of the prison camp where Lucas had been incarcerated.

After he read it, Lucas refolded the letter and stuffed it back in the envelope. His face gave away nothing and Aislinn couldn't stand not knowing. "Is it something important?"

He shrugged negligently. "Warden Dixon thinks I should be exonerated. He thinks he knows the men responsible for the violence that broke out at that demonstration. They've been convicted and sentenced for similar crimes. If he can get them to sign affidavits as to my innocence, he thinks he can get a judge to have me vindicated."

"Lucas, that's wonderful!" she cried. "That would mean you could be reinstated to the bar."

He whipped the towel from around his waist and got

into bed. "I've learned not to trust anybody's promises. Especially an Anglo's."

She got into bed beside him. His harsh words hadn't fooled her. She had seen his face a second before he switched off the light. He might pretend to be nonchalant over this unexpected ray of hope. But he wasn't.

Eleven

She had learned where the worst chuckholes were and how to avoid them. Recently Johnny and Linda Deer-inwater had gone to Scottsdale and offered to drive her car back when they returned. She and Lucas's pickup had never had a meeting of the minds, so driving her car again was a pleasure.

Today she barely noticed the pitching and rolling as she drove her car up the uneven road toward home. She was happy on several accounts, and when Lucas came riding up on a roan gelding to meet her and Tony, that was an extra bonus. She braked the car and lifted Tony out of his safety seat, just as Lucas swung his long leg over the saddle and dismounted.

"You were gone longer than I expected," he said.

Could that mean he was worried about her? she wondered. Or was he concerned only for Tony? She wanted to think she was included. "Gene's clinic was overflowing. There's a virus going around. He and Alice had their hands full."

"How are they?"

She grinned, her blue eyes glinting mischievously.

"Positively glowing. I've always thought your mother was beautiful, but wait until you see her now. She's radiant. And Gene wears a perpetually sappy grin."

Lucas smiled and chucked Tony under the chin. He was holding the reins of his horse in his free hand. "What did Gene say about Tony?"

"He has a slight cold. Actually Gene called it an upper respiratory something-or-other. He gave him a liquid decongestant that should take care of it in a few days."

"Is that why he's been crying so much?"

"Not solely. There's something else."

"What?" he asked, his brow beetling.

"Tony is hungry."

"Hungry?"

"Yes," Aislinn said, blushing under the tan she had acquired. "He's not getting enough milk. Gene suggested that I switch him to formula and start him on fruit and cereal."

Lucas shifted from one booted foot to another. "So you won't be, uh, breast-feeding him anymore?" Aislinn kept her eyes trained on the buttons of his shirt as she shook her head. "How do you feel about that?" he asked.

"I'll miss it. But of course I want to do what's best for Tony."

"Of course."

"I stopped at the grocery store and bought bottles and cans of formula and baby food."

"One little baby can eat all that?" he asked incredulously.

She followed the direction of his gaze into the back seat of her car and laughed when she noticed the cartons stashed there. "Only part of it. Most of those boxes contain the chemicals I had ordered. They were waiting for me at the post office."

"Will your darkroom be operable now?"

"Yes. All I needed were the chemicals." She had taken his silence on the subject of the darkroom as consent and had proceeded to convert the kitchen area of the derelict trailer.

Much to her surprise she had come out of the house one morning to find Lucas painting the trailer. Before she even posed the question, he said querulously, "This paint was left over from the house. No sense in letting it go to waste." Besides giving it the paint job, he had done some repairs that made the portable building more habitable.

"I won't be able to process color film," she told him now, "but I can do black and white. I thought I'd start with the snapshots I took at the wedding reception. If they're good, I'll give enlarged prints to Gene and Alice. I invited them to come to dinner soon."

"Good."

"And I took some pictures in town today. You know that housing area where the conditions are so bad?"

He nodded grimly. "All too well."

"There were some little girls playing beneath a clothesline. I think I got some good stuff, but it will take me a while to get back into practice."

"What did you do with Tony?"

"He was on my back in the sling carrier." She smiled up at her husband. "Just like a good little papoose."

His mouth twitched with the need to smile. He held it back as long as he could, but it overpowered his stubbornness and the remote face broke into a wide grin that dazzled his wife. His teeth were straight and white, a brilliant contrast to his dark face.

"I don't want the grandson of a chief to turn into a mama's boy. Give him to me."

He lifted the baby out of Aislinn's arms and turned

toward the horse, which was still standing by docilely. "Lucas, what are you doing? Lucas, you're not—"

"It's past time that Anthony Joseph Greywolf had a horseback-riding lesson."

"Don't you dare!" Aislinn cried.

Heedless of her protests, Lucas cradled the child in his right arm. Using his left hand to grasp the pommel, he pulled himself into the saddle. With one smooth motion he and Tony were sitting on the horse. Tony was waving his hands happily.

"Lucas, give me that baby before you break both your necks," Aislinn said sternly. Unconsciously, she laid both hands on Lucas's hard thigh to forestall him.

He grinned down at her teasingly. "Shall we race to the house?"

"Lucas!"

He wheeled the gelding around and nudged it with his knees. The horse cantered off. Aislinn propped her hands on her hips and glared after him with exasperation. Most of it was faked. Actually her heart had never been so full of love.

For several days after she had weaned Tony, she was uncomfortable and he was cranky. But he learned to like the pre-mixed formula. He was a creative eater, splattering her, Lucas, and anything within yards of him with mushy cereal and strained fruit, but he gobbled up the food greedily and soon Aislinn could tell he was gaining weight.

Lucas received another letter from Warden Dixon. He had been in consultation with a judge and was making progress toward having Lucas vindicated. Aislinn took heart; Lucas kept his feelings on the subject to himself.

Due to his hard work, the ranch was prospering. From

the hills surrounding the ranch, he had rounded up an impressive herd of horses that wore the Greywolf brand, but that had strayed since old Joseph's death. Several of the mares were pregnant. Those that weren't were artificially inseminated, a practice his grandfather had resisted.

The Greywolfs were fortunate to have a stream that flowed out of the mountains across one corner of their land. Water was the most valued commodity. Joseph had never sold water rights as a matter of principle, but Lucas was of the mind that what was good for one was good for all. There were several small ranchers, Indian and Anglo alike, who were now paying for the use of Greywolf water.

Nor did Lucas allow himself to become attached to the horses to the point of not being able to sell them, as his grandfather had. Customers who bought Greywolf horses got their money's worth. Lucas was a fair but shrewd dealer.

Aislinn spent a few hours every day in the trailer in her darkroom. She always took Tony with her, placing him in a playpen she had bought in a secondhand store. After she painted the slats and furnished it with a new pad, it looked as good as new.

One afternoon she was working in the darkroom, experimenting with different techniques, when she heard the distant rumble of thunder. At first she paid no attention to it. Her ears were trained to pick up any sound Tony made, but to tune out other distractions.

The thunder became louder, and she realized that a storm was fast approaching. Wending her way through the dark curtains surrounding the nucleus of her darkroom, she stepped into what had previously been the living area of the trailer.

Tony lay asleep in the playpen. Aislinn was alarmed

by how late it had gotten, but when she consulted her watch, she saw that it was only the middle of the afternoon, not nearly as late as the darkness indicated.

She went to the door of the trailer and looked out the small diamond-shaped window. Dark clouds were brewing over the mountains. Her first thought was for Lucas. He had left on horseback early that morning, saying he was going to ride up into the higher elevations to see if he could locate any more strays. Not liking the looks of the weather, she hoped he would return soon.

The wind was picking up. Dust was swirling in the wide yard between the trailer and the house. She decided to wait for Lucas before she tried carrying Tony and all his paraphernalia back to the house. Besides, the storm would probably blow over in a few minutes.

After checking on the baby again, she went back into the darkroom and became engrossed in her work. It took a jolt, literally, to rouse her. The trailer swayed as a gust of wind socked it like a mighty fist. Aislinn heard Tony whimper. Hurriedly, she left the darkroom. The trailer was lit by a ghostly, greenish light.

Tony began to cry. Aislinn rushed toward the door and opened it. The wind tore it from her hand, and it went crashing against the exterior wall of the trailer. Raindrops pricked her exposed skin like needles as she stepped out onto the concrete steps and reached for the door. Hailstones pelleted her. Within seconds the ground was white, covered with them.

"Oh, God," she cried, straining with all her might to pull the door closed against the wind. Inky black clouds boiled overhead. The sky was completely blocked out by the low clouds, which looked as opaque as a velvet curtain. Jagged forks of lightning struck the ground, dancing and popping, before disappearing again into the clouds.

Thunder roared so loudly that she could hardly hear Tony's piteous cries over the racket.

She finally got the door closed and latched, though it had required all her strength. Crouched over with fatigue, she practically crawled to the playpen and lifted Tony out. She didn't realize her clothes were wet until she held him against her. Her hair was plastered to her skull and dripping onto the child.

"Shh, shh, Tony, everything will be all right," she crooned, wishing she believed it herself.

Where is Lucas?

She squeezed her eyes shut as she envisioned him wandering lost in the storm, with the wind and rain and hail beating against him unmercifully.

Each time a fresh gust of wind buffeted the trailer, she feared it would overturn and she and Tony would be crushed. She could hear debris being hurled against the exterior and expected something to come crashing through one of the windows at any moment.

Tony was wailing, and she clutched him tightly against her breasts. That did nothing to comfort him because he could sense his mother's fear. Aislinn paced the length of the room, cringing each time she heard the lightning crack, knowing that it could very well strike the trailer.

"Lucas, Lucas," she chanted. Had his horse been spooked and thrown him? Was he lying unconscious somewhere? Had he fallen into a crevice and broken his leg?

The grisly possibilities were endless, yet she seemed to think of every conceivable one. She pressed her cheek to the top of Tony's head and bathed it with her tears.

She felt small and insignificant. God's wrath was awesome, and He was showing it off. What did He care if one woman and her child perished in a storm of His making?

The waiting was the worst part. But what else could she do? Getting across the clearing to the house would be hazardous even if she were alone. Carrying Tony and protecting him in her arms would make the trip impossible. The ground was already a sea of mud, unable to absorb the pelting rain quickly enough. Her vision would be hampered by the consuming darkness between blinding flashes of lightning. She could easily lose her way.

Why hadn't she left the trailer at the first signs of the impending storm? She would be frightened inside the house, but it would certainly provide more protection than the trailer.

Self-recriminations were useless now. She had made an unwise decision, and she would have to pay for it, possibly with her own life and that of her child.

Lucas. Lucas. Lucas.

She sat down in a rickety chair that had been left behind when Alice and Lucas moved from the trailer. Holding Tony against her, she rocked him, mindlessly humming, waiting for Fate to do with them what it would.

When she first heard the pounding noise, she thought it was another piece of debris banging against the trailer. But when she heard her name being shouted in accompaniment to the noise, she uttered a glad cry and went stumbling across the trailer.

"Lucas!"

"Open the door!" he shouted.

Holding Tony in one arm, she clumsily unlocked the door with her other hand. When the door opened, Lucas almost fell inside, propelled by the wind. Aislinn collapsed against him, sobbing uncontrollably. Only his surefootedness kept the three of them from toppling to the floor.

She repeated his name as she clung to him. His shirt

was soddenly molded to his body. His boots were caked with mud. His hat, secured to his head by a leather cord beneath his chin, dripped rainwater. He had never looked better to her.

They hugged each other tightly for a long moment, unmindful of the rain that fell in sheets through the open door. Between them, Tony squirmed and squalled. Lucas pressed Aislinn's face into his neck and rubbed his hands up and down her back until her wracking sobs subsided.

"Are you hurt anywhere?" he asked at last.

"No. I'm f...fine. Just scared."

"And Tony?"

"He's okay. He's frightened because he could tell I was." She bit her lower lip hard to keep it from trembling. "I thought something had happened to you."

"Something did. I got caught in the storm," he said wryly. "I could see it coming, but I couldn't get back in time. The horse threw a shoe and I had to walk him back. He was reluctant and scared."

She touched his face. It was wet. She didn't notice. "I thought you were lost. Or lying hurt somewhere. I didn't know what would happen to us without you."

"Well, it scared the hell out of me when I got to the house and you and Tony weren't there." He pushed a strand of her wet hair away from her mouth and touched her lips. "But we're all safe. Now our only problem is getting across the clearing to the house. I don't trust this trailer to stay in one piece much longer. We'll be safer outside than we are in here. Can you make it?"

She nodded without even having to consider the danger. Lucas was there. She felt safe again.

"Do you have something to wrap Tony in?" he asked.

She had stockpiled some extra baby blankets in the trailer. While Lucas stared out the door, planning the path of least resistance, she wrapped Tony in several of them until he looked like a living mummy. She ignored his crying, knowing that once he was fed and dry and calm, he would be all right.

Lucas took an extra blanket, draped it over Aislinn's head and tied it beneath her chin. "That won't give you much protection, but it's better than nothing. Now," he said, catching her shoulders in his hands and looking directly into her eyes, "your only job is to hang on to Tony. I'll do the rest." She nodded. "Okay, let's go."

She never remembered the details of that journey, which usually took less than sixty seconds. In her mind, it would forever be a blur of wind and rain and lightning and fear. No sooner had they left the steps of the trailer than her shoes got stuck in the mud. When she fished for them with her toes, Lucas shouted above the storm, "Leave them," and she went the remainder of the way barefoot. She slipped and slid in the oozing mud, but Lucas's strong arms kept her from falling. She held on to Tony so tightly that she was afraid she would break his ribs. She kept her head bowed and, for the most part, her eyes closed.

At last her shin rapped against something and she realized it was the porch of the house. With Lucas's assistance, she staggered up the steps and beneath the shelter of the overhang. He opened the front door and pushed her inside. He propped her against the wall and, while she regained her breath, pulled off his hat and boots and threw them out onto the porch.

He untied the blanket he had wrapped around her head and sent it the way of the boots and hat. "Don't move," he said sternly. "I'll get a blanket." Barefoot, he headed toward the bedrooms, his clothes dripping water onto the tile floors. While he was gone, Aislinn unwound the blankets covering Tony.

"My brave boy," she said, lifting him for her to kiss. "You and Daddy are so brave."

Lucas came back and threw a blanket around her shoulders, bundling her into it. "My teeth are chattering," she said needlessly.

"I noticed. Hurry, let's get Tony dried off. Then we'll work on you." Together they went into the nursery. The electricity wasn't working, but Lucas carried in two candles from their bedroom, which until now had served only as decoration. By candlelight, Aislinn swiftly undressed the baby and dried him off. While she was doing that, Lucas went to fetch a bottle from the kitchen. He waited for it to warm and came back with it just as Aislinn was snapping Tony into his sleeper.

"Let me feed him while you get into a tub of hot water. I've already turned the taps on. Take one of the candles." To keep the dry baby from getting wet and chilled again, Lucas was peeling off his clothes as he talked. When he was stripped to the skin, he took the towel Aislinn had used on Tony and whisked it over himself. Then he lifted Tony from the crib and carried him to the rocking chair.

Any other time, the sight of the huge, naked Indian man, sitting in the rocking chair with the gingham cushion, feeding a baby a bottle, would have been a hilarious sight. But Aislinn was still too benumbed by fright to notice the hilarity of it.

"Don't forget his medicine," she said, nodding toward the prescription Gene had ordered for the baby's congestion.

"I won't."

Knowing that Tony was in capable hands, she left the nursery to take her bath. It was almost a half-hour later when she came out of the bathroom carrying the candle. She had immersed herself in the tub until the hot water covered her shoulders. Its warmth had seeped into her comfortingly, relieving her chill and dulling the serrated edges of her nerves. Before she got out, she washed her hair. Brushing it back and leaving it to dry naturally, she wrapped herself in a long terry-cloth robe.

She checked the nursery first and found Tony sleeping soundly in his crib. She laid her hand on his head, tears forming in her eyes. He was so very precious to her. She couldn't imagine life without him now. What an empty, barren existence hers had been before she had been blessed with him.

She asked God to forgive her for her momentary lack of faith when she had been in the trailer. He had favored her by giving her Tony. He had brought them through a terrible ordeal safely. She would never doubt His grace and goodness again.

She left the sleeping child and tiptoed through the darkened rooms, which were illuminated only by occasional flashes of blue-white lightning and the faint, wavering glow of the candle she carried.

Lucas was in the kitchen, standing at the stove, stirring something in a saucepan. When she entered, he turned. She hadn't made a sound, and yet he had known she was there. "I knew this old gas stove was good for something. Just the other day I was wishing I could buy you a better one to cook on."

"I like that one." He had pulled on a pair of dry jeans. He was still bare-chested and barefoot. His hair was beginning to dry. She hoped he would never want to cut it short. She loved the way it shimmered each time he moved his head. "What are you cooking?"

"Cocoa. Sit down."

She set her candle on the table and pulled out a chair. "I didn't know you could cook."

He poured the steaming drink into a waiting mug and turned off the burner. "Better taste it before you make any snap judgments," he said, handing her the mug.

She sipped it cautiously because it was extremely hot. It was rich and sweet and delicious. It warmly trickled its way into her stomach and spread a welcome heat all through her. "It's delicious, Lucas. Thank you."

"Would you like something to eat?"

"No." Then she lifted her head quickly and looked up at him. "Would you? I'll fix—" She made a movement to get out of her chair, but he laid his hands on her shoulders.

"No. I'm not hungry. Drink your chocolate."

He removed his hands and soundlessly crossed the floor toward the window. "The storm is moving away." Rain was still falling, but the wind had died down considerably. The thunder sounded like low drumrolls coming from far away and the lightning was less sinister.

Aislinn raised the mug of chocolate to her lips and swallowed several sips. She tried to drink all of it, but the knot in her throat kept getting in the way. She couldn't take her eyes off Lucas. His profile was sharply outlined against the gray window. She thought he was a beautiful man.

The trauma of the day caught up with her. Emotions assailed her. She began to tremble, so drastically that the chocolate sloshed out of the mug onto her hand, burning it. She set the mug on the table. She was unable to stifle the whimper that escaped her trembling lips.

"Aislinn?"

She didn't answer because she knew her voice would only be a croak if she tried to speak. Cramming her fingers hard against her lips, she tried to contain the emotion that seemed determined to erupt.

"Aislinn?" Lucas repeated.

The concern in his voice was her undoing. Tears burst through the dam of her pride and false courage. Her shoulders shook. She buried her face in her hands.

"What's the matter? Is something wrong? Are you hurt?" Lucas knelt in front of her chair. He ran his hands up and down her arms, across her quaking shoulders, as though searching for injuries.

She lowered her hands from her face, but tears continued to stream down her cheeks. "No, no. I'm not hurt. I...I don't know why I'm doing this," she stammered. "Delayed reaction I guess. I was so scared." She dissolved into another bout of tears.

He reached up, touched her hair. "Don't," he whispered. "Don't. It's all over."

One side of his face was obscured by darkness, but the candle lit the other side. Aislinn extended both hands toward him. Reaching. Beseeching. She touched his face with feather-light fingertips. "I was afraid I'd never see you again. I didn't know how I would survive if anything happened to you."

"Aislinn—"

"More than fear for my safety, or even Tony's, I was frightened for yours." She ran her hands over his head and down his bare biceps before touching his face again.

"I was safe."

"But I didn't know that," she said with desperation.

He pressed three of his fingers against her lips to still their trembling. "I was frantic to get back to you, too."

"You were?"

"I was worried." His fingers moved over the delicate

features of her face, exploring it even as she was exploring his.

"Lucas?"

"What?"

He leaned forward and kissed her, briefly, softly. She made a tremulous, catchy sound in her throat and rested her hands on his shoulders. Reflexively her fingers clenched and unclenched. "I don't ever want to be alone and without you again."

"No."

"Don't ever leave me."

"I won't."

"I depend on you to protect Tony and me."

"I always will."

"Am I a fool? A coward?"

"You're very brave. I'm proud of you."

"You are?"

"Very."

"I love you, Lucas. I love you."

The declaration acted as a lever on a floodgate. Words came pouring out of her mouth, professions of love that had been fermenting inside her for weeks. Now they came frothing out of her like the bubbles in a bottle of uncorked champagne, undisciplined and uncontainable and beyond capture or control. And in between the rushing words, their lips met in brief little exchanges of breath.

But soon that wasn't nearly enough. His arms swept around her swiftly. He angled his head to one side, claiming her mouth in a searing kiss. His lips were hungry; hers were the feast. With a low groan, he pressed his tongue inside her mouth. He rubbed it against hers. The kiss was purely carnal.

His hands slid from her back to her front. He untied the belt of her robe and thrust his hands inside. She was warm and soft and womanly. Her breasts filled his hands and he massaged them.

He trailed kisses down her neck. She watched with wonder and love as he touched the tip of one breast with his tongue, flicking it softly. A small cry of joy escaped her. His mouth gave her even more reason to rejoice. Moving from side to side, it performed acts of love on her flesh.

From over his shoulders, Aislinn could see the smooth expanse of his back. The muscles beneath the sleek skin rippled with each movement he made. She smoothed her hands over his naked skin as though spreading on lotion.

Still kneeling in front of her, his hair brushed her belly. He touched it with his mouth. He kissed her navel. When he pressed his face into her lap, she threw her head back in a spasm of delight. She sobbed his name as he drew her hips forward.

Slowly, he parted her thighs and kissed her.

Aislinn was drawn into a maelstrom of passion. It welled up over her and she seemed to drown in it. She was barely conscious when he lifted her in his arms and carried her through the house.

Only when he gently deposited her on the bed did she become aware of her surroundings again. She heard the whispering sound of cloth as he unfastened his jeans. Her eyes opened in time to see him stepping out of them. As though for her benefit, lightning lit up the sky and provided her with enough light to see him, naked and splendid.

He didn't lie down as she expected, but knelt between her thighs. He lowered his head. "Lucas," she said in feeble protest.

"I owe you this, Aislinn. The first time, that morning so long ago, was for me. This is for you."

His mouth brought her to a crescendo of feeling, unlike anything she had ever experienced. Her head thrashed on the pillow as she tried unsuccessfully to draw breath, but wave after wave of ecstasy prevented that. He was relentless in his determination to give her ultimate satisfaction, but he withheld the finale until she thought she would die of pleasure almost unendurable.

When at last he released her from that glorious prison of rapture, her body was dewy with perspiration and her lips were bruised by her own teeth.

His lips were incredibly considerate of that as he brushed kisses over hers. He licked them gently, then bathed her entire face with his tongue. Once again, sensations began to ribbon their way through her body. Lucas lowered himself over her carefully.

His sex was hot and hard. She felt it against the inside of her thigh. She wanted him and conveyed that want by raising her hips and moving them against him.

"I won't hurt you?" he asked gruffly.

"No."

He was as hard as steel, but velvety smooth. His penetration was so complete that she winced. "I am hurting you," he said, alarmed. But when he tried to withdraw, she closed her thighs against his.

"I want to have all of you."

Burying his face in the curve of her shoulder, he groaned with immense pleasure, both at her words and at the way her body smoothly, tightly, and creamily gloved his. He wanted it to last forever, and he sustained it for as long as he could.

But his body was starved and wouldn't be delayed indefinitely. Once he began to move, the climax came quickly. It rushed upon them, as tempestuous as the storm had been.

When it was over, he rested atop her until their breathing subsided, then he rolled them to their sides, so they still faced each other.

Every time the lightning flickered through the windows, he enjoyed the reflection of her back and derriere in the mirror across the room. It made a provocative picture, her hair in wanton disarray, her skin so pale compared to his hands that moved over the curves of her body.

He touched her with astonishing familiarity, yet she murmured not a single word of protest. He was bold. He satisfied every curiosity he had entertained. The liberties she afforded him made him breathless and lightheaded. She didn't shrink from even the most intimate caresses, indeed she purred beneath his touch.

He remembered praying for death that first time, because he had thought then that nothing else in his life would ever be so good as being inside Aislinn. He felt equally good now, but selfishly he didn't want to die.

What a fool he had been to deny himself the privilege of making love with her. She had been healed from childbirth for weeks. Gene had even surreptitiously given him the go-ahead.

Yet he had stubbornly denied his desire for her, because he was terrified of the emotions that accompanied it. He didn't just want the woman's body; he wanted the woman. It was the first time in his life that he had felt a real need for another human being.

Now, mellow and languid in the sweet aftermath, he eased away from her, raised her chin with his finger and kissed her mouth. He thought it would be a benediction, a good-night, but her tongue initiated a deeper kiss and played with his lower lip.

"The day of your mother's wedding..." she whispered against his lips.

"Yes?"

"I knew you were outside when I undressed by the window." He leaned his head back and looked down at her. "I wanted you to see me," she confessed. "I wanted to seduce you."

His face remained remote, but after a lengthy silence, during which she was held captive by his compelling eyes, he said, "I was seduced."

Rolling quickly to his back, he pulled her atop him and rasped, "Ride me."

Taking him inside her, she fulfilled his fantasy. Eagerly, she carried him beyond his most vivid imaginings. It was a supreme effort, but Lucas kept his eyes open to enjoy the blond beauty of her skin and hair. He caressed her breasts, giving special care to their responsive peaks. And when she arched her back with the pleasure of that caress, he stroked her in places that caused her thighs to quiver against his.

At last, with a shudder, she collapsed on his chest. He wrapped himself around her and gave her all of himself that was in his power to give. Her body celebrated his gift.

Then, weak and spent, they lay there, his body nestled in hers, for a long time. And finally, when he moved her to his side and tucked her back against his chest, they fell into a sleep more peaceful than either had ever known.

Twelve

"I'm glad you chose my house to break into that night."

Greywolf tilted his head to look down at her. "So am I."

She lightly plucked at his chest hairs. They had made love frequently through the night, dozing in between. Their passions had been quick to kindle each time one touched the other. Now, their desire momentarily replete, they lay indolently among the tangled sheets. Last night's storm had long since passed. Morning light tinted the bedroom with a rosy glow.

"I was scared to death of you," she said.

"I was scared to death of you, too."

Laughing in surprise, she propped herself up on her elbows so she could look down on his face. "Of me? You were afraid of me? Why? Did you think I could overpower you?"

"Not in the sense you mean, but at that point in time, if anything could have overpowered me, it would have been a beautiful woman. You totally disarmed me. Why do you think I picked up that knife?"

"Did you think I was beautiful?" She glanced at him through a screen of demure lashes.

"Fishing?"

"Yes, husband. I'll never get tired of the compliments you continually shower on me." Her sarcasm was softened with a smile.

He had the grace to smile back. "I do think you're beautiful. But do you want to know what I thought when I first saw you?"

"Yes. What did you think?"

"Damn it all."

"What?"

"That's what I thought. *Damn it all.* Why did you have to be gorgeous and have the body and face of an angel? I wanted to curse you to perdition for looking the way you did. If you had been a man I would have clipped you on the chin and fled. Or if Miss Aislinn Andrews had been ugly, I would have tied her up, eaten her bread and sausage, drunk her milk, possibly stolen her car, and then hightailed it out of there."

"You did all that...but you spent the night, too."

He slanted a look down at her. "Even when I knew that multiplied my chances of getting caught."

"Why, Lucas?" Her fingers strummed his hard, flat stomach.

"Because I wanted to sleep with you."

She sucked in a short little breath. "Oh."

"But all the time I was wanting you, I hated myself for wanting you."

"Scruples?"

He laughed robustly. Aislinn loved the deep, rich sound still new to her ears. "Hardly. I've never had many scruples when it came to women."

"That's odd."

"Why?"

"After what happened to Alice."

He frowned. "I made sure I never got a woman pregnant." She gazed up at him inquiringly, and he gave her a rueful smile. "Except once."

They kissed.

"That time I wasn't thinking about anything but this." He touched her lower body, letting his fingers luxuriate in the soft, tawny hair. "I never took advantage of any woman. Until you. You were the exception to every rule I'd ever imposed on myself."

"It seems that way. I'm very glad. But why did you hate yourself for wanting me?"

"I didn't want to feel such desperate desire for any woman, much less an Anglo."

She looked pleased. "That's what you were feeling, a 'desperate desire'?"

"Yes," he admitted in a hoarse voice.

"The whole time we were together?"

He nodded seriously.

"And all that about my being your insurance policy?"

"Was my flimsy rationalization. Crazy as it was, I wanted to keep you with me. I felt guilty about disrupting your life and dragging you into that mess, but..." He gave a helpless shrug. "I couldn't bring myself to let you go even though all along I was so afraid you'd get hurt." He laid his hand on her throat and rubbed the soft skin. "I guess you got hurt anyway, didn't you?"

"I don't think so."

"Is that true, Aislinn?"

"That's true."

"God, I don't know why you haven't murdered me in my sleep."

She smiled down at him. "Because I was counting on that desperate desire still being there."

"It is. More desperate than ever." He wound her hair around his hand and, holding her head still for his fervent kiss, rolled her to her back.

After a lengthy kiss that left her breathless, she said, "We could have been doing this for weeks if you weren't so damned stubborn. You never give an inch, do you?"

He grinned lecherously. "Right now I know of several inches I could give you."

She pulled his hair by way of punishment for his ribaldry, but then she giggled. "I can't believe you actually made a joke."

"I can be extremely funny."

"With everyone but me. With me you're hardheaded and unbending. You can't be humorous because you're too busy being defensive about what happened that morning at Alice's house." He tensed up and started to move away, but she locked her arms across the small of his back. "You stay right where you are, Lucas Greywolf."

"I shamed myself."

"You needed me." The very softness with which she said it arrested his defensive reaction. "Needing someone is nothing to be ashamed of. Why is it so difficult for you to admit that you need another person occasionally, Lucas? None of us is entirely self-sufficient." Her finger touched his lips lovingly. "I liked being needed by you that morning. I wasn't offended by what you did. I was only sorry you didn't let me participate more."

She raised her head off the pillow and kissed him. At first he was resistant, but as her mouth continued to move over his, he began to thaw. When her head reclined on the pillow again, he followed it down and showed her just how much he needed her.

Later her hands glided down his sweat-dampened back, past his waist to his buttocks. "Do you hear something?"

"Yes," he mumbled into her neck. "My heart. It's still pounding."

She smiled against his shoulder, biting it softly, loving even the slightest trace of vulnerability he demonstrated. "Mine is pounding, too. But I was referring to something else."

"Like Tony?"

"Precisely Tony. Better let me up to check on him."

He moved away from her and lay sprawled on his back, watching with hot, possessive eyes as Aislinn pulled on the wrapper she'd been wearing the evening before and padded out of their bedroom.

Lucas didn't recall a time in his life when he'd been happy. He'd lived through happy occasions like birthdays and Christmases. He'd loved the times he and Joseph had hunted in the hills. He exulted in winning races at track meets. But happiness was something that other people had, people with normal families and backgrounds, people with undiluted blood, people who didn't live under stigmas, people who weren't labeled.

This morning Lucas Greywolf came as close to being happy as he ever had been. He even allowed himself to smile broadly just for the hell of it. He stretched like a sinuous mountain cat who had nothing more to worry about than what to eat for breakfast. Being happy wasn't nearly as frightening as he had thought it would be.

Aislinn, too, floated into Tony's bedroom on a cloud of joy. All the horrors of yesterday had been banished by Lucas's loving. Radiant sunlight was pouring through the windows. Her future looked sunny because she loved Lucas and had finally gotten him to accept her love.

He hadn't said he loved her, but one couldn't have everything at once. He desired her. He loved having her in his life and in his bed. Maybe love would grow out of that eventually. In the meantime, she would be satisfied with what she had. Life was good.

"Good morning, Tony," she called gaily as she entered the nursery. He was crying, whimpering actually. "Are you hungry? Hmm? Want a dry diaper? Wouldn't that feel better?"

The moment she bent over the crib, she realized that something was terribly wrong. With that inexplicable maternal instinct, she instantly realized that something wasn't right. The rattling sound of his breathing alerted her immediately. When she touched him, she screamed, "Lucas!"

He was pulling on a pair of jeans. He recognized Aislinn's cry as one of distress. He knew better than anyone that she didn't panic easily. Within heartbeats he was clearing the door of the nursery.

"What is it?"

"Tony. He's burning up with fever. And listen to his breathing."

His breath was making a hideous whistling sound as it rushed in and out of the tiny lungs. His respiration was quick and shallow. His face was mottled. And instead of making a lusty cry, which both his parents would have welcomed, he seemed barely to have the strength to mew pitiably.

"What do you want me to do?"

"Get Gene on the phone." Already Aislinn was stripping the infant and reaching for the rectal thermometer, which her baby books had advised she keep close at hand. Lucas didn't argue, deferring to her expertise in this situation. He raced through the house into the kitchen and quickly punched out the telephone number.

"Hello," Gene sleepily answered the second ring.

"Gene, Lucas. Tony's sick."

"A cold. I gave—"

"More than that. He can hardly breathe."

By now Gene had recognized the no-nonsense tone of Lucas's voice. "Does he have a temperature?"

"Just a minute." Lucas cupped his hand over the receiver and called out the question to Aislinn.

She appeared in the doorway of the kitchen, holding Tony against her chest. Her eyes were filled with fear. "One hundred and four," she whispered. "Lucas." It was a plea.

He reported the baby's temperature to Gene, who cursed. Lucas could hear Alice's voice in the background, asking of her husband who was calling and what was wrong.

"Dammit, Gene, what do we do?" Lucas demanded.

"You calm down for starters," Gene said reasonably. "Then you bathe Tony with cool water, try to get his temperature down. Bring him in as soon as you can get here."

"To the clinic?"

"Yes."

"We'll be there in half an hour or less."

Lucas hung up the phone without another word and repeated Gene's instructions to Aislinn. He finished dressing while she cupped cool water over Tony in the bathroom sink. Then they switched places. He took the baby and she slung on clothes, not caring what they were.

She diapered Tony, wrapped him in a light receiving blanket and left by way of the front door, where Lucas already had her car idling.

The clearing in front of the house was a quagmire

from the torrential rain the night before. The spongy ground sucked at the tires as Lucas plowed the car toward the road. It wasn't much better. He skidded into the ditch several times, the back tires fishtailing in the mire.

Lucas's hands were clenched around the steering wheel and his back was hunched. The hard expression on his face reminded Aislinn of another time he had driven her car with the same kind of concentration. At the time that had seemed like a life-or-death situation. How tame it seemed compared to this. Now she knew the real meaning of fear: when one's child is in life-threatening danger.

The drive into town seemed to take forever. Tony's little body generated so much heat that he branded himself into his mother's breasts. He was fretful. Every time he dropped off to sleep, he would come awake choking, struggling with his effort to breathe.

Gene and Alice came rushing out of the clinic the moment they saw the car race into the parking lot. "How is he?" Gene asked, opening Aislinn's door.

"Oh, Gene, help him," she pleaded. "He's burning up. I think his fever has gone back up."

They all hurried toward the doors of the clinic, scrambling over each other in their haste. Aislinn carried Tony into an examining room. The clinic wasn't open for business yet, so there were no other patients vying for the doctor's attention.

Alice and Gene methodically went about examining the baby, kindly elbowing his hovering mother aside. Aislinn looked toward Lucas for reassurance, but he was staring down at the baby. He had said little on the trip into town. She wanted to offer him comfort, but knew that anything she said would sound like just what it was, an empty platitude. And how could she comfort him when she was so terrified herself?

Gene listened to Tony's chest through a stethoscope. When he lowered the earplugs he said, "He's got fluid in his lungs. That upper-respiratory infection has gotten much worse."

"But he was getting better," Aislinn protested. "I've been giving him his medicine faithfully."

"No one's blaming you, Aislinn," Gene said kindly, laying a hand on her shoulder. "These things happen."

"He...he got wet last night. And chilled." She told them about the storm. "When Lucas took us back to the house, I kept Tony covered up as well as I could. Is that why this happened?"

There was a trace of hysteria in her high, thin voice. Both Alice and Gene hastened to assure her that the infection could have spread in any event. "He wasn't on any antibiotics," Gene said. "And it certainly wasn't negligence on your part."

"Make him well."

Lucas, who had remained silent until then, spoke from the side of the examination table where he continued to stare down at his son as though Tony were the center star of the universe and the light was about to burn out.

"I don't think I can, Lucas."

"What!" Aislinn gasped. She clasped her hands together and raised them to her white lips.

"I can't do much here," Gene said. "My suggestion would be to take him to one of the hospitals in Phoenix. Get him to a natal intensive-care unit where specialists can treat him. I'm not properly equipped."

"But that's hours from here," Aislinn said frantically.

"A guy I went to med school with heads up a helicopter ambulance service. I'll go call him. Alice, give the baby a shot to bring down the fever."

Unable to shake off the paralysis of fear, Aislinn

watched Alice prepare a syringe and give Tony an injection. When that was done, she rediapered him and
handed him to his anxiety-ridden mother. Aislinn leaned
against the examination table and rocked back and forth,
comforting the baby as best she could.

Gene returned and informed them, "He's dispatch-
ing a chopper immediately. It'll set down in that pasture
on the north side of the highway just outside town. The
pilot he's sending was here last year to pick up a snake-
bite victim, so he knows the way. Aislinn, Lucas, there
will be a pediatric nurse in the helicopter and specialists
standing by when you reach the hospital."

"Is he that critical?" Aislinn asked, her voice wavering.

Gene took her hands in his. "I wouldn't alarm you unnecessarily. Yes, he's that critical."

A few hours later, the specialist at the Phoenix hospital confirmed Gene's diagnosis. Those intervening hours
had been a nightmare for Aislinn. Lucas and she had met
the helicopter and were hustled aboard. From that moment on, she realized she would forever have a greater
appreciation for people in medicine. The nurse on board
the chopper began administering to Tony immediately;
by radio, she was in constant contact with the doctors at
the hospital, so that by the time they set down on the roof,
Tony was already getting the best of medical treatment.

As soon as he was carried into areas of the hospital
restricted to them, Aislinn turned to Lucas, seeking the
strength of his embrace. But even though he folded his
arms around her, it was a mechanical gesture. His heart
wasn't in it. She could feel the spiritual distance between
them, yawning as wide as a gulf. Since they had left their

home that morning, she had felt him slipping further and further away from her.

His face was closed, as though he had removed himself from the tragedy. But Aislinn knew he was suffering terribly. How he could enforce such rigid control over his emotions, she didn't know. She felt that at any moment she would begin banging her head against the wall, stamping her feet, tearing out her hair.

They waited, sharing a silence that was intolerable to Aislinn. Where was the loving comfort Lucas had given to Joseph and Alice when the old man had lain dying? Why was there none for her now? But Joseph had been an old man. Lucas had had years to prepare himself for the day his grandfather would die.

She was relieved when the specialist approached them. "Mr. and Mrs. Greywolf?" he asked politely. They nodded. "Your little boy is very sick," he began. He delivered a spate of medical terms that meant nothing to Aislinn, but he finished with, "Pneumonia."

"Then it's not so bad, is it?" Aislinn cried in relief. "I've known many people who have had pneumonia. They recovered without any difficulty."

The doctor glanced worriedly at Lucas before looking back into Aislinn's expectant face. "The recovery rate for pneumonia is high, but we're talking about a three-month-old pair of lungs. I'm afraid that reduces your child's ability to throw it off quite so easily."

"Then it *is* serious?"

"His current condition is extremely serious."

"Will he die?" She could barely control her wobbling lips long enough to ask the hateful question.

"I don't know," the doctor replied honestly. "I'm gonna fight like hell to keep him." He squeezed her shoulder in reassurance. "Excuse me, now. I should get back."

"May I see him?" she asked, clutching at the sleeve of his lab coat.

"I don't advise it. He's got tubes going in and out. To see him now would only frighten you more."

"She wants to see him." Lucas's sibilant whisper was more threatening than a shout. He and the doctor stared each other down for several seconds before the doctor relented.

"For one minute, Mrs. Greywolf. No more."

When she returned to the corridor, she was crying copiously. Lucas placed his arms around her and patted her gently on the back. But as before, she felt the invisible barriers between them, and there was little solace to be found in his aloof bearing and cool, gray eyes.

They spent the entire day and night in the hospital waiting room. Aislinn refused to leave even long enough to eat, though the nursing staff kindly urged her to. No one approached Lucas. Aislinn thought it was because they were afraid of him. What went on in the brain behind that implacable face remained a mystery to everyone but him.

Shortly after dawn on the second day, the doctor reported that Tony's condition was still serious. "But when he first arrived, I wouldn't have laid odds on him making it this long," he said, with a hint of optimism. "I think he's a fighter."

Aislinn took heart. She grasped at any straws of hope.

Gene and Alice arrived soon after that. They had posted notices that the clinic would be closed and had made the long drive, unable to stay away any longer. Their sudden appearance had such an impact on Aislinn that she dissolved into tears of gratitude.

The Dexters expressed alarm at how drawn and pale she looked and begged her to check into a hotel and rest.

She steadfastly refused. But they did talk her into eating the hot meal the hospital cafeteria sent up on trays for Lucas and her.

They were sitting in the waiting room, finishing their breakfast, when Lucas glanced up. He angrily tossed his napkin down and stood up, banging the table with his shin. "Who invited *them?*" he asked rudely, apparently not caring if the approaching couple overheard him.

"I did." Aislinn's voice was as unsteady as her knees as she stood up to confront her husband, who was obviously furious, and her parents, whom she hadn't seen or spoken to since her marriage. "Mother, Father," she said, stepping forward, "thank you for coming."

The Andrews seemed at a loss as to what to say or what to do. Eleanor fidgeted with the ivory handle of her purse, and Willard looked everywhere but at his daughter and son-in-law.

"We thought it was the least we could do," Eleanor said to break a silence that had grown uncomfortably long. "We're very sorry about the baby's illness."

"Do you need anything, Aislinn? Money?" Willard offered.

Lucas said something thoroughly obscene and went around them, shouldering them aside as he passed. "No thank you, Father," Aislinn said softly.

She was ashamed that her parents' solution to any problem was money, but she forgave them. Their being there was a comfort to her and, in light of their bigotry, more of a concession than she had had any right to expect from them.

She was relieved of having to deal with the awkward situation when Alice stepped forward. "I'm Alice Dexter, Tony's other grandmother. Please forgive my son's bad behavior. He's extremely upset."

She spoke softly. What impressed Aislinn, as it had from the night she met Alice in the hogan, was the absence of censure or prejudice in her tone. She looked directly at Eleanor, whose dress cost more than what Alice would spend on clothes in several years. She was neither hostile toward nor intimidated by the other woman. She extended her hand. "Please come meet my husband, Dr. Gene Dexter."

Aislinn left the four of them to get acquainted and went to find Lucas. He was standing at the end of the hall in front of a window. He was broodily staring out at a cloudless day very much the way Aislinn imagined he must have stared out the barred windows of the prison. For a man who enjoyed being outdoors as much as he did, it must have been hell.

"Lucas?" She saw his shoulders tense; otherwise he didn't respond. "Are you angry with me for notifying my parents?"

"We don't need them."

"Maybe you don't; I do."

He spun around. Only an act of will kept her from recoiling from the rage burning in his eyes. Taking her hand, he dragged her into a room that the nurses had made available to them, but which neither had used so far. When the heavy door silently swung closed, he faced Aislinn furiously.

"I guess you miss their damned money after all, don't you? What's the matter? Didn't you think I could provide sufficient medical care for my son? Did you call Daddy, begging forgiveness for marrying beneath you and asking him to please drop by with his checkbook?"

"I don't deserve that, Lucas!" She slapped him hard, hard enough for his head to follow the path her flying palm had taken. When his face came back around, his teeth were bared, and he raised his hand in retaliation. However, he stopped the downward arc of his hand before it could make contact with her cheek.

She threw herself against him and gripped handfuls of his shirt. "Go ahead. Hit me. Maybe then, just maybe, I'll know you're alive and not made of stone. I'll gladly invite you to strike me if that's what it takes for you to show some emotion, some feeling."

She shook him, grinding her white knuckles into the hard wall of his chest. "Damn you, Lucas! Talk to me! Yell. Scream. Show me your pain. I know it's there. I know you love Tony even if you love no one else. He might die and I know you're hurting because of it. Use me as your punching bag, as your sounding board. Let me share your grief."

She was crying, but the tears ran heedlessly down her cheeks. She licked them from the corners of her mouth. "You're so proud, aren't you? Nothing can touch you." She shook her head in denial of her own words. "I know differently. I heard you keening when Joseph died. I witnessed your pain. And that heartache can't begin to compare to what you're feeling now for your son. Your own stupid prejudice keeps you separate from the rest of the world, not the other way around. Are you so heartless that you can't even cry at your son's deathbed?

"You say you don't need anybody. But you do, Lucas. You just won't admit it. I needed my parents' support during this time, so I swallowed my pride and called them, having no guarantee that they wouldn't hang up on me. I need all the support I can muster today. I don't want to go through this crisis alone. Even if it meant losing face, I would have begged them to be here with me. You ridicule them, but you have more in common with them than you think. You're as cold and unyielding as they are. Only they relented. They're here for me now and you're not."

She gripped his shirt harder, almost tearing the fabric. "Whether you love me or not, you're my husband. I need you. Don't you dare withhold your support from me. You married me because you felt honor bound to do so. But is there any honor in deserting your wife when she needs you the most? Does it make you less a man to weep with me?"

She slapped him again. And again. Tears rained from her eyes and rolled down her face and dripped off her chin. "Cry, damn you! Cry!"

With a suddenness that snatched the breath from her body, he flung his arms around her and bent his head low. He buried his face in the crook of her shoulder. At first Aislinn didn't realize that her fondest wish had been granted. But then she felt his broad shoulders shaking and heard the wracking sounds of his weeping.

She encircled his waist with her arms and held him close while his tears bathed her neck and dampened her blouse. He cried on and on, and when she couldn't support his weight any longer, they sank to the floor, their arms still around each other. She pressed his head between her breasts, curved herself over it protectively and held him dearly, rocking back and forth as she often did with Tony. Her own tears were unstemmed and fell into his hair.

Lord, she loved him. She hurt with love.

"I want our baby to live," he sobbed. "You can't know what it was like for me to learn that I had a son. I want him to live. I want him to know me. When I was a kid, I wanted a father so badly, Aislinn. I want to be the kind of father to Tony that I used to dream about having." He burrowed his head deeper into her flesh. "Would God be so cruel as to take my son from me?"

"If he is taken from us, Lucas, I won't be able to bear your pain. I love you too much."

After a time, his tears ceased, but he kept his head nestled in her cleavage. He kissed her through the damp cloth of her blouse and murmured endearments, sometimes in English, sometimes in a language still foreign to her.

"I didn't want to love you."

"I know," she replied softly, combing her fingers through his hair.

"But I do."

"I know that, too."

He raised his head and looked at her through tear-washed eyes. "Do you?" For an answer, she lifted a tear off his glossy black eyelashes, looked at it, then at him, and gave him a bittersweet smile.

They shared one poignant second before there was a gentle knock at the door. Their expressions turned bleak. Lucas stood up and extended his hand down to her. Trustingly, she laid her hand in his, and he pulled her to her feet, placing a strong, supportive arm around her. They faced the door as though facing an executioner. "Come in," Lucas said. They expected the doctor.

But it wasn't the doctor who came through the door. It was Warden Dixon. Aislinn didn't recognize the man, but Lucas did. She could tell by the tensing of his muscled body.

"Hello, Mr. Greywolf. I know this is an awkward time for you." He was embarrassed, for it was apparent that they had both been crying. "I'm Warden Dixon," he said to Aislinn when it became obvious that Lucas wasn't going to make introductions.

"What are you doing here?" Lucas asked, curtailing the pleasantries.

"As I said, I know this is a terrible time for you. I apologize, Mrs. Greywolf, for the untimely intrusion. If I wasn't delivering good news I wouldn't trouble you at a time like this."

"How did you know I was here?"

"Mr. Andrews's secretary. I telephoned him this morning when I failed to contact you after trying all day yesterday."

"You've been diligent, Mr. Dixon," Aislinn said. "Have you come to see us about something important?"

"Your husband's exoneration." He looked at Lucas. "A judge has reviewed the transcripts of your trial. He has also considered the affidavits submitted to him freely by two men who have confessed to their crimes. The documents absolved you from any and all guilt. In fact, they stated that the only reason you were in the fracas at all was to break up the fighting. You were trying to prevent the violence, not perpetrate it. You are to be officially vindicated and immediately reinstated to the bar."

Aislinn slumped against her husband's arm with profound joy. Lucas, however, was barely able to support her. The news had made him weak-kneed.

Before either of them could voice their thanks to the warden, Gene came running into the room. "Lucas, Aislinn, come quickly. The doctor is looking for you."

Epilogue

"Smile!"

"Aislinn, my face is about to crack from smiling."

"I don't doubt it. It's so unusual an expression for you." She laughed at her husband's dark scowl. "Look this way, Tony. Look at Mommy."

She clicked off two pictures while Tony had his head turned in the right direction. He even proudly displayed his new front teeth in a slobbery grin.

"Now stop working with those cameras," Lucas said, moving toward his wife. "This is supposed to be a party."

"I'm having a wonderful time," she said happily, standing on her tiptoes to kiss his cheek. Her eyes were sparkling. "I'd rather be taking pictures of you and Tony than anything in the world."

Lucas looked at her with open skepticism. "Bet I can name something you'd rather be doing."

"Lucas!"

Now it was his turn to laugh…at his wife's exasperation. "However, I'll admit Tony and I do make good subjects, don't we?" he said, proudly looking at his son, who resembled him so remarkably.

Tony's eyes were already turning the same gray color as his father's, and they had a rim of blue around them which he had inherited from his mother. His hair was jet black, but not as straight as Lucas's. His cheekbones were just as prominent, but he had enough baby fat to round out the cheeks beneath them. He was a picture of good health.

"You are my favorite subjects anytime." Aislinn hugged them both, nuzzling her husband's strong throat, while her son tugged on fistfuls of her hair.

"Hey, will the three of you break it up?" Gene said, handing Aislinn a glass of punch. "You're supposed to mingle."

"Give Tony to me," Alice said, joining them. She had a cookie in her hand and that was bribery enough. Tony put up no fuss when Lucas passed him to his grandmother, though he was usually reluctant to leave his father's arms. "Willard and Eleanor want to see him."

"Now, stop making goo-goo eyes at each other and go shake some hands," Gene told Lucas and Aislinn, pushing them toward the crowd of people milling around the office.

The reception was to celebrate the official opening of Lucas's law office. The publicity surrounding his vindication, coupled with the publication of Aislinn's photographs in a national magazine, had brought renewed public awareness of the plight of many of the Indians who lived on the reservations.

Lucas wasn't deluded by this rush of interest. In his lifetime he wouldn't see an end to all the oppression, whether it was intentional or not. But every step he took in that direction was gratifying.

He was extremely conscientious about appearances. He never wanted it to seem that he had profited from his conviction and the subsequent reversal. He never forgot who his clients were. Even today, he had worn a white shirt, tie and sports jacket, but he had on jeans and boots with them. He hadn't worn a headband, but the silver earring was in his ear. And behind his desk, hanging on the wall, was a framed portrait of Joseph Greywolf dressed in the full regalia of a chief. Many of the attending dignitaries commented on the photograph, which had been taken when Joseph was in his prime.

"How much longer before we can go home?" Lucas asked Aislinn after an hour of smiles and handshakes.

"The invitations Alice sent out said from two till six. Why?"

"Because I want to get you home and in bed."

"Shh! Somebody might hear you."

In full view of their guests, he lowered his head and kissed her on the mouth.

"Behave, Lucas. This reception is in your honor." She tried to sound scolding, but couldn't mask her pleasure in his spontaneous display of affection.

He toyed with a strand of her hair. "I could just haul you out of here, you know."

"Kidnap me?"

"Uh-huh."

"You did that already."

"It was the smartest thing I ever did."

"It was the best thing that could have happened to me."

Unaware of the conversations buzzing around them, they stared searchingly into each other's eyes, finding the love they knew they would. Johnny Deerinwater finally broke them apart by coming up and thumping Lucas on the back while he heartily shook hands.

They played host and hostess for the time required and eventually the crowd began to dwindle. "We haven't spent any time with Mother and Father," Aislinn said, taking Lucas's arm and guiding him toward the couple who were sitting across the room talking to Gene. Lucas made a complaining sound. "They've come a long way, Lucas, and I'm not referring to the distance they drove today."

"I know," he conceded. "I'll be kind. After all, he's building that new wing to Gene's clinic."

As soon as Willard and Eleanor departed for Phoenix, Alice asked if she and Gene could keep Tony overnight. "We don't get to see him often enough. And you have to drive back tomorrow to clean up the office for Monday's business anyway. Please?"

They consented and left for home, just the two of them. It was a beautiful evening. The sky was star-studded and a full moon hung low over the mountains.

"You know, I think I've become part Indian myself," Aislinn said musingly. "I love all this," she said, nodding toward the horizon.

"You gave up a lot, Aislinn," Lucas said quietly, keeping his eyes on the narrow road that led to the ranch.

She took his hand from the steering wheel and held it, pressing it hard until he looked at her. "In that other life, I didn't have you. I didn't have Tony. I would never trade back."

Indeed, she had severed all her connections in Scottsdale. The condo had been sold. She used her equity in it to buy playground equipment for several of the schools on the reservation. She had sold the photography studio as well, and after using part of the profits to expand her darkroom and camera equipment, bought Lucas a magnificent stud for his herd. The day the animal was delivered, he had struggled with his pride to accept the gift.

Aislinn had laid her hands on his chest and gazed up

at him imploringly. "You've given me so much, Lucas. Let me give you this."

He had accepted the horse because it was a gift of love from her. Too, the stud would strengthen his herd. Its offspring would be valuable. The more profitable the ranch, the more young men Lucas could hire as hands who might otherwise go jobless. One of the first buildings to go up on his property had been a bunkhouse to house the six cowboys he had already hired. They ably ran the ranch so he could devote more time to his law practice.

Now, Aislinn looked at Lucas's stern profile etched against the moonlit sky and her heart swelled with love. She could barely contain the happiness that had been hers since Tony had survived the bout with pneumonia.

"I hope the pictures I took today turn out well. Especially the ones of Tony." Her husband seemed to sense that she wasn't finished, so he said nothing. "I still get the shivers when I think how close we came to losing him."

He withdrew his hand from hers and rubbed the backs of his fingers against her cheek. "We promised that we would never forget it, but we also promised that we wouldn't dwell on it either."

"I know," she said, softly kissing his knuckles as they stroked her lips. "I was just thinking about that day. You telling me that you loved me, then Warden Dixon showing up with his news, and almost immediately after that the doctor informing us that Tony would pull through." She smiled at him. "Whew! So much good stuff at one time nearly did me in."

"You're certainly in a reflective mood tonight."

"My way of celebrating how happy I am."

He pulled the car to a halt in front of the house and slid his gray eyes toward her. "Well, I've got another form of celebration in mind."

"And what would that be, Mr. Greywolf?"

They didn't even waste time turning on lights, but let the moonlight, shining in through the windows, guide them through the house into the bedroom.

Lucas whipped off his jacket and slung it onto a chair. He unbuttoned his shirt. That's as far as he got before his passions ruled him. He reached for Aislinn and pulled her into his arms. She dropped the jacket of her suit onto the floor, barely having had time to take it off.

His mouth retained the same hot fierceness it had had the first time he kissed her. His bitterness might have mellowed, his prejudices might have been tamped down, he might have come to accept and appreciate the Anglo half of himself, but Aislinn hoped that the savage nature of his lovemaking would never be tamed.

He touched the front of her blouse, groping for buttons. He released them one by one as she plowed all ten of her fingers through his hair, holding his mouth hard against hers. He tugged the blouse from the waistband of her skirt, unfastened the clasp of her bra and pushed the lacy cups aside, then covered her breasts with his hands.

His callused fingertips and palms were excitingly abrasive against her smooth flesh. They worked their magic, and when she was primed for his mouth, he took her between his lips and made her very wet.

They both groaned with pleasure when he lifted his mouth once again to hers and drew her breasts against his chest. He held her tight against him, wrapping his arms as far around her as he could reach, bending his head down low over hers.

"I don't ever want to remember when you weren't a part of my body," he said huskily, squeezing her closer. "I don't want to remember when I didn't love you."

The romantic speech was so unlike him that she treasured it all the more. He had learned that admitting to profound emotions didn't compromise his heritage or manhood. Still, he rarely voiced aloud his deepest feelings. When he did, as now, Aislinn cherished every precious word.

With their mouths fused in an ardent kiss, he slipped his hands beneath her skirt and moved them up her thighs. He played with the tops of her stockings and the suspenders of her garter belt, which he had expressed an extreme liking for and which she favored him by wearing often.

He cupped her derriere and positioned her against him, maximizing the sensations for both of them. Moments later, she stepped out of her panties. His hand slid between her thighs. And up. And inside. And he let her die a little before bringing her back down with soothing kisses and whispered endearments.

"Lucas," she murmured weakly, wilting against him like a flower that has experienced full bloom.

"God, you're beautiful." He wound his fingers through her hair, pulling hard. "My wife. My woman," he murmured possessively, and held her even tighter.

After sharing a violently passionate kiss, she backed away from him. To his eyes, she was a vision of sexy disarray, with her mouth dewy from their kiss, her hair tangled about her head and shoulders, her blouse and bra open but not off, her skirt rumpled.

He stood still, slightly surprised, when, keeping her eyes riveted to his, she peeled his shirt off his shoulders. After letting it trail from her fingertips to the floor, she pushed her hand beneath his ornate, turquoise-studded belt. "Remember when you carried the knife here?" she asked. "It was extremely phallic."

"It was?"

"It was."

She worked her hand into the waistband of his jeans, the backs of her fingers pleasantly gouging his hair-dusted belly. Then her eyes still focused on his, she backed toward the bed, towing him with her, until the backs of her knees touched the edge of it and she sat down.

He looked sinister and dangerous with the moonlight shining on his dark beauty. It made his hair appear blacker, his eyes lighter, his body lithe and sleek and menacing. The cross hanging from his neck only made his throat and chest appear stronger by contrast. The silver earring winked at her.

With an airy touch, her hands drifted over his chest, his nipples. Her fingers combed down the ridges of his lean ribs until they reached the shadowy dell of his navel. He raised his hands to his belt buckle.

"No," she said.

When his hands obediently moved back to his sides, she made a ballet of unfastening the belt buckle. Fingers had never been so nimble, yet so agonizingly controlled and unhurried. The metal clinked musically in the darkness. His rushing breath was the only other sound breaking the total stillness.

One by one she popped free the heavy metal buttons on his jeans until all were undone and the fly was open. The smell of his soap and his skin and his sex greeted her warmly, muskily. She wanted to swallow his smell.

"You are so beautiful," she whispered. "So tall and strong and...hard."

Tipping her head forward, she pressed her open mouth to his navel. She slid her hands inside his jeans and eased them down. Slowly. Seductively. Softly.

He gave a hoarse cry when her tongue touched him.

Again and again and again....

Much later, as they lay entwined, naked now, basking in each other's body heat, she kissed his neck and whispered into his pierced ear, "I love you, Lucas Greywolf."

"I know."

And because he did, she was content.

* * * * *

TWO ALONE

One

They were all dead.

All except her.

She was sure of that.

She didn't know how long it had been since the impact or how long she'd remained bent over with her head in her lap. It could have been seconds, minutes, light-years. Time *could* stand still.

Endlessly, it seemed, torn metal had shifted before settling with a groan. The dismembered trees—innocent victims of the crash—had ceased to quiver. Hardly a leaf was stirring now. Everything was frightfully still. There was no sound.

Absurdly she thought of the question about a tree falling in the woods. Would it make a sound? It did. She'd heard it. So she must be alive.

She raised her head. Her hair and shoulders and back were littered with chips of shattered plastic—what had previously been the window next to her seat. She shook her head slightly and the chips rained off her, making tinkling, pinging little noises in the quiet. Slowly she forced herself to open her eyes.

A scream rose in her throat, but she couldn't utter it. Her vocal cords froze. She was too terrified to scream. The carnage was worse than an air-traffic controller's nightmare.

The two men sitting in the seats directly in front of hers—good friends, judging by their loud and rambunctious bantering with each other—were now dead, their joking and laughter forever silenced. One's head had gone through the window. That fact registered with her, but she didn't look too closely. There was a sea of blood. She slammed her eyes shut and didn't open them until after she'd averted her head.

Across the aisle, another man lay dead, his head thrown back against the cushion as though he'd been sleeping when the plane went down. The Loner. She had mentally tagged him with that name before takeoff. Because the plane was small, there were strict regulations about weight. While the passengers and their luggage were being weighed before boarding, the Loner had stood apart from the group, his attitude superior and hostile. His unfriendliness hadn't invited conversation with any of the other passengers, who were all boisterously bragging about their kills. His aloofness had segregated him—just as her sex had isolated her. She was the only woman on board.

Now, the only survivor.

Looking toward the front of the cabin, she could see that the cockpit had been severed from the fuselage like a bottle cap that had been twisted off. It had come to rest several feet away. The pilot and copilot, both jovial and joking young men, were obviously, bloodily, dead.

She swallowed the bile that filled the back of her throat. The robust, bearded copilot had helped her on board, flirting, saying he rarely had women passengers on his airplane and when he did, they didn't look like fashion models.

The other two passengers, middle-aged brothers, were still strapped into their seats in the front row. They'd been killed by the jagged tree trunk that had cut into the cabin like a can opener. Their families would feel the tragedy with double intensity.

She began to cry. Hopelessness and fear overwhelmed her. She was afraid she would faint. She was afraid she would die. And she was afraid she wouldn't.

The deaths of her fellow passengers had been swift and painless. They had probably been killed on impact. They were better off. Her death would be long in coming because as far as she could tell, she was miraculously uninjured. She would die slowly of thirst, starvation, exposure.

She wondered why she was still alive. The only explanation was that she was sitting in the last row. Unlike the rest of the passengers, she had left someone behind at the lodge on Great Bear Lake. Her goodbye had been drawn out, so she was the last one to board the aircraft. All the seats had been taken except that one in the last row.

When the copilot assisted her aboard, the rowdy dialogues had ceased abruptly. Bent at an angle because of the low ceiling, she had moved to the only available seat. She had felt distinctly uncomfortable, being the only woman on board. It was like walking into a smoke-filled room where a heated poker game was in progress. Some things were innately, exclusively male, and no amount of sexual equality was ever going to change that. Just as some things were innately, exclusively female.

An airplane leaving a hunting and fishing lodge in the Northwest Territories was one of those masculine things. She had tried to make herself as inconspicuous as possible, saying nothing, settling in her seat and staring out the window. Once, just after takeoff, she had turned her head and inadvertently made eye contact with the man sitting across the aisle. He had looked at her with such apparent disfavor that she had returned her gaze to the window and kept it there.

Besides the pilots, she was probably the first one to notice the storm. Accompanied by dense fog, the torrential rain had made her nervous. Soon the others began to notice the jouncy flight. Their braggadocio was replaced with uneasy quips about riding this one out and being glad the pilot was "driving" instead of one of them.

But the pilots were having a difficult time. That soon became apparent to all of them. Eventually they fell silent and kept their eyes trained on the men in the cockpit. Tension inside the aircraft increased when the two-man crew lost radio contact with the ground. The plane's instruments could no longer be depended upon because the readings they were giving out were apparently inaccurate. Because of the impenetrable cloud cover, they hadn't seen the ground since takeoff.

When the plane went into a spiraling nosedive and the pilot shouted back to his passengers, "We're going in. God be with us," they all took the news resignedly and with an amazing calm.

She had bent double and pressed her head between her knees, covering it with her arms, praying all the way down. It seemed to take an eternity.

She would never forget the shock of that first jarring impact. Even braced for it, she hadn't been adequately prepared. She didn't know why she had been spared instantaneous death, unless her smaller size had allowed her to wedge herself between the two seats more securely and better cushion the impact.

However, under the circumstances, she wasn't sure that being spared was a favorable alternative. One could only reach the lodge on the northwestern tip of Great Bear Lake by airplane. Miles of virgin wilderness lay between it and Yellowknife, their destination. God only knew how far off the flight plan the plane had been when it went down. The authorities could search for months without finding her. Until they did—if ever—she was utterly alone and dependent solely on herself for survival.

That thought galvanized her into action. With near-hysterical frenzy she struggled to release her seat belt. It snapped apart and she fell forward, bumping her head on the seat in front of her. She eased herself into the narrow aisle and, on hands and knees, crawled toward the gaping tear in the airplane.

Avoiding any direct contact with the bodies, she looked up through the ripped metal seam. The rain had stopped, but the low, heavy, dark gray clouds looked so laden with menace they seemed ready to burst. Frequently they belched deep rolls of thunder. The sky looked cold and wet and threatening. She clutched the collar of her red fox coat high about her neck. There was virtually no wind. She supposed she should be grateful for that. The wind could get very cold. But wait! If there was no wind, where was that keening sound coming from?

Holding her breath, she waited.

There it was again!

She whipped her head around, listening. It wasn't easy to hear anything over the pounding of her own heart.

A stir.

She looked toward the man who was sitting in the seat across the aisle from hers. Was it just her wishful imagination or did the Loner's eyelids flicker? She scrambled back up the aisle, brushing past the dangling, bleeding arm of one of the crash victims. She had studiously avoided touching it only moments ago.

"Oh, please, God, let him be alive," she prayed fervently. Reaching his seat, she stared down into his face. He still seemed to be in peaceful repose. His eyelids were still. No flicker. No moaning sound coming from his lips, which were all but obscured by a thick, wide mustache. She looked at his chest, but he was wearing a quilted coat, so it was impossible to tell if he were breathing or not.

She laid her index finger along the top curve of his mustache, just beneath his nostrils. She uttered a wordless exclamation when she felt the humid passage of air. Faint, but definitely there.

"Thank God, thank God." She began laughing and crying at the same time. Lifting her hands to his cheeks, she slapped them lightly. "Wake up, mister. Please wake up."

He moaned, but he didn't open his eyes. Intuition told her that the sooner he regained consciousness the better. Besides, she needed the reassurance that he wasn't dead or going to die—at least not immediately. She desperately needed to know that she wasn't alone.

Reasoning that the cold air might help revive him, she resolved to get him outside the plane. It wasn't going to be easy; he probably outweighed her by a hundred pounds or more.

She felt every ounce of it as she opened his seat belt and his dead weight slumped against her like a sack of concrete mix. She caught most of it with her right shoulder and supported him there while she backed down the aisle toward the opening, half lifting him, half dragging him with her.

That seven-foot journey took her over half an hour. The bloody arm hanging over the armrest snagged them.

She had to overcome her repulsion and touch it, moving it aside. She got blood on her hands. It was sticky. She whimpered with horror, but clamped her trembling lower lip between her teeth and continued tugging the man down the aisle—one struggling, agonizing inch at a time.

It struck her suddenly that whatever his injury, she might be doing it more harm than good by moving him. But she'd come this far; she wouldn't stop now. Setting a goal and achieving it seemed very important, if for no other reason than to prove she wasn't helpless. She had decided to get him outside, and that's what she was going to do if it killed her.

Which it very well might, she thought several minutes later. She had moved him as far forward as possible. Occasionally he groaned, but otherwise he showed no signs of coming around. Leaving him momentarily, she climbed through the branches of the pine tree. The entire left side of the fuselage had been virtually ripped off, so it would be a matter of dragging him through the branches of the tree. Using her bare hands, she broke off as many of the smaller branches as she could before returning to the man.

It took her five minutes just to turn him around so she could clasp him beneath the arms. Then, backing through the narrow, spiky tunnel she had cleared, she pulled him along with her. Pine needles pricked her face. The rough bark scraped her hands. But thankfully her heavy clothing protected most of her skin.

Her breathing became labored as she struggled. She considered pausing to rest, but was afraid that she would never build up enough momentum to start again. Her burden was moaning almost constantly, now. She knew he must be in agony, but she couldn't stop or he might lapse into deeper unconsciousness.

At last she felt cold air on her cheeks. She pulled her head free of the last branch and stepped out into the open. Taking a few stumbling steps backward, she pulled the man the remainder of the way, until he, too, was clear. Exhausted beyond belief, the muscles of her arms and back and legs burning from exertion, she plopped down hard on her bottom. The man's head fell into her lap.

Bracing herself on her hands and tilting her head toward the sky, she stayed that way until she had regained her breath. For the first time, while drawing the bitingly cold air into her lungs, she thought that it might be good to still be alive. She thanked God that she was. And thanked Him, too, for the other life He'd spared.

She looked down at the man and saw the bump for the first time. He was sporting a classic goose egg on the side of his temple. No doubt it had caused his unconsciousness. Heaving his shoulders up high enough to get her legs out from under him, she crawled around to his side and began unbuttoning his bulky coat. She prayed that she wouldn't uncover a mortal wound. She didn't. Only the plaid flannel shirt that no game hunter would be without. There were no traces of blood on it. From the turtleneck collar of his undershirt to the tops of his laced boots, she could find no sign of serious bleeding.

Expelling a gusty breath of relief, she bent over him and lightly slapped his cheeks again. She guessed him to be around forty, but the years hadn't been easy ones. His longish, wavy hair was saddle brown. So was his mustache. But it and his heavy eyebrows had strands of blond. His skin was sunburned, but not recently; it was a baked-on, year-round sunburn. There was a tracery of fine lines at the corners of his eyes. His mouth was wide and thin, the lower lip only slightly fuller than the upper.

This rugged face didn't belong in an office; he spent

a good deal of time outdoors. It was an agreeable face, if not a classically handsome one. There was a hardness to it, an uncompromising unapproachability that she had also sensed in his personality.

She wondered uneasily what he would think when he regained consciousness and found himself alone in the wilderness with her. She didn't have long to wait to find out. Moments later, his eyelids flickered, then opened.

Eyes as flinty gray as the sky overhead focused on her. They closed, then opened again. She wanted to speak, but trepidation held her back. The first word to cross his lips was unspeakably vulgar. She flinched, but attributed the foul language to his pain. Again he closed his eyes and waited several seconds before opening them.

Then he said, "We crashed." She nodded. "How long ago?"

"I'm not sure." Her teeth were chattering. It wasn't that cold, so it must have been from fear. Of him? Why? "An hour, maybe."

Grunting with pain, he covered the lump on the side of his head with one hand and levered himself up, using the other hand as a prop. She moved aside so he could sit up straight. "What about everybody else?"

"They're all dead."

He tried to come up on one knee and swayed dizzily. She reflexively extended a helping hand, but he shrugged it off. "Are you sure?"

"Sure they're dead? Yes. I mean, I think so."

He turned his head and stared at her balefully. "Did you check their pulses?"

She changed her mind about his eyes. They weren't like the sky at all. They were colder and much more foreboding. "No, I didn't check," she admitted contritely.

He nailed her with that judgmental stare for several

seconds, then, with a great deal of difficulty, pulled himself to his feet. Using the tree behind him for support, he struggled to stand up and regain his equilibrium.

"How...how do you feel?"

"Like I'm going to puke."

One thing about him, he didn't mince words. "Maybe you should lie back down."

"No doubt I should."

"Well?"

Still holding his head in one hand, he raised it and looked at her. "Are you volunteering to go in there and check their pulses?" He watched the faint color in her cheeks fade and gave her a twisted smile of ridicule. "That's what I thought."

"I got *you* out, didn't I?"

"Yeah," he said dryly, "you got me out."

She didn't expect him to kiss her hands for saving his life, but a simple thank-you would have been nice. "You're an ungrateful—"

"Save it," he said.

She watched him lever himself away from the tree and stagger toward the demolished aircraft, pushing aside the branches of the tree with much more strength than she could have garnered in a month.

Sinking down onto the marshy ground, she rested her head on her raised knees, tempted to cry. She could hear him moving about in the cabin. When she raised her head and looked, she saw him through the missing windshield of the detached cockpit. He was emotionlessly moving his hands over the bodies of the pilots.

Minutes later, he thrashed his way through the fallen ~~ee~~. "You were right. They're all dead."

~~did~~ he expect her to respond? Nah-nah-nah? He ~~~~ a white first-aid box onto the ground and knelt beside it. He took out a bottle of aspirin and tossed three of them down his throat, swallowing them dry. "Come here," he ordered her rudely. She scooted forward and he handed her a flashlight. "Shine that directly into my eyes, one at a time, and tell me what happens."

She switched on the flashlight. The glass over the bulb was cracked, but it still worked. She shone the light directly into his right eye, then the left. "The pupils contract."

He took the flashlight away from her and clicked it off. "Good. No concussion. Just a rotten headache. You okay?"

"I think so."

He looked at her skeptically, but nodded.

"My name's Rusty Carlson," she said politely.

He barked a short laugh. His eyes moved up to take in her hair. "Rusty, huh?"

"Yes, Rusty," she replied testily.

"Figures."

The man had the manners of a pig. "Do you have a name?"

"Yeah, I've got a name. Cooper Landry. But this isn't a garden party so forgive me if I don't tip my hat and say, 'Pleased to meet you.'"

For two lone survivors of a disastrous plane crash, they were off to a bad beginning. Right now Rusty wanted to be comforted, reassured that she was alive and would go on living. All she'd gotten from him was scorn, which was unwarranted.

"What's with you?" she demanded angrily. "You act as though the crash was my fault."

"Maybe it was."

She gasped with incredulity. "What? I was hardly responsible for the storm."

"No, but if you hadn't dragged out that emotional, tearful goodbye to your sugar daddy, we might have beat it. What made you decide to leave ahead of him—the two of you have a lovers' spat?"

"None of your damned business," she said through teeth that had been straightened to perfection by an expensive orthodontist.

His expression didn't alter. "And you had no business being in a place like that—" his eyes roved over her "—being the kind of woman you are."

"What kind of woman is that?"

"Drop it. Let's just say that I'd be better off without you."

Having said that, he slid a lethal-looking hunting knife from the leather scabbard attached to his belt. Rusty wondered if he was going to cut her throat with it and rid himself of the inconvenience she posed. Instead, he turned and began hacking at the smaller branches of the tree, cutting a cleaner path to make the fuselage more accessible.

"What are you going to do?"

"I have to get them out."

"The…the others? Why?"

"Unless you want to be roommates with them."

"You're going to bury them?"

"That's the idea. Got a better one?"

No, of course she didn't, so she said nothing.

Cooper Landry hacked his way through the tree until only the major branches were left. They were easier to step around and over.

Rusty, making herself useful by dragging aside the branches as he cut them, asked, "We're staying here then?"

"For the time being, yeah." Having cleared a path of

sorts, he stepped into the fuselage and signaled her forward. "Grab his boots, will ya?"

She stared down at the dead man's boots. She couldn't do this. Nothing in her life had prepared her for this. He couldn't expect her to do something so grotesque.

But glancing up at him and meeting those implacable gray eyes, she knew that he did expect it of her and expected it of her without an argument.

One by one they removed the bodies from the aircraft. He did most of the work; Rusty lent him a hand when he asked for it. The only way she could do it was to detach her mind from the grisly task. She'd lost her mother when she was a teenager. Two years ago her brother had died. But in both instances, she'd seen them when they were laid out in a satin-lined casket surrounded by soft lighting, organ music, and flowers. Death had seemed unreal. Even the bodies of her mother and brother weren't real to her, but identical replicas of the people she had loved, mannequins created in their images by the mortician.

These bodies were real.

She mechanically obeyed the terse commands this Cooper Landry issued in a voice without feeling or inflection. He must be a robot, she decided. He revealed no emotion whatsoever as he dragged the bodies to the common grave that he'd been able to dig using his knife and the small hatchet he found in a toolbox beneath the pilot's seat. He piled stones over the shallow grave when he was finished.

"Shouldn't we say something?" Rusty stared down at the barbaric pile of colorless stones, put there to protect the bodies of the five men from scavenging animals.

"Say something? Like what?"

"Like a scripture. A prayer."

He shrugged negligently as he cleaned the blade of

his knife. "I don't know any scriptures. And my prayers ran out a long time ago." Turning his back on the grave, he stamped back toward the airplane.

Rusty mouthed a hasty prayer before turning to follow him. More than anything, she feared being left alone again. If she let the man out of her sight, he might desert her.

That was unlikely, however. At least not right away. He was reeling with fatigue and on the verge of fainting. "Why don't you lie down and rest?" she suggested. Her strength had deserted her long ago. She was running only on adrenaline now.

"Because night's coming on fast," he said. "We've got to remove the seats of the plane so we'll have room to stretch out in there. Otherwise you might have to spend a night in the great outdoors for the first time in your life." He sarcastically added the last as an afterthought before reentering the airplane. Moments later, Rusty heard him cursing viciously. He came out, his brows drawn together in a fierce scowl.

"What's the matter?"

He held his hand up in front of her face. It was wet. "Fuel."

"Fuel?"

"*Flammable* fuel," he said, impatient with her ignorance. "We can't stay in there. One spark and we'll be blown to China."

"Then don't build a fire."

He glared at her. "Once it gets dark, you'll want a fire," he said scornfully. "Besides, all it would take is a spark from anything. One piece of metal could scrape against another and we'd be history."

"What do we do?"

"We take what we can and move."

"I thought it was always best to stay with the airplane. I heard or read that once. Search parties will be looking for a downed plane. How will they find us if we leave the crash site?"

He cocked his head arrogantly. "You want to stay? Fine, stay. I'm going. But I'd better warn you that I don't think there's any water near here. The first thing I'm going to do in the morning is look for water."

His know-it-all attitude was insufferable. "How do you know there's no water?"

"No animal tracks around. I suppose you could exist on rainwater for as long as it held out, but who knows how long that will be."

When and how had he noticed that there were no animal tracks around? She hadn't even thought to look. In fact, having no water was almost as frightening as having to cope with wild animals to get it. Search for water? How did one go about that? Wild animals? How would she defend herself if one attacked?

She'd die without him. After several moments of deliberation, that was the grim conclusion she reached. She had no choice but to go along with whatever survival tactics he knew and be grateful that he was there to implement them.

Swallowing her pride, she said, "All right, I'll go with you." He didn't even glance up or otherwise acknowledge her. She had no way of knowing whether he was glad or sorry over her decision. By all appearances, he was indifferent. He was already making a pile of things he'd salvaged from the wreckage. Determined not to be ignored, Rusty knelt down beside him. "What can I do to help?"

He nodded toward the luggage compartment of the aircraft. "Go through the luggage. Everybody's. Take whatever might come in handy later." He handed her several tiny suitcase keys, which he had obviously taken off the bodies before he buried them.

She glanced warily at the suitcases. Some had already popped open as a result of the crash. The victims' personal belongings lay strewn on the damp ground. "Isn't that…violating their privacy? Their families might resent—"

He spun around so suddenly that she nearly toppled over backward. "Will you grow up and face facts?" He grabbed her by the shoulders and shook her. "Look around. Do you know what our chances are of coming out of this alive? I'll tell you: Nil. But before I go down, I'm going to fight like hell to stay alive. It's a habit I have."

His face moved closer to hers. "This isn't a Girl Scout outing gone awry; this is survival, lady. Etiquette and propriety be damned. If you tag along with me, you'll do what I tell you to, when I tell you to. Got that? And there won't be any time to spend on sentiment. Don't waste tears on those who didn't make it. They're gone and there's not a damn thing we can do about it. Now, move your butt and get busy doing what I told you to do."

He shoved her away from him and began collecting pelts that the hunters had been taking home as trophies. There was mostly caribou, but also white wolf, beaver, and one small mink.

Holding back bitter tears of mortification and accumulated distress, Rusty bent over the suitcases and began sorting through their contents as she'd been instructed. She wanted to strike out at him. She wanted to collapse in a heap and bawl her eyes out. But she wouldn't give him the satisfaction of seeing her do either. Nor would she provide him with an excuse to leave her behind; he would probably grab at the flimsiest.

A half-hour later she carried her findings and added

them to the pile of articles he had gathered. Apparently
he approved of her selection, which included two flasks
of liquor. She couldn't identify it by the smell, but Cooper
wasn't particular. He seemed to enjoy the healthy drink
he took from one of the flasks. She watched his Adam's
apple bob up and down as he swallowed. He had a strong
neck, and a solid, square jaw. Typical, she thought peevishly, of all stubborn mules.

He recapped the flask and tossed it down along with
the books of matches, a travel sewing kit, and the extra
clothing she had accumulated. He didn't remark on how
well she'd done. Instead he nodded down at the small
suitcase she was carrying. "What's that?"

"That's mine."

"That's not what I asked."

He yanked the suitcase from her hand and opened it.
His large hands violated her neat stacks of pastel silk
thermal underwear, nightgowns, and assorted lingerie.
He pulled one set of leggings through the circle he made
of his index finger and thumb. His gray eyes met hers.
"Silk?" Coldly, she stared back at him without answering. His grin was downright dirty. It insinuated things
she didn't even want to guess at. "Very nice."

Then his grin disappeared beneath his mustache and
he tossed the garment at her. "Take two sets of long johns.
A couple pairs of socks. A cap. Gloves. This coat," he
added, piling a ski jacket atop the other garments he'd
selected. "One extra pair of britches. A couple of sweat-
ers." He opened the zippered, plastic-lined travel bag
she'd packed her cosmetics and toiletries in.

"I need all of that," she said quickly.

"Not where we're going you don't." He rifled through
her cosmetics, heedlessly tossing a fortune's worth of
beauty-enhancing creams and makeup into the rotting,

wet leaves. "A hairbrush, toothpaste and toothbrush, soap. That's it. And, just because I'm merciful, these." He handed her a box of tampons.

She snatched it out of his hands and crammed it back into the cosmetic bag along with the other few items he had allowed her.

Again he grinned. The juxtaposition of his white teeth and wide mustache made him look positively wicked. "You think I'm a real son of a bitch, don't you? You're just too nice to say so."

"No, I'm not." Her russet brown eyes flashed hotly. "I think you're a real son of a bitch."

His smile merely deepened. "It's only gonna get worse before it gets better." He stood up, glancing worriedly at the darkening sky. "Come on. We'd better get going."

As soon as he turned his back, Rusty slipped a colorless lip gloss, a bottle of shampoo and a razor into the bag. He might not need to shave before they reached civilization, but she was sure she would.

She jumped guiltily when he turned back and asked her, "Do you know how to shoot one of these?" He held up a hunting rifle.

Rusty shook her head no. Only yesterday she'd seen a beautiful Dall ram being brought down with a rifle just like that. It was a distasteful memory. Rather than celebrating the kill, her sympathies had been with the slain animal.

"I was afraid of that," Cooper muttered. "But you can carry it anyway." He hooked the heavy rifle over her shoulder by its leather strap and placed another, presumably his own, over his shoulder. He shoved a fearsome-looking pistol into his waistband. Catching her wary glance he said, "It's a flare gun. I found it in the cockpit. Keep your ears open for search planes."

By seaming up the neck of a sweater with a shoelace, he had fashioned a backpack out of it. He tied it around her neck by the sleeves. "Okay," he said, giving her a cursory inspection, "let's go."

Rusty cast one last sad, apprehensive look at the wreckage of the airplane, then struck out after him. His broad back made an easy target to follow. She found that by keeping her eyes trained on a spot directly between his shoulder blades, she was able to put herself into a semitrance and ward off her memory of the bodies they had left behind. She wanted to lapse into forgetfulness.

She plodded on, losing energy with each step. Her strength seemed to be seeping out of her with alarming rapidity. She didn't know how far they had gone, but it couldn't have been very far before it seemed impossible for her to put one foot in front of the other. Her legs were trembling with fatigue. She no longer swatted aside the branches that backlashed, but indifferently let them slap into her.

Cooper's image grew blurry, then began wavering in front of her like a ghost. The trees all seemed to have tentacles that tried to catch her clothes, tear at her hair, ensnare her ankles, impede her in any way possible. Stumbling, she glanced down at the ground and was amazed to see that it was rushing up to meet her. How extraordinary, she thought.

Instinctively, she grasped the nearest branch to break her fall and called out weakly, "Coo...Cooper."

She landed hard, but it was a blessed relief to lie on the cool ground, damp and soggy as it was. The leaf mold seemed like a compress against her cheek. It was a luxury to let her eyes close.

Cooper murmured a curse as he shrugged off his backpack and let the strap of the rifle slide down his arm.

Roughly, he rolled her over onto her back and pried her eyelids open with his thumbs. She gazed up at him, having no idea that her face was as pale as death. Even her lips were as gray as the clouds overhead.

"I'm sorry to hold you back." She was vaguely surprised that her voice sounded so faint. She could feel her lips moving, but she wasn't sure she had actually spoken aloud. It seemed imperative to apologize for detaining him and being a nuisance in general. "I've got to rest for just a minute."

"Yeah, yeah, that's fine, uh, Rusty. You rest." He was working at the hook and eye buried deep in the fox-fur collar of her coat. "Do you hurt anywhere?"

"Hurt? No. Why?"

"Nothing." He shoved open her coat and plunged his hands inside. He slipped them beneath her sweater and began carefully pressing his fingers against her abdomen. Was this proper? she thought fuzzily. "You might be bleeding somewhere and don't know it."

His words served to clarify everything. "Internally?" Panicked, she struggled to sit up.

"I don't know. I don't— Hold it!" With a sudden flick of his hands, he flipped back the front panels of her full-length coat. His breath whistled through his teeth. Rusty levered herself up on her elbows to see what had caused him to frown so ferociously.

The right leg of her trousers was soaked with bright red blood. It had also made a sponge of her wool sock and run over her leather hiking boot.

"When did you do this?" His eyes, razor sharp, moved up to hers. "What happened?"

Dismayed, she looked at Cooper and wordlessly shook her head.

"Why didn't you tell me you were hurt?"

"I didn't know," she said weakly.

He slipped his knife from its scabbard. Pinching up the blood-soaked hem of her trousers, he slid the knife into the crease and jerked it upward. With one heart-stopping stroke, it cut straight up her pants leg, neatly slicing the fabric all the way from her hem to the elastic leg of her underpants. Shocked and fearful, she sucked in her breath.

Cooper, gazing down at her leg, expelled a long, defeated breath. "Hell."

Two

Rusty's head began to buzz. She felt nauseous. Her earlobes were throbbing and her throat was on fire. Each individual hair follicle on her head felt like a pinprick. The pads of her fingers and toes were tingling. She'd fainted once after having a root canal. She knew the symptoms.

But, damn, did they have to afflict her here? In front of him?

"Easy, easy." He grasped her shoulders and lowered her to the ground. "You don't remember hurting yourself?" She shook her head dumbly. "Must have happened when we crashed."

"I didn't feel any pain."

"You were too shocked. How does it feel now?"

Only then did she become aware of the pain. "Not bad." His eyes probed hers for the truth. "Really, it's not that bad. I've bled a lot, though, haven't I?"

"Yeah." Grim-faced, he rummaged through the first-aid kit. "I've got to sponge up the blood so I can see where it's coming from."

He tore into the backpack she'd been carrying and selected a soft cotton undershirt to swab up the blood. She felt the pressure of his hands, but little else as she gazed up through the branches of the trees overhead. Maybe she'd been premature to thank God for being alive. She might bleed to death lying here on the ground. And there wouldn't be anything Cooper or she could do about it. In fact, he would probably be glad to get rid of her.

His soft curse roused her from her macabre musings. She tilted her head up and looked down at her injured leg. Along her shinbone a gash ran from just below her knee to just above her sock. She could see flesh, muscle. It was sickening. She whimpered.

"Lie down, dammit."

Weakly, Rusty obeyed the emphatic order. "How could that happen without my feeling it?"

"Probably split like a tomato skin the moment of impact."

"Can you do anything?"

"Clean it with peroxide." He opened the brown opaque plastic bottle he'd found in the first-aid kit and soaked the sleeve of the T-shirt with the peroxide.

"Is it going to hurt?"

"Probably."

Ignoring her tearful, frightened eyes, he dabbed at the wound with the peroxide. Rusty clamped her lower lip with her teeth to keep from crying out, but her face twisted with anguish. Actually, the thought of the peroxide bubbling in the gash was as bad as the pain.

"Breathe through your mouth if you feel like vomiting," he told her tonelessly. "I'm almost finished."

She squeezed her eyes shut and didn't open them until she heard the sound of ripping cloth. He was tearing another T-shirt into strips. One by one he wrapped them around her calf, binding her lower leg tightly.

"That'll have to do for now," he said, more to himself than to her. Picking up his knife again, he said, "Raise your hips." She did, avoiding his eyes. He cut the leg of her trousers from around her upper thigh. His hands worked beneath her thighs and between them. His callused knuckles brushed against her smooth, warm skin, but she needn't have felt any embarrassment. He could have been cutting up a steak for all the emotion he showed.

"You damn sure can't walk."

"I can!" Rusty insisted frantically.

She was afraid that he would go off without her. He was standing over her, feet widespread, looking around. His brow was beetled and beneath his mustache she could tell that he was gnawing on the inside of his cheek as though giving something careful consideration.

Was he weighing his options? Deciding whether or not to desert her? Or maybe he was thinking of killing her quickly and mercifully instead of letting her die of her wound.

Finally he bent down and, cupping her armpits in his palms, lifted her into a sitting position. "Take off your coat and put on that ski jacket."

Without an argument, she let the fur coat slide from her shoulders. Using the hatchet he'd brought along, Cooper hacked down three saplings and stripped them of their branches. Silently Rusty watched as he fashioned them into an H, only placing the crossbar higher than normal. He bound the intersections with rawhide tongs, which he'd taken from the boots of the men they'd buried. Then he took her fur coat and ran a sleeve over each of the tops of the two longer poles. Rusty flinched when he stabbed through the fur and satin lining, gouging out a hole in the bottom of her precious fox coat.

He glanced up at her. "What's the matter?"

She swallowed, realizing that he was testing her. "Nothing. The coat was a gift, that's all."

He watched her for a few seconds more before making a similar hole in the other side. He then ran the poles through the holes. The finished product was a crude travois. No self-respecting American Indian would have claimed it, but Rusty was impressed with his ingenuity and skill. And vastly relieved that he obviously didn't plan to leave her behind or otherwise dispose of her.

He laid the rough contraption on the ground. Turning to her, he caught her under the knees and behind the back and lifted her. He laid her on the soft fur, then piled several pelts on top of her.

"I didn't see any animal up there with a hide that looked like this," she said, running her hand over a skin of short, fine wool.

"Umingmak."

"Pardon?"

"That's what the Inuit called the musk-ox. Means 'the bearded one.' It wasn't my kill; I just bought the pelt. It's very warm." He tucked the wool around her and threw another pelt on top of that. "It's up to you to stay on and keep covered."

Standing, he wiped perspiration off his brow with the back of his hand. He winced when he grazed the bump on his temple. Rusty would have gone to bed for a week if she had sustained a blow like that; it must be killing him.

"Thank you, Cooper," she said softly.

He froze, glanced down at her, nodded quickly, then turned and began gathering up their paraphernalia. He tossed both backpacks onto her lap, along with both rifles. "Hang on to those, too, will you?"

"Where are we going?"

"Southeast," was his succinct reply.

"Why?"

"Sooner or later, we'll bump into an outpost of civilization."

"Oh." She dreaded moving, anticipating that the journey wasn't going to be a joyride. "May I have an aspirin please?"

He unpocketed the plastic bottle and shook two aspirin tablets into her hands.

"I can't take them without water."

He made an impatient scoffing sound. "It's either dry or with brandy."

"Brandy, please."

He passed her one of the flasks, watching her closely. She bravely put the spout to her mouth and took a hefty swallow to wash down the aspirin tablets. She choked and sputtered. Tears filled her eyes, but with dignity and poise she returned the flask to him. "Thank you."

His narrow lips twitched with the need to smile. "You might not have any common sense, but you've got guts, lady."

And that, she thought, was as close to a compliment as she was ever likely to get from Cooper Landry. He secured the trunks of the saplings beneath his arms and moved forward, dragging the travois behind him. After having gone only a few teeth-jarring, butt-bruising yards, Rusty realized that she wasn't going to be much better off in the travois than she would have been walking. It required all her concentration just to keep from sliding off. Her bottom would be black and blue with bruises—legacies of the rocks it encountered every grueling step of the way. She dared not even think of the satin lining of her coat being ripped to shreds by the forest debris as it was hauled over the rough ground.

It grew progressively darker and colder. A light precipitation began—snow grains she thought the meteorologists called the stuff, pellets of ice no larger than grains of salt. Her injured leg began to ache, but she would have bitten her tongue in two before she complained. She could hear Cooper's labored breathing. He wasn't having an easy time of it either. If it weren't for her, he could cover three times the distance in the same amount of time.

Darkness closed in suddenly, making it perilous for them to continue over the unfamiliar terrain. He stopped in the next clearing he came to and dropped the poles of the travois. "How're you doing?"

She didn't think about how hungry, thirsty, and uncomfortable she was. She said, "Fine."

"Yeah, sure. How are you really?" He knelt down and whipped off the covering of furs. Her bandage was soaked with fresh blood. He quickly replaced the furs. "We'd better stop for the night. Now that the sun has set, I can't tell which direction I'm going in."

He was lying, only saying that to make her feel better. Rusty knew that he would keep going if it weren't for her. It was doubtful that he was afraid of the dark or that inclement weather would faze him. Even though he'd been dragging her for hours, he appeared to have enough stamina to go at least another two.

He circled the clearing and began shoveling pine needles into a pile. He spread the pelts over them and came back for Rusty.

"Cooper?"

"Hmm?" He grunted with the effort of lifting her off the travois.

"I have to go to the bathroom."

She couldn't see him clearly in the darkness, but she could feel his shocked stare. Embarrassed beyond belief, she kept her head down. "Okay," he replied after a moment. "Will your leg support you while—"

"Yes, I think so," she said in a rush.

He carried her to the edge of the clearing and gently lowered her to stand on her left leg. "Brace yourself against the tree," he instructed gruffly. "Call me when you're done."

It was much more difficult than she had expected it to be. By the time she had refastened what was left of her trousers, she was shaking with weakness and her teeth were chattering with cold. "All right, I'm finished."

Cooper materialized out of the darkness and lifted her into his arms again. She would never have thought a bed of pine needles and animal pelts could have felt so good, but she sighed with relief when he laid her on it and she was able to relax.

Cooper packed the furs around her. "I'll build a fire. It won't be much of one. There's not enough dry wood. But it'll be better than nothing and might help ward off visitors."

Rusty shivered and pulled the furs over her head, as much to protect her from the thought of wild animals as the icy precipitation that continued to dust the ground. But the increasing pain in her leg wouldn't let her doze. She grew restless and finally peeped out from beneath the covering. Cooper had succeeded in building a sputtering, smoky fire. He'd lined the shallow bowl he'd scooped out of the ground with rocks to keep it from igniting her bed.

He glanced over at her and, unzipping one of the many pockets in his coat, took something out and tossed it to her. She caught it one-handed. "What is it?"

"Granola bar."

At the thought of food, her stomach rumbled noisily. She ripped open the foil wrapper, ready to stuff the whole bar into her mouth. Before she did, she got hold of herself and paused. "You...you don't have to share with me," she said in a small voice. "It's yours and you might need it later."

His gray eyes looked as hard and cold as gunmetal when he turned his head. "It isn't mine. I found it in a coat pocket that belonged to one of the others."

He seemed to take brutal delight in telling her that, implying that if the granola bar were his, he'd think twice before sharing it with her.

Whatever his intention, he had spoiled it for her. The bar tasted like sawdust in her mouth; she chewed and swallowed it mechanically. The tastelessness was partially due to her thirst. As though reading her mind, Cooper said, "If we don't find water tomorrow, we're in trouble."

"Do you think we will?"

"I don't know."

She lay amid the furs contemplatively. "Why do you think the plane crashed?"

"I don't know. A combination of things, I guess."

"Do you have any idea where we are?"

"No. I might have a general idea if it hadn't been for the storm."

"You think we were off course?"

"Yes. But I don't know how far."

She rested her cheek against her hand and stared into the feeble flame that was struggling for life. "Had you ever been to Great Bear Lake before?"

"Once."

"When?"

"Several years ago."

"Do you do a lot of hunting?"

"Some."

He wasn't exactly an orator, was he? She wanted to draw him into conversation to keep her mind off the pain in her leg. "Do you think they'll find us?"

"Maybe."

"When?"

"What do you think I am, a damned encyclopedia?" His shout bounced around the ring of trees surrounding them. He came to his feet abruptly. "Stop asking me so many questions. I don't have the answers."

"I just want to know," she cried tearfully.

"Well, so do I. But I don't. I'd say the chances of them finding us are extremely good if the plane was still on the flight plan and extremely remote if it was too far off, okay? Now, shut up about it."

Rusty lapsed into wounded silence. Cooper prowled the clearing in search of dry tinder. He added a few sticks to the fire before moving toward her. "Better let me tend to your leg."

He brusquely threw the covers back. The fire shed meager light onto the bloody bandage. Expertly wielding the hunting knife, he cut through the knots he'd tied earlier and began unwinding the stained cloth. "Does it hurt?"

"Yes."

"Well, it has every right to," he said grimly as he gazed down at the wound. His expression wasn't very encouraging.

While she held the flashlight for him, he soaked the gash with peroxide again and wrapped it in fresh bandaging. By the time he had finished, tears were stinging her eyes and her lips were blotchy from biting them, but she hadn't cried out once. "Where'd you learn to bandage so well?"

"Nam." His answer was curt, indicating that the subject was closed. "Here, take two more aspirin." He passed her the bottle after shaking out two for himself. He hadn't complained, but his head must have felt as though it were splitting in two. "And drink some more brandy. At least two swallows. I think that by morning, you're going to need it."

"Why?"

"Your leg. Tomorrow will probably be the worst day. After that, maybe it'll start to get better."

"What if it doesn't?"

He said nothing; he didn't have to.

With trembling hands, Rusty held the flask of brandy to her lips and took an occasional sip from it. Now that the dry kindling had caught, Cooper stacked more wood on the fire. But it wasn't burning hot enough for him to take off his coat, which he surprised her by doing. He took off his boots, too, and told her to do the same. Then, making a bundle of the coats and boots, he stuffed them down between the furs.

"What's that for?" Her feet were already getting cold.

"If we sweat in our boots and it turns colder, we'll get frostbite. Scoot over."

She stared up at him apprehensively. "Huh?"

Sighing impatiently, he crawled in with her, forcing her to move over and allow him room beneath the pile of furs. Alarmed, Rusty exclaimed, "What are you doing?"

"Going to sleep. If you'll shut up, that is."

"Here?"

"Accommodations with separate beds were unavailable."

"You can't—"

"Relax, Miss... What was it again?"

"Carlson."

"Yeah, Miss Carlson. Our combined body heat will

help keep us warm." He snuggled close to her and pulled the furs up over their heads, effectively cocooning them inside. "Turn on your side, away from me."

"Go to hell."

She could almost hear him mentally counting to ten. "Look, I don't want to freeze. And I don't look forward to digging another grave to bury you in, either, so just do as I say. Now."

He must have been an officer in Vietnam, she thought petulantly as she rolled on to her side. He put his arm around her waist and drew her back against him, until they were lying together spoon fashion. She could scarcely breathe. "Is this really necessary?"

"Yes."

"I won't move away. There's nowhere to go. You don't have to keep your arm there."

"You surprise me. I thought you'd like this." He pressed against her stomach with the palm of his hand. "You're a real looker. Don't you expect men to get all hot and bothered when they're around you?"

"Let go of me."

"All that long hair, its unusual color."

"Shut up!"

"You're proud of your round little butt and perky tits, aren't you? I'm sure most men find you irresistible. That copilot sure did. He was salivating after you like a Doberman over a bitch in heat, almost stumbling over his tongue."

"I don't know what you're talking about."

He stroked her stomach. "Oh, yes, you do. You must have enjoyed stunning all those men on the plane into speechlessness when you climbed aboard with your fur collar pulled up, brushing against your flushed cheeks and sexy mouth."

"Why are you doing this?" she sobbed.

He cursed and when he spoke again, his voice wasn't lilting and teasing. It was weary. "So you'll rest assured that I'm not going to take advantage of you during the night. Redheads have never been my preference. Besides, your body is still warm from your sugar daddy's bed. All things considered, your virtue is safe with me."

She sniffed back tears of humiliation. "You're cruel and vulgar."

He laughed. "Now you sound offended that I'm not tempted to rape you. Make up your mind. If you have a hankering for sex tonight, I can oblige you. My body isn't as particular as my head. After all, it's awfully dark in here. And you know what they say about cats in the dark. But personally, I prefer safer, more comfortable surroundings to screw in. So just go to sleep, will you?"

Rusty grit her teeth in outrage. She held her body rigid and put a barrier between them, if not physically, then mentally. She tried to ignore his body heat, which permeated her clothing, and his breath that drifted over her neck each time he exhaled, and the latent power in the thighs that conformed to the backs of hers. Gradually, and with the help of the brandy she'd drunk, she relaxed. Eventually she dozed.

It was her own moan that woke her up. Her leg was throbbing painfully.

"What is it?"

Cooper's voice was gruff, but Rusty didn't think it was because he'd been roused from a deep sleep. Intuitively she knew that he had been lying there awake. "Nothing."

"Tell me. What's the matter? Your leg?"

"Yes."

"Is it bleeding again?"

"I don't think so. It's doesn't feel wet. It just hurts."

"Drink some more brandy." He angled himself away from her and reached for the flask of brandy, which he'd brought into the fur cocoon with them.

"I'm already woozy."

"Good. It's working." He poked her lips with the uncapped flask and tipped it forward. She either had to drink or drown.

The potent liquor burned a fiery path down her middle. At the very least, it took her mind off her painful wound for a few seconds. "Thanks."

"Open your legs."

"Pardon?"

"Open your legs."

"How much brandy have you had, Mr. Landry?"

"Do it."

"Why?"

"So I can get mine between them."

Without giving her another chance to argue, he slid his hand between her thighs and raised her injured leg. He wedged his knees between hers, then gently lowered her right leg to rest on top of his. "There. Keeping it elevated will help relieve the pressure. It'll also keep me from jostling it in the night."

She was too flabbergasted to fall back to sleep immediately; too uncomfortably aware of his nearness. And there was something else keeping her awake: a nagging guilt.

"Cooper, did you know any of the other men?"

"Those on board the plane? No."

"The men in the front two seats were brothers. While we were weighing our luggage, I heard them talking about getting their families together for Thanksgiving in a few weeks. They were going to show them the slides they'd taken this week."

"Don't think about it."

"I can't help it."

"Yes, you can."

"No, I can't. I keep asking myself why I'm alive. Why was I allowed to live? It doesn't make any sense."

"It doesn't have to make sense," he said bitterly. "That's just the way it *is*. It was their time, that's all. It's over, forgotten."

"Not forgotten."

"Force it out of your mind."

"Is that what you did?"

"Yes."

She shuddered. "How can you be so unfeeling about another human life?"

"Practice."

The word affected her like a hard slap on the cheek. It had been cruelly delivered to shut her up, and it did. But it didn't stop her from thinking. She wondered how many of his buddies Cooper had seen killed in Vietnam. Dozens? Scores? Hundreds? Still, she couldn't imagine ever becoming inured to death.

She'd had practice dealing with it, but not to the extent that he apparently had. It wasn't something she could block out, dismiss, by an act of will. When she thought about her losses, she still ached.

"My mother died of a stroke," she told him quietly. "Her death was almost a relief. She would have been severely incapacitated. I had a week to prepare myself for it. But my brother's death was sudden." Cooper wouldn't care to hear about any of this, but she wanted to talk about it.

"Brother?"

"Jeff. He was killed in a car wreck two years ago."

"No other family?"

"Only my father." She drew a gentle breath. "He was the man I was with at the lodge. The one I said goodbye to. Not a sugar daddy. Not a lover. My father."

She waited for an apology, but it never came. If his body hadn't been so tense, she might have thought he'd fallen asleep.

Finally he broke the silence by asking, "What is your father going to think when he's notified about the crash?"

"Oh, my God!" Reflexively, she clutched Cooper's hand where it still rested against her stomach. "I hadn't thought of that."

She could imagine her father's despair when he heard the news. He'd lost his wife. Then his son. Now his daughter. He would be disconsolate. Rusty couldn't bear to think of the suffering he would go through, the hell of uncertainty, of not knowing what had happened to her. Hopefully, as much for her father's sake as her own, they would be rescued soon.

"The guy looked like a real mover and shaker to me," Cooper said. "He'll ride the authorities until we're found."

"You're right. Father won't give up until he knows what happened to me."

Rusty was certain of that. Her father was a powerful man. He was dynamic and had both the talent and the means to get things done. His reputation and money could cut through miles of red tape. Knowing that he'd leave no stone unturned until she was rescued gave her an optimistic thread to cling to.

She was also surprised to discover that Cooper hadn't been as withdrawn and impervious as he had appeared to be. Before they boarded the plane, he had kept to himself. He hadn't mingled with the other passengers. But he'd noticed everything. Apparently her companion was an observant student of human nature.

Nature was having its way with him right now. While she'd been talking, Rusty became nervously aware of his sex snuggled solidly against her bottom. She blurted, "Are you married?"

"No."

"Ever?"

"No."

"Involved?"

"Look, I get my share of sex, okay? And I know why you're suddenly so curious. Believe me, I feel it too. But I can't do anything to help it. Well, actually I can, but as we discussed earlier, that isn't a very workable solution under the circumstances. The alternatives that come readily to mind would embarrass us both I'm afraid."

Rusty's cheeks grew hot and rosy. "I wish you wouldn't."

"What?"

"Talk like that."

"How?"

"You know. Dirty."

"You just left a big game hunting lodge. Didn't you intercept a few dirty jokes? Overhear some lewd comments? I thought you'd be used to bawdy language by now."

"Well, I'm not. And for your information, I went on that hunting trip for my father's sake. I didn't particularly enjoy myself."

"He forced you to go?"

"Of course not."

"Coerced you to? In exchange for that fur coat, maybe?"

"No," she grated with irritation. "The trip was my idea. I suggested that we take it together."

"And you randomly chose the Northwest Territories?

Why not Hawaii? Or St. Moritz? I can think of a thousand other places on the globe where you would have fit in better."

Her sigh was an admission that he had her correctly pegged. On a big game hunt she was as out of place as a rusty nail in an operating room. "My father and brother always went hunting together. Four weeks every year. It was a family tradition." Filled with remorse, she closed her eyes. "Father hadn't been hunting since Jeff was killed. I thought the trip would be good for him. I insisted that he go. When he hesitated, I offered to go with him."

She expected murmurs of sympathy and understanding—perhaps even whispered praise for her unselfish and noble gesture. Instead all she heard from him was a grumpy "Be quiet, will you? I'm trying to get some sleep."

"Stop it, Rusty."

Her brother's voice echoed through her dream. They were wrestling, as only brothers and sisters who either hate each other intensely or love each other intensely can. With Jeff and her, the latter had been true. They were barely a year apart in age. From the time Rusty took her first steps, they had been bosom buddies and playmates. Much to their father's delight and their mother's aggravation, they had often engaged in rowdy hand-to-hand combat and always came up laughing.

But there was no levity in Jeff's voice now as he clasped her wrists and anchored them to the floor on either side of her head. "Stop it, now." He shook her slightly. "You're going to hurt yourself if you don't stop flailing around."

She came awake and opened her eyes. It wasn't Jeff's

well-remembered, well-loved face she stared into, but the man's. The Loner's. She was glad he was alive, but she didn't like him very much. What was his name? Oh, yes, Cooper. Cooper...? Cooper something. Or something Cooper.

"Lie still," he commanded her.

She stopped thrashing. The air was cold on her exposed skin, and she realized that she'd kicked off all the furs he'd piled over them for the night. On his knees, he was straddling her chest and bending over her. Her wrists were stapled behind her head by his hard fingers.

"Get off me."

"Are you all right now?"

She nodded. She was as all right as a woman could be upon waking up to find a man the size and shape of Cooper Landry—that was it, Landry—straddling her with thighs that rose like columns above her, coming together... She averted her eyes from that mouth-drying juncture. "Please," she gasped. "I'm fine."

He eased himself off her. She sucked in frigidly cold air that hurt her lungs. But God, it felt good against her hot face. It felt good for only a second. Then she shivered with a chill and her teeth started clicking together. Cooper's brows were drawn together worriedly. Or crossly. She couldn't tell. He was either concerned or annoyed.

"You're burning up with fever," he told her bluntly. "I left the bed to build up the fire. You were delirious and started shouting for somebody called Jeff."

"My brother." Her shudders were convulsive. She pulled one of the furs around her.

It hadn't rained or drizzled anymore during the night. She could actually see flames and glowing coals beneath the sticks Cooper had added to the fire. The flames were so hot they burned her eyeballs until they hurt.

No, impossible. That must be the fever.

Leaving the fur covering her upper body alone, Cooper lifted the lower half of it off her leg. Once again he painstakingly unwrapped the bandage and stared down at the open wound. Rusty stared at him.

Finally he looked at her, his mouth set in a bleak line. "I won't try to fool you. It's bad. Infected. There's a bottle of antibiotics in the first-aid kit. I was saving them in case this happened, but I'm not sure they'll be adequate to take care of it."

She swallowed with difficulty. Even her feverish brain could assimilate what he was telling her. Raising herself to her elbows, she looked down at her leg. She wanted to gag. On either side of the deep gash, the skin was raised and puckered with infection. Flopping back down, she drew in shallow, rapid breaths. She wet her lips, ineffectually because the fever was making her mouth drier than it had been before. "I could get gangrene and die, couldn't I?"

He forced a half smile. "Not yet. We've got to do what we can to prevent that."

"Like cut it off?"

"God, you're morbid. What I had in mind was lancing out the pus and then closing the gash with stitches."

Her face turned ashen. "That sounds morbid enough."

"Not as bad as cauterizing it. Which it might come to." Her face went as colorless as chalk. "But, for right now, let's put some stitches in. Don't look relieved," he said, frowning deeply, "it's gonna hurt like hell."

She stared into the depths of his eyes. Strange as it was, rocky as their beginning had been, she trusted him. "Do whatever you have to do."

He nodded brusquely, then went to work. First he withdrew a pair of her silk long johns from the sweater cum

backpack. "I'm glad you wear silk undies." She smiled
waveringly at his mild joke as he began to unravel the
casing of the waistband.

"We'll use these threads for the sutures." He nodded
down toward the silver flask. "Better start on that brandy.
Use it to swallow one of those penicillin tablets. You're
not allergic to it, are you? Good," he said when she shook
her head. "Sip the brandy steadily. Don't stop until you're
good and drunk. But don't drink all of it. I'll have to ster-
ilize the threads and bathe the gash with it."

She wasn't anesthetized nearly enough when he bent
over her leg. The hunting knife, which he'd sterilized in
the fire, was held poised in readiness over the infected
wound. "Ready?" She nodded. "Try to keep still." She
nodded again. "And don't fight unconsciousness. We'd
both be better off if you passed out."

The first tiny puncture he made into the red, puffy
skin caused her to cry out and yank her leg back. "No,
Rusty! You've got to lie still."

It was an agonizing process and seemed to go on forever. He meticulously lanced the areas that needed it.
When he doused the entire wound with brandy, Rusty
screamed. After that, the stitches didn't seem so bad. He
used the sewing needle from the matchbook kit they'd
brought with them. After soaking individual threads in
brandy, he drew them through her skin and tied them,
firmly pulling the edges of the wound together.

Rusty stared at the spot where his tawny eyebrows
grew together above the bridge of his nose. His forehead
was sweating in spite of the cold. He never took his eyes
off his work except to occasionally glance down at her
face. He was sensitive to her pain. Even sympathetic toward it. His hands were amazingly tender for a man so

large, and for one who had a cold, unfeeling stone where his heart should have been.

Eventually that spot between his eyebrows began to swim in and out of focus. Although she was lying still, her head was spinning, reeling with pain and trauma and the anesthetizing effects of the brandy. Despite Cooper's advice, she struggled to stay awake, afraid that if she went to sleep she might never wake up. Finally, she gave up the fight and let her eyes drift closed.

Her last conscious thought was that it was a shame her father would never know how brave she'd been right up to the moment of her death.

"Well," Cooper said, sitting back on his heels and wiping his perspiring forehead, "it's not pretty, but I think it will work."

He looked down at her with a satisfied and optimistic smile. But she didn't see his smile. She was unconscious.

Three

She came to, actually surprised that she was alive. At first she thought that darkness had fallen, but she inched her head upward. The small mink pelt slid off her head. It was still daylight—exactly what time was impossible to pinpoint. The sky was gloomily overcast.

With a sense of dread, she waited for the pain from her leg to penetrate her consciousness, but miraculously it didn't. Dizzy from the brandy she'd consumed, she eased herself into a sitting position. It took every ounce of strength she had left to lift the furs off her leg. For one horrid moment she thought it might not be hurting because Cooper had amputated it after all.

But when she moved aside the largest caribou pelt, she found that her leg was still intact and bandaged in strips of white cotton. No signs of fresh blood. She was by no means ready to run a marathon, but it felt much better.

Sitting up had exhausted her and she fell back amid the furs, pulling them to her chin. Her skin was hot and dry, but she was chilled. She still had a fever. Maybe she should take more aspirin. But where were they? Cooper would know. He—

Where was Cooper?

Her lethargy vanished and she sprang into a sitting position. Frantically her eyes scanned the clearing. Not a trace. He was gone. His rifle was missing, too. The other one lay on the ground within her reach. The fire still had glowing coals and was giving off heat.

But her protector had deserted her.

Forcibly tamping down hysteria, she reasoned that she was jumping to conclusions. He wouldn't do that. He wouldn't have nursed her so meticulously only to leave her stranded and helpless in the wilderness.

Would he?

Not unless he was an unfeeling bastard.

Hadn't she decided that was exactly what Cooper Landry was?

No. He was hard. Tough. Cynical, certainly. But not completely lacking in feelings. If he were, he'd have deserted her yesterday.

So where was he?

He'd left a rifle behind. Why? Maybe that was the extent of his human kindness. He'd tended to her wound, done all he could on that score. He'd provided her with the means to protect herself. Maybe now it was every man for himself. Survival of the fittest.

Well, she would die. If not of fever, then of thirst. She had no water. She had no food. She had no shelter to speak of. In just a little while the supply of firewood, which he'd cut and stacked nearby, would be used up. She'd die of exposure if the weather turned even marginally colder.

Like hell she would!

Suddenly she was furious with him for going off and leaving her. She'd show him; she'd show her father. Rusty Carlson was not an easily expendable, spineless wimp.

She threw off the covers and pulled on her ski jacket. For the time being she'd leave off her left boot because the pair of them were still stashed farther down in the pile of furs, too far for her to reach. Besides, if one foot was bare, the other might just as well be, too. And on top of that, putting on her coat had sapped her energy.

Food and water.

Those essentials were necessary. That's what she had to find first. But where? At best, her surroundings were intimidating. At worst, terrifying. For three hundred and sixty degrees, all she could see was virgin forest. Beyond the nearby trees—some so tall she couldn't even see the tops of them—there stretched endless miles of more just like them.

Before she could go in search of water, she had to get to her feet. It seemed like an impossible task, but she gritted her teeth with the determination to do it.

When they discovered her body, it wouldn't be hunkered under a pile of furs!

Reaching out as far as she could, she closed her hand around a stick of firewood and pulled it toward her. Using it as a prop, she came up on her good knee, keeping the injured one straight out in front of her. Then she paused to catch her breath, which was forming clouds of white vapor in front of her face.

Repeatedly she tried to stand up, but failed. She was as weak as a newborn kitten. And light-headed. Damn Cooper Landry! No wonder he'd urged her to drink so much brandy. He'd wanted her to pass out so she wouldn't know when he sneaked away like the miserable skunk that he was.

Making a Herculean final effort, she put all her weight on her left foot and stood up on it. The earth tilted precariously. Closing her eyes, she clasped her supporting stick of firewood and held on for dear life. When she felt it was safe to reopen her eyes, she did—and let out a thin squeak of astonishment. Cooper was standing on the other side of the clearing.

"Just what the hell do you think you're doing?" he bellowed.

Dropping what he was carrying, including his rifle, he bore down on her like a sorely provoked angel. Catching her under her arms, he kicked the stick of wood out from under her and lowered her back into her sickbed. He packed the covers around her shivering body.

"What the hell were you trying to do?"

"F...find water," she stuttered through chattering teeth.

His muttered expletive was so vivid it was almost tangible. He laid his open hand on her forehead to gauge her temperature. "You're so cold, you're blue. Don't try another damn stupid stunt like that again, understand? It's *my* job to find water. *Yours* is to stay put. Got that?"

Swearwords continued to pour out of him like the payoff of a slot machine. He turned toward the fire and began stoking it, angrily throwing firewood onto the smoldering coals and fanning them to life. When the fire was blazing, he crossed the clearing and picked up the limp rabbit carcass he'd dropped on the ground. He was also carrying a thermos, one of the things he'd brought with them from the wreckage. Uncapping it, he poured water into the lid/cup and knelt on one knee beside Rusty.

"Here. I'm sure your throat is dry and sore. But don't drink too much too fast."

She cupped her hands around his and raised the cup to her parched lips. The water was so cold it hurt her teeth, but she didn't mind. She took three deep swallows before Cooper withdrew the cup.

"Easy, I said. There's plenty."

"You found a source?" She licked drops of water off her lips.

Watching that motion closely, Cooper said, "Yeah. A stream about three hundred yards that way." He indicated the direction with his head. "Must be a tributary of the Mackenzie."

She looked at the lifeless carcass lying next to his boot. "Did you shoot the rabbit?"

"Killed it with a rock. I didn't want to waste any ammo unless I had to. I'll dress it and put it on to cook. We can… Oh, hell. What's the matter?"

Rusty, much to her dismay, burst into tears. The sobs racked her entire body. She covered her face with her hands, but even as dehydrated as she was, tears leaked through her fingers.

"Look, it was either him or us," Cooper said with agitation. "We've got to eat. You can't be so—"

"It's not the rabbit," she blubbered.

"Then what? Does your leg hurt?"

"I thought you had de…deserted me. Left me behind beca…cause of my leg. And maybe you should. I'm holding you up. You probably could have wa…walked to safety by now if it weren't for me and my leg."

She hiccuped around several attempts to go on. "But my leg really doesn't make much difference because I'm a washout in situations like this anyway. I loathe the great outdoors and think it's anything but great. I hate it. Even summer camp never appealed to me. I'm cold. And scared. And guilty for complaining when I'm alive and everybody else is dead."

She dissolved into another torrent, her shoulders shaking. Cooper let out a long-suffering sigh, several florid curses, and then walked forward on his knees to take her into his arms. He pressed her shoulders between his large hands. Rusty's initial reaction was to tense up and try to pull away. But he kept his hands there and drew her against him. The promise of comfort was too much for her to resist. She slumped against his broad chest, clutching handfuls of his thick hunting coat.

The clean, fresh essence of pine clung to his clothes and hair—and that appealing, musty smell of damp leaves and fog. In Rusty's weakened, woozy state, he seemed unnaturally large, as fantastic as the hero in a children's tale. Powerful. Strong. Fierce but benevolent. Able to slay any dragon.

When one of his capable hands cupped the back of her head, she burrowed her face deeper into the quilted cloth of his coat and luxuriated in the first feeling of security she'd known since the plane went down—even before that, since leaving the hunting lodge and her disappointed father.

Finally the tumult passed. Her tears dried up. There was no excuse for Cooper to go on holding her, so she eased away from him. Embarrassed now, she kept her head down. He seemed reluctant to let her go, but at last his hands slid away.

"Okay now?" he asked gruffly.

"Yes, fine, thank you." She wiped her moist nose on the back of her hand, as though she did that all the time.

"I'd better get that rabbit ready to cook. Lie back down."

"I'm tired of lying down."

"Then turn your head. I want you to be able to eat this and I'm afraid you won't if you watch me gut it."

Carrying the rabbit to the edge of the clearing, he laid it on a flat rock and proceeded to dress it. Rusty wisely kept her eyes averted. "That's what we had our argument over," she said quietly.

Cooper looked at her over his shoulder. "You and who?"

"My father. He had brought down a ram." She laughed without humor. "It was a beautiful animal. I felt sorry for it, but I pretended to be ecstatic over the kill. Father hired one of the guides to field-dress it. He wanted to supervise, to make sure the guide didn't damage the hide." Blinking tears out of her eyes, she continued. "I couldn't watch. It made me physically ill. Father—" she paused to draw in a deep breath "—I think I disgusted and disappointed him."

Cooper was cleaning his hands on a handkerchief he'd soaked with water from the thermos. "Because you couldn't stomach a field-dressing?"

"Not just that. That capped it off. I proved to be a terrible marksman, but I couldn't have shot anything if it had walked up and put its nose against the barrel of my rifle. I didn't like anything about that whole scene." Softly, she added almost to herself, "I wasn't as good an outdoorsman as my brother Jeff."

"Did your father expect you to be?" He had skewered the rabbit on a green twig and was now suspending it over the coals.

"I think he was hoping I would be."

"Then he's a fool. You're not physically equipped to be a hunter."

His eyes dropped to her chest. And lingered. Heat rushed into her breasts, filling them like mother's milk, making them heavy and achy. Her nipples drew tight.

The reaction startled Rusty enormously. Instinctively she wanted to cover and press her breasts back to normalcy, but he was still looking at her, so she couldn't.

She didn't dare move at all. She was afraid that if she did, something terribly fragile would be broken—something that couldn't be replaced or repaired. Any reckless move would be disastrous and irrevocable. Something dreadful might happen as a result.

It was the first time he had made any sexual reference besides the vulgarities he'd spouted last night. He'd done that only to rile her. She realized that now. But this was something altogether different. This time, he was as much the victim as the perpetrator.

He yanked his eyes back toward the fire and the moment passed. But they didn't speak to each other for a long time. Rusty closed her eyes and pretended to doze, but she watched him as he busied himself around what was gradually coming to look like a bonafide camp. He sharpened the hatchet on a stone. He checked the roasting rabbit, turning it several times.

He moved with surprising agility for a man his size. She was sure that some women would consider him handsome, particularly now that his chin and jaw were deeply shadowed by a twenty-four-hour beard. The wide, curving mustache was sexy...if one liked facial hair. It sat directly on top of his lower lip, completely obscuring his upper one, making the thought of going in search of it intriguing.

She found herself staring at his mouth as he leaned down and spoke to her. "I...I beg your pardon?"

He looked at her strangely. "Your eyes are glassy. You're not going delirious again, are you?" He pressed his palm to her forehead.

Impatient with him and herself for her adolescent fantasies, she swatted his hand aside. "No, I feel fine. What did you say?"

"I asked if you were ready to eat."

"That's an understatement."

He assisted her into a sitting position. "This has been cooling for a minute or two. It should be about ready." He slid the rabbit off the spit and tore off a leg at the joint. He passed it to Rusty. Hesitantly she took it, staring at it dubiously.

"You're going to eat it if I have to force it down your throat." He tore off a bite of meat with his strong white teeth. "It's not half bad. Honest."

She pinched some of the meat off the bone and put it into her mouth, making herself chew and swallow it quickly. "Not so fast," he cautioned. "It'll make you sick."

She nodded and took another bite. With a little salt, it wouldn't have been bad at all. "There are some very nice restaurants in Los Angeles that have rabbit on the menu," she said conversationally. She instinctively reached for a napkin, remembered that she didn't have one, shrugged, and licked her fingers.

"Is that where you live, Los Angeles?"

"Beverly Hills, actually."

He studied her in the firelight. "Are you a movie star or something?"

Rusty got the impression that he wouldn't be impressed if she told him she was a three-time Oscar winner. She doubted if Cooper Landry put much stock in fame. "No, I'm not a movie star. My father owns a real-estate company. It has branches all over southern California. I work for him."

"Are you any good at it?"

"I've been very successful."

He chewed a mouthful and tossed the cleaned bone into the fire. "Being the boss's daughter, how could you miss?"

"I work hard, Mr. Landry." She took umbrage at his

sly implication that her father was responsible for the success she had achieved. "I had the highest sales record of the agency last year."

"Bravo."

Miffed that he was so obviously unimpressed, she asked snidely, "What do you do?"

He silently offered her another piece of the meat, which she tore into as though she'd been eating fresh, unseasoned roasted rabbit cooked over an open fire every day of her life.

"I ranch," Cooper replied.

"Cattle?"

"Some. Horses mostly."

"Where?"

"Rogers Gap."

"Where's that?"

"In the Sierra Nevada."

"Never heard of it."

"I'm not surprised."

"Can you make a living at just ranching?"

"I do all right."

"Is Rogers Gap close to Bishop? Do people ski there?"

"We have a few runs. Serious skiers consider them a real challenge. Personally I think they're some of the most spectacular on the continent."

"Then why haven't I ever heard of this place?"

"We're a carefully guarded secret and want to remain that way. We don't advertise."

"Why?" Her interest was piqued. She never passed up an opportunity to locate new and interesting property for her clients to invest in. "With the right developer handling it, you could make something out of Rogers Gap. If it's as good for skiing as you say, it could become the next Aspen."

"God forbid," he said under his breath. "That's the point. We don't want to be put on the map. We don't want our mountains to be littered with concrete condos or the peaceful community to be overrun by a bunch of pushing, shoving, rude skiers from Beverly Hills who are more interested in modeling their Rodeo Drive duds than preserving our landscape."

"Does everyone in town hold to this philosophy?"

"Fortunately, yes, or they wouldn't be living there. We don't have much going for us except the scenery and the tranquillity."

She tossed her denuded bones into the fire. "You sound like a holdover from the sixties."

"I am."

Her eyes were teasing. "Were you a flower child, advocating universal harmony? Did you march for peace and participate in war protests?"

"No," he replied sharply. Rusty's goading grin collapsed. "I couldn't wait to join up. I wanted to go to war. I was too ignorant to realize that I would have to kill people or get killed myself. I hadn't bargained on getting captured and imprisoned. But I did. After seven months in that stinking hole, I escaped and came home a hero."

He practically snarled the last sentence. "The guys in that POW camp would have killed each other for a meal like the one you just ate." His gray eyes looked like glittering knife blades as they sliced toward her. "So I'm not overwhelmed by your Beverly Hills glitz and glamour, Miss Carlson."

He stood up abruptly. "I'm going for more water. Don't wander off."

Don't wander off, she silently mimicked. All right, he had put her in her place, but she wasn't going to wear sackcloth and ashes for the rest of her life. Lots of men had fought in Vietnam and returned to lead happy, productive lives. It was Cooper's own fault if he was maladjusted. He thrived on his own bitterness. That's what fueled him. He nursed it. He cultivated his quarrel with society because he felt it owed him something.

Maybe it did. But it wasn't her fault. She wasn't responsible for whatever misfortune had befallen him. Just because he walked around with a chip on his shoulder the size of Mount Everest didn't make him a worthier human being than she was.

He returned, but they maintained a hostile silence while she drank her fill of water from the thermos. Just as wordlessly, he assisted her as she hobbled out of the clearing for a few minutes of privacy. When he eased her back down onto the thick pallet, which had become the nucleus of their world, he said, "I need to check your leg. Hold the flashlight for me."

She watched as he unbound the bandages and pulled them back to reveal a jagged, uneven row of stitches. She stared at it in horror, but he seemed pleased with his handiwork. With his hands around her calf muscles, he raised her leg to inspect it closer. "No signs of new infection. Swelling's gone down."

"The scar," she whispered roughly.

He looked up at her. "There wasn't much I could do about that." His lower lip thinned until it was hardly visible beneath his mustache. "Just be glad I didn't have to cauterize it."

"I am."

He sneered. "I'm sure a high-ticket plastic surgeon in Beverly Hills can fix the scar."

"Do you have to be so obnoxious?"

"Do you have to be so superficial?" He aimed a finger in the direction of the crashed plane. "I'm sure any of those guys we left up there would settle for a scar on their shin."

He was right, of course; but that didn't make his criticism any easier for her to swallow. She lapsed into sullen silence. He bathed her leg in peroxide and rebandaged it, then gave her one of the penicillin tablets and two aspirins. She washed them down with water. No more brandy for her, thank you.

Drunkenness, she had discovered, aroused her emotionally and sexually. She didn't want to think of Cooper Landry as anything but a wretched grouch. He was a short-tempered, surly ogre harboring a grudge against the world. If she didn't have to rely on him for her survival, she would have nothing to do with him.

She had already settled beneath the pile of furs when he slid in and embraced her as he had the night before.

"How much longer do we have to stay here?" she asked crossly.

"I'm not clairvoyant."

"I'm not asking you to predict when we'll be rescued; I was referring to this bed. Can't you rig up a shelter of some kind? Something we can move around in?"

"The accommodations aren't to m'lady's liking?"

She sighed her annoyance. "Oh, never mind."

After a moment, he said, "There's a group of boulders near the stream. One side of the largest of them has been eroded out. I think with a little ingenuity and some elbow grease, I could make a lean-to out of it. It won't be much, but it will be better than this. And closer to the water."

"I'll help," she offered eagerly.

It wasn't that she didn't appreciate this shelter. It had saved her life last night. But it was disconcerting to sleep this close to him. Since he had taken off his coat as he had the night before, Rusty was keenly aware of his muscled chest against her back. She could therefore assume that he was keenly aware of her body because she wasn't wearing her coat, either.

She could think of little else as his hand found a comfortable spot midway between her breasts and her waist. He even wedged his knees between hers, elevating her injured leg again. She started to ask him if that was necessary, but since it felt so much better that way, she let it pass without comment.

"Rusty?"

"Hmm?" His warm breath drifted into her ear and caused goose bumps to break out over her arms. She snuggled closer to him.

"Wake up. We've got to get up."

"Get up?" she groaned. "Why? Pull the covers back up. I'm freezing."

"That's the point. We're soaking wet. Your fever broke and you sweated all over both of us. If we don't get up and dry off, we stand a good chance of getting frostbite."

She came fully awake and rolled to her back. He was serious. Already he was tossing off the furs. "What do you mean, dry off?"

"Strip and dry off." He began unbuttoning his flannel shirt.

"Are you crazy? It's freezing!" Recalcitrantly, she pulled the pelt back over herself. Cooper jerked it off her.

"Take off all your clothes. Now!"

He shrugged off his flannel shirt and draped it over the nearest bush. With one fluid motion, he crossed his arms at his waist and peeled the turtleneck T-shirt over his head. It made his hair stick up funnily, but Rusty didn't feel like laughing. Laughter—in fact any sound at all—

got trapped inside her closed throat. Her first glimpse of the finest chest she'd ever seen rendered her speechless.

Hard as rocks those muscles were. Beautifully sculpted, too, beneath taut skin. His nipples were dark and pebbly from the cold, their areolae shriveled around them. It was all tantalizingly covered with a blanket of crisp hair that swirled and whorled, tipped and tapered beguilingly.

He was so trim she could count every single rib. His stomach was as flat and tight as a drum. She couldn't see his navel very well. It was deeply nestled in a sexy tuft of hair.

"Get started, Rusty, or I'll do it for you."

His threat plucked her out of her trance. Mechanically, she peeled off her sweater. Beneath it she was wearing a cotton turtleneck much like his. She fiddled with the hem while she watched him stand up and work his jeans down his legs. The long johns weren't the most alluring sight she'd ever seen.

But Cooper Landry unclothed had to be.

In seconds he was standing there, silhouetted against the dim glow of the fire, stark naked. He was beautifully shaped and generously endowed—so marvelously made that she couldn't help her gaping stare. He quite literally took her breath away.

He draped the articles of discarded clothing on the bush, then pulled a pair of socks over his hands and ran them over his body, drying it thoroughly—everything—before removing the socks from his hands.

Kneeling, he tore into one of the backpacks looking for underwear. He pulled on a pair of briefs, all with a supreme lack of self-consciousness, much less modesty.

When he turned toward her and noticed that she hadn't

moved, he frowned with irritation. "Come on, Rusty. Hurry up. It's damn cold out here."

He reached for her sweater, which, so far, was the only thing she'd taken off. She handed it to him and he hung it up to dry. Holding out his hand for more clothes, he snapped his fingers quickly and repeatedly to hurry her along. "Come on, come on." Casting one anxious glance up at him, she pulled the T-shirt over her head and passed it to him.

The cold air was a breathtaking shock to her system. Immediately she was chilled and started trembling so violently she couldn't handle the button on her one-legged trousers.

"Here, let me do that, dammit. Or I'll be standing out here all night." Cooper dropped to his knees and straddled her thighs. Impatiently he pushed her hands out of the way so he could unfasten the button and pull down the zipper. With a detached air he eased the trousers down her legs and tossed them haphazardly toward the nearest bush.

But he was brought up short by what he obviously hadn't expected. A pair of extremely feminine, extremely scanty bikini panties. He'd seen the lace-edged leg, but that was all. For what seemed like an eternity, he stared at them before saying gruffly, "Take them off."

Rusty shook her head. "No."

His face became fierce. "Take them off." Rusty shook her head emphatically. Before she could brace herself for it, he pressed his open hand directly over the triangular scrap of silk and lace. "They're wet. Take them off."

Their eyes, like their wills, clashed. It was as much the chill in his stare as the chill in the air that prompted Rusty to slide the damp garment down her legs.

"Now dry off."

He handed her a cotton sock like the ones he'd used. She ran it over her lower body and her legs. Keeping her head bowed, she groped blindly for the underwear Cooper handed her. He hadn't chosen long johns because they would chafe her injury. She pulled on a pair of panties similar to the ones she'd just taken off and which were now dangling from the lower branches of the bush, fluttering like a victory banner the morning after a fraternity beer bust.

"Now the top."

Her brassiere was just as frivolous as the panties that matched them. The morning she left the lodge, she had dressed in clothes befitting her return to civilization. After having to wear thermal underwear for several days, she had been good and sick of it.

Leaning forward, she grappled with the hook at her back, but her fingers were so numb from the cold she couldn't get it to open. Muttering curses, Cooper reached around her and all but ripped the hook from its mooring. The brassiere fell forward. She peeled the straps down her arms, flung it away and faced him defiantly.

Beneath his mustache, his mouth was set in a hard, unyielding line. He paused for only a heartbeat before he began roughly rubbing the cotton sock over her throat, chest, breasts, and stomach. Then, reaching around her again, he blotted the sweat off her back. They were so close that her breath stirred his chest hair. Her lips came perilously close to touching one of his distended nipples. Hers, hard and peaked from the cold, grazed his skin.

He pulled back quickly and angrily dragged a thermal top over her head. While she was working her arms into the sleeves, he ripped the damp fur they'd been lying on off the pallet and replaced it with another one. "It's not as soft, but it's dry."

"It'll be fine," Rusty said hoarsely.

Finally they were cocooned again. She didn't resist when he pulled her close to him. She was shivering uncontrollably and her teeth were chattering. But it wasn't long before they began to warm up. Their bodies were in chaos because of what their eyes had seen. Erotic impressions lingered in their minds.

Lying in his embrace fully dressed had been unnerving enough. Lying there with him wearing only underwear wreaked havoc on Rusty's senses. Her fever had broken, but her body was burning like a furnace now.

His bare thighs felt delicious against hers. She liked their hair-smattered texture. Because she was braless, she was sharply aware of his hand resting just beneath her breasts, almost but not quite touching them.

He wasn't immune to the enforced intimacy. He'd exerted himself by switching out the pelts and changing clothes so quickly, but that wasn't the only reason he was breathing heavily. His chest swelled and receded against her back rhythmically but rapidly.

And then there was that other inexorable evidence of his arousal.

It prompted her to whisper, "I don't think I need to… uh…prop my leg on top of yours."

A low moan vibrated through his chest. "Don't even talk about it. And for God's sake, don't move." His distress was obvious.

"I'm sorry."

"For what? You can't help being beautiful any more than I can help being a man. I guess we'll just have to tolerate that from each other."

She honored his request and didn't move so much as a muscle. She didn't even reopen her eyes once they were closed. But she did fall asleep with a tiny smile on her lips. Inadvertently, perhaps, but he had told her that he thought she was beautiful.

Four

It made a difference in their relationship.

The forced intimacy of the night before didn't draw them closer together. Rather, it created a schism of uneasiness between them. Their conversation the following morning was stilted. They avoided making eye contact. They dressed with their backs to each other. They moved awkwardly. Their motions were jerky and unsure, like those of invalids who had just regained the use of their limbs.

Taciturn and withdrawn, Cooper whittled her a pair of crutches out of two stout tree branches. Aesthetically, they weren't much to rave about, but Rusty was immensely grateful for them. They allowed her mobility. She would no longer be confined to the bed.

When she thanked him, he only grunted an acknowledgement and stamped off through the underbrush toward the stream to get water. By the time he returned, she was accustomed to the crutches and was hobbling around the clearing on them.

"How does your leg feel?"

"Okay. I cleaned it with peroxide myself and took another pill. I think it's going to be okay." She had even managed to dress in her one remaining pair of slacks and put her boots on. Enough of the soreness was gone that the additional pressure of clothing didn't irritate the wound.

They drank from the thermos in turn. That passed for breakfast. Cooper said, "I'd better start building that shelter today."

They had awakened to find their cocoon dusted with snow. This time the flakes weren't merely grains; they were real and ominous, harbingers of the first winter storm. Both knew how harsh the winters in this area could be. It was imperative that they have a shelter to use until they were rescued. If they weren't rescued, a temporary shelter would be of little consequence, but neither wanted to think about that.

"What can I do to help?" she asked.

"You can cut up that suede jacket into strips." He nodded toward a jacket that had belonged to one of the crash victims and handed her an extra knife. "I'll need plenty of thongs to tie the poles together. While you're doing that, I'd better see if we've got food for dinner." She looked at him quizzically. "I set some snares yesterday."

She glanced around her apprehensively. "You won't go far, will you?"

"Not too far." He shouldered his rifle and checked to see that he had pocketed a box of ammunition. "I'll be back before the fire needs to be refueled. Keep the knife and rifle handy, though. I haven't seen any bear tracks, but you never know."

Without another word he turned and dissolved into the dense screen of trees. Rusty stood leaning on her crutches, her heart thumping fearfully.

Bears?

After several moments, she shook off her paralyzing fright. "This is silly," she muttered to herself. "Nothing's going to get me."

She wished she had a radio, a television set, anything to relieve the oppressive silence. It was only occasionally broken by the cracking of twigs and the rustling of leaves as unseen forest animals scurried about on their daily forages. Rusty's eyes searched out these silence-breakers, but they remained hidden and thereby more intimidating. She couldn't put Cooper's mention of bears out of her mind.

"He probably said that on purpose just to frighten me," she said out loud as she viciously sliced through the tough suede with the knife he'd left behind for her use. It was smaller than the one that constantly rode in the scabbard attached to his belt.

Her stomach growled. She thought about fresh, hot and buttery breakfast croissants, toasted bagels and cream cheese, warmed glazed donuts, pancakes and bacon, ham and eggs. That only made her hungrier. The only thing she could do was to fill her empty stomach with water.

Soon, however, drinking so much water created another problem. She put it off as long as possible, but finally had no choice but to set aside her handiwork. Painstakingly, and without a smidgen of grace or coordination, she stood up and propped her arms on her crutches. Going in the direction opposite to that Cooper had taken, she found a spot in which to relieve herself.

As she struggled with her crutches and her clothes, at the same time checking for creepy crawlies on the ground, she marveled that this was really Rusty Carlson, real-estate princess of Beverly Hills, seeking a place in the woods to pee!

Her friends would never have guessed she could

come this far without going stark, staring mad. Her father would never believe it. But if she lived to tell about it, he would be so proud of her.

She was in the process of refastening her pants when she heard the nearby movement. Swiveling her head in that direction, she listened. Nothing.

"Probably just the wind." Her voice sounded unnaturally loud and cheerful. "Or a bird. Or Cooper coming back. If he's creeping up on me as a joke, I'll never forgive him."

She ignored the next rustling noise, which was louder and nearer than the last one, and moved as fast as she could back toward the camp. Determined not to do anything so cowardly as to whimper or cry out, she clenched her jaw in fear as she stumbled along over the uneven ground.

All her bravery deserted her when the form materialized from between the trunks of two pines and loomed directly in her path. Her head snapped up, she looked into the beady eyes, the hairy, leering face, and let out a bloodcurdling scream.

Cooper was in a hurry to get back, but he decided to dress the two rabbits before he returned. He had told himself that he wasn't testing her fortitude when he'd gutted the rabbit where she could see it.

But he knew deep down inside that's exactly what he'd been doing. Perversely, he had wanted her to cringe, to retch, to get hysterical, to demonstrate some feminine weakness.

She hadn't. She'd borne up well. Far better than he'd expected her to.

He tossed away the entrails and began scraping the insides of the pelts. They would come in handy later.

The fur was warm and he could always use it to make Rusty—Rusty. Her again. Couldn't he think of anything else? Did his every single thought have to come full circle back to her? At what point had they become a pair as inseparable as Adam and Eve? Couldn't he think of one without thinking immediately of the other?

He remembered the first thought that had registered when he regained consciousness. Her face, alluringly framed in that tumble of russet curls, had been bending over him, and he'd thought of the vilest obscenity the marine corps had ever coined and came just short of saying it out loud.

He'd been glad to be alive—but barely. He had thought he'd be better off dead rather than having to put up with this airhead swathed in expensive fur and sexy perfume. In the wilderness she wouldn't stand a marshmallow's chance at a bonfire. He'd figured that before it was over, he'd probably have to kill her to put them both out of their misery.

That was an unsettling and unappetizing thought, but he had been forced to do worse in order to save his own life in Nam. The plane crash had caused him to automatically revert to the law of the jungle, to slip back into the role of survivor.

Rule number one: You either killed or got killed. You stayed alive no matter what it cost. The survival tactics taught to the army's special services knew no conscience. You did whatever was necessary to live one more day, one more hour, one more minute. He had been steeped in that doctrine and had practiced it more times than he wanted to remember—but too many times to let him forget.

But the woman had surprised him. That leg injury had caused her a great deal of pain, but she hadn't whined about it. She hadn't nagged him about being hungry and thirsty and cold and scared, although God knew she must have been. She'd been a tough little nut and she hadn't cracked yet. Unless things got drastically worse, he doubted now that she would.

Of course that left him with a whole new set of problems. Few people had ever won his admiration. He didn't want to admire Rusty Carlson, but found himself doing so.

He was also coming to acknowledge that he was stranded in the middle of nowhere with a tempting piece of womanhood, and that they might be alone and dependent on each other for a long time.

The demons who had guided his fate were having a huge laugh at his expense this time. They'd run amok many times in the past, but this was the clincher. This was the big punch line that had made his whole life a joke.

Traditionally, he despised women like Rusty Carlson. He had no use for wealthy, silly, superficial society broads who'd been born with silver spoons in their mouths. They didn't know, or want to know, about anything outside their gilded cages. Wasn't it just his luck to draw one who had earned his grudging respect by bearing up under the worst of circumstances?

But even that wasn't enough for the malicious gods. She could have been a silly society broad who wouldn't have given a warthog any competition in the looks department. She could have had a voice that would shatter glass.

Instead, the fates had forced on him a woman who looked like a dream. Surely the devil had designed her. Temptation incarnate. With cinnamon-colored hair a man could wrap himself in and nipples that looked so sweet they must taste like candy. Her voice would melt butter. That's what he thought about every time she spoke.

What a cruel joke. Because he would not touch her. Never. He'd been down that road. Women like her followed vogue. Not only in clothes; in everything. When he'd met Melody it had been fashionable to love a veteran. She had, until it became convenient not to.

Scratch the silky surface of Rusty Carlson and you'd find another Melody. Rusty was only sucking up to him now because she depended on him for her survival. She looked like a tasty morsel, but inside she was probably as rotten and devious as Melody had been.

Slinging the rabbit pelts over his shoulder and folding the meat in a cloth, he headed back toward their camp. She wasn't going to get to him. He couldn't afford to start feeling soft toward her. Last night he'd let her cry because he felt that she deserved one good, cleansing cry. But no more. He'd held her during the night because it was necessary for them to keep warm. But he would keep his distance from now on. Once the shelter was built, they wouldn't have to sleep together like that. He wouldn't have to endure any more nights with her curled against his front and her bottom cushioning his involuntary reaction to her.

Stop thinking about it, he told himself. Forget how smooth her belly felt beneath your hand. Forget the shape of her breasts and the color of the hair between her thighs.

Groaning, he thrashed through the woods, viciously determined to keep his thoughts on track. As soon as he built the shelter, such close proximity wouldn't be necessary. He would keep his eyes and his hands—

The piercing scream brought him up short.

If he'd walked into an invisible wall, he couldn't have stopped more abruptly. When Rusty's next scream rent the stillness, he instinctively slipped into the role of jungle fighter as easily as well-greased gears fitting into their notches. Silently, he slithered through the trees in the direction of her scream, knife drawn and teeth bared.

"Who...who are you?" Rusty's hand was gripping her own throat, where her pulse was beating wildly.

The man's bearded face split into a wide grin. He turned his head and said, "Hey, Pa, *she* wants to know who *I* am."

Chuckling, another man, an older version of the first, stepped out from between the trees. The two gaped at Rusty. Both had small, dark eyes embedded in deep sockets.

"We could ask you the same question," the older one said. "Who are you, little girl?"

"I...I...I survived the airplane crash." They gazed back at her with perplexity. "You didn't know about the crash?"

"Can't say that we did."

She pointed with a shaking finger. "Back there. Two days ago. Five men were killed. My leg was injured." She indicated the crutches.

"Any more women?"

Before she could answer, Cooper lunged up behind the older of the two men and laid the gleaming blade of his knife against the whiskered throat. He grasped the man's arm, twisted it behind him and shoved his hand up between his shoulder blades. The man's hunting rifle clattered to the ground at his feet.

"Move away from her or I'll kill him," he said to the stunned younger man.

He was staring at Cooper as though he were Satan himself, who had sprung up out of the ground straight from hell. Even Rusty was quelled by the evil threat in Cooper's eyes. But she was trembling with relief to see him.

"I said to move away from her." Cooper's voice seemed as deadly as his knife. It was void of inflection, emotionless. The younger man took two exaggerated steps away from Rusty. "Now, drop the rifle," Cooper told him.

Since it appeared that the attacker was human after all, the younger man's face puckered with rebellion. He whined, "Pa, do I have to do—"

"Do as he says, Reuben."

Reluctantly the younger man tossed down his hunting rifle. Cooper kicked the two rifles now on the ground out of reach and gradually released his stranglehold on the man. He stepped around him and stood beside Rusty, facing the two. "Rusty?" She jumped. "Are you okay?"

"Fine."

"Did they hurt you?"

"They scared me, that's all. I don't think they meant to."

Cooper didn't take his eyes off the two men, but regarded them warily. "Who are you?"

His bark carried more authority than Rusty's feeble question. The older man answered him at once. "Quinn Gawrylow and my son, Reuben. We live here." Cooper didn't even blink. The man went on. "Across the deep ravine." He hitched his chin in that direction.

Cooper had discovered the ravine the day before. The stream where he'd been getting water lay at the bottom of it. He hadn't crossed it to explore because he hadn't wanted to leave Rusty alone that long. He thanked God now that he hadn't. These men might be perfectly harmless. Then again, they might not be. His suspicious nature had served him well on more than one occasion. Until they proved to be otherwise, he'd consider this duo the enemy. They hadn't done anything harmful so far, but he didn't like the way the younger one was staring at Rusty as though she were a celestial vision.

"What brought you across the ravine?" Cooper asked.

"We smelled your wood smoke last night and this morning came to investigate. We don't usually see other people in our woods."

"Our plane crashed."

"That's what the young lady said."

She'd been elevated from a little girl to a young lady. Rusty silently thanked Cooper for that. She, too, was unnerved by the younger man's stare and inched closer to Cooper, taking shelter behind his arm. "How far are we from the nearest town?" she asked.

"A hundred miles." Her hopes plummeted. The man obviously noticed. "But the river isn't too far."

"The Mackenzie?"

"Right. If you reach that before it freezes closed, you'll catch a boat on its way down to Yellowknife."

"How far to the river?" Cooper asked.

The man scratched his head beneath his wool stocking cap. "Ten, fifteen miles, wouldn't you say, Reuben?"

The younger man bobbed his head, never taking his lustful eyes off Rusty. Cooper squinted at him, his stare malevolent and dangerous. "Could you direct us to the river?"

"Yes," the elder Gawrylow said. "Tomorrow. Today we'll feed you. Let you rest up." He glanced down at the fresh meat Cooper had dropped. "Would you like to follow us to our cabin?"

Rusty glanced up at Cooper expectantly. His face remained a mask as he studied the two men cautiously. At last he said, "Thanks. Rusty could use the food and rest before we strike out. You go on ahead." Using his rifle, he pointed them toward their camp.

The two men bent to pick up their rifles. Rusty felt Cooper's muscles tense with precaution. But the father and son shouldered their rifles and turned in the direction Cooper had indicated. Cooper glanced down at her and spoke from the side of his mouth. "Stay close. Where's the knife I gave you?"

"I left it behind when I went—"

"Keep it with you."

"What's the matter with you?"

"Nothing."

"You don't act very glad to see them. I'm delighted. They can lead us out of here."

His only comment was a thin-lipped "Yeah."

The Gawrylows were impressed with Cooper's improvisations. They helped gather up the pelts and the belongings Cooper and Rusty had salvaged from the crash. Nothing in the wilderness was ever wasted. Reuben kicked stones into the fire to make certain it was out.

The band, under Quinn's guidance, with his son following closely, set out for their cabin. Cooper brought up the rear so he could keep an eye on both Gawrylows and on Rusty, who was making admirable if awkward progress on her crutches.

The men seemed to be well-meaning, but Cooper had learned the hard way never to trust anyone. He'd seen too many soldiers blown to bits by hand grenades handed to them by smiling children.

At the stream they paused to rest. Rusty's lungs felt as though collapse were imminent; her heart was beating double time; and the crutches were chafing her armpits, even though Cooper had tried to prevent that by padding the tops of them with articles of extra clothing.

"How are you doing?" he asked her, uncapping the thermos and passing it to her.

"Fine." She forced a smile.

"Does your leg hurt?"

"No, it just feels like it weighs a ton."

"It can't be much farther. Then you can lie down for the rest of the day."

The Gawrylows waited patiently nearby until she had regained her breath and was ready to start again. "We'll cross at the easiest point," the elder one informed Cooper.

They walked along the streambed for several hundred yards. At any other time, Rusty would have been entranced with the landscape. The stream was crystal clear. It gurgled over rocks that had been polished as smooth as mirrors by the gallons of water that had rushed across them. Towering trees interlaced and formed canopies overhead. The evergreens were so deeply green that they appeared blue. The leaves of the deciduous trees ranged from vivid red to vibrant yellow. Encroaching winter had already caused many leaves to fall. They provided a crunchy carpet beneath their feet.

Rusty's chest was burning with exertion by the time the Gawrylows drew to a halt. She laid her crutches on the ground and gratefully sank down onto a rock beside the stream, which ran shallow at this point. The side of the ravine rising up on the other side of the brook looked as high as the Himalayas.

"This is it," Quinn said. "I'll lead the way. Reuben can carry the woman. You can bring your gear."

"Reuben can bring the gear. I'll carry the woman," Cooper amended in a steely voice.

The older man shrugged and ordered his son to take the bundles from Cooper. Reuben did so, but not without shooting Cooper a sour look. Cooper stared back at him unmoved. He didn't care whether Reuben liked it or not; he wasn't going to let those grubby hands get anywhere near Rusty.

When the father and son had moved out of earshot, he bent over her and whispered, "Don't be shy of using that knife." She looked up at him with alarm. "Just in case these Good Samaritans turn on us." He laid the crutches across her lap and picked her up in his arms.

The Gawrylows were already well up the side of the ravine. He started after them, keeping one eye on them and the other on the treacherously steep incline. If he fell, Rusty would go with him. She had put up a brave front, but he knew her leg must be causing her considerable discomfort.

"Do you really think we'll be rescued tomorrow, Cooper?"

"Looks like there's a good chance. If we make it to the river and if a boat of some kind happens by." He was breathing with difficulty. Sweat had popped out on his forehead. His jaw was set with determination.

"You need a shave." The remark came from nowhere, but it indicated to them both how carefully she'd been studying his face. Without moving his head, he cast his eyes down toward her. Embarrassed, she looked away and murmured, "Sorry I'm so heavy."

"Hardly. Your clothes weigh more than you do."

That comment reminded them that he knew just how much of her was clothing and how much was flesh and bone. He'd seen her without any clothes, hadn't he? Rusty decided that if all their conversations were going to result in awkwardness, it was safer not to engage in conversation at all.

Besides, by this time they had reached the top of the ravine. Quinn was biting off a chaw of tobacco. Reuben had removed his stocking cap and was fanning himself with it. His dark hair was greasily plastered to his head.

Cooper set Rusty down. Wordlessly Quinn offered him the brick of tobacco. Rusty was grateful when, with a shake of his head, Cooper turned it down.

"We'll wait until you're rested," Quinn said.

Cooper looked down at Rusty. Her face was pale with fatigue. Her leg was probably hurting. The moist wind had picked up, making the temperature noticeably colder. No doubt she needed to take it slow and easy, but all things considered, the sooner he got her under a roof, fed, and lying down, the better.

"No need to wait. Let's go," he said tersely.

He pulled Rusty to her feet and propped her up on her crutches. He noticed her wince with pain, but steeled himself against compassion and indicated to their hosts that they were ready to proceed.

At least the remaining distance to the cabin was level ground. By the time they reached it, however, Rusty's strength was totally spent. She collapsed on the sagging porch like a rag doll.

"Let's get the woman inside," Quinn said as he pushed open the door.

The rickety door was attached to its frame by leather hinges. The interior of the cabin looked as uninviting as an animal's lair. Rusty eyed the opening with trepidation and a sense of dread. Then and there she decided that there were worse things than being exposed to the outdoors.

Cooper remained expressionless as he scooped her into his arms and carried her into the gloomy interior. The small windows were so blackened by grime that they let in little light. A dim, smoky fire gave off meager illumination, but what Rusty and Cooper saw would have been better left hidden in darkness.

The cabin was filthy. It stank of wet wool, rancid grease, and unwashed men. The only merit it had was that it was warm. Cooper carried Rusty toward the stone hearth and set her down in a cushionless, straight-backed chair. He upended an aluminum bucket and propped the foot of her injured leg on it. He stirred the fire with an iron poker. The desultory flames showed new life when he added sticks of firewood from the wooden box on the hearth.

The Gawrylows stamped in. Reuben closed the door behind them, deepening the darkness inside. In spite of the warmth the fire was now giving off, Rusty shivered and shrank deeper into her coat.

"You must be hungry." Quinn went to the wood-burning stove in one corner. He lifted the lid on a simmering pot and peered inside. "Stew smells done. Want some?"

Rusty was on the verge of refusing but Cooper answered for both of them. "Yes, please. Got any coffee?"

"Sure. Reuben, start a pot of coffee to boiling."

The younger man hadn't stopped staring at Rusty since he'd slunk in and dropped Cooper's and her belongings just inside the door.

Cooper followed Reuben's gawking stare back to Rusty. He wished to hell the firelight didn't shine through her hair, making it shimmer. Pale and drawn as her face was, her eyes looked huge, vulnerable, female. To the young man, who apparently lived alone in this wilderness with his father, a woman wouldn't even have to be pretty to be enticing. Rusty must have embodied his wildest fantasies.

With his bare hand, Reuben reached into a metal canister of coffee and tossed a handful into an enamel pot.

He filled the pot with water from the pump in the dry sink and set it on the stove to boil. Within a few minutes Rusty and Cooper were handed plates filled with an unidentifiable stew. She was sure she was better off not knowing what meat was in it, so she refrained from asking. She chewed and swallowed quickly. It was at least hot and filling. The coffee was so strong that she grimaced as she swallowed, but she drank most of it.

While they ate, Cooper and she had a captivated audience. The older man's stare was more subtle than his son's, but possibly more observant. His deep-set eyes didn't miss a single move they made.

He broke a long silence by asking, "You married?"

"Yes," Cooper lied easily. "Five years."

Rusty swallowed the last bite she'd taken, hoping that the Gawrylows didn't notice how difficult it was to get down. She was glad Cooper had taken the initiative to answer. She didn't think she could have uttered a word.

"Kids?"

This time Cooper got tongue-tied, so it was left to Rusty to say "No," hoping that that answer was satisfactory to her "husband." She planned on asking him later why he had lied, but for now she would play along. His wariness was out of proportion, she thought; but she would still rather ally herself with him than with the Gawrylows.

Cooper finished eating and set his plate and cup aside. He glanced around the cabin. "You don't have a transmitter, do you? A ham radio?"

"No."

"Have you heard any airplanes flying over lately?"

"I haven't. Reuben?" Gawrylow nudged his gawking son in the knee. The younger man dragged his eyes away from Rusty.

"Planes?" he asked stupidly.

"We crashed two days ago," Cooper explained. "They're bound to have figured that out by now. I thought there might have been search planes out looking for survivors."

"I haven't heard any planes," Reuben said abruptly and returned his unwavering attention to Rusty.

"How can you stand to live so far away from everything?" she asked. Such self-imposed isolation dismayed her. She couldn't imagine doing without the amenities a city had to offer, particularly by choice. Even rural living would be tolerable if one could get to a city every now and then. But to deliberately sever all contact with civilization—

"We walk to the river and hitch a ride to Yellowknife twice a year," Quinn told them. "Once in April and once in October. We stay for a few days, sell a few pelts, buy what supplies we'll need, and hitch a ride back. That's all the dealings we want with the outside world."

"But why?" Rusty asked.

"I got a bellyful of towns and people. I lived in Edmonton, worked on a freight dock. One day the boss accused me of stealing."

"Were you?"

Rusty was amazed at Cooper's audacity, but the old man didn't seem to take offense at the blunt question. He merely cackled and spat a stringy wad of tobacco juice into the fireplace.

"It was easier to disappear than to go to court and prove my innocence," he said evasively. "Reuben's mother was dead. He and I just up and left. Took nothing with us but what money we had and the clothes on our backs."

"How long ago was this?"

"Ten years. We drifted for a while, then gradually migrated here. We liked it. We stayed." He shrugged. "We've never felt the urge to go back."

He concluded his story. Rusty had finished eating, but the Gawrylows seemed content to continue staring at Cooper and her.

"If you'll excuse us," Cooper said after an awkward silence, "I'd like to check my wife's injury."

Those two words, *my wife's*, seemed to come easily to his lips, but they jangled with falsehood in Rusty's ears. She wondered if the Gawrylows were convinced that they were a couple.

Quinn carried their plates to the sink where he pumped water over them. "Reuben, do your chores."

The young man seemed inclined to argue, but his father shot him a baleful, challenging glance. He shuffled toward the door, pulling on his coat and cap as he went. Quinn went out onto the porch and began stacking firewood against the wall of the cabin.

Rusty leaned close to Cooper where he knelt in front of her. "What do you think?"

"About what?"

"About them," she replied with asperity. He pinched the hem of her slacks between his fingers and sliced a knee-high tear in them with his knife. She reacted angrily. "Why'd you do that? This is my last pair of slacks. I won't have any clothes left by the time you get through cutting them to shreds."

He raised his head. His eyes were hard. "Would you rather take them off and give Reuben an eyeful of those nothing-to-them panties you wear?"

She opened her mouth, but discovered that she had no proper comeback, so she fell silent while he unwrapped her bandages and checked her stitched wound. It seemed to have suffered no ill effects as a result of her hike. But it was sore again. Lying to him about it was useless since she was grimacing by the time he finished rewrapping it.

"Hurt?"

"A little, yes," she admitted.

"Stay off it for the rest of the day. Either sit here or lie on the pallet I'm about to make."

"Pallet? What about the beds?" She glanced across the room to where two beds stood against adjacent walls. "Don't you think they'll offer me one?"

He laughed. "I'm sure Reuben would love for you to join him in his. But unless you want lice, I'd advise you to stay out of it."

She jerked her leg back. Cooper just couldn't be nice, could he? They were comrades because they had to be, but they were not—no, definitely not—friends.

Five

It seemed to take forever for bedtime to arrive. Early in the evening they shared another meal with the Gawrylows. Their discussion about the extensive hike to the Mackenzie River carried over long after they were finished eating.

"There's no path to follow. It's rugged terrain, so it's a full day's walk," Quinn told them.

"We'll leave as soon as it's light enough." Cooper hadn't let Rusty out of his sight. He'd kept an eagle eye on her all afternoon. Now, as she sat in the straight-backed chair, he sat beside her on the floor, a proprietary arm draped over her thigh. "We won't need to pack much. I don't plan to take everything—only what's absolutely necessary."

Quinn asked, "What about the woman?"

Rusty felt Cooper's biceps contract against her leg. "What about her?"

"She'll slow us down."

"I'll stay here with her, Pa," Reuben offered gallantly.

"No." Cooper's response was as sharp as a jab made

with a hat pin. "She goes. I don't care how slow we have to travel."

"It's all the same to us," Quinn said with his characteristic shrug, "but I thought you were in a hurry to contact your friends and family. They must be worried about you."

Rusty glanced down at the top of Cooper's head. "Cooper?" He looked up at her. "I don't mind staying here alone. If you can cover more ground without me hobbling along, it only makes sense, doesn't it? You could call my father as soon as you get to a telephone. He'll send someone to pick me up. This could all be over by tomorrow night."

He regarded her wistful expression. She'd go along and bear up under the hardships stoically if he insisted. But it wouldn't be easy for her to cover fifteen miles of forested ground even if she weren't injured. Through no fault of her own, she would cause them endless delays that might necessitate making camp for a night.

Still, he didn't like the idea of being separated from her. No matter how feisty she was, she couldn't effectively defend herself. In this environment she was as helpless as a butterfly. He wasn't being sentimental, he assured himself. It was just that she had survived this long against incredible odds; he would hate for something to happen to her now that rescue was a probability instead of a pipe dream.

His hand folded around her knee protectively. "Let's wait and see how you feel in the morning."

The next several hours crawled by. Rusty didn't know how the Gawrylows maintained their sanity. There was nothing to do, nothing to read, nothing to listen to or to look at—except each other. And when that became boring, they all stared at the sputtering kerosene lamp that put out more smelly black smoke than light.

One would expect these hermits to ply them with a million questions about the outside world, but the Gawrylows showed a marked absence of interest in anything that was going on beyond their boundaries.

Feeling grimy and unwashed, Rusty timidly asked for a bowl of water. Reuben stumbled over his own long feet while fetching it for her and slopped some of it in her lap before successfully setting it down.

She pushed the sleeves of her sweater up to her elbows and washed her face and hands with the bar of soap Cooper had permitted her to bring along. She would have liked to savor the luxurious feeling of cupping handful after handful of water over her face, but three pairs of eyes were focused on her. When Cooper thrust one of his own T-shirts into her wet hands, she accepted it regretfully and dried her face.

Picking up her hairbrush, she began pulling it through her hair, which was not only dirtier than it had been in her life, but also matted and tangled. She was just beginning to work all the snarls out when Cooper jerked the brush out of her hands and said bossily, "That's enough."

She rounded on him, ready to protest, but his stony face stopped her. He'd been behaving strangely all day— more so than usual. She wanted to ask what the hell was wrong with him, why he was so edgy, but wisely decided that now wasn't an opportune time for an argument.

She did, however, show her irritation by angrily snatching her hairbrush back and repacking it in her precious bag of toiletries. They were her only reminders that somewhere in the world hot water, cream rinse, perfume, bubble bath and hand lotion were still realities.

At last, they all settled down for the night. She slept

with Cooper as she had the past two nights. Lying curled on her side, her injured leg the uppermost, she faced the fire. Beneath her was the pallet Cooper had made using the pelts they'd carried with them. He had tactfully declined to use the bedding Quinn had offered them.

Cooper didn't curve his body around hers as he had been doing. He lay on his back tensely, never completely relaxed, and ever watchful.

"Stop twitching," she whispered after about half an hour. "What's your problem?"

"Shut up and go to sleep."

"Why don't you?"

"I can't."

"Why?"

"When we get out of here I'll explain it to you."

"Explain it to me now."

"I shouldn't have to. Read the signs."

"Does it have anything to do with why you told them we were married?"

"It has everything to do with that."

She pondered that for a moment. "I'll admit that they're kinda spooky, the way they keep staring at us. But I'm sure they're only curious. Besides, they're sound asleep now." The chorus of loud snores should have been his assurance that the Gawrylows were harmlessly asleep.

"Right," he said dryly, "and so should you be. Nighty-night."

Exasperated with him, she rolled back onto her side. Eventually she sank into a deep sleep. It was mercilessly short-lived. It seemed only minutes after her eyes closed that Cooper was nudging her awake. She groaned in protest, but remembering that today was the day her ordeal would come to an end, she sat up.

The cabin was still in total darkness, although she

could see the shadowy outlines of Cooper and the Gawrylows moving about. Quinn was at the stove brewing coffee and stirring the pot of stew. It must never run out but he continually added to, she thought, hoping that she didn't return home with a case of ptomaine poisoning.

Cooper knelt beside her. "How do you feel?"

"Cold," she replied, rubbing her hands up and down her arms. Even though she hadn't slept in his embrace, his body heat had kept her warm throughout the night. He was better than any electric blanket she'd ever slept with.

"I meant health-wise. How does your leg feel?"

"Stiff, but not as sore as yesterday."

"You sure?"

"Positive."

"Get up and move around on it. Let's give it a test run."

He helped her to her feet. Once she had slipped her coat on and propped herself on her crutches, they went outside so she could have some privacy; the Gawrylows' cabin didn't have indoor plumbing.

When she emerged from the outhouse, the rising sun had turned the overcast sky a watery gray. That light only emphasized her wanness. Cooper could tell that the effort of leaving the cabin to go to the bathroom had taxed her. Her hard breathing created clouds of vapor around her head.

He cursed beneath his breath. "What?" she asked him anxiously.

"You'll never make it, Rusty. Not in days." Hands on hips, he expelled his frustration in a gust of ghostly white breath and said, "What the hell am I going to do with you?"

He didn't soften the question with any degree of tenderness or compassion. His inflection intimated that he'd far rather not be bothered with her at all.

"Well, I'm sorry to inconvenience you further, Mr. Landry. Why don't you bait a bear trap with me? Then you can jog all the way to that damn river."

He stepped forward and put his face close to hers. "Look, Pollyanna, you're apparently too naive to see it, but there's a lot more at stake here than just getting to the river."

"Not as far as I'm concerned," she shot back. "If you sprouted wings and flew there, it couldn't be fast enough for me. I want to get out of here, away from you, and back home where I belong."

His stern lip all but disappeared beneath his mustache. "All right, then." He spun around and stamped back toward the cabin. "I'll get there much faster without having you tagging along. You'll stay here."

"Fine," she called after him.

Then, setting her own chin as stubbornly as his, she made her halting progress up the incline toward the cabin. The men were in the midst of an argument by the time she reached the door, which Cooper, in his haste or anger, had left ajar. Turning sideways and using her elbows, she maneuvered her way inside.

"Be reasonable, Gawrylow," Cooper was saying. "Reuben is twenty or so years younger than you. I want to move fast. He goes with me. You stay with my...my wife. I can't leave her here alone."

"But, Pa—" Reuben whined.

"He's right, Reuben. You'll move much faster than I could. If you're lucky, you might reach the river by midafternoon."

The plan wasn't to Reuben's liking at all. He gave Rusty one last, hungry glance, then ambled out, muttering under his breath. Cooper didn't appear much happier. He drew Rusty aside and handed her the flare gun, curtly instructing her on how to use it.

"Think you can manage that?"

"I'm not an idiot."

He seemed prone to argue, but changed his mind. "If you hear an airplane, get outside as fast as you can and fire the flare straight up."

"Why aren't you taking it with you?"

The flare gun had been within Cooper's reach since they left the wreckage. "Because the roof of the cabin would be easier to spot than two men on foot. Keep this with you, too." Before she knew what he was about, he pulled the waistband of her slacks away from her body and slid the sheathed skinning knife inside. The smooth leather was cold against the naked skin of her abdomen. She gasped and sucked in her breath. He smiled at her startled reaction. "That should keep you mindful of where it is at all times."

"Why should I be mindful of that?"

He stared into her eyes for a long moment. "Hopefully you'll never have to know why."

She returned his stare. Up until that moment, she hadn't realized how much she hated the thought of his leaving her behind. She had put up a courageous front, but the idea of covering miles of wilderness on crutches had been overwhelming. In a way she was glad he had opted to go without her. But now that he was actually leaving, she wanted to cling to him and beg him not to.

She didn't, of course. He had little enough respect for her as it was. He thought she was a petted, pampered, city girl. Obviously he was right, because at that moment, she was sorely dreading the hours she would have to spend until he came back for her.

Cooper broke the telling stare and, with an impatient curse, turned away.

"Cooper!"

He spun back around. "What?"

"Be...be careful."

Within a heartbeat, she was anchored against his chest and his mouth was above hers, taking from it a scorching kiss that burned her soul. It surprised her so that she slumped against him. His arms tightened around her waist and drew her up so close and high that her toes dangled inches above his boots. She sought to regain her balance by clutching handfuls of his coat.

His lips ground against hers. They were possessive and hard. But his tongue was soft and warm and wet. It filled her mouth, explored, stroked. A desire that had been building for forty-eight hours overcame his iron control. His self-discipline snapped, but he was still masterful. This was a no-nonsense kiss that had nothing to do with romance. It was a kiss of passion. Raw. Carnal. Selfish.

Dizzily Rusty threw one of her arms around his neck and tilted her head back to give him deeper access, which he took. His stubbled jaw scraped her skin, but she didn't care. His mustache was surprisingly silky. It tickled and tantalized.

All too soon for her, he broke the kiss, pulling his head back abruptly and leaving her lips parted and damp and wanting more. "I'll be back as soon as possible. Goodbye, honey."

Honey? *Honey?*

He released her and turned toward the door. That's when she noticed Quinn Gawrylow sitting at the table, mindlessly chewing his perpetual wad of tobacco and watching them with the still, silent concentration of a cougar.

Rusty's heart sank like lead. Cooper had kissed her

for the old man's benefit—not for his own. And certainly not for hers.

She shot his broad back a venomous look as he went through the door. It slapped closed behind him. Good riddance, she thought. How dare he—

Then, realizing that the old man's eyes were still on her, she looked at him with a vapid good-little-wife smile. "Do you think he'll be all right?"

"Reuben knows what he's doing. He'll take care of Mr. Landry." He waved down at the pallet still spread out in front of the hearth. "It's early yet. Why don't you go back to sleep?"

"No, I, uh—" she cleared her throat noisily "—I'm too keyed up to sleep. I think I'll just sit here for a while."

"Coffee?" He moved toward the stove.

"Please."

She didn't want any, but it would give her something to do and help pass the time. She set her crutches and the flare gun on the hearth within easy reach and lowered herself into the chair. The knife's scabbard poked her lower abdomen. Why it hadn't plunged right into her when Cooper had pulled her against his—

Her heart fluttered with the memory. It hadn't been only the knife's hardness she'd felt against her middle. He'd probably derived a lot of joy out of humiliating her like that.

Feeling rebellious, she defiantly took the knife out of her waistband and laid it on the hearth. Accepting the cup of steaming coffee from Quinn, she settled down to wait through what would probably be the longest day of her life.

Cooper calculated that they'd gone no farther than a mile when Reuben commenced to talk. Cooper could have gone the whole fifteen miles without a conversation, but maybe talking would make the time pass more quickly and help take his mind off Rusty.

"How come you don't have any kids?" Reuben asked him.

Cooper's instincts slipped into overdrive. Each of his senses was on the alert. That prickle at the back of his neck, which could always be relied upon to warn him that something wasn't quite right, hadn't gone away. Ever since he'd heard Rusty's scream and found her in a standoff with the Gawrylows, he had been suspicious of the two men. He might be doing them a grave injustice. They were probably on the level. But probabilities weren't worth a damn. Until he had Rusty safely turned over to the authorities, he wasn't giving either of the recluses the benefit of the doubt. If they proved to be reliable, then they would have earned his undying gratitude. Until then—

"Huh?" Reuben probed. "How come you—"

"I heard you." Cooper was following Reuben's lead. He didn't let the man get too far ahead of him, nor did he crowd up too close behind him. "Rusty has a career. We're both busy. We'll get around to having kids one of these days."

He hoped that would end the discussion. Children and families were topics Cooper always avoided talking about. Now, he didn't want to talk at all. He wanted to pour every ounce of energy into reaching that river as soon as possible.

"If I'd been married to her for five years, we'd have five kids by now," Reuben bragged rashly.

"But you're not."

"Maybe you ain't doing it right."

"What?"

Reuben gave him a sly wink over his shoulder. "You know, screwing."

The word crawled over Cooper like a loathsome insect. It wasn't that he was offended by the word. He used far worse on a daily basis. It was that he was offended by the word in connection with Rusty. It didn't occur to him that only the night before last he'd used it himself. He was too busy hoping that before the day was out, he wouldn't have to pound Reuben's face to mush; but if he made many more references to Rusty in that context, he just might.

"If she was my woman—"

"But she isn't." Cooper's voice cracked like a bullwhip.

"She will be, though."

With that, Reuben, wearing the grin of a madman, spun around and aimed his rifle at Cooper's chest. Cooper had subconsciously been bracing himself all morning for such an attack. He raised his rifle a split second after Reuben, but Reuben got off the first shot.

"What was that?" Rusty jumped, realizing that she'd been drowsing in her chair.

Quinn was sitting where she'd last seen him, at the table. "Hmm?"

"I thought I heard something."

"I didn't hear anything."

"I could swear—"

"The logs in the fireplace shifted. That's all."

"Oh." Chagrined by her nervousness, she relaxed again in her chair. "I must have dozed off. How long ago since they left?"

"Not long."

He got up and moved toward her, kneeling down on the hearth to add logs to the fire. The warmth seeped into

Rusty's skin and her eyes drifted closed again. Sad and dirty as this cabin was, at least it provided a roof over her head and protection from the cold west wind. She was grateful for that. After spending days—

Her eyes popped open at his touch. Quinn, still kneeling in front of her, had his hand folded around her calf. "I thought you might want to prop up your leg again," he said.

His voice was as gentle as a saint's, but his eyes were Lucifer's own as they stared up at her from within their cavelike sockets. Terror gripped her, but common sense warned her not to show it.

"No, thank you. In fact," she said in a thin voice, "I think I'll walk around a bit to exercise it."

She reached for her crutches, but he grabbed them up first. "Let me help you."

Before she could protest, he caught her arm and pulled her out of the chair. He had caught her off guard and the momentum caused the front of her body to bump against his. She backed away instantly, but found that she couldn't go far because his other hand was at the small of her back, urging her forward.

"No!"

"I'm only trying to help you," he said smoothly, obviously enjoying her mounting distress.

"Then please let me go, Mr. Gawrylow. I can manage."

"Not without help. I'll take your husband's place. He told me to take care of you, didn't he?" He ran his hand over her hip and Rusty went cold with fear.

"Don't touch me like that." She tried to squirm away from him but his hands were everywhere. "Get your hands off me."

"What's wrong with my hands?" His expression suddenly turned mean. "Aren't they clean enough for you?"

"No...yes...I...I just meant that Cooper will—"

"Cooper won't do anything," he said with a sinister smile. "And from now on I'll touch you however I want."

He yanked her against him. This time there was no doubt about his intention. Rusty funneled all her strength into getting away from him. She placed the heels of her hands on his shoulders and arched her back, trying to push herself away and at the same time to dodge his kiss.

The crutches slid out from under her arms and fell to the floor. She had to support herself on her sore leg and a pain shot up the jagged scar. She cried out.

"Go ahead, scream. I won't mind." His breath was foul and hot against her face. She turned her head away, but he caught her jaw between iron fingers and pulled it back around. Just before his mouth made contact with hers, they heard thudding footsteps outside.

"Help me," Rusty screamed.

"Reuben?" the old man shouted. "Get in here."

Quinn turned his head toward the door, but it wasn't Reuben who came crashing through. Cooper's sweating face was a fierce mask of hatred and rage. His hair was littered with twigs and leaves. There were bleeding scratches on his cheeks and hands. His shirt was specked with blood. To Rusty, no one had ever looked better.

Feet wide apart, Cooper barked, "Let her go, you filthy animal."

Rusty collapsed to the floor when Gawrylow released her. He spun around. As he did so, he reached behind his back. Before Rusty fully realized what had happened, she heard a solid thunk. Then she saw the handle of Cooper's knife in the center of Quinn's chest. The blade was fully buried between his ribs.

The old man was wearing a startled expression. He groped for the handle of the knife. His searching fingers closed around it as he dropped to his knees. Then he fell face down onto the floor and was still.

Rusty gathered her arms and legs against her body, forming herself into a ball. She clapped her hands over her mouth and stared at the still form with wide, unfocusing eyes. Her breath was trapped in her lungs.

Cooper, knocking furniture aside, rushed across the room and crouched in front of her. "Are you all right?" He laid a hand on her shoulder. She recoiled in fright.

He froze. His eyes went as hard as slate as he said, "No need to thank me."

Gradually Rusty lowered her hands and released her breath. She gazed up at Cooper, her lips white with fear. "You killed him." The words had no sound; she mouthed them.

"Before he killed me, you little fool. Look!" He pointed down at the dead man's back. There was a small handgun tucked into the waistband of his pants. "Don't you get it yet?" he roared. "They were going to waste me and keep you. They planned to share you between them."

She shuddered with revulsion. "No!"

"Oh, yeah," Cooper said, nodding his head. Apparently exasperated with her, he stood up and rolled the body over. Squeezing her eyes shut, Rusty averted her head. She heard the body being dragged across the floor and out the door. She heard Quinn's boots thump on the steps as Cooper dragged him down them.

She wasn't sure how long she stayed curled up in that fetal position on the floor. But she still hadn't moved when Cooper returned. He loomed over her. "Did he hurt you?"

Miserably she shook her head.

"Answer me, dammit! Did he hurt you?"

She raised her head and glared up at him. *"No!"*

"He was about to rape you. You *do* realize that, don't you? Or are the stars in your eyes still keeping you from seeing the light?"

Not stars, but tears filled her eyes. She was experiencing a delayed reaction to her horror. "What are you doing here? Why did you come back? Where's Reuben? What are you going to say to him when he gets back?"

"Nothing. Reuben won't be coming back."

She clamped her teeth over her quivering lower lip and closed her eyes. Tears rolled down her cheeks. "You killed him, too, didn't you? That's his blood on you."

"Yes, dammit," he hissed, bending over her. "I shot him in self-defense. He walked me into the woods just far enough to separate us, then he turned a gun on me with every intention of killing me and making you his 'woman.'" Staring up at him, she shook her head in disbelief, which seemed to infuriate him. "And don't you dare pretend to be surprised. You had whipped them into a sexual froth and you know it."

"Me? How? What did I do?"

"Brushing your hair for God's sake!"

"'Brushing'—"

"Just being you. Just looking the way you do."

"Stop yelling at me!" she sobbed. "I didn't do anything."

"Except cause me to kill two men!" he shouted. "Think about that while I'm out burying them."

He stalked out. The fire in the fireplace burned out and the cabin grew cold. But Rusty didn't care.

She was still sitting in a heap on the floor and crying hard when he came back. She was tired. There wasn't a place on her body that didn't ache either from sleeping on the ground or walking on crutches or suffering Quinn Gawrylow's squeezing caresses.

She wanted good, honest food. She'd gladly trade her Maserati for a glass of milk. Her clothes had been ripped by tree branches or ravaged by this barbaric hoodlum she was marooned with. The fur coat she had prized so highly had been used as a litter.

And she had seen men die.

Five in the plane crash. Two at the hands of the man who now threw himself down beside her. He roughly raised her head by placing his callused fingers beneath her chin.

"Get up," he ordered. "Dry your face. You're not going to spend the rest of the day sitting around crying like a baby."

"Go to hell," she spat, lifting her chin out of his grasp.

He was so furious, his lips hardly moved when he spoke. "Look, if you had a good thing going with Reuben and his pa, you should have told me. I'm sorry I ruined it for you."

"You bastard."

"I would have been all too glad to leave you in this paradise and strike out for the river by myself. But I think I should tell you that Reuben had a lot of children in mind. Of course you might not have ever known if the kids you hatched were his or his daddy's."

"Shut up!" She raised her hand to slap him.

He caught it in midair and they stared at each other for several tense seconds. Finally Cooper relaxed his fingers from around her wrist. Snarling angrily, he stood up and kicked a chair as far across the cabin as he could.

"It was either them or me," he said in a voice that vibrated with rage. "Reuben fired first. I got lucky and deflected his rifle just in time. I had no choice."

"You didn't have to kill them."

"No?"

An alternative didn't leap into her mind, but she was sure that if she thought about it long enough she would come up with one. Temporarily conceding, she lowered her eyes. "Why didn't you just keep going?"

His eyes narrowed to slits as he looked down at her. "Don't think I didn't consider it."

"Oh," she ground out. "I can't wait until I'm rid of you."

"Believe me, the feeling is mutual. But in the meantime we've got to tolerate each other. First thing on the agenda is to get this place cleaned up. I'm not spending another night in this stink hole."

Her jaw went slack with disbelief. Slowly her eyes roamed the grimy interior of the cabin. "Clean this place up? Is that what you said?"

"Yeah. We'd better get started, too. The day's getting away."

He righted the chair he'd just kicked over and made his way toward the pile of dingy bedding where Reuben had slept the night before. Rusty started laughing and her laughter was tinged with impending hysteria.

"You're not serious?"

"Like hell I'm not."

"We're spending the night here?"

"And every night from now on until we're rescued."

She came to her feet, propping herself up on one crutch while she watched him strip both beds and pile the bedding in the middle of the floor. "What about the river?"

"That might have all been a lie."

"The Mackenzie River is real, Cooper."

"But where is it from here?"

"You could keep walking in the direction they said until you found it."

"I could. I could also get terribly lost. Or injured and stranded. If you went with me, we might not make it out before the first real snow, in which case we'd probably die of exposure. If you stayed here and something happened to me, you'd die of starvation before the winter was over. And I'm not even sure the direction Reuben led me in was the right one. I've got 359 other choices from this cabin, and getting around to them all would take over a year."

Hands braced on his hips, he faced her. "None of those alternatives sounds very appealing to me. On the other hand if we clean this place up, we can survive. It's not the Beverly Hills Hotel, but it's shelter and there's a constant supply of fresh water."

She didn't appreciate his sarcasm and her mutinous expression let him know it. His whole demeanor suggested that she was foolish not to see all that without his having to explain it, and issued a challenge she wasn't about to back down from. She had been weak this morning, but she never would be again. Pushing up the sleeves of her sweater, she said, "What do you want me to do?"

He hitched his head backward. "Start with the stove."

Without another word, he gathered up the foul bedding and carried it outside.

Rusty attacked the black iron stove with a vengeance, scouring it from top to bottom, using more elbow grease than soap, since she had more of that. It was hard work, especially since she had to keep herself propped up on one crutch. She moved from the stove to the sink, then to the windows, then every stick of furniture got washed down.

After he had boiled the bedding in a caldron outside

and hung it up to dry—or freeze, if the temperature turned much colder—Cooper came inside and washed the stones of the hearth. He found a colony of dead insects beneath the woodpile. They had no doubt died of old age since it was almost a certainty that the hearth had never been swept. Keeping the door and windows open to air the place out, he shored up the front porch and stacked firewood on the cabin's south side to protect it from the weather's brunt.

Rusty couldn't sweep the floor, so he did. But when he was finished, she got down on hands and knees and scrubbed it. Her sculptured nails broke off one by one. Where a mere chip would have sent her into a tizzy not long ago, she merely shrugged and went on with her scrubbing, taking satisfaction in the results of her labor.

Cooper brought in two beheaded and plucked birds— she didn't recognize the species—for their dinner. She had made an inventory of the Gawrylows' hoard and was pleased to find a fair amount of canned goods. They had apparently made their October trip to Yellowknife and were well stocked for the winter. A gourmet cook she wasn't, but it didn't take much talent to boil the fowl together with two cans of vegetables and a sprinkling of salt. By the time the stew was done, the aroma was making her mouth water. Darkness was settling in before Cooper carried in the bedding.

"Is it deloused?" she asked, turning from the stove.

"I think so. I boiled the hell out of it. I'm not sure it's quite dry, but if I leave it out any longer, it's going to freeze. We'll check it after dinner and if it's not dry, we'll hang it up in front of the fire."

He washed his hands at the sink, which was sparkling compared to what it had been.

They sat down to eat at the table Rusty had sanded

clean. Cooper smiled when he unfolded what had once been a sock and was now acting as a napkin and placed it in his lap, but he didn't comment on her ingenuity. If he noticed the jar with the arrangement of autumn leaves serving as a centerpiece, he said nothing to indicate it. He ate two portions of the stew but didn't say a word about it.

Rusty was crushed. He could have said something nice—one single word of encouragement. Even a puppy needs to be patted on the head now and then.

She dejectedly carried their tin dishes to the sink. While she was pumping water over them, he moved up behind her. "You worked hard today."

His voice was soft and low and came from directly above her head. He was standing very close. His sheer physicality overwhelmed her. She felt tremulous. "So did you."

"I think we deserve a treat, don't you?"

Her stomach rose and fell as weightlessly as a balloon. Memory of the kiss he had given her that morning filled her mind, while a potent desire to repeat it flooded her veins. Slowly she turned around and gazed up at him. Breathlessly she asked, "What did you have in mind, Cooper?"

"A bath."

Six

"A…bath?" Dorothy couldn't have said "Oz?" with any more awe and wistfulness.

"A real one. The works. Hot water, soap." He went to the door, opened it, and came back in rolling a large washtub. "I found this behind the cabin and cleaned it out."

She didn't remember feeling this grateful when she opened the present from her father and found her full-length, red fox coat folded amid tissue paper. She clasped her hands beneath her chin. "Oh, Cooper, thank you."

"Don't get gushy," he said querulously. "We'll get as disgusting as the Gawrylows if we don't bathe. Not every day, though."

Rusty didn't let him spoil her good mood. He didn't allow people to get even close enough to thank him. Well, that was his problem. He'd done something very thoughtful for her. She had thanked him. Beyond that, what else could she do? He must know how much this meant to her, even if he chose to act like a heel about it now.

She filled several pots and kettles with water from the pump. He carried them to the stove to heat them up, refueling the fire to hurry them along. He then dragged the tub across the wooden floor and placed it directly in front of the fireplace. The metal was icy cold, but in a few minutes the fire would warm it up.

Rusty watched him making all these preparations with expectation, then a growing concern. "What do I do about, uh…"

Saying nothing, expressionless, Cooper unfurled one of the rough muslin bed-sheets he'd boiled and aired that day. The ceiling of the cabin had bare beams. Apparently the Gawrylows had hung meat from it because there were several metal hooks screwed into the dark wood.

Cooper stood on a chair and pushed one of the sharp hooks through a corner of the sheet. Repositioning the chair several times, he soon had the sheet hanging like a curtain behind the tub.

"Thank you," Rusty said. She was glad to have the sheet there but couldn't help but notice that with the fireplace behind it, it was translucent. The tub was silhouetted against it. Anybody in the tub would be, too.

Cooper must have noticed that at the same time, because he shifted his eyes away from it and ran his hands nervously up and down his pants legs. "I think the water's just about ready."

Rusty assembled her precious cache of toiletries—a bar of scented soap, a small plastic bottle of shampoo, her razor—on the seat of the chair near the tub.

Earlier in the day, she had separated the meager clothing they had left and neatly folded and stacked it on separate shelves, one for her, one for Cooper. She took a fresh pair of long johns and a tank top from her stack now and draped them over the back of the chair.

When everything was ready, she stood awkwardly by while Cooper carefully carried the heavy pots of boiling water across the room and poured them into the tub. Steam rose out of it, but as far as Rusty was concerned it couldn't be too hot. She had four days' accumulation of grime and fatigue to soak away. Besides, she was accustomed to spending several minutes each day in her hot tub at home.

"What do I dry with?" she asked.

Cooper tossed her a coarse, dingy towel from the pile of bedding he'd carried in earlier. "I found a couple of these hanging from nails outside the cabin. I boiled them, too. They've never known fabric softener, but they're better than nothing."

The towel did feel more like sandpaper than terry cloth, but Rusty accepted it without comment.

"There, that should do it," Cooper said brusquely, emptying the contents of the last kettle into the tub. "Ease into it carefully. Don't scald yourself."

"Okay."

Standing at opposite sides of the tub, they faced each other. Their eyes met through the rising steam. The humidity was already curling Rusty's hair and making her complexion look dewy and rosy.

Cooper turned his back abruptly and impatiently swatted aside the curtain. It fell back into place. Rusty could hear his stamping, booted footsteps against the uneven flooring. He went outside and slammed the door closed behind him.

She sighed with resignation. He had a sour disposition and that's all there was to it. And while she was lolling in her first bath in four days, she certainly wasn't going to dwell on his personality flaws. She wouldn't let him spoil this for her, no matter how disagreeable he became.

Because she still avoided putting any weight on her leg, it was a challenge to get out of her clothes. When she had managed that, it was an even greater challenge to ease herself into the bathtub. She was finally able to do so by supporting herself on her arms and sitting down slowly, pulling her sore leg in behind her.

It felt more heavenly than she had allowed herself to anticipate. Cooper had been right to caution her; the water was hot, but deliciously so. The corrugated bottom of the tub felt odd against her buttocks and took some getting used to, but before long the luxury of being submerged in hot, soothing water took her mind off that one minor discomfort.

She immersed as much of herself as possible and rested her head against the rim. Her eyes slid closed. She was so relaxed that she didn't even flinch when she heard Cooper come back inside. She only frowned slightly when a breath of cold air reached her before he shut the door behind him.

Eventually she extended one dripping arm and took the bar of soap off the seat of the chair. She was tempted to lather herself liberally, wantonly, wastefully. But she thought better of it. This bar of soap might have to last a long time. Better not squander it, she decided, as she worked up an adequate lather and soaped herself all over.

Propping her feet one at a time on the rim of the tub, she shaved her legs, carefully maneuvering the razor around Cooper's stitching. With anguish she realized what an unsightly scar she was going to have but was ashamed of her vanity. She was lucky to be alive. As soon as she got back to Beverly Hills, she would have a plastic surgeon repair Cooper's well-intentioned, but unattractive, handiwork.

It struck her then that he was being awfully noisy. "Cooper, what are you doing?"

"Making up the beds," he said, grunting with the effort. "These frames are made of solid oak and weigh a ton."

"I can't wait to lie down on one."

"Don't expect it to be much better than the ground. There're no mattresses. Just canvas platforms like cots. But mattresses would have had lice, so it's just as well."

Laying aside her razor, she picked up the bottle of shampoo and after dunking her head beneath the water, squeezed out a dollop. The shampoo would have to be rationed even more sparingly than the soap. She worked it through her thick hair, scrubbing ruthlessly from her scalp to the ends. She dunked her head to rinse it, then wrung out as much water as she could.

Laying her head against the tub's rim again, she fanned her hair out behind her so it could begin to dry. It would drip on the floor, but water was probably the least offensive substance to ever be dripped on it.

Again, her eyes closed as she luxuriated in the warmth of the water, the floral fragrance of shampoo and soap, and the deliciousness of feeling clean again.

Eventually the water began to cool and she knew it was time to get out. Anyway, she doubted that Cooper would go to bed before she did. He must be exhausted after all he'd done since getting up before daybreak that morning. She had no idea what time it was. The crash had stopped both their watches. Time was measured by the sun coming up and going down. The days were short, but today had been long—emotionally as well as physically taxing.

She braced her arms on the rim of the tub and tried to push herself up. To her dismay, her arms collapsed like wet noodles. She had stayed in the hot water too long; her muscles were useless. Several times she tried, but to no avail. Her arms simply wouldn't support her. She devised other plans, but none of them worked because of her sore leg, which she couldn't put any weight on.

Finally, growing chilled and knowing that the inevitable couldn't be postponed indefinitely, she bashfully called his name.

"What?"

His irritable response wasn't too encouraging, but she had no choice. "I can't get out."

After a silence long enough for a telephone pole to stretch out in, he said, "Huh?"

Rusty squeezed her eyes shut and repeated, "I can't get out of the tub."

"Get out the same way you got in."

"I'm too weak from the hot water. My arms won't hold me up long enough to step out."

His curses were so scorching, she didn't know why the bed-sheet curtain didn't combust. When she heard his approaching footsteps, she crossed her arms over her breasts. Cool air fanned across her wet, bare back as he moved the curtain aside. She stared straight ahead into the fireplace, feeling his eyes on her as he moved toward the tub.

For a long time he just stood there, saying nothing. Rusty's lungs were almost ready to burst from internal tension by the time he said, "I'll slide my hands under your arms. Come up on your left leg. Then while I'm holding you up, lift it out of the tub and set it on the floor. Okay?"

His voice was low and of the same texture as the towel he'd given her to use—as rough as sandpaper. "Okay." She eased her arms slightly away from her body. Even though she'd been expecting it, the first touch of his fingertips against her slippery, wet skin, came as a shock. Not because it felt awful, but because it didn't.

And it only got better from there. Confident and strong, his hands slid into the notches of her armpits and cupped them supportively. He braced his legs wide apart, almost straddling the tub, and lifted her. She sucked in her breath sharply.

"What's the matter?"

"My...my underarms are sore," she told him breathlessly. "Because of the crutches." He muttered a curse. It was so vile she hoped she hadn't heard it correctly.

His hands slipped over her wet skin and encased her ribs. "Let's try it this way. Ready?"

Rusty, according to his instructions, supported herself on her left leg, letting the injured one dangle uselessly as he raised her out of the water.

"Okay so far?" She nodded. "Ready?" She replied in the same soundless way. He took all her weight on his hands as she lifted her left foot over the edge of the tub and set it on the floor.

"Oh!"

"What now?"

He was just about to release her when she made the exclamation and tipped forward slightly. With lightning reflexes, his arm slid around her, clasping her just below her breasts.

"The floor is cold."

"Christ, don't scare me like that."

"Sorry. It was a shock."

Each was thinking, "You can say that again."

Rusty groped for the back of the chair to lend her support and hastily clutched the towel to the front of her body. Of course that still left her back naked to his eyes, but she trusted that he was being a gentleman and wasn't taking advantage.

"All right?"

"Yes."

His hands moved from her front to her sides, but he didn't release her entirely. "Sure?"

"Yes," she answered thickly, "I'm fine."

He withdrew his hands. Rusty sighed with relief—as it turned out, prematurely.

"What the hell is this?" She gasped when his hand cupped the side of her hip. His thumb made a long, slow sweep across her buttock, sluicing off water. Then the other buttock was similarly examined. "What the devil happened to you? I thought you said he didn't hurt you?"

"I don't know what you mean." Breathless and dizzy, she turned her head and looked up at him over her shoulder. His brows were pulled together into a deep V and his mustache was curved downward with displeasure.

"You're black-and-blue."

Rusty looked over her shoulder and down the length of her back. The first thing that registered with her was that Cooper's dark hands against her pale flesh made a very sensuous picture. Only when he made another solicitous movement with his thumb did she see the bruises.

"Oh, those. They're from the ride in the travois."

His eyes swung up to hers and penetrated her with their heat. He kept his hands against her flesh. His voice was as soft as his touch. "You should have said something."

She became entranced with the movements of his mustache as his mouth formed words. Perhaps that's why she whispered, "Would saying something have changed anything?"

A strand of her hair got caught in the stubble on his chin. It connected them like a filament of light. Not that they needed it. Their stare was almost palpable. It lasted forever and wasn't broken until a log in the fireplace popped loudly. They both jumped guiltily.

Cooper resumed his broody expression and growled. "No. It wouldn't have changed anything."

Seconds later the drape fluttered back into place behind him. Rusty was trembling. *From the cold,* she averred. He had kept her standing here long enough to get chilled. She wrapped the towel around her and dried quickly. The cloth was so coarse it left her skin tingling. It chafed the delicate areas of her body, especially her nipples. When she finished drying, they were abnormally rosy and pointed. Achy. And throbbing. And hot.

"It's the *towel,*" she muttered as she pulled on her silk long johns.

"What is it this time?" The cantankerous question came from the other side of the drape.

"What?"

"I heard you say something."

"I said this towel would make a great scouring pad."

"It was the best I could come up with."

"I wasn't being critical."

"That'd be a first."

She muttered something else beneath her breath, making sure he didn't overhear it this time, since it was an epithet grossly unflattering to his lineage and personality.

Aggravated, she ungracefully pulled the tank top over her head. Her nipples poked darkly against the clinging fabric. The silkiness, which should have felt soothing after the towel, only seemed to irritate them more.

She repacked her toiletries in their carrying case and dropped down into the chair. Bending at the waist, she flipped all her hair forward and rubbed it vigorously with the towel, alternately brushing it. Five minutes later, she flung her head back and her semidried hair settled against her shoulders in russet waves. It wasn't styled, but it was clean, and that was a definite improvement.

It was when she was replacing her hairbrush in the cosmetic kit that she noticed the condition of her nails. They had been jaggedly broken or torn away. She groaned audibly.

Within a heartbeat, the curtain was thrown back and Cooper was standing there. "What's the matter? Is it your leg? Is it—"

He broke off when he realized that Rusty wasn't in any pain. But even if that realization hadn't shut him up, the sight of her sitting silhouetted against the golden firelight, a halo of wavy cinnamon-colored hair wreathing her head like an aura would have. She was wearing a top that was more alluring than concealing. The shadows of her nipples drew his eyes like magnets. Even now, he could feel the heaviness of her breasts where they had rested on his forearms minutes ago.

His blood turned to molten lava, hot and thick and rampant. It surged toward his sex where it collected and produced the normal, but currently unwanted, reaction. It was painful in its intensity.

And since he couldn't alleviate it, he released his sexual tension by another means: fury. His face grew dark with menace. His heavy brows, more gold than brown in the firelight, were intimidatingly drawn into a frown over his eyes. Since he couldn't taste her with his tongue— as he was dying to do—he'd use it to verbally lash her.

"You were groaning over your damn fingernails?" he shouted.

"They're all chipped and broken," Rusty yelled back at him.

"Better them than your neck, you little fool."

"Stop calling me that, Cooper. I'm not a fool."

"You couldn't even figure out that those two hillbillies wanted to rape you."

Her mouth drew up into a sullen pout that only inflamed him further because he wanted to kiss it so badly. His unquenchable desire prompted him to say ugly, hurtful things. "You did all you could to entice them, didn't you? Sitting near the fire when you know what it does to your eyes and complexion. Brushing your hair until it crackled. You know what that kind of thing does to a man, don't you? You know it drives him crazy with lust." Then, realizing that his tirade was as good as a confession, he sneered, "I'm surprised you didn't come out in that getup last night and flaunt yourself in front of Reuben, the poor jerk."

Rusty's eyes smarted with tears. His estimation of her was far lower than she had thought. Not only did he think she was useless, he thought she was no better than a whore.

"I didn't do anything on purpose. You know that, no matter what you say." Instinctively, in self-defense, she crossed her arms over her chest.

Suddenly he dropped to his knees in front of her and jerked her arms away. In the same motion, he whipped the lethal knife from its scabbard at his waist. Rusty squealed in fright when he clasped her left hand tightly and raised the glittering blade to it. He made a short, efficient job of paring her nails down even with the tops of her fingers. When he dropped that hand, she looked at it remorsefully.

"That looks awful."

"Well, I'm the only one here to see them and I don't give a damn. Give me your other hand."

She complied. She had no choice. In an arm-wrestling match, she could hardly win against him. And now her breasts were fair game for his condemning gaze again. But when his eyes glanced up from the bizarre manicure he was giving her, they weren't condemning. Nor were they cold with contempt. They were warm with masculine interest. A lot of interest. So much interest that Rusty's stomach took another of those elevator rides that never quite took it to the top or the bottom but kept it bobbing up and down somewhere in between.

Cooper took his time trimming the nails on her right hand, as if they needed more care and attention than those on her left. His face was on a level with her chest. In spite of the awful things he'd said to her just moments ago, she wanted to run her fingers through his long, unruly hair.

As she watched his lips, set firmly in a scowl, she couldn't help but remember how soft they could become in a kiss—how warm and damp—and how marvelous his mustache had felt. If it had felt that good against her upper lip, how good would it feel against other parts of her body? Her neck? Her ear? Her areola—while his lips tugged at her nipple with the gentle fervency of a baby hungry for milk?

He finished cutting her nails and sheathed his knife. But he didn't release her hand. He held it, staring down at it, then laid it on her thigh, pressing it there with his own hand. Rusty thought her heart would explode from the pressure inside her chest.

He kept his head down, staring at the spot where his hand covered hers high on her thigh. His eyes looked closed from Rusty's angle. The lashes were thick and crescent shaped. She noticed that they, like his mustache and eyebrows, were tipped with gold. In the summertime his hair would be naturally streaked, bleached from the sun.

"Rusty."

He said her name. There was a slight creak in his voice, a groaning protest of the raw emotion behind his saying it. Rusty didn't move, but her heart was beating so fast and wildly that it stirred the silk that wasn't doing a very adequate job of covering her.

He removed his hand from hers and placed each of his on either side of the chair seat, bracketing her hips. His knuckles pressed into their flaring shape. He remained staring fixedly at her hand, which still lay on her thigh. He looked ready to lower his head and wearily rest his cheek against it, or to bend down and tenderly kiss it, or to nibble on the very fingers he'd just cut the nails from.

If he wanted to, Rusty wouldn't stop him. She knew that positively. Her body was warm and moist and receptive to the idea. She was ready for whatever happened.

No, she wasn't.

Because what happened was that Cooper came to his feet hastily. "You'd better get to bed."

Rusty was stunned by his about-face. The mood had been shattered, the intimacy dispelled. She felt like arguing, but didn't. What could she say? "Kiss me again, Cooper," "Touch me"? That would only confirm his low opinion of her.

Feeling rejected, she gathered her belongings, including the pile of dirty clothes she'd left beside the tub, and walked around the curtain. Each of the two beds had been spread with sheets and blankets. A fur pelt had been left at the foot of each. At home her bed was covered in designer sheets and piled with downy pillows, but it had never looked more inviting than this one.

She put her things away and sat down on the bed. In the meantime, Cooper had made several trips outside with buckets of bathwater. When the water level was low enough, he dragged the tub to the door and out onto the porch, then tipped it over the edge and emptied the rest of it. He brought the tub back into the room, replaced it behind the curtain, and from the pump in the sink began filling the pots and kettles again.

"Are you going to take a bath, too?"

"Any objections?"

"No."

"It's been a while since I chopped firewood and my back is sore. Besides that, I think I'm beginning to stink."

"I didn't notice."

He looked at her sharply, but when he could see that she was being honest, he came close to smiling. "You will now that you're clean."

The kettles had begun to boil. He lifted two of them off the stove and headed toward the tub.

"Do you want me to massage it?" Rusty asked guilelessly.

He stumbled, sloshed boiling water on his legs, and cursed. *"What?"*

"Massage it?" He gazed at her as though he'd been hit between the eyes with a two-by-four. "Your back."

"Oh, uh…" His eyes moved over her. The tank top left her throat and shoulders bare, cloaked only with a mass of reddish-brown curls. "No—" he refused curtly "—I told you to go to sleep. We've got more work to do tomorrow." He rudely returned to his task.

Not only was human courtesy impossible for him, he wouldn't let anybody be nice to him. Well he could rot, for all she cared!

Rusty angrily thrust her feet between the chilly sheets and lay down, but she didn't close her eyes. Instead she watched Cooper sit down on the edge of his bed and unlace his boots while he was waiting for more water to boil. He tossed his socks onto the pile of dirty clothing she had made and began unbuttoning his shirt. He was wearing only one today because he'd been working so hard outside. He pulled the tails of it from his jeans and took it off.

Rusty sprang to a sitting position. "What happened to you?"

He flung his shirt down onto the pile of clothes to be washed. He didn't have to ask what she was referring to. If it looked as bad as it felt, the bruise was noticeable even in the dim light.

"My shoulder came into contact with the barrel of Reuben's rifle. I had to deflect it that way, so my hands would be free to get my own rifle up."

Rusty winced. The fist-size bruise at the outer edge of his collarbone was black-and-blue and looked extremely painful. "Does it hurt?"

"Like hell."

"Did you take an aspirin?"

"No. We need to conserve them."

"But if you're hurting—"

"You aren't taking them for the bruises on your butt."

That remark shocked her speechless. But it didn't last long. After a moment she said stubbornly, "I still think two aspirin would help."

"I want to save them. You might have fever again."

"Oh, I see. You don't have any aspirin to take for your shoulder because I wasted them on my fever."

"I didn't say you wasted them. I said, oh—" Then he said a word that described something neither was in the mood to do, a word that should never be spoken aloud in polite company. "Go to sleep, will you?"

Wearing only his jeans, he went to the stove, apparently decided that the water was hot enough even though it wasn't quite boiling, and emptied it all into the tub.

Rusty had lain back down, but she watched his shadow moving on the curtain as he shucked off his jeans and stepped naked into the tub. Her imagination got the night off because his shadow left nothing up to it, especially in profile.

She heard cursing as he lowered himself into the water. The tub didn't accommodate him as easily as it had her. How he expected her to go to sleep with all that splashing going on, she didn't know. He had splashed more water on the floor than was left in the bottom of the tub by the time he stood up to rinse off.

Rusty's throat went dry as she watched his shadow. He bent at the waist, repeatedly scooping handfuls of water over himself to rinse off the soap. When he stepped out, he dried with masculine carelessness. The only attention he gave his hair was to make one pass over it with the towel, then to comb his fingers through it. He finished by wrapping the towel around his waist.

He went through the laborious procedure of emptying the tub again. After the last trip to the porch, he left the tub outside. Rusty could tell he was shivering when he moved back to the fire and added several logs. Using the chair as his ladder, he took down the screen the same way he'd put it up. He folded the sheet, placed it on one of the several shelves against the wall, and blew out the lantern on the table. The last thing he did before sliding into his bed was yank the towel from around his waist.

During all that time, he never looked at Rusty. She was hurt that he hadn't even said good-night. But then, she might not have been able to answer him.

Her mouth was still dry.

Counting sheep didn't help.

Reciting poetry didn't help, especially since the only

poems he knew by heart were limericks of a licentious nature.

So Cooper lay there on his back, with his hands stacked beneath his head, staring at the ceiling, and wondering when his stiff manhood was going to stop tenting the covers and relax enough to let him fall asleep. He was exhausted. His overexerted muscles cried out for rest. But his sex wasn't listening.

Unlike the rest of him, it was feeling great. He felt like taps all over, but it felt like reveille: alert and alive and well. Too well.

In desperation, he put one hand beneath the covers. Maybe… He yanked his hand back. Nope. Uh-uh. Don't do that. Trying to press it down only made the problem worse.

Furious with Rusty for doing this to him, he rolled to his side. Even that movement created unwanted friction. He uttered an involuntary groaning sound, which he hastily turned into a cough.

What could he do? Nothing that wouldn't be humiliating. So he'd just have to think about something else.

But dammit, he'd tried. For hours, he'd tried. His thoughts eventually meandered back to her.

Her lips: soft.

Her mouth: vulnerable but curious; then hungry, opening to him.

He clenched his teeth, thinking of the way her mouth had closed around his seeking tongue. God, she tasted good. He'd wanted to go on and on, thrusting his tongue inside her, sending it a little farther into her mouth each time, until he decided exactly what it was she tasted like. It would be an impossible task and therefore endless— because she had her own unique taste.

He should have known better than to kiss her—not

even for the sake of fooling the old man. Who had been fooling whom? he asked himself derisively. He had kissed her because he'd wanted to and he *had* known better. He had suspected that one kiss wouldn't satisfy him and now he knew that for sure.

What the hell? Why was he being so hard on himself? He was sleeplessly randy because she was the only woman around. Yeah, that was it.

Probably. Possibly. Maybe.

But the fact still remained that she had a knockout face. Sexy-as-hell hair. A body that begged to be mated. Breasts that were created for a man's enjoyment. A cute, squeezable derriere. Thighs that inspired instant arousal. And what lay nestled between them—

No! his mind warned him. Don't think about that or you'll have to do what you have miraculously, and with considerable self-discipline, refrained from doing tonight.

All right, that's enough. *Finis. No mas.* The end. Stop thinking like a sex-crazed kid at worst and a redneck sexist at best, and go to sleep.

He closed his eyes and concentrated so hard on keeping them closed that at first he thought the whimpering sound that issued from the other bed was his imagination. Then Rusty sprang up out of the covers like a jack-in-the-box. That wasn't his imagination. Nor was it something he could ignore by playing possum.

"Rusty?"

"What is that?"

Even with no more to light the room than the dying fire, he could see that her eyes were round and huge with fear. He thought she was having a nightmare. "Lie back down. Everything's okay."

She was breathing erratically and clutching the covers to her chest. "What is that noise?"

Had he made a noise? Had he failed to camouflage his groans? "Wha—"

But just as he was about to ask, the mourning, wailing sound came again. Rusty covered her ears and bent double. "I can't stand it," she cried.

Cooper tossed back the covers on his bed and reached hers in seconds. "Wolves, Rusty. Timber wolves. That's all. They're not as close as they sound and they can't hurt us."

Gently he unfolded her and eased her back until she was lying down again. But her face was far from restful. Her eyes apprehensively darted around the dark interior of the cabin as though it had been invaded by demons of the night.

"Wolves?"

"They smell the—"

"Bodies."

"Yes," he replied with regret.

"Oh, God." She covered her face with her hands.

"Shh, shh. They can't get to them because I covered the graves with rocks. They'll eventually go away. Hush, now, and go to sleep."

He'd been so miserable with his own problem that he'd paid scant attention to the barking of the pack that lurked in the woods surrounding the cabin. But he could see that Rusty's fear was genuine. She clasped his hand and drew it up under her chin as a child might hold his teddy bear to help ward off the terrors of a recent nightmare.

"I hate this place," she whispered.

"I know."

"I've tried to be brave."

"You have been."

She shook her head adamantly. "No, I'm a coward.

My father saw it. He was the one who suggested that I return home ahead of schedule."

"Lots of people can't stand seeing animals killed."

"I broke down and cried today in front of you. You've known all along that I'm useless. I'm no good at this. And I don't want to be good at it." Her voice was defiant, incongruous with the tears that washed her cheeks. "You think I'm a terrible person."

"No, I don't."

"Yes, you do."

"No, honest."

"Then why did you accuse me of enticing those men?"

"I was angry."

"Why?"

Because you entice me, too, and I don't want to be enticed. He didn't tell her that. Instead he muttered, "Never mind."

"I want to go home. Where everything is safe and warm and *clean*."

He could argue that the streets of Los Angeles couldn't always been considered safe, but knew that now wasn't the time for teasing—even gentle teasing.

It went against his grain to compliment her, but he felt she'd earned it. "You've done exceptionally well."

She lifted watery eyes to his. "No, I haven't."

"Far better than I ever expected."

"Really?" she asked hopefully.

The breathlessness of her voice and the feminine appeal on her face was almost too much for him. "Really. Now, ignore the wolves and go back to sleep." He pulled his hand from her grasp and turned away. Before he could move, however, another wolf howled. She cried out and reached for him again, throwing herself against him when he turned back to her.

"I don't care if I am a coward. Hold me, Cooper. Please hold me."

Reflexively his arms went around her. Like that other time he had held her while she wept, he felt the same sense of helplessness steal over him. It was lunacy to hold her for any reason, but it would be abominably cruel to turn away. So even though it was as much agony as ecstasy, he drew her close and buried his lips in her wealth of hair.

As he spoke them, his words were sincere. He was sorry this had happened to her. He wished they would be rescued. He wanted her to be returned safely home. He was sorry she was frightened. If there was something he could do to get them out of their predicament, he would.

"You've done everything possible. But just hold me a minute longer," she begged.

"I will."

He continued to hold her. His arms remained around her. But he didn't move his hands. He didn't trust himself to rub them over her back and stop with that. He wanted to touch her all over. He wanted to knead her breasts and investigate the warm, soft place between her thighs. Desire made him shiver.

"You're freezing." Rusty ran her hands over the goose-flesh on his upper arms.

"I'm fine."

"Get under the covers."

"No."

"Don't be silly. You'll catch a cold. What's the big deal? We've slept together for the past three nights. Come on." She pulled back the covers.

"Uh-uh. I'm going back to my own bed."

"You said you'd hold me. Please. Just until I fall asleep."

"But, I'm—"

"Please, Cooper."

He swore, but slid beneath the covers with her. She cuddled against him, nuzzling her face against the fuzzy security of his chest. Her body became pliant against his. He gritted his teeth.

Seconds after she had relaxed against him, she pushed herself away. "Oh!" she exclaimed softly. "I forgot that you were—"

"Naked. That's right. But it's too late now, baby."

Seven

Masculine urges governed him now. His mouth moved over hers in a deep, long, questing kiss while his body settled heavily against hers. Angling his head first to one side, then the other, he made heated love to her mouth with his greedy tongue.

Shock was Rusty's initial reaction. His wonderful nakedness was a stunning surprise. Then, before she could recover from that, she was swept up into his tempestuous kiss.

Her next reaction was spontaneous longing. It surged up through her middle, overwhelming her heart and mind, obliterating all else but the man who was ravishing her mouth so expertly. Her arms encircled his neck and drew him closer. Reflexively she arched against him, bringing her body in contact with his hard, rigid flesh.

Groaning in near pain, he buried his face in her neck. "God, it's so full it's about to burst."

"What do you want, Cooper?"

He laughed harshly. "That's obvious, isn't it?"

"I know; but, what do you want me to do?"

"Either touch me all over or don't touch me at all." His

breath struck her face in hot, rapid gusts. "But whatever you decide, decide now."

Rusty hesitated only half a heartbeat before she ran the fingers of one hand up through his hair and settled them against his scalp. She used the other to comb through the crisp hair on his chest, massaging the muscles that had beguiled her.

Their lips met in another rapacious kiss. He ran his tongue over her lower lip, then drew it between his lips and sucked it lightly. The sheer sexuality of it electrified her. He took her moaning whimper as encouragement and began kissing his way down her throat and chest. He wasn't a man to ask permission. Boldly he lowered his hand to her breast, cupped it, and pushed it up.

"I've been going out of my mind wanting you," he rasped. "I thought I'd go insane before I touched you, tasted you."

He opened his mouth over the smooth flesh that swelled above her tank top. He kissed it fervently, applying enough suction to draw it up against his teeth. He tickled it with his tongue at the same time he unhurriedly whisked his thumb back and forth across her nipple. When it began to respond and grow hard, he accelerated that fanning caress until Rusty was almost delirious.

"Stop, Cooper," she gasped. "I can't breathe."

"I don't want you to be able to breathe."

He lowered his head and, through the cloth of her tank top, flicked his tongue against her raised nipple, playfully nudging it. Rusty's heels ground into the bed beneath her and her back came off it. But even that revealing response didn't satisfy him.

"Say you want me," he said in a low, vibrating voice.

"Yes, I want you. Yes, yes."

Driven by a wild, uncontrollable hunger, heedless of the consequences, she pushed him back and became the aggressor. Her lips moved down his throat and over his chest and stomach, striking as randomly as raindrops on parched earth. Each time her mouth touched his hair-smattered skin, she whispered his name. It became like a prayer, growing in fervency with each kiss.

"You're beautiful, beautiful," she whispered over his navel. Then, moving her head lower and rubbing her cheek in the hair that grew dense and dark, she said with a sigh, "Cooper."

The passion she'd unleashed stunned him. He tilted his head up and gazed down at her. Her hair was sweeping across his belly. Her breath was disturbing his body hair. The love words she was chanting had more erotic rhythm than any he'd ever heard. Her lips...God, her lips...were leaving dewy patches on his skin.

Her head moving over him was the most erotic, most beautiful sight he'd ever seen. And it scared the hell out of him. He pushed her away from him and rolled off the bed. Standing at the side of it, he trembled visibly, swearing beneath his breath.

Hard, passionate, mindless coupling he could handle, but not this. Not this. He didn't want any real yearning and feeling and emotion to be involved, thank you. He'd done every sensual thing that was physically possible to do with a woman. But no woman had ever expressed such honest longing. What Rusty had done suggested an intimacy between them that went beyond the physical.

He didn't need that. No romance. No love. No thanks.

He was temporarily responsible for Rusty Carlson's survival, but he damned sure wasn't going to assume responsibility for her emotional stability. If she wanted to mate, fine, but he didn't want her fooling herself into

thinking that it meant something more than physical gratification. She could do whatever she wanted to with his
body. He would permit, even welcome her, to indulge her
most carnal desires. But that's where it stopped. No one
was allowed to trespass on his emotions.

Rusty stared up at him, bewildered and hurt. "What's
wrong?" Self-conscious now, she raised the sheet up to
her chin.

"Nothing."

He crossed the room and tossed another log on the
fire. It sent up a shower of sparks that threw a brief, but
bright, glow into the room. In that light, she saw that he
was still fully aroused.

He saw that her eyes were inquiring and disillusioned.
"Go to sleep," he said crossly. "The wolves are gone. Besides, I told you they can't hurt you. Now stop being a
crybaby and don't bother me again."

Returning to his own bed, he pulled the covers up
around his ears. In seconds he was drenched with sweat.
Damn her. His body was still on fire.

Damn her, why had she responded that way? So honestly. With no coyness. No affectation. Her mouth had
been so receptive. Her kisses so generous. Her breasts
so soft and her nipples so hard.

He clenched his teeth against the memories. Was he
a fool? A damn fool for not taking what she had offered
so unconditionally?

But that was the hitch. It wasn't unconditional. Otherwise he'd be lying between her silky thighs now instead
of in a pool of his own sweat. That dazed expression on
her face had told him that it meant more to her than simple rutting. She was reading things into it that he would
never be able to deliver.

Oh, he could imbed himself deeply into that sweet

feminine body and succeed in pleasing both of them physically. But he couldn't *feel*, and that's what she wanted. Maybe even what she deserved. He didn't have it to give. His heart was the Sahara of emotional wastelands.

No, better to hurt her now and get it over with. Better to be a bastard now than to take advantage of the situation. He didn't engage in long-term affairs. Certainly not in anything more. A relationship between them could go nowhere once they were rescued.

Until then, he'd live. Contrary to popular myth, a man couldn't die from being perpetually hard. It wouldn't be comfortable, but he'd live.

The following morning, Rusty's eyes were so swollen from crying that she could barely open them. With an effort, she pried them apart and noticed that the cabin's other bed was empty. The covers had already been neatly smoothed into place.

Good. He wouldn't notice her puffy eyes until she had had a chance to bathe them in cold water. The weakness she'd exhibited last night made her furious with herself. Unreasonably, the crying wolves had frightened her. They personified all the threats surrounding her and made the precariousness of her situation very real.

For some inexplicable reason, her terror had manifested itself in desire. Cooper had responded. Then she had. Thank heaven he'd come to his senses before something drastic had happened.

Rusty only wished that she had been the one to come to her senses first. He might erroneously think that she'd wanted *him*—when in fact, what she had wanted was *someone*. He was just the only one around. And if he thought anything else, he was sorely mistaken.

Imitating him by making her bed—never let it be said that he was a superior survivor—she went to the sink and pumped enough water to bathe her face and brush her teeth. She dressed in the same pair of slacks she'd worn yesterday—air conditioning provided by Jack the Ripper, she thought peevishly—but put on a fresh flannel shirt. She brushed her hair and tied it back with a shoelace. It was when she was pulling on her socks that she realized she had been moving about without the aid of her crutches. There was very little soreness left in her leg. They might not be pretty, but Cooper's stitches had worked to heal her injury.

Not wanting to feel any kindness toward him, she moved to the stove and fed short sticks of firewood into it. She filled a kettle with water and spooned coffee into it, sadly thinking about the automatic coffee maker with the built-in digital timer that she had in her kitchen at home.

Forcibly tamping down a wave of homesickness, she began making a breakfast of oatmeal. Reading the directions on the side of the cylindrical box that she'd found among the food supplies, she was glad to discover that oatmeal didn't require any cooking skills beyond boiling water and pouring in the correct portion of oats.

Unfortunately her guess was off a trifle.

Cooper came stamping in and without preamble demanded, "Have you got breakfast ready yet?"

None too charitably, she answered, "Yes. Sit down."

She wanted to serve him a steaming bowl of creamy oatmeal like the ones in the commercials on TV. Instead, when she lifted the lid on the pot, she gazed down into a gooey mess about the color and consistency of setting concrete, except lumpier.

Dismayed, but determined not to show it, she squared her shoulders and dug out two spoonfuls. When she dumped them into the tin bowls, they landed in the bottom of them like lead. She carried the bowls to the table, set them on the rough wood plank with forceful disdain, and took her chair across from him.

"Coffee?" he said.

She bit her lip in consternation, but got up, poured their coffee and returned to the table without saying a single word. She let her body language convey her dislike for his lord-of-the-manor attitude.

He scooped up a bite of the oatmeal and weighed it in his spoon, eyeing her skeptically. Silently, she challenged him to say anything derogatory about her oatmeal. He put the bite in his mouth.

As though instructing him on what to do with it once it was there, Rusty took a bite of hers. She almost spat it out immediately. Instead, knowing he was watching her with his eagle eyes, she chewed it. It seemed to expand instead of get smaller. Finally she had no recourse but to swallow it to get rid of it. Her stomach must have thought she was eating golf balls. She swilled down a scalding gulp of coffee.

Cooper's spoon clattered against his bowl. "Is this the best you can do?"

Rusty wanted to come back with, "Was last night the best *you* could do?" But she reasoned that aiming such an insult at a man's lovemaking abilities might be justifiable grounds for homicide, so she judiciously said, "I don't cook that much at home."

"Too busy flitting from one expensive, fancy restaurant to another, I guess."

"Yes."

Making a terrible face, he forced down another swallow of the foul stuff. "This isn't that presalted, presweetened oatmeal that comes in the cute little packages with teddy bears and bunnies on them; this is the real stuff. Add salt to the water next time. Use only about half as much oatmeal, and then sprinkle sugar over it. But not too much. We've got to ration our supplies."

"If you know so much about cooking, Scoutmaster, why don't you do it?" she asked sweetly.

He shoved his bowl aside and propped his forearms on the table. "Because I've got to do the hunting and fishing and firewood cutting. But, now that I think about it, cooking is a whole lot easier. Want to swap? Or do you plan to make me do *all* the work while you lounge around and watch your fingernails grow back?"

In a flash and a scraping sound of wood on wood, Rusty was out of her chair and leaning across the table. "I don't mind doing my share of the work and you know it. What I *do* mind is having my best efforts criticized by you."

"If this is any indication of your best efforts, we'll be dead of starvation inside a week."

"I'll learn to do better," she shouted.

"It can't be soon enough for me."

"Oh!"

She spun away and when she did, the flannel shirt, which she'd left unbuttoned, flared open. Cooper's arm shot out and grabbed her arm.

"What's that?" Reaching inside the open shirt, he pulled down the strap of her tank top.

Rusty followed the direction of his gaze down to the slight discoloration on the upper curve of her breast. She looked at the round bruise, then lifted her eyes up to his. "That's where you…kissed…" Unable to go on, she made a helpless gesture with her hands. "Last night," she added huskily.

Cooper snatched his hand back, as guilty as Adam

when caught sampling the forbidden fruit. Rusty could feel the blush rising in her neck. It spread as evenly and thoroughly as his eyes were moving over her. He noticed the rosy abrasions that his whiskered jaw had made around her mouth and against her face and throat. He grimaced with regret and raised his hand to his chin. When he rubbed it, the scratching noise filled the silence.

"Sorry."

"It's okay."

"Does it…do they hurt?"

"Not really."

"Did it, you know, when…?"

She shook her head. "I didn't notice then."

They quickly glanced away from each other. He moved to the window. It was drizzling outside. Occasionally a pellet of sleet would ping against the glass.

"I guess I should explain about last night," he said in a low, deep voice.

"No. No explanation is necessary, really."

"I don't want you to think I'm impotent or anything like that."

"I know you're not impotent."

His head snapped around and their gazes locked. "I don't guess I could keep it a secret that I was ready and able."

Rusty swallowed with difficulty and lowered her head. "No."

"That leaves willing." She kept her head bowed. "Well, aren't you even curious as to why I didn't go through with it?" he asked after a lengthy moment.

"I didn't say I wasn't curious. I only said that you didn't have to explain. We're strangers, after all. We owe each other no explanations."

"But you wondered." He pointed an accusing finger

at her. "Don't deny that you wondered why I didn't finish it."

"I assumed that there is someone back home. A woman."

"No woman," he barked. At her shocked expression, he smiled crookedly. "No man, either."

She laughed uneasily. "That never occurred to me."

The injection of humor didn't last. His smile inverted itself into a frown. "I don't make sexual commitments."

Her chin went up a notch. "I don't remember asking for one."

"You didn't have to. If we... If I... With just the two of us here, for God knows how long, that's what it would amount to. We're already dependent on each other for everything else. We don't need to make the situation any more complicated than it already is."

"I couldn't agree with you more," she said breezily. She had never taken rejection very well, but neither had she ever let her hurt feelings show. "I lost my head last night. I was frightened. More exhausted than I realized. You were there, you did the humane thing and rendered comfort. As a result, things got out of hand. That's all there was to it."

The lines running down either side of his mouth pulled in tighter. "Exactly. If we'd met anywhere else, we wouldn't have looked at each other twice."

"Hardly," she said, forcing a laugh. "You wouldn't exactly fit in with my cosmopolitan crowd. You'd stick out like a sore thumb."

"And you in your fancy clothes would be laughed off my mountain."

"So, fine," she said testily.

"Fine."

"It's settled."

"Right."

"We've got no problem."

One might wonder, then, why they were facing each other like pugilists squaring off. The air was redolent with animosity. They'd reached an agreement. They'd figuratively signed a peace treaty. But by all appearances they were still at war.

Cooper was the first to turn away and he did so with an angry jerk of his shoulders. He pulled on his coat and picked up his rifle. "I'm going to see what the stream has to offer in the way of fish."

"Are you planning to shoot them?" She nodded at his rifle.

He frowned at her sarcasm. "I rigged up a trotline while you were languishing in bed this morning." He didn't give her time to offer a rebuttal before he added, "I also started a fire under that caldron outside. Do the laundry."

Rusty followed his gaze down to the tall pile of dirty clothes and looked at it with unconcealed astonishment. When she turned back to him, the spot he'd been standing in was empty. She hurried to the door as quickly as her limp would allow.

"I was going to do the laundry without you telling me to," she shouted at his retreating back. If he heard her, he gave no indication of it.

Cursing, Rusty slammed the door shut. She cleared the table. It took her almost half an hour to scrub clean the pot she'd cooked the oatmeal in. Next time she would remember to pour hot water in it as soon as she'd spooned the oatmeal out.

She then attacked their pile of dirty clothes with a vengeance. By the time he came back, she wanted to be finished with the chore she'd been summarily assigned.

It was mandatory that she prove to him that last night's breakdown was a fluke.

After putting on her coat, she carried the first load of clothes outside and dropped it into the caldron. Previously, she had thought that such black iron pots suspended over smoldering coals existed only in movies. She used a smooth stick to swish the clothes around. When they were as clean as she thought they'd get, she lifted them out of the water with the stick and tossed them into a basket that Cooper had washed out the day before.

By the time she'd finished washing all the clothes using this archaic method, her arms were rubbery with fatigue. And by the time she had wrung them out and hung them up to dry on the wire that stretched from the corner of the house to the nearest tree, her arms felt as if they were about to fall off. Not only that, her wet hands were nearly frozen, as was her nose, which dripped constantly. Her leg, too, had begun to ache again.

A rewarding sense of accomplishment helped relieve some of her miseries. She took comfort in the thought of having done her job well. Once again inside the cabin, she warmed her hands by the fire. When circulation returned to them, she tugged off her boots and wearily climbed onto her bed. If anyone deserved a nap before dinner, it was she.

Apparently she'd been in a much deeper sleep than she had planned on. When Cooper came barging through the door shouting her name, she sprang up so suddenly that her head reeled dizzily and yellow dots exploded in front of her eyes.

"Rusty!" he shouted. "Rusty, did you— Dammit, what are you doing in bed?" His coat was open, his hair wild.

His cheeks were ruddy. He was breathing hard, as though he'd been running.

"What am I doing in bed?" she asked around a huge yawn. "I was sleeping."

"Sleeping! *Sleeping!* Didn't you hear the plane?"

"Plane?"

"Stop repeating every damn word I say! Where's the flare gun?"

"The flare gun?"

He was all but foaming at the mouth. "Where's the flare gun? There's a plane buzzing overhead."

Her feet hit the floor. "Is it looking for us?"

"How the hell should I know?" He tore through the cabin, uprighting everything he laid his hands on in his frantic search for the flare gun. "Where is that...here!" Brandishing the gun, he raced outside, leaped over the porch, and scanned the sky. In stocking feet, Rusty hobbled after him.

"Do you see it?"

"Shut up!" He cocked his head to one side while he listened carefully. The unmistakable hum of the engine reached them at the same time. They turned simultaneously and were met with a dismal sight.

It was an airplane, all right. Obviously a search plane, because it was flying low. But it was flying in the opposite direction. Firing the flares now would serve no purpose except to waste them. Two pairs of eyes remained on the diminishing speck until it grew too small to see and the whine of the engine could no longer be heard. It left a deafening silence in its wake. As the noise had died, so had their chances for a probable rescue.

Cooper came around slowly. His eyes looked cold and colorless and so laden with murderous intent that Rusty took a step backward.

"Just what the *hell* were you doing asleep?"

Rusty preferred him shouting. Ranting and raving she knew how to deal with and respond to. This soft, hissing, sinister-as-a-serpent voice terrified her. "I...I finished the wash," she said hastily. The words tripped over themselves. "I was exhausted. I had to lift—"

It suddenly occurred to her that she owed him no stuttering apologies. From the beginning, he'd assumed charge of the flare gun. It hadn't been out of his possession since they'd left the wrecked aircraft.

Belligerently, she placed her hands on her hips. "How dare you blame this on *me!* Why did you go off without the flare gun?"

"Because I was mad as hell this morning when I left. I forgot it."

"So it's your fault the flare wasn't fired, not mine!"

"It was your fault that I was so damn mad when I left."

"If you can't control your short temper, how can you expect me to?"

His eyes turned dark. "Even if I'd had the gun and fired it, they could have missed it. But they damn sure could have seen smoke from our chimney. But, no. You needed a beauty rest. So you went to sleep and let the fire burn out."

"Why haven't you built a signal fire, a big one, one a potential rescuer couldn't miss?"

"I didn't think I'd need one. Not with a chimney. Of course I didn't count on you taking afternoon naps."

She faltered, then said defensively, "Chimney smoke wouldn't have attracted their attention anyway. That's nothing out of the ordinary."

"This far off the beaten track it is. They would have at least circled around to investigate."

Rusty groped for another valid alibi. "The wind is too

strong for a column of smoke to form. Even if the fire had been going, they wouldn't have spotted our smoke."

"There was a *chance*."

"Not as good a chance as seeing a flare, if you had had the gun with you."

It would have been prudent not to point out his dereliction of duty at that particular moment. His lower lip disappeared beneath his mustache and he took a menacing step forward. "I could easily murder you for letting that plane go by."

She tossed her head back. "Why don't you? I'd rather you do that than keep harping about my shortcomings."

"But you provide me with such a wealth of material. You've got so many shortcomings that if we were stranded here for years I would never get around to harping on all of them."

Her cheeks grew pink with indignation. "I admit it! I'm not qualified to live in a rustic cabin in the middle of nowhere. It wasn't a life-style I chose for myself."

His chin jutted out. "You can't even cook."

"I've never wanted to or needed to. I'm a career woman," she said with fierce pride.

"Well, a helluva lot of good your career is doing me now."

"Me, me, me," Rusty shouted. "You've thought only of yourself through this whole ordeal."

"Ha! I should be so lucky. Instead I've had you to think about. You've been nothing but an albatross."

"It was not my fault that my leg got hurt."

"And I suppose you're going to say it wasn't your fault that those two men went dotty over you."

"It *wasn't*."

"No?" he sneered nastily. "Well, you haven't stopped

putting out signals that you'd like to have me in your pants."

Later, Rusty couldn't believe she'd actually done it. She'd never guessed that she had a latent violent streak. Even as a child, she'd always given in to other children to avoid a confrontation. By nature she was a pacifist. She'd never been physically aggressive.

But at Cooper's intentionally hurtful words, she launched herself at him, fingers curled into claws aimed for his smirking face. She never reached him. She came down hard on her injured leg. It buckled beneath her. Screaming with pain, she fell to the frozen ground.

Cooper was beside her instantly. He picked her up. She fought him so strenuously that he restrained her in an armlock. "Stop that or I'll knock you unconscious."

"You would, wouldn't you?" she asked, breathless from her efforts.

"Damn right. And I'd enjoy it."

Her struggles subsided, more out of weakness and pain than capitulation. He carried her indoors and set her down in the chair near the fire. Casting her a reproachful look, he knelt on the cold hearth and painstakingly coaxed the fire back to life.

"Does your leg still hurt?"

She shook her head no. It hurt like hell, but she'd have her tongue cut out before admitting it. She wasn't going to speak to him, not after what he'd said, which was patently untrue. Her refusal to speak was childish, but she clung to her resolution not to, even as he separated her torn pants leg, rolled down her sock, and examined the zigzagging incision on her shin.

"Stay off it for the rest of the day. Use your crutches if you move around." He patted her clothes into place, then stood up. "I'm going back to get the fish. I dropped them in my pell-mell rush to the cabin. I hope a bear hasn't already made them his dinner." At the door he turned back. "And I'll cook them if it's all the same to you. They look like good fish and you'd probably ruin them."

He slammed the door behind him.

They were good fish. Delicious, in fact. He'd cooked them in a skillet until they were falling-off-the-bones tender, crusty on the outside and flaky on the inside. Rusty regretted passing up the second one, but she wasn't about to devour it ravenously, as she had done the first. Cooper added insult to injury by eating it when she refused it. She wished he would choke on a bone and die. Instead, he complacently licked his fingers, smacking noisily, and patted his stomach.

"I'm stuffed."

Oh, boy, did she have some excellent comebacks for that leading line. But she maintained her stony silence.

"Clean up this mess," he said curtly, leaving the dirty table and stove to her.

She did as she was told. But not without making a terrible racket that echoed off the rafters. When she had finished, she threw herself down on her bed and gazed at the ceiling overhead. She didn't know if she were more hurt or angry. But whichever, Cooper Landry had coaxed more emotion from her than any other man ever had. Those emotions had run the gamut from gratitude to disgust.

He was the meanest, most spiteful human being she'd ever had the misfortune to meet, and she hated him with a passion that appalled her.

True, she had begged him to get into bed with her last night. But for comfort, not sex! She hadn't asked for it; she hadn't wanted it. It had just happened. He was bound to realize that. His puffed-up, colossal ego just kept him from admitting it.

Well, one thing was for certain: from now on she was going to be as modest as a nun. He'd see the skin of her face, possibly her neck, surely her hands, but that was it. It wasn't going to be easy. Not living together in this—

Her thoughts came to an abrupt halt as she spied something overhead that provided the solution to her problem. There were hooks over her bed, exactly like the ones Cooper had used to drape the curtain in front of the bathtub.

Filled with sudden inspiration, she left the bed quickly and retrieved an extra blanket from the shelf against the wall. Completely ignoring Cooper, who she knew was watching her covertly, she dragged a chair across the floor and placed it beneath one of the hooks.

Standing on the chair, she had to stretch her calf muscles—more than they'd ever been stretched in aerobics class—in order to reach the hook, but eventually she managed it. Moving the chair directly beneath another hook, she repeated the procedure. When she was done, she was left with a curtain of sorts around her bed, which would give her privacy.

She shot her cabin mate a smug glance before she ducked behind the blanket and let it fall into place behind her. There! Let him accuse her of asking for "it."

She shuddered at the memory of the crude thing he'd said to her. Add *uncouth* to all his other disagreeable traits. She undressed and slid into bed. Because of her nap, she couldn't fall asleep right away. Even after she heard Cooper go to bed and his steady breathing indicated that he was fast asleep, she lay there awake, watching the myriad flickering patterns the fire cast on the ceiling.

When the wolves began to howl, she rolled to her side,

covered her head with the blanket, and tried not to listen. She clamped her finger between her teeth and bit down hard to keep from crying, to keep from feeling lost and alone, and to keep herself from begging Cooper to hold her while she slept.

Eight

Cooper sat as perfectly still as a hunter in a deer stand. Motionless, feet planted far apart, elbows propped on widespread knees, fingers cupped around his chin. Above them, his eyes stared at her unblinkingly.

That was the first sight Rusty saw when she woke up the following morning. She registered surprise, but managed to keep from jumping out of her skin. Immediately she noticed that the screen she had so ingeniously devised and hung around her bed the night before had been torn down. The blanket was lying at the foot of her bed.

She levered herself up on one elbow and irritably pushed her hair out of her eyes. "What are you doing?"

"I need to talk to you."

"About what?"

"It snowed several inches last night."

She studied his expressionless face for a moment, then said with a great deal of pique, "If you're wanting to build a snowman, I'm not in the mood."

His eyes didn't waver, although she could tell that he was willfully restraining himself when he was sorely tempted to strangle her.

"The snowfall is important," he said calmly. "Once winter gets here our chances of being rescued are greatly reduced."

"I understand that," she replied in a serious tone befitting his observation. "What I don't understand is why it has such grave implications at this very minute."

"Because before we spend another day together, we've got to get some things straight, lay down some ground rules. If we're going to be marooned up here together all winter—which looks like a very real possibility—then we must reach an understanding on several points."

She sat up but kept the blanket raised to her chin. "Such as?"

"Such as no more pouting spells." His brows were drawn together in a straight, stern line of admonition. "I won't put up with that kind of brattiness from you."

"Oh, you won't?" she asked sweetly.

"No, I won't. You're not a child. Don't act like one."

"It's all right for you to insult me, but I'm supposed to turn the other cheek, is that it?"

For the first time, he looked away, apparently chagrined. "I probably shouldn't have said what I did yesterday."

"No, you shouldn't have. I don't know what evil thoughts you've cultivated in your dirty little mind, but don't blame me for them."

He gnawed on the corner of his mustache. "I was mad as hell at you."

"Why?"

"Mainly because I...I don't like you very much. But I still want to sleep with you. And by 'sleep' I don't mean just sleep." If he had slapped her, she couldn't have been more astounded. Her lips parted with a sudden intake of breath, but he didn't give her a chance to say anything.

"Now isn't the time to beat around the bush or to mince words, right?"

"Right," she repeated hoarsely.

"I hope you can appreciate my honesty."

"I can."

"Okay, concede this point. We're physically attracted to each other. Bluntly stated, we want to get off together. It doesn't make any sense, but it's a fact." Rusty's gaze dropped to her lap. He waited until his patience gave out. "Well?"

"Well, what?"

"Say something for God's sake."

"I'll concede both points."

He let out a long breath. "All right then, knowing that, and knowing that it's unreasonable to do anything about it, and knowing, too, that's it's going to be a helluva long winter, we've got some things to iron out. Agreed?"

"Agreed."

"First, we'll stop the mudslinging." Her russet eyes treated him to a frosty stare. Grudgingly he added, "I'll admit to being guilty of that more than you. Let's just promise not to be verbally abusive to each other from here on."

"I promise."

He nodded. "The weather will be our enemy. A fearsome one. It will require all our attention and energy. We can't afford the luxury of fighting each other. Our survival depends on living together. Our sanity depends on doing it peaceably."

"I'm listening."

He paused to collect his thoughts. "As I see it, our roles should be traditional."

"You Tarzan, me Jane."

"Sort of. I'll provide the food. You'll cook it."

"As you've so untactfully pointed out, I'm not a very good cook."

"You'll get better."

"I'll try."

"Don't get defensive if I offer you advice."

"Then don't make snide remarks about my lack of talent. I'm good at other things."

His eyes lowered to her lips. "I can't argue that." After a long, silent moment, he roused himself. "I don't expect you to wait on me hand and foot."

"I don't expect that from you, either. I want to pull my weight."

"I'll help you keep the cabin and our clothes clean."

"Thank you."

"I'll teach you to shoot more accurately so you can protect yourself when I'm gone."

"Gone?" she asked faintly, feeling that the rug had just been pulled out from under her.

He shrugged. "If the game gives out, if the stream freezes over, I might have to go in search of food."

She would face with fear and dread the times she might have to stay in the cabin alone, perhaps for days. Even a vulgar and insulting Cooper was better than no Cooper at all.

"And this is the most important point." He waited until he had her full attention, until her dazed eyes had refocused on him. "I'm the boss," he said, tapping his chest. "Don't let's kid ourselves. This is a life-or-death situation. You might know all there is to know about residential real estate and California chic and the life-styles of the rich and famous. But up here, all that knowledge isn't worth a damn. On your turf you can do whatever the hell you please and I say, more power to you, 'You've come a long way, baby,' and all that. But up here, you obey me."

She was stung by his implication that her field of expertise wasn't much use outside Beverly Hills. "As I recall, I haven't tried to usurp your position as the macho provider."

"Just see that you don't. In the wilderness there's no such thing as equality between the sexes."

He stood up and happened to catch sight of the blanket lying on the foot of the bed. "One more thing: No more silly screens. The cabin is too small and we're living too close together to play coy games like that. We've seen each other naked. We've touched each other naked. There're no more secrets. Besides," he said, raking his eyes over her, "if I wanted you bad enough, no damn blanket would keep me from you. And if rape was what I had in mind, I would have done it a long time ago."

Their eyes locked and held. Finally, he turned his back. "It's time you got up. I've already started the coffee."

That morning the oatmeal was considerably better than it had been the day before. At least it didn't stick to the palate like a day-old peanut-butter sandwich. It had been frugally seasoned with salt and sugar. Cooper ate every bite of his, but didn't offer her a compliment.

She didn't take umbrage as she once would have done. His failure to criticize was tantamount to a compliment. They had only promised not to be verbally abusive; they hadn't promised to shower each other with flattery.

He went outside after breakfast and by the time he came in for a lunch of biscuits and canned soup, he had made himself a pair of snowshoes out of bent greenwood and woven dead vines. He strapped them to his boots and clumped around the cabin, modeling them for her. "These will make it a lot easier to navigate the ravine between here and the river."

He spent the afternoon away from the cabin. She

straightened it, but the housekeeping didn't take more than half an hour. That left her with nothing to do but fret until she saw him through the window at dusk, making awkward progress toward the cabin in the homemade snowshoes.

She rushed out on the porch to greet him with a cup of hot coffee and a tentative smile, feeling slightly foolish for being so pleased to see him return safe and sound.

Unstrapping the snowshoes and propping them against the cabin's outside wall, he looked at her strangely and took the proffered coffee. "Thanks." He stared at her through the cloud of rising steam as he took a sip.

She noticed, as he held the cup to his lips, that they were chapped and that his hands were raw and red despite the shearling gloves he always wore when he was outdoors. She wanted to commiserate, but decided against it. His lecture that morning discouraged anything except mutual tolerance.

"Any luck at the stream?" she asked.

He nodded down toward the creel, which had belonged to the Gawrylows. "It's full. We'll leave some out to freeze and save them for days when I can't get down the ravine. And we should start filling containers with water in case the pump freezes up."

Nodding, she carried the basket of fish inside, proud of the appetizing aroma of her stew. She had made it with dried beef found among the hermits' stock of canned food. Its aroma filled the cabin. Cooper ate two full bowls of it and made her day by saying, "Pretty good," at the conclusion of the meal.

The days followed that basic pattern. He did his chores. She did hers. He helped her with hers. She helped him with his. They were scrupulously polite, if politely distant.

But while they could fill the short days with activity, the evenings seemed endless. They came early. First the sun sank below the tree line and cast the area surrounding the cabin in deep shadow, making outdoor chores hazardous and forcing them indoors.

The instant the sun was swallowed by the horizon, it was dark, even though it was still officially afternoon. Once dinner was eaten and the dishes were washed, there was little to do. There weren't enough inside chores to keep them occupied and separated. They had nothing to do except stare into the fire and avoid staring at each other—something that required supreme concentration on both their parts.

That first snowfall melted the next day, but the night following that, it snowed again and continued into the day. Because of the steadily dropping temperature and blowing snow, Cooper returned to the cabin earlier than usual, which made the evening stretch out unbearably long.

Rusty, her eyes swinging back and forth like twin pendulums, watched him as he paced the length of the cabin like a caged panther. The four walls were making her claustrophobic, and his restlessness only irritated her further. When she caught him scratching his chin, something she'd noticed him doing repeatedly, she asked with asperity, "What's the matter?"

He spun around as though spoiling for a fight and delighted that someone had finally picked one with him. "With what?"

"With you?"

"What do you mean?"

"Why do you keep scratching your chin?"

"Because it itches."

"Itches?"

"The beard. It's at the itchy stage."

"Well, that scratching is driving me crazy."

"Tough."

"Why don't you shave it off if it itches?"

"Because I don't have a razor, that's why."

"I—" She broke off when she realized that she was about to make a confession. Then, noticing that his eyes had narrowed suspiciously, she said haughtily. "I do. I have one. I brought it along and now I'll bet you're glad I did."

Leaving her chair near the fireplace, she went to the shelf where she had stored her toiletries. She treasured them as a miser did his bag of gold coins. She brought the plastic, disposable razor back to Cooper. And something else besides. "Put this on your lips." She passed him the tube of lip gloss. "I noticed that your lips are chapped."

He took the tube from her and rolled the stick of lip balm out. He seemed pressed to make several comments, but said none of them. She laughed at the awkward way he applied the gloss. When he was done, he handed the capped tube back to her. She gave him the razor. "Be my guest."

"Thanks." He turned the razor over in his hand, studying it from every angle. "You didn't by chance sneak some hand lotion, too, did you?"

She held up her hands. Like his, they had been ravaged by water, wind and cold. "Do these look like they've seen any lotion lately?"

His smiles were so rare that her heart melted beneath the one he flashed her now. Then, in what seemed like a reflexive gesture, he captured one of her hands and lightly kissed the backs of her fingers with lips made soft by shiny gloss.

His mustache tickled her fingers. And in a bizarre correlation that made absolutely no sense, it tickled the back of her throat as well. Her stomach executed a series of somersaults.

Suddenly realizing what he'd done, he dropped her hand. "I'll use the razor in the morning."

Rusty hadn't wanted him to let go of her hand. In fact, she'd been tempted to turn it and cover his mustache and lips with her palm. She wanted to feel their caress in that vulnerable spot. Her heart was pounding so hard she had difficulty speaking. "Why not shave now?"

"There's no mirror. With this much stubble, I'd lacerate myself."

"I could shave you."

For a moment neither of them said anything, only filled the narrow space between them with leaping arcs of sexual electricity. Rusty didn't know where the impulse had sprung from. It had just popped up from nowhere and she'd acted on it before thinking—maybe because it had been days since they'd touched each other for any reason. She was feeling deprived. As the body gets hungry for a certain food when it needs the vitamins and minerals it contains, she'd unconsciously expressed her desire to touch him.

"All right." Cooper's permission was granted in a ragged voice.

Nervous, now that he had agreed to her suggestion, she clasped her hands at her waist. "Why...why don't you sit over there by the fire. I'll bring the stuff."

"Okay."

"Roll the collar of your shirt in and tuck a towel inside," she said over her shoulder as she poured water from the kettle on the stove into a shallow bowl. She pulled a chair up close to his and set the bowl and razor on the seat. She also got her bar of soap from the shelf, and a spare towel.

"I'd better soak it first." He dipped the extra towel into the bowl of hot water. "Ouch, damn," he cursed when he tried to wring it out.

"It's hot."

"No foolin'?"

He juggled the scalding towel from one hand to the other before finally slapping it against the lower portion of his face, letting out a yelp when he did so. He held it there, although Rusty didn't know how he could stand it.

"Doesn't that burn?" Without removing the towel, he nodded solemnly. "You do it to soften the whiskers, right?" Again, he nodded. "I'll try to work up a good lather."

Tentatively she wet her hands in the bowl of hot water and picked up the cake of soap. Cooper watched her every move as she rubbed the soap between her hands until they were covered with honeysuckle-scented suds. The foam looked rich and creamy as she slid it between her palms. It oozed between her fingers, looking intensely sexy, although exactly why, he didn't know.

"Whenever you're ready," she said, moving behind him.

Gradually Cooper lowered the towel. Just as gradually, Rusty raised her hands to his face. Gazing down at him from her position above and behind him, the planes and ridges of his face looked even more harsh, more pronounced. But there was a vulnerability to his eyelashes that gave her enough courage to lay her palms against his prickly cheeks.

She felt him tense up in reaction to her touch. She

didn't move her hands at first, but kept them still, resting lightly against his cheeks, while she waited to see
if he was going to tell her that this wasn't a good idea.

It was a given that it wasn't a good idea.

She just wondered which one of them was going to
admit it first and call a halt to the proceedings. But Cooper said nothing, and she didn't want to stop, so she began
to rotate her hands over his cheeks.

The sensation of that scratchy surface against her
palms was enticing. She moved her hands to encompass
more area and found that the bones of his jaw were just as
chiseled and rigid to the touch as they looked. His square
chin had a shallow indentation in its center. She slipped
the edge of her fingernail into it, but didn't investigate it
nearly as long as she wanted to.

She ran her hands simultaneously down his throat,
smoothing on the lather as she went. Her fingers glided
over his Adam's apple and toward the base of his neck,
where she felt his pulse pounding. Dragging her fingers
back up his neck and over his chin again, she encountered
his lower lip and, beyond it, the brush of his mustache.

She froze and drew in a quick, hopefully inaudible
breath. "Sorry," she murmured. Removing her hands, she
dipped them in the water to rinse them off. She leaned
forward and inspected her handiwork from another angle.
There was a speck of soap on his lower lip and some bubbles clinging to several of the blond hairs in his mustache.

With her wet finger, she whisked away that speck from
his lip, then rubbed her finger over his mustache until
the bubbles disappeared.

A low sound emanated from him. Rusty froze, but her
eyes flew to his. "Get on with it," he growled.

With his face partially obscured by white foam, he
shouldn't have posed any threat. But his eyes were alight.

They glittered in the firelight. She could see the flames dancing in their depths and sensed a coiled violence over which he exercised tenuous control. It prompted her to step behind him again and out of harm's way.

"Don't cut me," he warned as she lifted the razor to his jaw.

"I won't if you'll be still and shut up."

"Have you ever done this before?"

"No."

"That's what I was afraid of."

He stopped talking as she drew the first swipe up his cheek. "So far so good," she said softly as she dipped the razor in the bowl. He mumbled something, trying to keep his mouth still, but Rusty didn't catch what he said. She was concentrating too hard on giving him a clean shave without nicking his skin. When the lower part of his face was clean, she let out a deep sigh of relief and satisfaction. "Smooth as a baby's bottom."

A laugh rolled up from the depths of his chest. Rusty had never heard him actually laugh with pure humor before. His infrequent laughs were usually tinged with cynicism. "Don't start bragging yet. You're not finished. Don't forget my neck. And for God sake, be careful with that blade."

"It's not that sharp."

"That's the worst kind."

She swished the razor in the water to dampen it, then placed one hand beneath his chin. "Tilt your head back."

He did. It rested heavily against her breasts. Rusty, unable to move for a moment, kept the razor poised above his throat. His Adam's apple bobbed with a hard, involuntary swallow. To take her mind off their position, she turned her attention to the task at hand, which only made matters worse. She had to come up on her toes and lean forward to see well. By the time she'd shaved his neck clean, his head was cushioned between her breasts and they were both keenly aware of it.

"There." She stepped back and dropped the razor as though it were the single piece of incriminating evidence in a murder trial.

He yanked the towel out of his collar and buried his face in it. For what seemed like hours he didn't move or lower the towel.

"How does it feel?" she asked.

"Great. It feels great."

Then, he stood up abruptly and tossed the towel onto the chair. Tearing his coat from the peg near the door, he pulled it on, ruthlessly shoving his arms into the sleeves.

"Where are you going?" Rusty asked anxiously.

"Outside."

"What for?"

He shot her a sizzling glance that wasn't in keeping with the blizzard blowing beyond the open door. "Believe me, you don't want to know."

He continued to behave in that volatile manner until noon the next day. All morning the weather had been prohibitive to beast and man, so they'd been snowbound in the cabin. For the most part, Cooper ignored her. She responded in kind. After several unsuccessful attempts to make conversation with him, she gave up and lapsed into a moody silence that matched his.

It was a relief when the snowy wind stopped its incessant howling and he announced that he was going out to take a look around. She was concerned for his safety, but refrained from persuading him to stay indoors. They needed the breathing space away from each other.

Besides, she needed some privacy. Cooper wasn't the

only one who'd been itching lately. The incision on her leg was giving her fits. As the skin began to knit, it had become tight and dry. Her clothing only aggravated it further. She decided that the stitches had to come out. She also decided that she was going to pull them out herself rather than involve Cooper, especially since their relationship was so rocky and his mood shifts so unpredictable.

He'd been gone only a few minutes when she stripped off all her clothes, having decided to use this opportunity to give herself a thorough sponge bath. When she finished washing, she sat down in front of the fire, wrapped in a blanket for warmth. She propped her injured leg over the knee of the other and examined it. How hard could it be to clip those stitches and pull them out?

Where before, the thought would have given her qualms the size of goose eggs, she approached the chore pragmatically. The first obstacle was to find something to clip the silk stitches with. The knife Cooper had given her was too cumbersome. The only thing in the cabin sharp enough and delicate enough was her razor.

It had seemed like a good idea, but when she held the razor lengthwise over the first stitch, poised and ready to saw into it, she realized that her hand was perspiring with apprehension. Drawing a deep breath, she touched the silk thread with the razor.

The door burst open and Cooper tramped through it, snowshoes and all. He'd covered his head with a fur pelt and was bundled up from his neck to his boots. His own breath had frozen on his mustache, making it appear ghostly white. Rusty emitted a squeak of alarm and momentary fright.

But her surprise couldn't compare to his. She was just as supernatural a vision as he, in an entirely different way. Silhouetted as she was against the fireplace, the flames shone through her hair. One leg was propped up, exposing a tantalizing length of naked thigh. The blanket she'd wrapped herself in after her sponge bath had slipped off her shoulder, revealing most of one breast. As his eyes fastened on it, the nipple grew taut with the chilly air he was letting in.

He closed the door. "What the hell are you doing sitting there like that?"

"I thought you'd be gone longer."

"I could have been anybody," he roared.

"Like who?"

"Like...like..."

Hell, he couldn't think of a single other person who might have barged in the way he just had, never guessing that he'd find a breathtaking sight like this one in a rude cabin in the Canadian wilds. He felt the front of his pants strain with his instant erection. Either she genuinely had no idea what effect she had on him, or she did know and was maliciously using it to slowly drive him crazy. Whichever, the result was the same.

Frustrated, he tore the pelt from his head and shook snow out of it. Gloves went flying. He tore at the tongs tying on his snowshoes. "Back to my original question, what the hell are you doing?"

"Taking my stitches out."

The peg in the wall caught the coat he tossed in that general direction. *"What?"*

His stance—that know-it-all, arrogant, condescending, masculine stance—grated on her like a pumice stone. Not to mention his superior tone of voice. She looked him directly in the eye. "They're itching. The wound has closed. It's time they came out."

"And you're using a razor?"

"What do you suggest?"

He crossed the floor in three angry strides, pulling his hunting knife from its scabbard as he came. When he dropped to his knees in front of her, she recoiled and drew the blanket tightly around herself. "You can't use *that!*"

His expression was forbearing as he unscrewed the handle of his knife and shook out several implements that Rusty hadn't known until now were in there. Among them was a tiny pair of scissors. Instead of being pleased, she was furious: "If you had those all along, why did you cut my fingernails with that bowie knife?"

"I felt like it. Now, give me your leg." He extended his hand.

"I'll do it."

"Give me your leg." He enunciated each word as he glared up at her from beneath his brows. "If you don't, I'll reach into that blanket and bring it out myself." His voice dropped to a seductive pitch. "No telling what I might encounter before I find it."

Mutinously she thrust her bare leg out from under the blanket. "Thank you," he said sarcastically.

"Your mustache is dripping on me."

The frost was beginning to melt. He wiped it dry on his shirt sleeve, but he didn't release her bare foot. It looked small and pale in his large hand. Rusty loved the feeling, but she fought against enjoying it. She waged a war within when he tucked her heel into the notch of his thighs. She gasped over the firm, solid bulge that filled her arch.

He raised sardonic eyes up to hers. "What's the matter?"

He was daring her to tell him. She would die before she even let him know she had noticed. "Nothing," she said nonchalantly. "Your hands are cold, that's all."

The glint in his eyes told her that he knew she was lying. Grinning, he bent his head to his task. Clipping the silk threads presented no problems to either of them. Rusty was thinking that she could just as easily have done it herself. But when he picked up a small pair of tweezers and pinched the first clipped thread between them, she realized that the worst was yet to come.

"This won't hurt, but it might sting a little," he cautioned. He gave one swift tug to pull the stitch out. Reflexively Rusty's foot made a braking motion against him.

"Ah, God," he groaned. "Don't do that."

No, she wouldn't. She definitely would not. She would keep her foot as still as stone from now on, even if he had to tear the stitches out with his teeth.

By the time the tweezers had picked the last thread out, tears of tension and anxiety had filled her eyes. He'd been as gentle as he could be, and Rusty was grateful, but it hadn't been pleasant. She laid her hand on his shoulder. "Thanks, Cooper."

He shrugged her hand off. "Get dressed. And hurry up with dinner," he ordered with the graciousness of a caveman. "I'm starving."

Soon after that, he started drinking.

Nine

The jugs of whiskey had been among the Gawrylows' supplies. Cooper had discovered them the day they cleaned out the cabin. He had smacked his lips with anticipation. That was before he tasted the whiskey. He had tossed back a healthy gulp and swallowed it without chewing—the stuff had looked viscous enough to chew. It was white lightning, moonshine, rotgut, and it had crashed and burned inside his stomach like a meteor.

Rusty had laughed at his coughing/wheezing spasm. He wasn't amused. After he'd recovered the use of his vocal cords, he had darkly informed her that it wasn't funny, that his esophagus had been seared.

Until now, he hadn't touched the jugs of whiskey. This time, there was nothing funny about his drinking it.

After he had built up the fire, he uncorked a jug of the smelly stuff. Rusty was surprised, but said nothing as he took a tentative swig. Then another. At first she thought he was drinking it in order to get warm. His expedition outside had been brief, but long enough to freeze his mustache. He was no doubt chilled to the marrow.

That excuse didn't serve for long, however. Cooper

didn't stop with those first two drinks. He carried the jug with him to the chair in front of the fireplace and drank what must have equaled several cocktails before Rusty called him to the table. To her irritation, he brought the jug with him and poured an intemperate amount of the whiskey into his coffee mug. He sipped from it between bites of the rabbit stew she had cooked.

She weighed the advisability of cautioning him not to drink too much, but after a time, she felt constrained to say something; the regularity with which he drank from the tin mug was making her uneasy.

What if he passed out? He'd have to lie where he fell because she'd never be able to lift him. She remembered how much effort it had taken to drag him out of the crashed fuselage of the airplane. A great deal of her strength then had come from adrenaline. What if he ventured outside and got lost? A thousand dreadful possibilities elbowed their way through her mind.

Finally she said, "I thought you couldn't drink that."

He didn't take her concern at face value. He took it as a reprimand. "You don't think I'm man enough?"

"What?" she asked with bewilderment. "No. I mean yes, I think you're man enough. I thought you didn't like the taste of it."

"I'm not drinking it because I like the taste. I'm drinking it because we're out of the good stuff and this is all I've got."

He was itching for a fight. She could see the invitation to one in his eyes, hear it in his snarling inflection. Rusty was too smart to pull a lion's tail even if it was dangling outside the bars of the cage. And she was too smart to wave a red flag at Cooper when his face was as blatant a warning of trouble as a danger sign.

In his present mood he was better left alone and unprovoked, although it was an effort for her to keep silent. She longed to point out how stupid it was to drink something that you didn't like just for the sake of getting drunk.

Which was apparently what he intended to do. He nearly overturned his chair as he pushed himself away from the table. Only trained reflexes that were as quick and sure as a striking rattler's kept the chair from landing on the floor. He moved back to the hearth. There he sipped and sulked while Rusty cleaned up their dinner dishes.

When she was finished, she swept the floor—more to give herself something to do than because it needed it. Unbelievable as it seemed, she'd come to take pride in how neatly she had arranged and maintained the cabin.

Eventually she ran out of chores and stood awkwardly in the center of the room while deciding what to do with herself. Cooper was hunched in his chair, broodily staring into the fireplace as he steadily drank. The most sensible thing to do would be to make herself scarce, but their cabin had only one room. A walk was out of the question. She wasn't a bit sleepy, but bed was her only alternative.

"I, uh, think I'll go to bed now, Cooper. Good night."

"Sit down."

Already on her way to her bed, she was brought up short. It wasn't so much what he'd said that halted her, but the manner in which he'd said it. She would prefer a strident command to that quiet, deadly request.

Turning, she looked at him inquisitively.

"Sit down," he repeated.

"I'm going—"

"Sit down."

His high-handedness sparked a rebellious response, but Rusty quelled it. She wasn't a doormat, but neither was she a dope. Only a dope would tangle with Cooper while he was in this frame of mind. Huffily, she crossed the room and dropped into the chair facing his. "You're drunk."

"You're right."

"Fine. Be ridiculous. Make a fool of yourself. I couldn't care less. But its embarrassing to watch. So if you don't mind, I'd rather go to bed."

"I do mind. Stay where you are."

"Why? What difference does it make? What do you want?"

He took a sip from his cup, staring at her over the dented rim of it. "While I'm getting plashtered, I want to sit here and shtare at you and imagine you…" He drank from the cup again, then said around a juicy belch, "Naked."

Rusty came out of her chair as though an automatic spring had ejected her. Apparently no level of drunkenness could dull Cooper's reflexes. His arm shot out. He grabbed a handful of her sleeve, hauled her back, and pushed her into the chair.

"I told you to shtay where you are."

"Let go of me." Rusty wrested her arm free. She was as apprehensive now as she was angry. This wasn't a silly drunk's prank, or an argumentative drunk's unreasonableness. She tried convincing herself that Cooper wouldn't hurt her, but then she really didn't know, did she? Maybe alcohol was the catalyst that released his controlled violence. "Leave me alone," she said with affected courage.

"I don't plan on touching you."

"Then what?"

"Call this a masochistic kind of…self-fulfillment." His eyelids drooped suggestively. "I'm sure you can substitute the correct name for it."

Rusty went hot all over with embarrassment. "I know the correct name for *you*. Several, in fact."

He laughed. "Save them. I've heard them all. Instead of thinking up dirty names to call me," he said, after sipping from his mug, "let's talk about you. Your hair, for instance."

She crossed her arms over her middle and looked toward the ceiling, a living illustration of supreme boredom.

"You know what I thought about the first time I saw your hair?" He was undaunted by her uncooperative spirit and refusal to answer. Leaning forward from the waist, he whispered, "I thought about how good it would feel sweeping over my belly."

Rusty jerked her eyes back to his. His were glazed, and not entirely from liquor. They didn't have the vacuous look of the seasoned drunk. The dark centers of them were brilliant, fiery. His voice, too, was now clear. He wasn't slurring his words. He made it impossible for her to misunderstand him—even to pretend to.

"You were standing in the sunshine out on the tarmac. You were talking to a man…your father. But then I didn't know he was your father. I watched you hug him, kiss his cheek. I was thinking, 'That lucky bastard knows what it's like to play with her hair in bed.'"

"Don't, Cooper." Her fists were clenched at her sides. She was sitting as tall and straight as a rocket about to be launched.

"When you got on the plane, I wanted to reach out and touch your hair. I wanted to grab handfuls of it, use it to move your head down even with my thighs."

"Stop this!"

Abruptly he ceased speaking and took another draught

of whiskey. If anything, his eyes grew darker, more sinister. "You like hearing that, don't you?"

"No."

"You like knowing you've got that kind of power over men."

"You're wrong. Very wrong. I felt extremely self-conscious about being the only woman on that airplane."

He muttered an obscenity and took another drink. "Like today?"

"Today? When?"

He set his cup aside without spilling a single drop. His coordination, like his reflexes, was still intact. He was a mean, nasty drunk, but he wasn't a sloppy one. He leaned forward, beyond the edge of his chair, putting his face within inches of hers.

"When I came in and found you bundled up naked in that blanket."

"That wasn't calculated. It was an error in judgment. I had no way of knowing you would come back so soon. You never do. You're usually away for hours at a time. That's why I decided to take a sponge bath while you were gone."

"I knew the minute I came through the door that you had bathed," he said in a low, thrumming voice. "I could smell the soap on your skin." His eyes moved down over her, as though seeing bare skin rather than her heavy, cable-knit sweater. "You favored me with a peek at your breast, didn't you?"

"No!"

"Like hell."

"I didn't! When I realized the blanket had slipped, I—"

"Too late. I saw it. Your nipple. Pink. Hard."

Rusty drew in several uneven breaths. This bizarre

discussion was having a strange effect on her. "Don't say any more. We promised each other not to be abusive."

"I'm not being abusive. Maybe to myself, but not to you."

"Yes, yes, you are. Please, Cooper, stop this. You don't know—"

"What I'm saying? Yes, I do. I know exactly what I'm saying." He looked directly into her eyes. "I could kiss your nipples for a week and never get tired of doing it."

The whiskey huskiness of his voice barely made the words audible, but Rusty heard them. They intoxicated her. She swayed unsteadily under their impact. She whimpered and shut her eyes in the hopes of blocking out the outrageous words and the mental pictures they inspired.

His tongue moving over her flesh, soft and wet, tender and ardent, rough and exciting.

Her eyes popped open and she glared at him defensively. "Don't you dare speak to me like that."

"Why not?"

"I don't like it."

He gave her a smug and skeptical smile. "You don't like me telling you how I've wanted to put my hands all over you? How I've fantasized about your thighs being opened for me? How I've lain in that damn bed night after night listening to your breathing and wanting to be so deep inside you that—"

"Stop it!" Rusty leaped from her chair and pushed past him, trying to make good an escape out the door of the cabin. She would survive the bitter cold far better than she would his heat.

Cooper was too quick for her. She never reached the door. Before she'd taken two steps, he had her locked in an inescapable embrace. He arched her back as he bent over her. His breath struck her fearful features hotly.

"If it was my destiny to be stranded in this godforsaken place, why did it have to be with a woman who looked like you? Huh?" He shook her slightly as though expecting a logical explanation. "Why'd you have to be so damn beautiful? Sexy? Have a mouth designed for loving a man?"

Rusty tried to wiggle free. "I don't want this. Let me go."

"Why couldn't I be trapped here with someone ugly and sweet? Somebody I could have in bed and not live to regret it. Somebody who would be grateful for my attention. Not a shallow little tart who gets off by driving men crazy. Not a socialite. Not *you*."

"I'm warning you, Cooper." Gritting her teeth, she struggled against him.

"Somebody far less attractive, but *useful*. A woman who could cook." He smiled nastily. "I'll bet you cook all right. In bed. That's where you cook. I'll bet that's where you serve up your best dishes."

He slid his hands over her buttocks and brought her up hard against himself, thrusting his hips forward and making contact with her lower body.

"Does it give you a thrill, knowing you do that to me?"

It gave her a thrill, but not the kind of which he spoke. This intimacy with his hardness stole her breath. She grabbed his shoulders for support. Her eyes clashed with his. For seconds, they held there.

Then Rusty broke their stare and shoved him away. She despised him for putting her through this. But she was also ashamed of her own, involuntary reaction to everything he'd said. It had been fleeting, but for a moment there, her choice could have gone either way.

"Keep away from me," she said in a voice that trembled with purpose. "I mean it. If you don't, I'll turn that knife you gave me on you. Do you hear me? Don't lay a hand on me again." She strode past him and threw herself face down on her bed, using the coarse sheet to cool her fevered cheeks.

Cooper was left standing in the center of the room. He raised both hands and plowed them through his long hair, painfully raking it back off his face. Then he slunk back to his chair in front of the fireplace and picked up the jug and his tin cup.

When Rusty dared to glance at him, he was still sitting there morosely sipping the whiskey.

She panicked the following morning when she saw that his bed hadn't been slept in. Had he wandered out during the night? Had something terrible happened to him? Throwing off the covers—she didn't remember pulling them up over herself last night—she raced across the floor and flung open the door.

She slumped against the jamb in relief when she saw Cooper. He was splitting logs. The sky was clear. The sun was shining. What had been icicles hanging from the eaves the day before were now incessant drips. The temperature was comparatively mild. Cooper wasn't even wearing his coat. His shirttail was hanging out loose, and when he turned around Rusty saw that his shirt was unbuttoned.

He spotted her, but said nothing as he tossed several of the split logs onto the mounting pile near the edge of the porch. His face had a greenish cast and there were dark crescents beneath his bloodshot eyes.

Rusty stepped back inside, but left the door open to let in fresh air. It was still cold, but the sunshine had a cleansing effect. It seemed to dispel the hostility lurking in the shadows of the cabin.

Hastily Rusty rinsed her face and brushed her hair. The fire in the stove had gone out completely. By now she was skilled at adding kindling and starting a new one. In minutes she had one burning hot enough to boil the coffee.

For a change, she opened a canned ham and fried slices of it in a skillet. The aroma of cooking pork made her mouth water; she hoped it would tantalize Cooper's appetite, too. Instead of oatmeal, she cooked rice. She would have traded her virtue for a stick of margarine. Fortunately she didn't have an opportunity to barter it, so she settled for drizzling the ham drippings over the rice, which miraculously came out just right.

Splurging, she opened a can of peaches, put them in a bowl, and set them on the table with the rest of the food. She could no longer hear the crunching sound of splitting logs, so she assumed Cooper would be in shortly.

She was right. He came in moments later. His gait was considerably more awkward than usual. While he was washing his hands at the sink, Rusty took two aspirin tablets from the first-aid kit and laid them on his plate.

He stared down at them when he reached the table, then took them with the glass of water beside his plate. "Thanks." Gingerly he settled himself into his chair.

"You're welcome." Rusty knew better than to laugh, but the careful way he was moving was indicative of how severe his hangover was. She poured a cup of strong, black coffee and passed it to him. His hand was shaking as he reached for it. The log-splitting exercise had been self-imposed punishment for his whiskey-drinking binge. She was glad he hadn't chopped off a toe. Or worse.

"How do you feel?"

Without moving his head, he looked over at her. "My eyelashes hurt."

She held back her smile. She also resisted the compulsion to reach across the table and lift the sweaty strands of hair off his forehead. "Can you eat?"

"I think so. I should be able to. I spent what seemed like hours, uh, out back. If the lining of my stomach is still there, it's all that's left."

While he sat with his shoulders hunched and his hands resting carefully on either side of his plate where he'd planted them, she dished up the food. She even cut his ham into bite-size pieces before scooting the plate in front of him. Taking a deep breath, he picked up his fork and took a tentative bite. When he was certain that it was going to stay down, he took another, then another, and was soon eating normally.

"This is good," he said after several minutes of silence.

"Thank you. Better than oatmeal, for a change."

"Yeah."

"I noticed the weather is much warmer."

Actually, what she had noticed was that the exercise had caused the hair on his chest to curl damply. He'd re-buttoned most of the buttons on his shirt before coming to the table, but it was open far enough for her to get a glimpse of that impressive chest.

"We might get lucky and have a few more days of this before the next storm blows through."

"That would be nice."

"Hmm. I could get a lot done around here."

They'd never had a pointless, polite conversation before. This exchange of meaningless chitchat was more awkward than any of their arguments had been, so both dropped it. In a silence so profound they could hear the water dripping off the eaves outside, they finished their meal and drank their second cups of coffee.

When Rusty stood up to clear the table, Cooper said, "I think the aspirin helped. My headache's almost gone."

"I'm glad."

He cleared his throat loudly and fiddled with the knife and fork he'd laid on his empty plate. "Look, about last night, I, uh, I don't have an excuse for it."

She smiled at him with understanding. "If I could have stood the taste of that whiskey, I might have gotten drunk myself. There have been numerous times since the crash when I've wanted that kind of escape. You don't have to apologize."

Moving back to the table, she reached for his plate. He caught her hand. The gesture, unlike anything else he'd done since she met him, was unsure, hesitant. "I'm trying to apologize to you for the things I said."

Staring down at the crown of his head, where his hair grew around a boyish swirl, Rusty asked softly, "Did you mean them, Cooper?"

She knew what she was doing. She was inviting him to make love to her. She wanted him to. There was no sense in fooling herself any longer. He appealed to her like no man ever had. And apparently the attraction was mutual.

They would never maintain their sanity if they didn't satisfy this physical craving. They might live through the winter without becoming lovers, but by spring they would both be raving maniacs. This passionate wanting, unreasonable as it was, could no longer be suppressed.

A relationship between them would be unworkable under ordinary circumstances. Their circumstances were far from ordinary. It simply wasn't practical to examine whether their life-styles or politics or philosophies were compatible. It didn't matter. What mattered—very much so—was a basic human need for intimacy with the opposite sex.

Cooper raised his head slowly. "What did you say?"

"I asked if you meant them—the things you said."

His eyes didn't even flicker. "Yes. I meant them."

He was a man of action, not of words. He reached up and curled his fingers around the back of her neck, pulling her head down for his kiss. He made a sound like that of a feasting wild animal as he used his lips to rub hers apart. His tongue went searching inside her mouth. Rusty welcomed it.

He stood up, stumbling and off balance. This time his chair did topple backward. It landed on the floor with a crash. Neither of them noticed. His arms slid around her waist, hers around his neck. He drew her body tightly against his. Where hers was bowed, his arched to complement it.

"Oh, God." He tore his mouth from hers and pressed it against her neck. The fingers of one hand ravaged her hair, threading through it and weaving it between his fingers. It became hopelessly ensnared in his grip, which was exactly what he wanted. He pulled her head back and stared down into her face. His was taut with desire.

She met his gaze without shyness. "Kiss me again, Cooper."

His mouth claimed hers again, hotly and hungrily. It drew breath from her. As he kissed her, his hand moved to the front of her slacks. He fumbled with the button and zipper until they were undone. When his hand slid into the elastic waistband of her panties, Rusty gasped. She had thought there would be a sensual buildup, a flirtatious progression, extended foreplay.

She didn't regret that there wouldn't be. His boldness, his impatience, was a powerful aphrodisiac. It set off explosions of desire deep within her. She tilted her hips forward and filled his palm with her softness.

He muttered swearwords that were in themselves arousing because they so explicitly expressed the height of his arousal. Like a Rod Stewart song, they were viscerally sexy; one couldn't hear them without thinking of a male and a female mating.

He struggled with the fly of his jeans until his manhood was freed—a hot, hard fullness probing between her thighs. "I feel your hair against me," he rasped in her ear. "It's so soft."

The erotic message made Rusty weak. She leaned back against the edge of the table and lowered her hands to his hips, inside his jeans. "Please, Cooper, now."

One swift and sure stroke planted him solidly inside her. She gasped at the splendid pleasure/pain. He caught his breath and held it. They clung together like the survivors of a catastrophe—which, in fact, they were—as though their very existence depended on never letting go of each other. Oneness was essential to survival.

It was impossible to say who moved first. Perhaps it was simultaneous. After that initial instant of sheer delight in his total possession, Cooper began to delve deeper yet. He ground his hips against hers, extending himself, stretching her, his goal seemingly to be to reach the very nucleus of her soul.

Rusty, crying out in ecstasy, flung her head back. He randomly kissed her exposed throat and moved his mouth over her breasts, though she was still wearing her sweater.

But love play was unnecessary. Nothing could heighten this fire. Cooper's plunging body became hotter and harder with each savage thrust.

Then he had no choice in the matter.

* * *

"You're a very beautiful woman."

Rusty gazed up at her lover. One of her arms was folded beneath her head. The other hand was draped over his shoulder. Her pose was provocative. She wanted it to be. She didn't mind that her breasts were fully revealed and wantonly inviting. She wanted to display them for his entertainment. She enjoyed seeing his eyes turn lambent every time he looked at them and their pouting tips.

Maybe he'd been right all along. She'd shown a marked lack of modesty since she'd met him. Maybe she had been deliberately seductive because she had wanted him from the beginning. She had wanted this—this languishing aftermath of a coupling that had left her replete.

"You think I'm beautiful?" she asked coyly, running her fingers through his hair and smiling like the cat who had just lapped up the cream.

"You know I do."

"You don't have to sound so angry about it."

His fingers trailed down the groove between her ribs all the way to her navel. "I am, though. I didn't want to give in to your charms. I lost the battle with my own lust."

"I'm glad you did." She raised her head and kissed his mouth softly.

He dusted his fingertips over her navel. "For the time being, so am I."

Rusty didn't want them to be restricted to a time limit. "Why 'for the time being'?"

It hadn't taken them long to undress and make up the pallet in front of the fire. Stretched out naked on the pile of furs, hair a rumpled heap of reddish curls, lips rosy and wet from frequent kissing, eyes drowsy with lovemaking, Rusty looked like a conquering vandal's battle prize. Cooper had never waxed poetic, surely not right after having sex. The thought brought an involuntary smile to his lips.

He surveyed her alluring body. "Never mind."

"Tell me."

"It has something to do with you and me and who we are. But I really don't want to talk about that now." He bent his head low and kissed the ginger curls between her thighs. They were damp. They smelled and tasted of himself and he felt his body respond. Her low moan worked as surely as a velvet-fisted caress on his rising sex. He sighed his pleasure. "Did you know that you're very small?" he whispered into the fleecy delta. Her thighs relaxed and parted. His fingers slipped inside her.

"I am?"

"Yes."

"I'm not all that experienced."

He gazed down at her doubtfully, but her face was guileless. Abruptly he asked, "How many?"

"How indelicate!"

"How many?"

Rusty wrestled with her decision to tell him. Finally, eyes evasive, she said quietly, "Less than I could count on one hand."

"In a year?"

"Total."

Cooper stared down at her, searching for any trace of duplicity in her eyes. God, he wanted to believe her, but couldn't. His probing caress was telling him what his mind wasn't ready to accept, what he should have known the moment he entered her, but couldn't reconcile with his image of her.

"Less than five?"

"Yes."

"Less than three?" She looked away. "Just one?" She

nodded. His heart did an odd little dance, and the emotion that surged through him felt like happiness. But he'd known so little of it, he couldn't be sure. "And you didn't live with him, did you, Rusty?"

"No." She tossed her head to one side and bit her lower lip at his thumb's indolent stroking. The callused pad of it had been gifted with a magical and intuitive touch that paid honor to a woman's body.

"Why not?"

"My father and brother wouldn't have approved."

"Does everything you do have to meet with your father's approval?"

"Yes... No... I... I... Cooper, please stop," she gasped breathlessly. "I can't think while you're doing that."

"So don't think."

"But I don't want to...to, you know...oh, please... no..."

After the last shimmering beam of light had finally burned out, she opened her eyes and met his teasing smile. "That wasn't so bad, was it?"

She discovered that she had just enough energy to answer his smile and reach up and touch his mustache with her fingertips. "I didn't want to do that so soon. I wanted to look at you some more."

"I guess that ends the discussion of you and your father."

Her brows drew into a frown. "It's very complex, Cooper. He was devastated when Jeff was killed. So was I. Jeff was..." She searched for the all-encompassing word. "He was wonderful. He could do everything."

Cooper brushed her lips with his mustache. "Not everything," he said mysteriously. "He couldn't—" He bent down and whispered what Jeff couldn't do with him, using a street word that brought color rising all the way to Rusty's hairline. But she blushed with pleasure, not with affront. "So, see? There's no reason for you to feel inferior to your brother."

Before she could expound on the subject, he sealed her lips closed with an arousing, eating kiss. "Now, what was that about looking at me?"

Her breath was insufficient. She drew in a deep, long one before saying, "I haven't looked my fill." Her eyes, shining as brightly as copper pennies, roved down his chest. She lifted her hand to touch him, glanced up at him as though asking permission, then laid her fingers against the springy hair.

"Go on, coward. I don't bite." The glance she gave him was eloquently sensual. He laughed. "Touché. I do. But not all the time." He leaned down and whispered, "Only when I'm buried inside the sweetest silk I've ever found between two thighs."

While she explored, he nibbled her ear and took love bites out of her neck. When her fingers flitted across his nipple, he sucked in a sharp breath. She jerked her hand back quickly. He recaptured it and pressed it back against his chest.

"That wasn't alarming or painful," he explained in a hoarse, thick voice. "It's like connecting two live wires. I wasn't prepared for the shock. Do it again. All you want."

She did. And more. She dallied with him until his breath became choppy. "Something else needs your attention, but we'd better not," he said, catching her hand on its downward slide. "Not if we want to take this one slow and easy."

"Let me touch you."

Against such a breathy request, he exercised no willpower. He squeezed his eyes shut and withstood her curious caresses until he couldn't bear anymore. Then he lifted her hand off him and satisfied them both with a fervent kiss.

"My turn." One of her arms was still bent behind her head. Her breasts rose off her chest, perfect domes crowned with delicate, pink crests. He covered each with a hand and squeezed. "Too hard?" he asked in response to Rusty's change in facial expression.

"Too wonderful." She sighed.

"That night I kissed you…here…" He touched the curving softness of her breast.

"Yes?"

"I meant to make the mark."

Her sleepy eyelids opened wide. "You did? Why?"

"Because I'm mean, that's why?"

"No, you're not. You just want everyone to think you are."

"It works, doesn't it?"

She smiled. "Sometimes. Sometimes I've thought you were very mean. Other times I knew you were feeling a lot of pain and that being deliberately mean was your only way of coping with it. I think it goes back to your days as a POW."

"Maybe."

"Cooper?"

"Hmm?"

"Make another mark if you want to."

His eyes darted up to hers. Then he moved above her and kissed her mouth thoroughly while his hands continued to massage her breasts. He brushed her wet and swollen lips with his mustache before dragging it down her neck, nipping her lightly with his teeth as he went. He kissed his way across her collarbone and down her chest until he reached the upper curve of her breast.

"I'm responsible for the bruises on your bottom. Then the passion mark. I guess in a primitive way I wanted to brand you mine. I don't have to put a mark on you now," he said, moving his lips lightly over her skin. "You belong to me. For a little while, anyway."

Rusty wanted to take issue with his choice of words and tell him that she would belong to him for as long as he liked, but his roving lips emptied her mind of the correct phrases. He kissed every inch of her breasts, avoiding the nipples. Then he licked them all over and at once, like a greedy child with a quickly melting ice-cream cone. When Rusty didn't think she could stand any more, she clutched handfuls of his hair and pulled his mouth directly above one of the achy, stiff peaks.

His tongue flicked over it, lightly, deftly, until her head was thrashing from side to side. He used his mustache to tickle and tease. When he closed his lips around her nipple and surrounded it with the scalding, tugging pressure of his mouth, she cried his name out loud.

"Oh, baby, you're nice." He moved his head from one side of her body to the other. His mouth was ravenous, but tender.

"Cooper?"

"Hmm?"

"Cooper?"

"Hmm?"

"Cooper?" She curled her fingers around his ears and pulled his head up even with hers. "Why'd you do it?"

"Do what?"

He avoided looking at her by staring at a spot beyond the top of her head. "You know what." She wet her lips anxiously. "Why did you…withdraw…before…?"

She felt apprehensive and disappointed, just as she had earlier when, at the last possible heartbeat, he'd cheated her out of the ultimate high, that of feeling him come inside her.

He became perfectly still. For a moment she was afraid she'd made him angry and that he was going to leave the pallet. After a long, tense moment, he cut his eyes back to hers. "I guess you're due an explanation." She said nothing. He released her name on a sigh. "We might be here for a long time. I don't think either of us wants or needs another mouth to feed."

"A baby?" Her voice was hushed with awe. She played with the idea of having a baby and didn't find it repugnant at all. In fact her lips formed a winsome smile. "I hadn't thought of that."

"Well, I had. We're both young, healthy adults. I know you're not using a contraceptive because I know everything that we brought into this cabin with us. Am I right?"

"Yes," she said timidly, like a child confessing a small transgression.

"I didn't pack anything to take with me to the hunting lodge."

"But it probably won't even happen."

"We can't be sure. I'm taking no chances. So—"

"But if it should," she interrupted excitedly, "we'd be found before the child was born."

"Probably, but—"

"Even if we weren't, I'd be the one responsible for feeding it."

This talk about a child had his stomach churning. His mouth was set in its familiar, firm, hard line. It softened now when he saw how earnest Rusty was. Almost naive. "That's just it," he said roughly, his mouth moving toward her breasts. "I can't stand the thought of sharing you with anyone."

"But—"

"I'm sorry. That's the way it's got to be."

She wanted to protest and pursue the argument. But he used his hands and lips and tongue with such prurient talent that they dissolved in a mutual, simultaneous orgasm before she realized that once again he had withdrawn from her just in time.

They kept each other so sated with sex that they didn't get hungry or cold or tired. They made love all that day and into the evening. Finally, exhausted, they wrapped themselves in fur and each other, and slept.

Only the unexpected rat-a-tat drumbeat of helicopter blades could have disturbed their dreams.

Ten

He was going to miss the chopper. He knew that. He always did. But he kept running anyway. He always did that, too. Jungle foliage blocked his path. He clawed his way through it toward the clearing. He was running so hard his lungs were on fire. His breathing sounded loud to his own ears.

But he could still hear the rotating blades of the chopper. Close. So close. Noisy.

I've got to make it this time, *he cried to himself.* I've got to make it or I'll be captured again.

But he knew he wouldn't make it, although he kept running. Running. Running...

As always, after having the nightmare, Cooper sat up, chest heaving with exertion and drenched with sweat. God, it had been real this time. The racket of those chopper blades seemed—

Suddenly he realized that he could still hear the helicopter. Was he awake? Yes, he was. There lay Rusty, sleeping peacefully beside him. This wasn't Nam; this was Canada. And, by God, he heard a helicopter!

He scrambled to his feet and crossed the cabin's chilly

floor with running footsteps. Since the day they'd missed the search plane, the flare gun had remained on a shelf next to the door. He grabbed it on his way out. When he dashed across the porch and leaped to the ground, he was still naked, but the flare gun was clutched tightly in his right hand.

Shading his eyes with his left, he scanned the sky. The sun was brilliant and just even with the tops of the trees. His eyes teared because it was so bright. He couldn't see a damn thing. He only had six flares. He mustn't waste them. Each one had to count. But he could still hear the chopper. So he acted on impulse and fired two of the flares directly overhead.

"Cooper, is it—"

"A chopper."

Rusty ran out onto the porch and tossed him a pair of jeans. When she had awakened, first with the intuitive knowledge that her lover was no longer lying beside her, then with the sound of the helicopter, she had hastily pulled on her tattered slacks and bulky sweater. Now she, too, shaded her eyes and searched the sky in every direction.

"He must have seen the flares," Cooper cried excitedly. "He's coming back."

"I don't see him. How do you know?"

"I recognize the sound."

Apparently he did. Within seconds, the helicopter swept over the tops of the trees and hovered above the cabin. Cooper and Rusty began waving their arms and shouting, even though it was obvious that they'd been spotted by the two men sitting in the chopper. They could even see their wide smiles through the bubble.

"They see us! Oh, Cooper, Cooper!"

Rusty launched herself against him. He caught her in

a fierce bear hug and, lifting her off her feet, swung her around. "We made it, baby, we made it!"

The clearing surrounding the cabin was large enough to accommodate the helicopter. It set down. Hand in hand, Rusty and Cooper ran toward it. She was heedless of the twinge of pain in her leg. The pilot in the right-hand chair unbuckled his seat belt and stepped out. Ducking under the rotating blades, he ran to meet them.

"Miz Carlson, ma'am?" His Southern accent was as thick as corn syrup. Rusty bobbed her head up and down, suddenly shy and speechless. Timidly she clung to Cooper's arm.

"Cooper Landry," Cooper said, sticking out his hand and pumping the pilot's in a hearty handshake. "We're damn sure glad to see you guys."

"We're kinda glad to see you, too. Miz Carlson's daddy hired us to look for her. The authorities weren't doing the job to his satisfaction."

"That sounds like Father," Rusty shouted over the clapping sound of the turning blades.

"Y'all the only ones who made it?" They nodded somberly. "Well, unless y'all want to stick around, let's git you home. Your daddy sure is gonna be glad to see ya."

At the mention of the young woman's father, the congenial pilot gave Cooper a worried glance, taking in his unfastened jeans. It was obvious that they'd been pulled on in haste and that the man wearing them was naked underneath. Rusty had the debauched, disheveled look of a woman who'd been making love all night. The pilot summed up the situation readily enough; it didn't have to be spelled out to him.

They returned to the cabin only long enough to dress properly. Cooper retrieved his expensive hunting rifle. Beyond that, they came away empty-handed. As she went through the door for the last time, Rusty gave the cabin a wistful backward glance. Originally she had despised the place. Now that she was leaving it, she felt a trace of sadness.

Cooper didn't seem to share her sentiment. He and the pilot were laughing and joking, having discovered that they were veterans of the same war and that their tours of duty had overlapped. Rusty had to run to catch up with them. When she did, Cooper slipped an arm around her shoulders and smiled down at her. That made everything all right. Or at least better.

"I'm Mike," the pilot told them as he assisted them into their seats. "And that's my twin brother Pat." The other pilot saluted them.

"Pat and Mike?" Cooper shouted. "You gotta be kidding?"

That seemed hilariously funny and they were all laughing uncontrollably as the chopper lifted off the ground and skimmed the tops of the trees before gaining altitude.

"The crash site was spotted by a search plane several days ago," Mike shouted back at them and pointed down.

Rusty viewed the sight. She was surprised that they had covered so much distance on foot, especially with Cooper dragging her in the handmade travois. She would never have survived if it hadn't been for him. What if he had died in the crash? Shuddering at the thought, she laid her head on his shoulder. He placed his arm around her and pulled her close. Her hand curled around the inside of his thigh in a subconscious gesture of trust.

"The other five died on impact," Cooper told the pilots. "Rusty and I were sitting in the last row. I guess that's why we lived through it."

"When the report came back that the plane wasn't

burned or anything, Mr. Carlson insisted on searching for survivors," Mike said. "He hired my brother and me out of Atlanta. We specialize in rescue missions." He propped his elbow on the back of his seat and turned his head to address them. "How'd you happen onto the cabin?"

Cooper and Rusty exchanged a troubled glance. "We'll save that story and tell it only once, if you don't mind," Cooper said.

Mike nodded. "I'm gonna radio that you've been rescued. Lots of people have been lookin' for ya. The weather's been a real bitch. Sorry, Miz Carlson."

"That's okay."

"We were grounded until yesterday when the weather cleared. Didn't see anything. Then got an early start again this morning."

"Where are you taking us?" Cooper asked.

"Yellowknife."

"Is my father there?"

Mike shook his head. "He's in L.A. My guess is that he'll have y'all hustled down there before the day is out."

That was good news to Rusty. She couldn't say why, but she had dreaded having to relate the details of her ordeal to her father. Knowing that she wouldn't have to face him right away came as a relief—perhaps because of what had happened last night. She hadn't had time to analyze it. She wanted to savor the experience she had had with Cooper.

Their rescue had been an intrusion. She'd been glad about it, of course. Still, she wanted to be alone with her thoughts. The only person she wanted to distract her was Cooper. With that thought, the uncharacteristic shyness stole over her again and she snuggled against him.

He seemed to read her mind. He tipped her face up and peered at her closely. Bending his head, he kissed her soundly on the lips, then pressed her head against his chest. He gathered her hair in a gentle fist. His actions were both protective and possessive.

They stayed in that position for the remainder of the flight. Neither pilot tried to engage them in conversation, but respected their need for privacy. Pertinent questions could wait.

"You've drawn quite a crowd." Mike glanced at them over his shoulder and nodded toward the ground as they approached the airport, which was small when compared to metropolitan airports, but large enough to accommodate jet aircraft.

Rusty and Cooper saw that the airport below was teeming with people. The milling crowd was showing no respect for restricted areas of the tarmac. Vans labeled as portable television-broadcast units were parked end to end. In this remote area of the Northwest Territories, such media hype was virtually unheard of.

Cooper muttered a curse. "Who the hell is responsible for this?"

"The plane crash made big news," Mike told him with an apologetic smile. "Y'all were the only survivors. I reckon everybody wants to hear what y'all've got to say about it."

The instant Pat set the chopper down, the crowd of reporters surged forward against the temporary barriers. Policemen had a difficult time forcing them back. Several official-looking men ran forward. The helicopter's twirling blades plastered their business suits against their bodies and slapped their neckties against their faces. The rotors finally wound down.

Mike jumped to the concrete and helped Rusty climb down. She cowered bashfully against the side of the helicopter until Cooper jumped down beside her. Then, after profusely thanking the twin pilots from Georgia, they moved forward. Their hands were clasped together tightly.

The men who greeted them were representatives of the Canadian Aviation Safety Board and the National Transportation Safety Board. The U.S. agency had been invited to investigate the crash since the passengers involved were all American.

The bureaucrats deferentially welcomed Cooper and Rusty back to civilization and escorted them past the squirming, shouting wall of reporters whose behavior was anything but civilized. They bombarded them with questions fired as rapidly as machine-gun bullets.

The dazed survivors were escorted through one of the building's employee entrances, down a corridor, and into a private suite of offices that had been provided for their use.

"Your father has been notified, Miss Carlson."

"Thank you very much."

"He was delighted to hear that you are well," the smiling official told her. "Mr. Landry, is there anyone we should notify for you?"

"No."

Rusty had turned to him, curious to hear his reply. He had never mentioned a family, so she had assumed that there was none. It seemed terribly sad to her that no one had been waiting for Cooper's return. She longed to reach out and lay a compassionate hand along his cheek. But the officials were crowded around them.

One stepped forward. "I understand you were the only two to survive the crash."

"Yes. The others died immediately."

"We've notified their families. Some are outside. They want to speak with you." Rusty's face turned as white as the knuckles of her fingers, which were still linked with Cooper's. "But that can wait," the man said hastily, sensing her distress. "Can you give us a clue as to the cause of the crash?"

"I'm not a pilot," Cooper said shortly. "The storm was a factor, I'm sure. The pilots did everything they could."

"Then you wouldn't blame the crash on them?" the man probed.

"May I have a glass of water, please?" Rusty asked softly.

"And something to eat," Cooper said in that same clipped tone. "We haven't had any food this morning. Not even coffee."

"Surely, right away." Someone was dispatched to order them a breakfast.

"And you'd better bring in the proper authorities. I've got the deaths of two men to report."

"What two men?"

"The ones I killed." Everyone froze. He had succeeded in winning their undivided attention. "I'm sure someone should be notified. But first, how about that coffee?" Cooper's voice rang with authority and impatience. It was almost amusing how it galvanized everyone into action. For the next hour, the officials flapped around them like headless chickens.

They were brought huge breakfasts of steak and eggs. More than anything on the tray Rusty enjoyed the fresh orange juice. She couldn't drink enough of it. As they ate, they answered the endless rounds of questions. Pat and Mike were brought in to verify the location of the cabin relative to the crash site. While the weather was still co-operating, crews were dispatched to view the wreckage and exhume the bodies that Cooper had buried.

In the midst of the chaos a telephone receiver was

thrust into Rusty's hand and her father's voice boomed into her ear. "Rusty, thank God. Are you all right?"

Tears filled her eyes. For a moment she couldn't speak. "I'm fine. Fine. My leg feels much better."

"Your leg! What happened to your leg? Nobody told me anything about your leg."

She explained as best she could in brief, disjointed phrases. "But it's fine, really."

"I'm not taking your word for it. Don't worry about anything," he told her. "I'll handle everything from here. You'll be brought to L.A. tonight and I'll be at the airport to meet you. It's a miracle that you survived."

She glanced at Cooper, and said softly, "Yes, a miracle."

Around noon they were taken across the street to a motel and assigned rooms in which to shower and change into clothes provided by the Canadian government.

At the door to her room, Rusty reluctantly let go of Cooper's arm. She couldn't bear to let him out of her sight. She felt alien, apart. None of this seemed real. Everything and everybody swam toward her like distorted faces out of a dream. She had difficulty matching words to concepts. Everything was strange—except Cooper. Cooper alone was her reality.

He seemed no more pleased with the arrangements than she, but it would hardly be suitable for them to share a motel room. He squeezed her hand and said, "I'll be right next door."

He watched her enter her room and safely close and lock the door before he went to his own. Once inside, he dropped into the only chair and covered his face with his hands.

"Now what?" he asked the four walls.

If only he had held off for one more night. If only she

hadn't asked that question of him yesterday morning after breakfast. If only she hadn't been so desirable in the first place. If only they hadn't been on the same airplane. If only it hadn't crashed. If only some of the others had survived and they hadn't been alone.

He could come up with thousands of "if onlys," and the bottom line would still be that they'd made love all day yesterday and last night until the wee hours.

He didn't regret it—not a single breathless second of it.

But he didn't know how in the hell he was going to handle it from here. Rightfully, he should pretend that it hadn't happened and ignore the shining recognition of mutual passion in her eyes. But that was just it: he couldn't ignore her melting looks.

Nor could he callously disregard her dependency on him. The rules they'd laid down in the cabin were still in effect. She hadn't acclimated yet. She was apprehensive. She had just survived a trauma. He couldn't subject her to another one so soon. She wasn't tough like him; she had to be treated with delicacy and tact. After the rough time he'd given her, he thought she deserved that much consideration.

Of course he was reconciled to having to turn his back on her. He wished she would turn hers on him first. That would relieve him of the responsibility of hurting her.

But dammit, she wouldn't. And he couldn't. Not yet. Not until it was absolutely necessary for them to part. Until then, even though he knew it was foolhardy, he'd go on being her Lancelot, her protector and lover.

God, he loved the role.

It was just too damn bad it was temporary.

The hot shower felt wonderful and worked to revive her physically and mentally. She scrubbed her hair with shampoo twice and rinsed it until it squeaked. When she stepped out of the tub, she felt almost normal.

But she wasn't. Normally she wouldn't have noticed how soft the motel towels were. She would have taken soft towels for granted. She was changed in other ways, too. When she propped her foot on the edge of the tub to dry, she noticed the unsightly, jagged scar running down her shin. She bore other scars. Deeper ones. They were indelibly engraved on her soul. Rusty Carlson would never be the same.

The clothes she'd been given were inexpensive and way oversize, but they made her feel human and feminine again. The shoes fit, but they felt odd and unusually light on her feet. It was the first time in weeks that she'd worn anything but hiking boots. Almost a week at the lodge and almost two since the crash.

Two weeks? Is that all it had been?

When she emerged from the motel room, Cooper was waiting outside her door. He had showered and shaved. His hair was still damp and well combed. The new clothes looked out of place on his rangy body.

They approached each other warily, shyly, almost apologetically. Then their eyes met, the familiarity sparked. And something else, too.

"You're different," Rusty whispered.

He shook his head. "No, I'm not. I might look different, but I haven't changed."

He took her hand and drew her aside, giving the people who would have rushed to cluster around them a "back off" glance. They moved out of hearing distance. Cooper said, "In all this confusion, I haven't had a chance to tell you something."

Clean and smelling like soap and shaving cream, mouth giving off the fresh scent of peppermint, he was very handsome. Her eyes moved hungrily over him, unable to take in this new Cooper. "What?"

He leaned closer. "I love the way your tongue feels flicking over my navel."

Rusty sucked in a startled breath. Her eyes darted toward the group that was huddled a discreet distance away. They were all watching them curiously. "You're outrageous."

"And I don't give a damn." He inched even closer. "Let's give them something to speculate about." He curled his hand around her throat and placed his thumb beneath her chin to tilt it up.

Then he kissed her unsparingly. He took what he wanted and gave more than she would have had the audacity to ask for. Nor was he in any hurry. His tongue plumbed her mouth slowly and deliciously in a purely sexual rhythm.

When he finally pulled away, he growled, "I want to kiss you like that all over, but," he shot a look in the direction of their astounded observers, "that'll have to wait."

They were driven back to the airport, but Rusty never remembered leaving the motel. Cooper's kiss had entranced her.

The hours of the afternoon dragged on forever. They were catered another meal. Rusty ordered an enormous chef's salad. She was starved for cold, crisp, fresh vegetables, but found that she could only eat half of it.

Her lack of appetite was partially due to the breakfast she'd eaten only hours before, but mostly to her anxiety over the interrogation she and Cooper were put through regarding the deaths of Quinn and Reuben Gawrylow.

A court reporter was brought in to take down Cooper's testimony. He told how they had met the two recluses, were given shelter by them, promised rescue, and then were attacked. "Our lives were in danger," he said. "I had no choice. It was self-defense."

Rusty gauged the reactions of the policemen and saw that they weren't convinced. They murmured among themselves and kept casting suspicious glances toward Cooper. They began asking him about his stint in Vietnam and brought up the fact that he was a former POW. They asked him to recount the events leading to his escape from the prison camp. He refused, saying that it had no bearing on this issue.

"But you were forced to...to..."

"Kill?" Cooper asked with ruthless candor. "Yes. I killed a lot of them on my way out of there. And I'd do it again."

Telling looks were exchanged. Someone coughed uncomfortably.

"He's leaving out a vital point," Rusty said abruptly. Every eye in the room turned to her.

"Rusty, no," he said. His eyes speared into hers in a silent plea for caution and discretion. "You don't have to."

She looked back at him lovingly. "Yes, I do. You're trying to spare me. I appreciate it. But I can't let them think you killed those two men without strong motivation." She faced her listeners. "They, the Gawrylows, were going to kill Cooper and...and keep me."

Shock registered on the faces encircling the table where she was seated with Cooper. "How do you know that, Ms. Carlson?"

"She just knows it, okay? You might suspect me of lying, but you have no reason to think she is."

Rusty laid a restraining hand on Cooper's arm. "The older one, Quinn, attacked me." In plain language, she told them what Gawrylow had done to her that morning in the cabin. "My leg was still seriously injured. I was virtually helpless. Cooper returned just in time to prevent a rape. Gawrylow reached for a gun. If Cooper hadn't acted when and how he did, he would have been killed instead of Gawrylow. And I would still be at the old man's mercy."

She exchanged a long stare of understanding with Cooper. She had never deliberately inflamed the hermits. He had known that all along. He silently asked her to forgive him his insults and she silently asked him to forgive her for ever being afraid of him.

Cooper's hand splayed wide over the top of her head and moved it to his chest. His arms wrapped around her. Ignoring everybody else in the room, they held each other tight, rocking slightly back and forth.

Half an hour later, Cooper was relieved of all legal responsibility for the deaths of the Gawrylows. Facing them now was their meeting with the victims' families. The weeping, somber group was led into the office. For nearly an hour Rusty and Cooper spoke with them and provided what information they could. The bereaved derived some comfort from the fact that their loved ones had died immediately and without having suffered. They tearfully thanked the survivors for sharing their knowledge about the crash. It was a moving experience for everyone involved.

The meeting with the media was something altogether different. When Rusty and Cooper were escorted into the large room that had been set up for the press conference, they were greeted by a restless crowd. A pall of tobacco smoke obscured the ceiling.

Seated behind a table with microphones, they answered the barrage of questions as thoroughly, but as concisely, as possible. Some of the questions were silly, some were intelligent, and some were painfully personal. When one gauche reporter asked what it was like to share a cabin with a total stranger, Cooper turned to one of the officials and said, "That's it. Get Rusty out of here."

The bureaucrat didn't move fast enough to suit him. Taking it upon himself to remove Rusty from the carnival atmosphere, he slipped his arm beneath hers and assisted her out of her chair. As they made their way toward the exit, a man came rushing up and shoved a business card into Cooper's face. It identified him as a reporter for a newsmagazine. He offered them an enormous sum of money for exclusive rights to their story.

"But if that's not enough," he stammered hastily when Cooper glared at him with icy malevolence, "we'll up the ante. I don't suppose you took any pictures, did you?"

Emitting a feral growl, Cooper pushed the reporter aside and told him what he could do with his magazine, using descriptive words that couldn't be misunderstood.

By the time they were boarded onto the L.A.-bound jet, Rusty was so exhausted she could barely walk. Her right leg was aching. Cooper had to practically carry her aboard. He buckled her into her first-class seat next to the window and took the aisle seat beside her. He asked the flight attendant to bring a snifter of brandy immediately.

"Aren't you having any?" Rusty asked after taking a few fiery and restorative sips.

He shook his head. "I've sworn off the booze for a while." The corner of his mouth lifted into a slight smile.

"You're very handsome, Mr. Landry," she remarked softly, gazing up at him as though seeing him for the first time.

He removed the snifter from her listless fingers. "That's the brandy talking."

"No, you are." She raised her hand and touched his hair. It slid through her fingers silkily.

"I'm glad you think so."

"Dinner, Ms. Carlson, Mr. Landry?"

They were surprised to realize that the airplane was already airborne. They'd been so preoccupied with each other that they hadn't even noticed the takeoff. Which was just as well. The helicopter ride hadn't been so bad for her because she hadn't had time to anticipate it. But as the day stretched out, the thought of flying to Los Angeles had filled Rusty with apprehension. It would be a while, if ever, before she was a completely comfortable flyer.

"Dinner, Rusty?" Cooper asked. She shook her head. To the flight attendant he said, "No, thanks. They fed us several times today."

"Buzz me if you need anything," she said graciously before moving down the aisle. They were the only passengers in the first-class cabin. When the flight attendant returned to the galley, they were left alone for the first time since being rescued.

"You know, it's funny," Rusty said musingly, "we were together so much that I thought I'd welcome the time when we could be apart. I thought I missed being with other people—" she fingered the pocket of his shirt "—but I hated the crowds today. All that pushing and shoving. And every time I lost sight of you, I panicked."

"Natural," he whispered as he tucked a strand of hair behind her ear. "You've been dependent on me for so long, you're in the habit. That'll go away."

She angled her head back, "Will it, Cooper?"

"Won't it?"

"I'm not sure I want it to."

He said her name softly before his lips settled against

hers. He kissed her ardently, as though this might be his last chance. There was a desperation behind his kiss. It persisted when Rusty looped her arms around his neck and buried her face in the hollow of his shoulder.

"You saved my life. Have I thanked you? Have I told you that I would have died without you?"

Cooper was frantically kissing her neck, her ears, her hair. "You don't need to thank me. I wanted to protect you, to take care of you."

"You did. Well. Very well." They kissed again until they were forced to break apart breathlessly. "Touch me."

He watched her lips whisper the words. They were still glistening from their kiss. "Touch you? Here? Now?"

She nodded rapidly. "Please, Cooper. I'm frightened. I need to know you're here—really and truly here."

He opened the coat that the Canadian government had supplied and slipped his hand inside. He covered her breast. It felt womanly and warm and full beneath her sweater.

He laid his cheek against hers and whispered, "Your nipple is already hard."

"Hmm."

His fingers played with the tight little bead through the knit. "You don't seem surprised."

"I'm not."

"Are they always like this? Where were you when I was fourteen?"

She laughed softly. "No, they're not always like this. I was thinking about last night."

"Last night lasted a lifetime. Be specific."

"Remember when…" She whispered a sultry reminder.

"Lord, yes," he groaned, "but don't talk about that now."

"Why?"

"If you do, you'll have to sit on my lap."

She touched him. "To cover this?"

"No, Rusty," he said through gritted teeth. And when he told her what they would be doing if she sat on his lap, she chastely removed her hand.

"I don't think that would be proper at all. For that matter, neither is what you're doing. Maybe you'd better stop." He withdrew his hand from her sweater. By now both her breasts were showing up hard and pointed beneath it. They gazed at each other, their eyes reflecting a sense of loss. "I wish we hadn't been so stubborn. I wish we'd made love before last night."

He sighed deeply. "I've thought about that, too."

A sob rose in her throat. "Hold me, Cooper." He clasped her tightly and burrowed his face in her hair. "Don't let me go."

"I won't. Not now."

"Not ever. Promise."

Sleep claimed her before she got his promise. It also spared her from seeing the bleak expression on his face.

It seemed that the entire population of the city was waiting for their arrival at LAX. They had landed only briefly in Seattle and hadn't had to deplane. None of the boarding passengers had joined them in first class. That takeoff had been uneventful.

Now, anticipating a mob scene, the senior flight attendant advised them to let all the other passengers disembark first. Rusty welcomed the delay. She was terribly nervous. Her palms were wet with perspiration. Jitters like this were foreign to her. At ease on every social occasion, she couldn't imagine why she was sick with anxiety now. She didn't want to release her grip on Cooper's arm, although she kept flashing insincere, confident smiles up at him. If only she could slip back into her regular life without a lot of fuss.

But it wasn't going to be that easy. The moment she stepped through the opening of the jet way and entered the terminal, her worst expectations were realized. She was momentarily blinded by television lights. Microphones were poked into her face. Someone inadvertently bumped her sore shin with a camera bag. The noise was deafening. But out of that cacophony, a familiar voice beckoned her. She turned toward it.

"Father?"

Within seconds she was smothered in his embrace. Her arm was jostled away from Cooper's. Even as she returned her father's hug, she groped for Cooper's hand, but she couldn't find it. The separation left her panicked.

"Let me review the damage," Bill Carlson said, pushing his daughter away and holding her at arm's length. The reporters widened the circle around them, but cameras snapped pictures of this moving reunion. "Not too bad, under the circumstances." He whipped the coat from around her shoulders. "As grateful as I am to the charitable Canadian government for taking such good care of you today, I think you'll feel much better in this."

One of his lackeys materialized and produced a huge box, from which Carlson shook out a full-length red fox coat exactly like the one she'd been wearing when the plane crashed. "I heard about your coat, darling," he said as he proudly draped the fur around her shoulders, "so I wanted to replace it."

Oohs and aahs rose out of the crowd. Reporters pressed closer to take pictures. The coat was gorgeous but far too heavy for the balmy southern California evening. It felt like chain mail weighting her down. But Rusty was oblivious to it, to everything, as her eyes frantically probed the circle of light surrounding her in search of Cooper. "Father, I want you to meet—"

"Don't worry about your leg. It will be seen to by expert doctors. I've arranged a room for you at the hospital. We're going there immediately."

"But Cooper—"

"Oh, yes, Cooper Landry, isn't it? The man who also survived the crash. I'm grateful to him, of course. He saved your life. I'll never forget that." Carlson spoke in a booming voice that was guaranteed to be overhead by the newspaper reporters and picked up by microphones.

Diplomatically his assistant wielded the long coatbox to clear a path for them through the throng of media people. "Ladies and gentlemen, you'll be notified if anything else comes out about the story," Carlson told them as he ushered Rusty toward a golf cart that was waiting to transport them through the terminal.

Rusty looked everywhere, but she didn't see Cooper. Finally she spotted his broad-shouldered form walking away from the scene. A couple of reporters were in hot pursuit. "Cooper!" The cart lurched forward and she grabbed the seat beneath her for balance. "Cooper!" she called again. He couldn't hear her above the din.

She wanted to leap off the cart and chase after him, but it was already in motion and her father was speaking to her. She tried to assimilate his words and make sense of them, but it seemed that he was speaking gibberish.

She fought down her rising panic as the cart rolled down the concourse, beeping pedestrians out of the way. Finally Cooper was swallowed up by the crowd and she lost sight of him altogether.

Once they were inside the limousine and cruising toward the private hospital where Carlson had arranged for a room, he clasped Rusty's clammy hand. "I was very afraid for you, Rusty. I thought I'd lost you, too."

She rested her head on her father's shoulder and squeezed his arm. "I know. I was as worried about how you'd take the news of the crash as I was about my own safety."

"About our tiff that day you left—"

"Please, Father, don't let's even think about that now." She lifted her head and smiled up at him. "I might not have survived the gutting of that ram, but I survived a plane crash."

He chuckled. "I don't know if you remember this— you were very young—but Jeff sneaked out of his cabin at Boy Scout camp one summer. He spent the entire night in the woods. He got lost and wasn't found until well into the next day. But that little scrapper wasn't the least bit scared. When we found him, he had made camp and was calmly fishing for his dinner."

Rusty returned her head to his shoulder, her smile gradually fading. "Cooper did all that for me."

She felt the sudden tension in her father's body. He usually bristled like that when something didn't meet with his approval. "What kind of man is this Cooper Landry, Rusty?"

"What kind?"

"A Vietnam veteran, I understand."

"Yes. He was a POW, too, but managed to escape."

"Did he…handle you well?"

Ah, yes, she was thinking. But she capped the fountain of passionate memories that bubbled inside her like uncorked champagne. "Yes, Father. Very well. I wouldn't have survived without him."

She didn't want to tell him about her personal involvement with Cooper so soon after her return. Her father would have to be apprised of her feelings gradually. They might be met with resistance, because Bill Carlson was an opinionated man.

He was also intuitive. One didn't easily pull the wool over his eyes. Keeping her tone as casual as possible, Rusty said, "Will you try to locate him for me tonight?" It wasn't an unusual request. Her father had contacts all over the city. "Let him know where I am. We got separated at the airport."

"Why is it even necessary for you to see this man again?"

He might just as well have asked her why it was necessary for her to go on breathing. "I want to thank him properly for saving my life," she said as a diversion.

"I'll see what I can do," Carlson told her just as the chauffeur wheeled under the porte cochere of the private clinic.

Even though her father had paved the way, it was two hours later before Rusty was left alone in her plush room. Decorated with original works of art and contemporary furniture, it resembled a chic apartment more than it did a hospital room. She lay in a firm, comfortable, mechanized bed with soft pillows beneath her head. She was wearing a new designer nightgown, one of several her father had packed in the suitcase that had been waiting for her when she checked in. All her favorite cosmetics and toiletries had been placed in the bathroom. She had the staff at her beck and call. All she had to do was pick up the phone on her nightstand.

She was miserable.

For one thing, her leg was sore as a result of the surgeon's examination. As a safety precaution X-rays had been taken, but they revealed no broken bones. "Cooper said nothing was broken," she quietly informed the doctor. He had frowned over the jagged scar. When he lamented the crude stitching that had been done, Rusty jumped to Cooper's defense. "He was trying to save my leg," she snapped.

Suddenly she was fiercely proud of that scar and not all that excited about seeing it erased, which, she was told, would require at least three reconstructive operations—maybe more. To her, the scar was like a badge of courage.

Besides, Cooper had spent a great deal of time with it the night before, kissing the raised, puckered skin and telling her that it didn't turn him off in the slightest and, in fact, made him "horny as hell" every time he looked at it. She had contemplated telling *that* to the pompous plastic surgeon.

She hadn't. Indeed, she hadn't said much of anything. She simply didn't have the energy. All she could think about was how blessed it was going to be when she was left alone to go to sleep.

But now that she had the opportunity, she couldn't. Doubts and fears and unhappiness were keeping her awake. Where was Cooper? Why hadn't he followed her? It had been a circus at the airport, but surely he could have stayed with her if he'd really wanted to.

When the nurse came in offering her a sedative, she gladly swallowed the pill. Otherwise she knew she'd never fall asleep without Cooper's hard, warm presence embracing her.

Eleven

"I mean, my God! We couldn't believe it! Our Rusty in a plane crash!"

"It must have been dreadful."

Rusty looked up from the pillows of her hospital bed at the two well-dressed women and wished they would vanish in a puff of smoke. As soon as her breakfast tray had been carried out by an efficient and ebullient nurse, her two friends had breezed into her room.

Reeking of exotic perfume and avid curiosity, they said they wanted to be the first to commiserate. Rusty suspected that what they really wanted was to be the first to hear the delicious details of her "Canadian caper," as one had called it.

"No, I couldn't say it was much fun," Rusty said tiredly.

She had awakened long before breakfast was served. She was accustomed to waking up with the sun now. Thanks to the tranquilizing pill she'd been given the night before, she had slept soundly. Her lack of animation stemmed from dejection more than fatigue. Her spirits were at an extremely low ebb, and her friends' efforts to raise them were having the opposite effect.

"As soon as you get out of here, we're treating you to a day of self-indulgence at the salon. Hair, skin, massage. Just look at your poor nails." One lifted her listless hand, clicking her tongue against the roof of her mouth. "They're ravaged."

Rusty smiled wanly, remembering how upset she'd been when Cooper had pared off her fingernails with his hunting knife. "I didn't get around to having a manicure." It was meant to be facetious, but her friends were nodding sympathetically. "I was too busy trying to stay alive."

One shook her intentionally tousled blond head and shuddered delicately, causing the Hermès scarf around her neck to slip. The dozen or so silver bangle bracelets on her wrist jingled like the harness on a Christmas reindeer. "You were so brave, Rusty. I think I would rather have died than go through all that you did."

Rusty was about to refute that remark, when she remembered that not too long ago she could have said something that shallow. "I always thought I would, too. You'd be amazed how strong the human animal's survival instincts are. In a situation like the one I was in, they take over."

But her friends weren't interested in philosophy. They wanted to hear the nitty-gritty. The get-down-and-get-dirty good stuff. One was sitting on the foot of Rusty's bed; the other was leaning forward from the chair beside it. They looked like scavenger birds perched and ready to pick her bones clean the second she succumbed.

The story of the crash and the events following it had appeared on the front page of that morning's newspaper. The writer had, with only a few minor errors, meticulously chronicled Rusty's and Cooper's ordeal. The piece had been serious in tone and journalistically sound. But the public had a penchant for reading between the lines;

it wanted to hear what had been omitted. Her friends included, the public wanted the facts fleshed out.

"Was it just *awful?* When the sun went down wasn't it terrifyingly dark?"

"We had several lanterns in the cabin."

"No, I mean outside."

"Before you got to the cabin. When you had to sleep outdoors in the woods."

Rusty sighed wearily. "Yes, it was dark. But we had a fire."

"What did you eat?"

"Rabbits, mostly."

"Rabbits! I'd *die.*"

"I didn't," Rusty snapped. "And neither would you."

Now, why had she gone and done that? Why hadn't she just left it alone? They were looking wounded and confused, having no idea why she had jumped down their throats. Why hadn't she said something cute, something glib, such as telling them that rabbit meat is served in some of the finest restaurants?

Following on the heels of that thought, of course, came one of Cooper. A pang of longing for him seized her. "I'm awfully tired," she said, feeling the need to cry and not wanting to have to explain why.

But subtlety didn't work with this duo. They didn't pick up on the hint to leave. "And your poor leg." The one with the bracelets clapped her hand to her cheek in horror. "Is the doctor sure he can fix it?"

Rusty closed her eyes as she answered, "Reasonably sure."

"How many operations will it take to get rid of that hideous scar?" Rusty felt the air stir against her face as the other friend waved frantically to the untactful speaker. "Oh, I didn't mean it that way. It's not that hideous. I mean—"

"I know what you mean," Rusty said, opening her eyes. "It is hideous, but it's better than a stump, and for a while I was afraid that's what I'd end up with. If Cooper—"

She broke off, having inadvertently spoken his name. Now that it was out, the carrion birds flocked to it, grasping it in their avidly curious talons.

"Cooper?" one asked innocently. "The man who survived the crash with you?"

"Yes."

The two women exchanged a glance, as though mentally tossing a coin to see who was going to pose the first of numerous questions about him.

"I saw him on the TV news last night. My God, Rusty, he's gorgeous!"

"'Gorgeous'?"

"Well not gorgeous in the *perfect* sense. Not *model* gorgeous. I mean rugged, manly, sweaty, hairy, sexy kind of gorgeous."

"He saved my life," Rusty said softly.

"I know, my dear. But if one's life must be saved, better it be by someone who looks like your Cooper Landry. That mustache!" She grinned wickedly and licked her chops. "Is what they say of mustaches true? Remember the joke?"

Rusty did remember the joke. Her cheeks went pink while her lips went pale. What they said about mustaches *was* true.

"Are his shoulders really this broad?" The friend held her hands a yard apart.

"He's rather brawny, yes," Rusty admitted helplessly. "But he—"

"Are his hips really this narrow?" The hands closed to less than a foot apart. The ladies giggled.

Rusty wanted to scream. "He knew things to do that I would never have thought about. He built a travois, using my fur coat, and dragged me away from the crash site—for miles. I didn't even realize how far until I saw the distance from the helicopter."

"There's something deliciously dangerous about him." One friend gave a delicate shiver. She hadn't heard a single word Rusty had said. "Something threatening in his eyes. I've always found that primitive streak wildly sexy."

The one sitting in the chair closed her eyes in a near swoon. "Stop. You're making me hot."

"This morning's paper said he killed two men in a fight over you."

Rusty nearly got out of her bed. "That's not what the paper said at all!"

"I put two and two together."

"It was self-defense!"

"Honey, calm down." She patted Rusty's hand. "If you say it was self-defense, then it was self-defense." She winked down at Rusty. "Listen, my hubby knows Bill Friedkin. He thinks your story would make a terrific movie. He and Friedkin are having lunch next week and—"

"A movie!" Rusty was aghast over the thought. "Oh, no. Please tell him not to say anything. I don't want anything to come of this. I just want to forget about it and get on with my life."

"We didn't mean to upset you, Rusty." The one who had been sitting in the chair rose to stand beside the bed. She laid a comforting hand on Rusty's shoulder. "It's just that we're your two best friends. If there *was* something dreadful that you wanted to discuss, some—you know—

personal aspect of the disaster that you couldn't tell your father, we wanted to make ourselves available."

"Like what?" Rusty shrugged off her friend's hand and glared up at them. They exchanged another telling glance.

"Well, you *were* alone with that man for almost two weeks."

"And?" Rusty asked tetchily.

"And," she said, drawing a deep breath, "the paper said it was a one-room cabin."

"So?"

"Come on, Rusty." The friend's patience gave out. "The situation lends itself to all kinds of speculation. You're a very attractive young woman, and he's positively yummy and certainly virile. You're both single. You were hurt. He nursed you. You were almost totally dependent on him. You thought you might be stranded up there for the duration of the winter."

The other took up the slack and said excitedly, "Living together like that, in such close proximity, in the wilderness—well, it's positively the most romantic thing I ever heard of. You know what we're getting at."

"Yes, I know what you're getting at." Rusty's voice was cold, but her brown eyes were smoldering. "You want to know if I slept with Cooper."

Just then the door swung open and the topic of their discussion came striding in. Rusty's heart nearly jumped out of her chest. Her friends spun around, reacting to the radiant smile that broke across her face. He barely took notice of them. His gray eyes found and locked upon Rusty. The sizzling look they exchanged should have answered any questions regarding their level of intimacy.

Rusty finally composed herself enough to speak. "Uh, Cooper, these are two of my closest friends." She introduced them by name. He gave each of the women a dis-interested, terse nod to acknowledge the introductions.

"Oh, Mr. Landry, I'm *so* honored to meet you," one of them gushed, round-eyed and breathless. "The *Times* said that you are an escaped POW. That just blows my mind. I mean, all that you've been through already. Then to survive a plane crash."

"Rusty claims that you saved her life."

"My husband and I would like to give the two of you an intimate little dinner party when Rusty gets up and around. Please say you'll let us."

"When did you decide that?" the other asked with pique. "*I* wanted to give them a dinner party."

"I spoke first."

The silly chatter was irritating and embarrassing. Their squabbling made them sound like the two step-sisters in *Cinderella*. "I'm sure Cooper can't stay long," Rusty interrupted, noticing that he was growing increasingly impatient. As was she. Now that he was here, she wanted to get rid of her so-called friends so she could be alone with him.

"We've stayed long enough," one of them said as she gathered up her handbag and coat. She bent over Rusty and kissed the air just above her cheek, whispering, "You sly thing, you. You won't get away with this. I want to know *everything*."

The other one leaned down and said, "I'm sure he was well worth the plane crash. He's divine. So raw. So... Well, I'm sure I don't have to tell *you*."

They stopped on their way to the door to say good-bye to Cooper. One even tapped his chest with a flirta-tious hand as she reminded him about the dinner party she was planning in his honor. They glided out, smiling smugly at Rusty over their shoulders before the door closed on them.

Cooper watched them go, then approached the bed. "I'm not going to any damned dinner party."

"I didn't expect you to. Once the novelty has worn off, I'll advise her to drop that idea."

Looking at him proved to be hazardous. She was dismayed to feel tears stinging her eyes. Self-consciously she brushed them off her cheeks.

"Something wrong?"

"No, I'm..." She hesitated to tell him, but decided to take the plunge. The time for secrets between them was long past. Bravely she lifted her eyes back to his. "I'm just very glad to see you."

He didn't touch her, although he might just as well have. His gaze was as possessive as a caress. It passed down her form lying beneath the thin blanket, then moved back up again. It lingered on her breasts, which were seductively outlined by the clinging silk nightgown.

She nervously raised her hand and fiddled with the lace neckline. "The, uh, the gown was waiting here for me when I checked in."

"It's nice."

"Anything is better than long johns."

"You look all right in long johns."

Her smile wavered. He was here. She could see him, smell his soapy clean smell, hear his voice. He was wearing new clothes—slacks and a casual shirt and jacket. But they weren't responsible for his distant attitude. She didn't want to acknowledge it, but it was undeniably there—as obvious to her as an unbreachable wall.

"Thank you for coming to see me," she said for lack of anything better. "I asked my father to locate you and tell you where I was."

"Your father didn't tell me anything. I found you on my own."

She took heart. He'd been looking for her. Maybe all night. Maybe while she'd lain sleeping a drug-induced sleep, he'd been combing the city streets in a frantic search.

But then he shot down her soaring hopes by adding, "It was in the morning paper that you were here. I understand that a plastic surgeon is going to correct the stitches I made."

"I defended your stitching."

He shrugged indifferently. "It worked, that's all I care about."

"That's all I care about, too."

"Sure."

"It is!" She sat up straighter, angry over his righteous condescension. "It wasn't my idea to come straight here from the airport. It was my father's. I would rather have gone home, checked my mail, watered my plants, slept in my own bed."

"You're a big girl. Why didn't you?"

"I just told you. Father had made these arrangements. I couldn't demand that he change them."

"How come?"

"Don't be obtuse. And why shouldn't I want this scar removed?" she cried angrily.

He glanced away, gnawing on the corner of his mustache. "You should. Of course you should."

Slumping with misery, Rusty settled back on her pillows and blotted her eyes with the corner of the sheet. "What's wrong with us? Why are we behaving like this?"

His head came back around. He wore a sad expression, as though her naiveté was to be pitied. "You shouldn't have to go through the rest of your life with that scar on your leg. I didn't mean to suggest that you should."

"I'm not talking about the scar, Cooper. I'm talking about everything. Why did you disappear at the airport last night?"

"I was there, in plain sight."

"But you weren't with me. I called out. Didn't you hear me?"

He didn't answer directly. "You didn't seem to be lacking attention."

"I wanted *your* attention. I had it until we stepped off the airplane."

"We could hardly do in that crowd what we were doing on the airplane." His eyes raked down her insultingly. "Besides, you were otherwise occupied." His mouth was set in a cynical smirk again. It looked unfamiliar now because Rusty hadn't seen that expression since they'd made love.

She was bewildered. Where and when had things between them gone wrong? "What did you expect to happen when we arrived in L.A.? We were and are news, Cooper. It wasn't my fault that the reporters were there. And my father. He was worried sick about me. He helped fund our rescue. Did you think he'd treat my return casually?"

"No." He raked his fingers through his hair. "But did it have to be such a goddamn sideshow? Why the big production? That coat, for instance."

"That was a very thoughtful thing for him to do."

It embarrassed her even now to recall her father's flamboyant gesture, but she sprang to defend him. The coat had been an expression of his love and joy at having her safely returned to him. That it had been a tasteless display of affluence wasn't the point. It was aggravating that Cooper couldn't see that and simply overlook her father's idiosyncrasies.

Cooper was moving around the room restlessly, as though he found it confining. His motions were abrupt and self-conscious, like those of a man ill at ease because his clothes didn't fit him well. "Look, I've got to go."

"Go? Now? Why? Where are you going?"

"Home."

"To Rogers Gap?"

"Yeah. Back to where I belong. I've got a ranch to look after. No telling what shape I'll find it in when I get there." Almost as an afterthought he glanced down at her right leg. "What about your leg? Is it going to be all right?"

"Eventually," she replied dully. *He's leaving. He's going. Away from me. Possibly forever.* "It's going to take a series of operations. The first of them is being done tomorrow."

"I hope I didn't do you more harm than good."

Her throat was tight with emotion. "You didn't."

"Well, I guess this is goodbye." He edged toward the door, trying not to make it look like an escape.

"Maybe sometime I can drive up to Rogers Gap and say hello. You never can tell when I might get up that way."

"Yeah, sure. That'd be great." His forced smile told her otherwise.

"How...how often do you come to L.A.?"

"Not very often," he was honest enough to say. "Well, so long, Rusty." Turning on the heels of his new shoes, he reached for the door handle.

"Cooper, wait!" He turned back. She was sitting up in bed, poised to chase after him if necessary. "Is this how it's going to end?"

He nodded curtly.

"It can't. Not after what we've been through together."

"It has to."

She shook her head so adamantly that her hair flew in every direction. "You don't fool me anymore. You're being insensitive to protect yourself. You're fighting it. I know you are. You want to hold me just as much as I want to hold you."

His jaw knotted as he ground his teeth together. At his sides, his hands formed fists. He warred with himself for several seconds before losing the battle.

He lunged across the room and pulled her roughly into his arms. Lowering himself onto the side of the bed, he hugged her against him tightly. With their arms wrapped around each other, they rocked together. His face was buried in the cinnamon-colored hair. Hers was nestled against his throat.

"Rusty, Rusty."

Thrilling to the anguish in his voice, she told him, "I couldn't go to sleep last night without a sedative. I kept listening for your breathing. I missed being held in your arms."

"I missed feeling your bottom against my lap."

He bent his head at the same moment she lifted hers and their mouths sought each other. Their kiss was desperate with desire. He plowed all ten fingers through her hair and held her head still while he made love to her open mouth with his tongue.

"I wanted you so bad last night, I thought I'd die," he groaned when they moved apart.

"You didn't want to be separated from me?"

"Not that way."

"Then why didn't you answer me when I called out to you at the airport? You heard me, didn't you?"

He looked chagrined, but nodded his head yes. "I couldn't be a performer in that circus, Rusty. I couldn't get away from there fast enough. When I came home from Nam, I was treated like a hero." He rubbed a strand of her hair between his fingers while he reflected on the painful past. "I didn't feel like a hero. I'd been living in hell. In the bowels of hell. Some of the things I'd had to do... Well, they weren't very heroic. They didn't deserve a spotlight and accolades. *I* didn't deserve them. I just wanted to be left alone so I could forget it."

He tilted her head back and pierced her with a silvery-gray stare. "I don't deserve or want a spotlight now, either. I did what was necessary to save our lives. Any man would have."

She touched his mustache lovingly. "Not any man, Cooper."

He shrugged away the compliment. "I've had more experience at surviving than most, that's all."

"You just won't take the credit you deserve, will you?"

"Is that what you want, Rusty? Credit for surviving?"

She thought of her father. She would have enjoyed hearing a few words of praise for her bravery. Instead he had talked about Jeff's Boy Scout escapade and told her how well her brother had reacted to a potentially fatal situation. Comparing her to Jeff hadn't been malicious on her father's part. He hadn't meant to point out how she fell short of Jeff's example. But that's what it had amounted to. What would it take, she wondered, to win her father's approval?

But for some reason, winning his approval didn't seem as important as it once had been. In fact, it didn't seem important at all. She was far more interested in what Cooper thought of her.

"I don't want credit, Cooper. I want..." She stopped

short of saying "you." Instead, she laid her cheek against his chest. "Why didn't you come after me? Don't you want me anymore?"

He laid his hand over her breast and stroked it with his fingertips. "Yes, I want you." The need that made his voice sound like tearing cloth wasn't strictly physical.

Rusty perceived the depth of his need because she felt it too. It came out of an emptiness that gnawed at her when he wasn't there. It caused her own imploring inflection. "Then why?"

"I didn't follow you last night because I wanted to speed up the inevitable."

"The inevitable?"

"Rusty," he whispered, "this sexual dependency we feel for each other is textbook normal. It's common among people who have survived a crisis together. Even hostages and kidnap victims sometimes begin to feel an unnatural affection for their captors."

"I know all that. The Stockholm syndrome. But this is different."

"Is it?" His brows lowered skeptically. "A child loves whoever feeds him. Even a wild animal becomes friendly with someone who leaves food out for it. I took care of you. It was only human nature that you attach more significance—"

Suddenly and angrily, she pushed him away. Her hair was a vibrant halo of indignation, her eyes bright with challenge. "Don't you dare reduce what happened between us with psychological patter. It's crap. What I feel for you is real."

"I never said it wasn't real." Her feistiness excited him. He liked her best when she was defiant. He yanked her against him. "We've always had this going for us."

He cupped her breast again and impertinently swept his thumb across the tip.

She wilted, murmuring a weak "Don't," which he disregarded. He continued to fondle her. Her eyes slid shut.

"We get close. I get hard. You get creamy. Every damned time. It happened the first time we laid eyes on each other in the airplane. Am I right?"

"Yes," she admitted.

"I wanted you then, before we ever left the ground."

"But you didn't even smile, or speak to me, or encourage me to speak to you."

"That's right."

"Why?" She couldn't take any more of his caresses and stay sensible. She moved his hand aside. "Tell me why."

"Because I guessed then what I know for fact now: we live worlds apart. And I'm not referring to geography."

"I know what you're talking about. You think I'm silly and superficial, like those friends of mine you just met. I'm not!"

She laid her hands on his forearms and appealed to him earnestly. "They irritated me, too. Do you know why? Because I saw myself—the way I used to be. I was judging them just as you did me when we first met.

"But please be tolerant toward them. Toward me. This is Beverly Hills. Nothing is real. There are areas of this city I couldn't relate to. The Gawrylows' cabin was beyond my realm of comprehension. But I'm changed. I really am. I'm not like them anymore."

"You never were, Rusty. I thought so. I know better now." He framed her face between his hands. "But that's the life you know. It's the crowd you run with. I couldn't. Wouldn't. Wouldn't even want to try. And you wouldn't belong in my life."

Hurt by the painful truth of what he was saying, she reacted with anger and threw off his hands. "Your life! What life? Shut away from the rest of the world? Alone and lonely? Using bitterness like an armor? You call that a life? You're right, Cooper. I couldn't live like that. The chip on my shoulder would be too heavy to bear."

His lower lip narrowed to a thin, harsh line beneath his mustache. She knew she'd hit home, but there was no victory in it.

"So there you have it," he said. "That's what I've been trying to tell you. In bed we're great, but we'd never make a life together."

"Because you're too damned stubborn to try! Have you even considered a compromise?"

"No. I don't want any part of this scene." He spread his hands wide to encompass the luxurious room and all that lay beyond the wide window.

Rusty aimed an accusing finger at him. "You're a snob."

"A snob?"

"Yes, a snob. You snub society because you feel superior to the masses. Superior and righteous because of the war and your imprisonment. Scornful because you see all that's wrong with the world. Locked up there on your solitary mountain, you play God by looking down on all of us who have the guts to tolerate each other despite our human failings."

"It's not like that," he ground out.

"Isn't it? Aren't you just a trifle self-righteous and judgmental? If there's so much wrong with our world, if you ridicule it that much, why don't you do something to change it? What are you accomplishing by withdrawing from it? Society didn't shun you. You shunned it."

"I didn't leave her until she—"

"Her?"

Cooper's face cleared of all emotion and became as wooden and smooth as a mask. The light in his eyes flickered out. They became hard and implacable.

Shocked, Rusty laid a hand against her pounding heart. *A woman was at the source of Cooper's cynicism.* Who? When? A hundred questions raced through her mind. She wanted to ask all of them, but for the time being she was occupied only with enduring his icy, hostile stare. He was furious with himself and with her. She had goaded him into resurrecting something he had wanted to keep dead and buried.

Her overactive heart pumped jealousy through her system as rich and red as her blood. Some woman had wielded enough influence over Cooper to alter the course of his life. He might have been a happy-go-lucky chap before this unnamed she-wolf got her claws into him. For his bitterness to be this lasting, she must have been some woman. He was still feeling her influence. Had he loved her that much? Rusty asked herself dismally.

A man like Cooper Landry wouldn't go long without having a woman. But Rusty had imagined his affairs to be fleeting, physical gratification and little else. It had never occurred to her that he'd been seriously involved with someone. But he had been, and her departure from his life had been wrenching and painful.

"Who was she?"

"Forget it."

"Did you meet her before you went to Vietnam?"

"Drop it, Rusty."

"Did she marry someone else while you were a prisoner?"

"I said to forget it."

"Did you love her?"

"Look, she was good in the sack, but not as hot as you, okay? Is that what you're itching to know—how the two of you compare? Well, let's see. She wasn't a redhead, so she lacked your fiery spirit. She had a great body, but it didn't come close to yours."

"Stop it!"

"Her breasts were fuller, but no more responsive. Nipples? Larger and darker. Thighs? Hers were just as smooth, but not nearly as strong as yours." He stared at the spot where hers came together. "Yours can squeeze the life out of a man."

She covered her mouth to trap a sob of anguish and outrage. Her breath was coming as hard and fast as his. They glared at each other with an animosity as fierce as the passion they'd shared while making love.

It was into that seething atmosphere that Bill Carlson made his inopportune entrance. "Rusty?"

She jumped at her father's voice. "Father!" His name came out as a gusty exhalation. "Come...good morning. This..." She discovered that her mouth was dry and the hand she raised to gesture toward Cooper was trembling. "This is Cooper Landry."

"Ah, Mr. Landry." Carlson extended his hand. Cooper shook it. He did so firmly, but with a noticeable lack of enthusiasm and a great deal of dislike. "I've had several people trying to track you down." Cooper offered no explanations as to his whereabouts overnight, so Carlson blustered on. "I wanted to thank you for saving my daughter's life."

"No thanks is necessary."

"Of course it is. She means the world to me. The way she tells it, you meant the difference between her life and death. In fact she's the one who urged me to locate you last night."

Cooper glanced down at Rusty, then back at Carlson, who was reaching into the breast pocket of his suit coat. He withdrew a white envelope. "Rusty wanted to say thank-you in a special way."

He handed the envelope to Cooper. Cooper opened it and glanced inside. He stared at the contents for a long moment before lifting his eyes to Rusty. They were frigid with contempt. One corner of his mustache curled into a nasty smile. Then, in one vicious motion, he ripped the envelope and the cashier's check inside in half. He tossed the two halves into the valley of her thighs.

"Thanks all the same, Miss Carlson, but on our last night together I was paid in full for my services."

Twelve

Turning back to his daughter after watching Cooper storm from the room, Carlson said, "What an unpleasant individual."

"Father, how could you have offered him money?" Rusty cried in dismay.

"I thought you wanted and expected me to."

"Whatever gave you that impression? Cooper…Mr. Landry… He is a proud man. Do you think he saved my life for profit?"

"I wouldn't be surprised. He's an unlikeable character from what I've heard of him."

"You asked around?"

"Certainly. As soon as he was identified as the man with you when you were rescued. Being marooned with him couldn't have been easy for you."

"We had our differences," Rusty replied with a rueful smile. "But he could have deserted me and saved himself at any time."

"He wasn't about to. Not when there might be a reward for saving you."

"He didn't know that."

"He's clever. He deduced that I'd spare no expense to rescue you if you were still alive. Maybe he was offended by the amount." He picked up the ripped check and studied it. "I thought it was a generous reward, but maybe he's greedier than I suspected."

Rusty closed her eyes and let her head fall back onto the pillows in defeat. "Father, he doesn't want your money. He's all too glad to be rid of me."

"The feeling is mutual." Carlson sat down on the edge of her bed. "However, it's unfortunate that we can't capitalize on your mishap."

Her eyes came open again. "'Capitalize'? What in the world are you talking about?"

"Don't jump to conclusions until you've heard me out."

She'd already jumped to several conclusions, none of which were to her liking. "You're not referring to a movie are you?" When her friend had mentioned the idea, she'd been appalled.

Carlson patted her hand. "Nothing so crass, my dear. We've got more style than that."

"Then, what?"

"One of your problems has always been your lack of vision, Rusty." Affectionately, he cuffed her on the chin. "Your brother would have immediately seen the enterprising possibilities this situation has opened up to us."

As usual, the comparison to her brother left her feeling inferior. "Like what?"

Patiently Carlson explained. "You've made a name for yourself in real estate. And not by riding my coattails, either. I might have placed a few opportunities in your path, but you took advantage of them."

"Thank you, but what is this leading to, Father?"

"In your own right, you're something of a celebrity in this town." She shook her head scoffingly. "I mean it. Your name is well-known in important circles. And in recent days your name and picture have appeared in newspapers and on television. You've been made into a sort of folk heroine. That kind of free publicity is as good as money in the bank. I propose that we use this disaster to our advantage."

On the verge of panic, Rusty wet her lips. "You mean promote the fact that I survived an airplane crash to generate business?"

"What could it hurt?"

"You must be joking!" He wasn't. There was nothing in either his expression or demeanor to indicate that he was only fooling. She bowed her head, shaking it. "No, Father. Absolutely not. The idea doesn't appeal to me at all."

"Don't say no right away," he said patronizingly. "I'll get our advertising agency to work up a few ideas. I promise not to move on any of them until you've been consulted and I have your approval."

He was suddenly a stranger to her. The voice, the face, the polished manner—all were familiar. But she didn't really know the heart and soul of the man behind the veneer. She didn't know him at all.

"I'll never approve. That plane crash killed five people. *Five men*, Father. I met their families—their grieving widows and children and parents. I talked to them. I offered them my heartfelt condolences. To turn their misfortune to my own advantage—" she shuddered with repugnance "—no, Father. That's something I can't do."

Bill Carlson pulled on his lower lip, as he always did when he was deep in thought. "Very well. For the time being, we'll table that idea. But another has occurred to me."

He pressed both her hands between his. Rusty got the

distinct impression that she was being restrained as a pre-
cautionary measure, as if what he was about to suggest
would precipitate a fit.

"As I've told you, I had Mr. Landry thoroughly
checked out yesterday. He owns a large ranch in a beautiful area of the Sierras."

"So he's said."

"No one has developed the land around it."

"That's the beauty of it. The region has remained virtually untouched. I fail to see what that has to do with us."

"Rusty, what's the matter with you?" he asked teasingly. "Have you become a conservationist after two
weeks in the woods? You're not going to circulate peti-
tions accusing builders of raping the land every time a
new tract of homes goes up, are you?"

"Of course not, Father." His teasing bordered on criticism. There was a trace of reproach behind his smile.
Rusty didn't want to disappoint him, but she hastened
to eliminate any ideas he was nursing regarding Cooper
and enterprise. "I hope you aren't considering any com-
mercial development in Mr. Landry's part of the state.
I can promise you, he wouldn't welcome it. In fact he'd
fight you."

"Are you sure? How does the idea of a partnership
strike you?"

She stared at him incredulously. "A partnership between Cooper and me?"

Carlson nodded. "He's a war veteran. That's very pro-
motable. You survived a plane crash together and endured
unbelievable hardships in the Canadian wilds before you
were rescued. That, too, has high drama and marketabil-
ity. The buying public will eat it up."

Everyone, even her own father, seemed to regard the
plane crash and the life-threatening experiences follow-

ing it as a grand adventure, a melodrama starring Cooper and herself in the principal roles—*The African Queen* set in a different time and locale.

Carlson was too caught up in his plans to notice Rusty's negative reaction to them. "I could make a few calls and by dark today put together a group of investors who would love to build condos in that area. There's a ski lift at this Rogers Gap, but it's ill-managed. We'd modernize and improve that and build around it.

"We'd bring Landry into it, of course. That would smooth the way with the other locals. He's not a mixer, but my investigators reported back that he wields a lot of influence. His name means something up there. Once the condos are under construction, you could start selling them. We'd all stand to make millions."

Her objections to his proposal were too many to enumerate, so she didn't even try. She had to shoot down the idea before it even took off. "Father, in case you didn't get the message a minute ago, Mr. Landry isn't interested in making money." She picked up the two halves of the check and shook them in front of his face as a reminder. "Making money off a real-estate venture will be anathema to him. He loves that country up there. He wants it left alone, kept the way it is, unspoiled by land developers. He loves the way nature developed it."

"He might pay lip service to that Walden Pond philosophy," her father remarked skeptically. "But every man has his price, Rusty."

"Not Cooper Landry."

Carlson stroked his daughter's cheek. "Your naiveté is endearing."

The twinkle in his eyes was familiar and alarming. It indicated that he was on the scent of a Big Deal. In a community of capitalist sharks, her father was among

those with the most deadly jaws. She grasped his hand
and squeezed it hard. "Promise me, *promise*, that you
won't do this. You don't know him."

"And you do?" The glint in his eyes dimmed and the
lids narrowed. Gradually she released his hands. He
backed away from her suspiciously, as though he'd just
learned that what was confining her to the hospital bed
might be contagious.

"I haven't posed any questions that might have been
embarrassing for you to answer, Rusty. I wanted to spare
us both that. However, I'm not blind. Landry is almost a
caricature of the macho male. He's the kind of belligerent loner that women swoon over and fancy themselves
able to tame."

He cupped her chin and tilted it up so he could read
her eyes. "Surely you're too intelligent to fall for a pair
of broad shoulders and a broody disposition. I hope that
you didn't form any sort of emotional attachment to this
man. That would be most unfortunate."

Unwittingly her father had echoed Cooper's theory—
that their feelings were due largely to their dependency
on each other. "Under the circumstances, wouldn't forming an attachment to him be natural?"

"Yes. But the circumstances have changed. You're
no longer isolated with Landry in the wilderness; you're
home. You have a life here that mustn't be jeopardized
by a juvenile infatuation. Whatever happened up there,"
he said, hitching his perfectly groomed head in the direction of the window, "is over and should be forgotten."

Cooper had said as much, too. But it wasn't over. Not
by a long shot. And it couldn't be forgotten. What she felt
for him wasn't going to weaken and eventually die from
lack of nurturing. She hadn't formed a psychological de-

pendency on him that would disappear as she gradually resumed her previous life.

She'd fallen in love. Cooper was no longer her provider and protector, but something so much more. He was the man she loved. Whether they were together or apart, that would never change.

"Don't worry, Father. I know exactly what I feel for Mr. Landry." That was the truth. Let her father draw his own conclusions.

"Good girl," Carlson said, patting her shoulder. "I knew I could count on you to come out of this stronger and smarter than ever. Just like your brother, you've got your head on straight."

She had been home for a week after spending almost a week in the hospital recovering from the first operation on her shin. The scar didn't look much better than it had before the surgery, but the doctor had assured her that after the series of operations, it would be virtually undetectable.

Aside from a little tenderness in her leg, she felt perfectly fine. The bandages had been removed, but the surgeon had advised her to keep clothing off the leg and to continue to use crutches for support.

She had regained the few pounds she'd lost after the plane crash. She spent a half hour or so each day lying in the sun on the redwood deck of her pool to restore her light tan. Her friends had been true to their promise, and since she couldn't easily get to a salon, they'd brought the salon to her. A hairdresser had trimmed and conditioned and restored her hair to its usual glossy sheen. A manicurist had resculptured her nails. She'd also massaged a pound of cream into Rusty's dry, rough hands.

As she watched the manicurist smoothing away the

scaly redness, Rusty thought about the laundry she had washed by hand, then hung up to dry on a crude outdoor clothesline. It had always been a contest to see if the clothes would dry before they froze. It hadn't been all that bad. Not really. Or did memory always make things seem better than they actually had been?

That could be applied to everything. Had Cooper's kisses really been that earth-moving? Had his arms and whispered words been that comforting in the darkest hours of the night? If not, why did she wake up frequently, yearning for his nearness, his warmth?

She had never been so lonely.

Not that she was ever alone—at least not for prolonged periods of time. Friends dropped in to bring trifling presents that would hopefully amuse her because she seemed so morose. Physically she was coming along nicely, but her spirits hadn't bounced back yet.

Friends and associates were worried about her. Since the airplane crash, she was not her usual, jovial self at all. They kept her stuffed with everything from Godiva chocolates to carry-out tacos to covered dishes from Beverly Hills's finest restaurants, prepared especially for her by the head chefs who knew personally what her favorite foods were.

She had lots of time on her hands, but she was never idle. Her father's prediction had come true: she was suddenly a celebrity real-estate agent. Everybody in town who wanted to sell or buy sought her advice on the fluctuating market trends. Each day she took calls from prospective clients, including an impressive number of movie and television people. Her ear grew sore from the hours spent on the telephone. Ordinarily she would have leaped over the moon for a client list of this caliber. Instead she was plagued with an uncharacteristic ennui that she couldn't explain or overcome.

Her father hadn't said any more about developing the area around Rogers Gap. She hoped that idea was officially a dead issue. He came by her house each day, ostensibly to check on her progress. But Rusty suspected, perhaps unfairly, that her father was more interested in quickly harvesting this crop of new business than in her recovery.

The lines around his mouth became tense with impatience, and his jocular encouragement for her to get back to work was beginning to sound forced. Even though she was following doctor's orders, she knew that she was stretching her recovery time for as long as she could. She was determined, however, not to return to her office until she felt good and ready.

On this particular afternoon, she groaned in dread when the doorbell pealed through her house. Her father had called earlier to say that because of a business commitment he wouldn't be able to come by that day. Rusty had been relieved. She loved her father but had welcomed the break from his daily visit, which never failed to exhaust her.

Obviously his meeting had been canceled and she wasn't going to get a reprieve after all.

Hooking her arms over her crutches, she hobbled down the hallway toward her front door. She'd lived in this house for three years. It was a small, white stucco building with a red tile roof, very southern California in design, tucked into an undercliff and shrouded with vividly blooming bougainvillea. Rusty had fallen in love with it the minute she saw it.

Propping herself up on one crutch, she unlatched and opened the door.

Cooper said nothing. Neither did she. They just stared at each other for a long time before she silently moved aside. He stepped through the arched doorway. Rusty closed the door and turned to face him.

"Hi."

"Hi."

"What are you doing here?"

"I came to see about your leg." He looked down at her shin. She stuck it out for his inspection. "It doesn't look much better."

"It will." His skeptical gaze moved up to meet hers. "The doctor has promised it will," she said defensively.

He still seemed doubtful, but let the subject drop. He took in his surroundings, pivoting slowly. "I like your house."

"Thank you."

"It's a lot like mine."

"Really?"

"Mine looks sturdier, maybe. Not decorated as fancy. But they're similar. Large rooms. Lots of windows."

She felt she had recovered enough to move. Upon seeing him, her one good knee, which she relied on for support, had threatened to buckle beneath her. Now, she felt confident enough to move forward and indicated for him to follow her. "Come on in. Would you like something to drink?"

"Something soft."

"Lemonade?"

"Fine."

"It'll only take a minute to make."

"Don't bother."

"No bother. I was thirsty for some anyway."

She maneuvered herself through the dining room and into the kitchen at the back of the house. He followed. "Sit down." She nodded toward the butcher-block table that formed an island in the center of the kitchen and moved toward the refrigerator.

"Can I help?" he asked.

"No thanks. I've had practice."

She turned her head, ready with a smile, and caught him staring at the backs of her legs. Thinking that she was going to be alone all day, she'd dressed in a ragged pair of cutoffs and hadn't bothered with shoes. The tails of a chambray shirt were knotted at her waist. She'd pulled her hair up into a high, scraggly ponytail. The effect was a Beverly Hills version of Daisy Mae.

Caught staring at her smooth, bare legs, Cooper shifted guiltily in his chair. "Does it hurt?"

"What?"

"Your leg."

"Oh. No. Well, some. Off and on. I'm not supposed to walk or drive or anything like that yet."

"Have you gone back to work?"

Her ponytail swished against her neck as she shook her head. "I'm conducting some business here by telephone. The messenger services love me. I've kept them busy. But I haven't quite felt up to dressing and going to the office."

She took a can of lemonade concentrate out of the refrigerator where she'd had it thawing. "Have you been busy since you got home?"

She poured the thick pink concentrate into a pitcher and added a bottle of chilled club soda. When some of it splashed on the back of her hand, she raised it to her mouth and sucked it off. That's when she turned with the question still in her eyes.

Like a hawk, Cooper was watching every move. He was staring at her mouth. Slowly, she lowered her hand

and turned back to her task. Her hands were trembling as she took glasses down out of the cabinet and filled them with ice cubes.

"Yeah, I've been busy."

"How was everything when you got back?"

"Okay. A neighbor had been feeding my livestock. Guess he would have gone on doing that indefinitely if I'd never turned up."

"That's a good neighbor." She had wanted to inject some levity into the conversation, but her voice sounded bright and brittle. It didn't fit the atmosphere, which was as heavy and oppressive as a New Orleans summer. The air was sultry; she couldn't draw enough of it into her lungs.

"Don't you have any help running your ranch?" she asked.

"Off and on. Temporary hands. Most of them are ski bums who only work to support their habit. When they run out of money they work a few days so they can buy lift tickets and food. The system works for both them and me."

"Because you don't like a lot of people around."

"Right."

An abysmal depression came over her. She staved it off by asking, "Do you ski?"

"Some. Do you?"

"Yes. Or I did." She glanced down at her leg. "I may have to sit this season out."

"Maybe not. Since the bone wasn't broken."

"Maybe."

And that, it seemed, was all they had to say. By tacit agreement, they ended the inane small talk and did what they really wanted to do—look at each other.

His hair had been cut, but was still unfashionably long.

She liked the way it brushed the collar of his casual shirt. His jaw and chin were smoothly shaven, but if one single hair in his mustache had been altered, she couldn't tell it. The lower lip beneath it was as stern and unyielding as ever. If anything, the grooves bracketing his mouth looked deeper, making his face appear more unrelievedly masculine. She couldn't help but wonder what particular worry had carved those lines deeper.

His clothes weren't haute couture, but he would turn heads on Rodeo Drive and be a refreshing change from the dapper dressers. Blue jeans still did more for a male physique than any other garment ever sewn together. They did more for Cooper's body than for most. Of course, there was more to work with—so much more that the bulging denim between his thighs made Rusty's stomach flutter.

His cotton shirt was stretched over a chest she still dreamed about. The sleeves had been rolled back to reveal his strong forearms. He had carried a brown leather bomber jacket in with him. It was now draped over the back of his chair, forgotten. Indeed, he seemed to have forgotten everything except the woman standing only a few feet, yet seemingly light-years, away from him.

His eyes tracked down her body, stripping her as they went. As though he were actually peeling away layer after layer of clothing, her skin began to burn with fever. By the time his eyes paused on the uneven, stringy hems of her cutoffs, where the soft threads tickled her bare thighs, Rusty was warm and moist.

His gaze moved back up to her face and the desire he saw registered there reflected his own. His eyes were like magnets drawing her into their field. On her crutches, she closed the distance between them, never breaking their stare. He didn't either. As she drew nearer, he had to tilt his head back to maintain eye contact. It seemed to take a lifetime but was actually only a few seconds before she stood directly in front of him, leaning on her crutches for support.

She said, "I can't believe you're really here."

Groaning, he lowered his head and pressed it hard against her breasts. "Rusty. Damn you. I couldn't stay away."

Overwhelming emotions caused her eyes to close. Her head tipped forward in total surrender to her love for this complex man. She whispered his name.

He folded his arms around her waist and nuzzled his face in the soft, fragrant valley between her breasts. His hands opened wide over her back, drawing her body closer even though she couldn't move her feet.

"I've missed you," she admitted hoarsely. She didn't expect him to make a similar confession, and he didn't. But the ardency of his embrace was unspoken evidence of how much he'd missed her. "I'd hear your voice and turn, expecting you to be there. Or I'd start to say something to you before I realized you weren't there."

"God, you smell good." Openmouthed, he gnawed on the soft inner curves of her breasts, catching cloth and all between his strong, white teeth.

"You smell like the mountains," she told him, kissing his hair.

"I've got to have—" he was frantically untying the knot at her waist "—just one—" it came undone and he ripped the buttons apart "—bite." His mouth fastened on the fleshy part of her breast, which was overflowing the cup of her brassiere.

At the first hot contact of his mouth with her skin, she arched her back and moaned. Her knuckles turned white where they gripped the handles of her crutches.

She longed to drop them and plunge her fingers into his hair. She felt it dusting her skin when he turned his head and kissed her other breast. He took gentle love bites through the sheer cups of her brassiere and delicately sipped at the tips.

She released a keening sound much like a sob. It was both frustrating and thrilling not to have the use of her hands. The sense of helplessness was titillating. "Cooper," she gasped imploringly.

He reached around her and unhooked her bra strap, working it down as far as it would go before the straps got caught in her sleeves. But that was sufficient. He had completely uncovered her. His eyes drank their fill before his lips surrounded one taut, pink crest and drew it into his mouth. He sucked it lovingly, then sponged the very tip of it with his tongue before drying it with his mustache. His whole face moved over her breasts, rubbing them with cheek and chin and mouth and nose and brow. Rusty, leaning precariously on her crutches, chanted his name with religious fervor.

"Tell me what you want. Anything," he said huskily. "Tell me."

"I want you."

"Woman, you've got me. What do you want?"

"To touch. To be touched."

"Where?"

"Cooper..."

"Where?"

"You know where," she cried.

He brusquely unsnapped her cutoffs and slid down the zipper. Her brief panties did little more than cover the triangle of curls. He wanted to smile, but his face was too set with passion, so he couldn't. He merely growled his approval as he pulled down the panties along with her cutoffs. He kissed the gingery down.

Rusty's strength deserted her. She let go of the crutches. They clattered to the floor. She fell forward slightly, breaking her fall by placing her hands on Cooper's shoulders. As she did so, he slid off the seat of the chair and sank to his knees in front of her.

She caught her lower lip between her teeth to keep from screaming with pleasure as he parted her dewy flesh with his thumbs and buried his tongue in the softness.

He didn't stop there. He didn't stop at all. Not after the first wave of ecstasy swept over her. Not even after the second had claimed her. He didn't stop until her body was glistening with a fine sheen of perspiration, until tendrils of russet hair were clinging damply to her temples and cheeks and neck, until she was quivering with aftershocks.

Only then did he rise to his feet and take her in his arms. "Which way?" His face was softer than she'd ever seen it as it bent over hers. The guarded chill was no longer in his eyes. In its place were sparks of some strong emotion she dared to hope was love.

She raised her hand and pointed in the general direction of the bedroom. He found it without difficulty. Since she'd spent a great deal of time in that room recently, it had a homey, lived-in aspect that apparently appealed to him. He smiled as he carried her through the doorway. Gently he stood her on her left leg and threw back the covers on the bed. "Lie down."

She did, watching as he went into the bathroom. She heard water running. Moments later, he came back carrying a damp cloth. He didn't say a word, but his eyes spoke volumes as he drew her into a sitting position and eased off her blouse. Removing her brassiere only required sliding the straps off her arms. She sat before him totally naked, and marvelously unashamed.

He ran the cool, damp cloth over her arms and shoulders and around her neck. After he had eased her back onto the pillows, he raised her arms over her head and washed the shallow cups of her armpits. She purred in surprised satisfaction; he ducked his head and kissed her moaning mouth.

He moved the cloth over her chest, then her breasts. Her nipples drew up again and he smiled. He touched a rosy whisker-burn on her tender flesh.

"I always seem to leave a mark on you," he said with a trace of regret. "I'm sorry."

"I'm not."

His eyes glowed hotly as they moved down her stomach to her navel. He licked the sweat out of it before bathing the rest of her abdomen with the cloth. Then he washed her legs, being careful of her new scar. "Turn over."

Rusty gazed up at him inquisitively, but she turned over on her stomach and rested her cheek on her stacked hands. Leisurely, he washed her entire back with the cloth. At the small of her back, he paused, then ran the cloth over the cheeks of her bottom.

"Hmm," she sighed.

"That's for me to say."

"Go right ahead."

"Hmm." He spent far more time than was necessary to wash away any perspiration. He sponged the backs of her legs all the way down to the soles of her feet, which he discovered were ticklish. On his way back up, he lingered to taste the backs of her knees.

"Just relax a minute," he told her as he left the bed to undress.

"Easy for you to say. You haven't been subjected to heavy petting."

"Brace yourself, baby. You've got more coming."

Rusty wasn't quite braced for him to lie naked and warm along the length of her back. She drew in a jagged breath and shivered with the startling impact of his hair-roughened skin against the smoothness of her back. His opened thighs sandwiched hers. Her bottom fit snugly against his sex. It was solid with desire and as smooth as velvet-sheathed steel as it rubbed against her.

He covered the backs of her hands with his palms, interlacing their fingers, and used his nose to move aside her ponytail so his lips could get to her ear.

"I can't do anything for wanting you," he whispered gruffly. "Can't work. Sleep. Eat. There's no comfort in my getaway house anymore. You ruined it for me. The mountains aren't beautiful anymore. Your face has blinded me to them."

He rocked against her and made an upward thrust, settling himself more firmly against her. "I thought I'd work you out of my system, but so far I've failed. I even went to Vegas and bought a woman for the evening. When we got to the hotel room, I just sat there staring at her and drinking, trying to work up desire. She practiced some of her fanciest tricks, but I felt nothing. I couldn't do it. Didn't want to. Finally I sent her home before she became as disgusted with me as I was with myself."

He buried his face in the back of her neck. "You redheaded witch, what'd you do to me up there? I was fine, understand? Fine, until you came along with your wet-satin mouth and silky skin. Now my life isn't worth a damn. All I can think about, see, hear, touch, smell, taste, is you. *You*."

He rolled her over and pinned her beneath him. His

mouth slanted against hers. He parted her lips with his hard, invasive, possessive tongue. "I've got to have you. Got to. Now."

He ground his body against hers as though to meld them into one. Nudging her knees apart and giving one long, smooth, plunging motion of his hips, he delved into the giving folds of her womanhood.

Groaning with pleasure, he lowered his head to her chest. He called upon every prince of Heaven and hell to release him from his torment. His breath fell hot and labored on her breasts and when the nipples responded, he loved them with his mouth.

His skin was flushed. It burned her hands as she moved them over the rippling, supple muscles of his back and hips. She cupped his hard buttocks and drew him deeper yet. He moaned her name and brought their mouths together again. His kiss was carnally symbolic.

Rusty didn't feel vanquished by his virile power, though she could well have. On the contrary, she felt free and unfettered, strong enough to fly, to soar to the limits of the universe. Just as her body was opened to him, so was her heart and soul. Love poured out of them abundantly. He must feel it. He must know.

She was sure he did, because he was saying her name in cadence to his thrusts. His voice was raw with emotion. But a heartbeat before he lost his ability to reason, she felt him about to withdraw.

"No! Don't you dare."

"Yes, Rusty, yes."

"I love you, Cooper." She crossed her ankles at the small of his back. "I want you. All of you."

"No, no," he groaned in misery as well as ecstasy.

"I love you."

Clenching his teeth and baring them, he threw his

head back and surrendered to orgasm with a long, low, primal groan that worked its way up from the bottom of his soul. He filled this woman who loved him with his hot, rich seed.

Thirteen

Sweat dripped from his face. He was drenched in it. His body hair was curled with it. He collapsed atop her. She held him tightly. Her maternal instinct asserted itself; she wanted to cuddle him like a child.

It was an endless forever before he regained enough strength to move, but neither was in a hurry for him to leave her. Finally, he rolled away from her and lay on his back, replete. Rusty gazed at his beloved face. His eyes were closed. The lines on either side of his stern mouth had relaxed considerably since he'd come through her front door.

She laid her head on his chest and smoothed her hand over his stomach, combing through the crinkled, damp hair. "It wasn't just me you withdrew from, was it?" Somehow she knew that this was the first time in a long time that Cooper had completed the love act.

"No."

"It wasn't because I might get pregnant, was it?"

"No, it wasn't."

"Why did you make love that way, Cooper?" He opened his eyes. She stared down into them. They were guarded. He, who she had assumed was fearless, was afraid of her, a naked woman, lying helplessly beside him, utterly fascinated by him and under his spell. What threat could she possibly represent?

"Why did you impose that kind of discipline on yourself?" she asked gently. "Tell me."

He stared at the ceiling. "There was a woman."

Ah, *the* woman, Rusty thought.

"Her name was Melody. I met her soon after I got back from Nam. I was messed up. Bitter. Angry. She—" he made a helpless gesture "—she put things back into perspective, gave focus to my life. I was attending college on the GI bill. We were going to get married as soon as I finished. I thought that everything was going well for us. It was."

He closed his eyes again and Rusty knew he was approaching the difficult part of the story. "Then she got pregnant. Without my knowledge, she had an abortion." His hands curled into fists and his jaw grew rigid with fury. Rusty actually jumped when he turned to her abruptly.

"She killed my baby. After all the death I'd seen, she…" His breathing became so harsh that Rusty was afraid he'd go into cardiac arrest. She laid a comforting hand on his chest and softly spoke his name.

"I'm so sorry, Cooper, darling. I'm so sorry."

He breathed deeply, until he had filled his lungs with sufficient air. "Yeah."

"You've been angry at her ever since."

"At first. But then I came to hate her too much to be angry at her. I'd shared so many confidences with her. She knew what was going on inside my head, how I felt about things. She'd urged me to talk about the prison camp and everything that happened there."

"Did you feel that she abused that confidence?"

"Abused and betrayed it." With the pad of his thumb, he caught a tear rolling down Rusty's cheek and swept it away. "She'd held me in her arms while I cried like a baby, telling her about buddies I'd seen...killed," he finished in a hoarse whisper.

"I'd told her about the hell I went through to escape and then what I did to survive until I was rescued. Even after that, after I'd described how I'd lain in a heap of rotting, stinking corpses to keep from being recaptured—"

"Cooper, don't." Rusty reached for him and drew him close.

"She went out and had our baby destroyed. After I'd seen babies torn apart, probably had killed some myself, she—"

"Shh, shh. Don't."

Rusty cradled his head against her breasts and crooned to him as she smoothed his hair. Tears blurred her vision. She felt his suffering, and wished she could take it all on herself. She kissed the crown of his head. "I'm sorry, my darling. So very sorry."

"I left Melody. I moved to the mountains, bought my livestock, built my house."

And a wall around your heart, Rusty thought sadly. No wonder he'd spurned society. He'd been betrayed twice— once by his country, which didn't want to be reminded of its mistake, and then by the woman he had loved and trusted.

"You didn't take a chance on any woman getting pregnant by you again."

He worked his head free and looked into her eyes. "That's right. Not until now." He placed his hands on either side of her face. "Until you. And I couldn't stop

myself from filling you." He kissed her hard. "I wanted
it to last forever."

Smiling, she turned her head and bit the meaty part of
his hand just below his thumb. "I thought it was going to."

He smiled, too, looking boyishly pleased with himself. "Really?"

Rusty laughed. "Really."

He slid his hand between her thighs and worked his
fingers through the nest of russet curls before intimately
palming her sex. "I left a special mark on you this time.
You're carrying part of me inside you." He raised his
head off the pillow and brushed his mouth across her
kiss-swollen lips.

"That's what I wanted. I wouldn't have let you leave
me this time."

"Oh, no?" There was an arrogant, teasing glint in his
eyes. "What would you have done?"

"I would have given you one hell of a fight. That's
how much I wanted you. All of you."

He pulled her lower lip between his teeth and worried
it deliciously with his tongue. "One of the things I like
most about you..." His mouth went for her neck.

"Yes?"

"Is that you always look like you've just been royally..." He finished his sentence with a gutter word that
only he could make sound sexy.

"Cooper!" Pretending to be offended, Rusty sat back
on her heels and placed her hands on her hips.

He laughed. The wonderful, rare sound of his laughter was so encouraging that she assumed an even prissier expression. He only laughed harder. His laughter
was real, not tainted by cynicism. She wanted to draw it
around her like a blanket. She wanted to bask in it as one
would the first hot day of summer. She'd made Cooper

Landry laugh. That was no small feat, particularly in the past few years. Probably few could lay claim to having made this man laugh.

His mouth was still split into a wide grin beneath his mustache. He mimicked her in an old maid's whine. "Coo-per!" Piqued by his imitation of her, she smacked his bare thigh. "Hey, it's not my fault that you've got bedroom hair and smoky brown eyes." He reached out and ran his thumb along her lower lip. "I can't help it if your mouth always looks recently kissed and begging for more; if your breasts are always aquiver."

"'Aquiver'?" she asked breathlessly as he cupped one.

"Hmm. Is it my fault that your nipples are always primed and ready?"

"In fact it is."

That, he liked. Smiling, he plucked at the dusky pearl, rolling it gently between his fingers.

"But primed and ready for what, Cooper?"

He leaned forward and, using his lips and tongue, demonstrated.

Rusty felt the familiar sensations unwinding in her midsection like a spool of silk ribbon. Sighing, she clasped his head and pushed it away from her. He looked at her in bewilderment, but didn't resist as she pressed him back against the pillows. "What are we doing?" he asked.

"I'm going to make love to you for a change."

"I thought you just did."

She shook her tousled head. At some point her ponytail had come down. "You made love to me."

"What's the difference?"

Smiling a feline smile, her eyes full of promise, she stretched out alongside him and began nibbling his neck. "Wait and see."

* * *

In the peaceful aftermath, they lay together, their arms and legs entangled. "I thought only hookers knew how to do that right." His voice was still scratchy from crying out her name, and he barely had the energy to strum her spine with his fingertips.

"Did I do it right?"

He tilted his head back and gazed down at the woman who lay sprawled across his chest. "Don't you know?"

Her eyes were glazed with love as she looked up at him and shook her head with shy uncertainty.

"That's the first time you ever...?" She nodded yes. He hissed a soft curse and drew her up for a gentle, loving kiss. "Yeah. You did it just fine," he said with a trace of humor when he finally released her lips. "Just fine."

After a long silence, Rusty asked him, "What kind of family life did you have?"

"Family life?" As he collected his thoughts, he absently rubbed his leg against her left one, ever careful not to bump the sore one. "It's been so long ago I barely remember. Practically all I remember of my dad was that he went to work every day. He was a salesman. His job finally caused a massive heart attack that killed him instantly. I was still in elementary school."

"Mother never got over being mad at him for dying prematurely and leaving her a widow. She never got over being mad at me for...existing, I guess. Anyway, all I meant to her was a liability. She had to work to support us."

"She never remarried?"

"No."

His mother had probably blamed her blameless son for that, too. Rusty could paint in the numbered spaces and get the complete picture. Cooper had grown up unloved.

It was little wonder that now, when a hand was extended to him in kindness, he bit it instead of accepting it. He didn't believe in human kindness and love. He'd never experienced them. His personal relationships had been fouled with pain, disillusionment, and betrayal.

"I joined the Marines as soon as I graduated from high school. Mother died during my first year in Nam. Breast cancer. She was the kind of woman who was too stubborn to have that lump checked before it was too late."

Rusty stroked his chin with her thumbnail, occasionally dipping it into the vertical cleft. She was filled with remorse for the lonely, unloved child he'd been. Such unhappiness. By comparison she'd had it so easy.

"My mother died, too."

"And then you lost your brother."

"Yes. Jeff."

"Tell me about him."

"He was terrific," she said with an affectionate smile. "Everybody liked him. He was friendly—the kind of person who never met a stranger. People were automatically drawn to him. He had outstanding leadership qualities. He could make people laugh. He could do everything."

"You've been reminded of that often enough."

Quickly her head popped up. "What's that supposed to mean?"

Cooper seemed to weigh the advisability of pursuing this conversation, but apparently decided in favor of it. "Doesn't your father continually hold your brother up as an example for you to follow?"

"Jeff had a promising future in real estate. My father wants that for me, too."

"But is it *your* future he wants for you, or your brother's future?"

She disengaged herself and swung her legs over the side of the bed. "I don't know what you mean."

Cooper caught a handful of her hair to keep her from leaving the bed. He came up on his knees behind her where she sat on the edge of it. "Like hell you don't, Rusty. Everything you've said about your father and brother leads me to believe that you're expected to fill Jeff's shoes."

"My father only wants me to do well."

"What *he* considers well. You're a beautiful, intelligent woman. A loving daughter. You have a career, and you're successful. Isn't that enough for him?"

"No! I mean, yes, of course it's enough. It's just that he wants me to live up to my potential."

"Or Jeff's." She tried to move away, but he held her back by her shoulders. "Like that hunting trip to Great Bear Lake."

"I told you that that was my idea, not Father's."

"But why did you feel that it was necessary to go? Why was it your responsibility to uphold the tradition he had shared with Jeff? You only went because you thought it might please your father."

"What's wrong with that?"

"Nothing. If it was strictly a gesture of self-sacrifice, of love. But by going, I think you set out to prove something to him; I think that you wanted your father to see that you're as marvelous as Jeff was."

"Well, I failed."

"That's my point!" he shouted. "You don't like hunting and fishing. So what? Why should that make you a failure?"

She managed to wrest herself free. Once she was on her feet, she spun around to face him. "You don't understand, Cooper."

"Obviously I don't. I don't see why being exactly what you are isn't enough for your father. Why do you continually have to prove yourself to him? He lost his son: unfortunate; tragic. But he's still got a daughter. And he's trying to shape her into something she isn't. You're both obsessed with Jeff. Whatever else he did, I'm fairly sure he didn't walk on water."

Rusty aimed an accusing finger at him. "You're a fine one to preach about other people's obsessions. You nurse your hurt obsessively. You actually take pleasure in your despair."

"That's nuts."

"Precisely. It's easier for you to sit up there on your mountain than it is to mix with other human beings. Then you might have to open yourself up a little, let people get a peek at the man you are inside. And that terrifies you, doesn't it? Because you might be found out. Somebody might discover that you're not the hard, cold, unfeeling bastard you pretend to be. Someone might decide that you're capable of giving and receiving love."

"Baby, I gave up on the idea of love a long time ago."

"Then what was that all about?" She gestured toward the bed.

"Sex." He made the word sound as dirty as possible.

Rusty recoiled from the ugliness of his tone, but tossed her head back proudly. "Not to me. I love you, Cooper."

"So you said."

"I meant it!"

"You were in the throes of passion when you said it. That doesn't count."

"You don't believe that I love you?"

"No. There's no such thing."

"Oh, there is." She played her trump card. "You still love your unborn child."

"Shut up."

"You grieve for it still because you loved it. You still love all those men you saw die in that prisoner-of-war camp."

"Rusty…" He came off the bed and loomed over her threateningly.

"You watched your mother spend her life nursing her anger and bitterness. She thrived on her misfortune. Do you want to waste your life like that?"

"Better that than to live like you, constantly striving to be someone you're not."

Hostility crackled between them. It was so strong that at first they didn't even notice the doorbell. It wasn't until Bill Carlson called out his daughter's name that they realized they weren't alone.

"Rusty!"

"Yes, Father." She dropped back onto the edge of the bed and started yanking on her clothes.

"Is everything okay? Whose beat-up old car is that out front?"

"I'll be right out, Father."

Cooper was pulling on his clothes with considerably more composure than she. She couldn't help but wonder if this was the first time he had found himself in an awkward situation like this, maybe with the untimely appearance of a husband.

Once they were dressed, he helped her to her feet and handed her her crutches. Together they went through the bedroom door and down the hall. Red-faced, knowing that her hair was in wild tumble and that she smelled muskily of sex, Rusty entered the living room.

Her father was impatiently pacing the hardwood floor. When he turned around and saw Cooper, his face went taut with disapproval. He treated Cooper to a frigid stare before casting his judgmental eyes on his daughter.

"I hated to let a day go by without coming to see you."

"Thank you, Father, but it really isn't necessary for you to stop by every day."

"So I see."

"You...you remember Mr. Landry."

The two men nodded to each other coolly, taking each other's measure like opposing champion warriors who would decide the outcome of a battle. Cooper kept his mouth stubbornly shut. Rusty couldn't speak; she was too embarrassed. Carlson was the first to break the stressful silence.

"Actually, this is an opportune meeting," he said. "I have something to discuss with both of you. Shall we sit down?"

"Surely," Rusty said, flustered. "I'm sorry. Uh, Cooper?" She gestured toward a chair. He hesitated, then dropped into the overstuffed armchair. His insolence grated on her raw nerves. She gave him a baleful look, but he was staring at her father. He'd watched the Gawrylow men with that same kind of suspicious caution. The memory disturbed Rusty. What correlation between them and her father was he making in his mind? She moved toward a chair near Carlson.

"What do you want to discuss with us, Father?"

"That land deal I mentioned to you a few weeks ago."

Rusty's lungs caved in. She could feel each membrane giving way, collapsing one on top of the other. Her cheeks paled, and her palms became immediately slick with nervous perspiration. A choir of funeral bells started tolling in her ears. "I thought we had that all settled."

Carlson chuckled amiably. "Not quite. But now we do. Now the investors have had a chance to put some concrete ideas on paper. They'd like to present these ideas for Mr. Landry's consideration."

"Somebody want to tell me what the hell is going on?" Cooper rudely interrupted.

"No."

"Of course." Carlson overrode his daughter's negative reply and seized the floor. In his typically genial manner, he outlined his ideas for developing the area around Rogers Gap into an exclusive ski resort.

Summing up, he said, "Before we're done, working with only the most innovative architects and builders, it will rival Aspen, Vail, Keystone, anything in the Rockies or around Lake Tahoe. In several years I'll bet we could swing the Winter Olympics our way." Leaning back in his chair and smiling expansively, he said, "Well, Mr. Landry, what do you think?"

Cooper, who hadn't so much as blinked an eye during Carlson's recital, slowly rolled off his slouching spine and came to his feet. He circled the island of furniture several times as though considering the proposal from every angle. Since he owned some of the land that would be used—Carlson had done his homework—and had been offered the salaried, figurehead position as local coordinator of the project, he stood to make a great deal of money.

Carlson glanced at his daughter and winked, assured of capitulation.

"What do I think?" Cooper repeated.

"That's what I asked," Carlson said jovially.

Cooper looked him straight in the eye. "I think *you* are full of garbage, and I think your *idea* sucks." He dumped those words in the middle of the floor like a ton of bricks, then added, "And for your information, so does your daughter."

He gave Rusty a look that should have turned her to stone. He didn't even deign to slam the door shut behind himself after he stamped out. They heard his car roar to life, then the crunch of gravel as he steered out of her driveway.

Carlson harrumphed and said, "Well, I see that I was right about him all along."

Knowing that she would never recover from the wound Cooper had inflicted on her, Rusty said dully, "You couldn't be more wrong, Father."

"He's crude."

"Honest."

"A man without ambition or social graces."

"Without pretenses."

"And apparently without morals. He took advantage of your solitude and confinement."

She laughed softly. "I don't remember exactly who dragged whom into the bedroom, but he certainly didn't force me into bed with him."

"So you *are* lovers?"

"Not anymore," she said tearfully.

Cooper thought she had betrayed him, too, just like that other woman, Melody. He thought she had been her father's instrument, using bedroom tactics to turn a profit. He would never forgive her, because he didn't believe that she loved him.

"You've been his lover all this time? Behind my back?"

She started to point out that at the ripe old age of twenty-seven she shouldn't have to account to her father for her private life. But what was the use? What did it matter? The starch had gone out of her. She felt sapped of strength, of energy, of the will to live.

"When we were in Canada, yes. We became lovers.

When he left my hospital room that day, he went home and hasn't been back since. Not until this afternoon."

"Then apparently he has more sense than I gave him credit for. He realizes that the two of you are completely incompatible. Like most women, you're looking at the situation through a pink fog of romance. You're letting your emotions rule you instead of your head. I thought you were above that female frailty."

"Well, I'm not, Father. A female is what I happen to be. And I have all the frailties, as well as all the strengths, that go with being a woman."

He came to his feet and crossed the room. He gave her a conciliatory hug. She was standing on her crutches so he didn't notice how stiffly she held herself in resistance to his embrace. "I can see that Mr. Landry has upset you again. He truly is a scoundrel to have said what he did about you. You're better off without him, Rusty, believe me.

"However," he continued briskly, "we won't let his lack of charm keep us from doing business with him. I intend to move forward with our plans in spite of his objections to them."

"Father, I beg you—"

He laid a finger against her lips. "Hush, now. Let's not talk anymore tonight. Tomorrow you'll feel better. You're still emotionally overwrought. Having surgery so soon after the plane crash probably wasn't such a good idea. It's perfectly understandable that you're not quite yourself. One of these days you'll come to your senses and return to being the old Rusty. I have every confidence that you won't disappoint me."

He kissed her forehead. "Good night, my dear. Look over this proposal," he said, withdrawing a file folder from his lizard briefcase and laying it on the coffee table.

"I'll drop by tomorrow morning, eager to hear your opinion."

After he left, Rusty locked up her house and returned to the bedroom. She bathed, languishing in a hot bubble bath. She'd taken one every day since the doctor had said it was okay to get her leg wet. But once she was dried, lotioned, and powdered, she still hadn't rid her body of the traces of Cooper's lovemaking.

She was pleasantly sore between her thighs. The blemish he'd left on her breast still showed up rosily, as indelible as a tattoo. Her lips were tender and puffy. Every time she wet them with her tongue, she could taste him.

Looking at herself in the mirror, she admitted that he was right. She *did* look as if she'd just been engaged in rowdy lovemaking.

Her bed seemed as large and empty as a football field during the off-season. The linens still smelled like Cooper. In her mind she relived every moment they'd spent together that afternoon—the giving and taking of pleasure; the exchange of erotic dialogue. Even now, his whispered, naughty words echoed through her mind, causing her to flush hotly all over.

She yearned for him and could find no comfort in the thought that her life would be a series of empty days and joyless nights like this one.

She'd have her work, of course.

And her father.

Her wide circle of friends.

Her social activities.

It wouldn't be enough.

There was a great big hole where the man she loved should be.

She sat up in bed and clutched the sheet against her, as

though the realization she'd just had would get away from
her if she didn't hold on to it until she could act upon it.

Her choices were clear. She could either roll over and
play dead. Or she could fight for him. Her main adversary would be Cooper himself. He was mule-headed and
mistrustful. But eventually she would wear him down and
convince him that she loved him and that he loved her.

Yes, he did! He could deny it until he gasped his dying
breath, but she would never believe that he didn't love
her—because right after her father had made that hateful
disclosure, just before Cooper's face had hardened with
contempt, she'd seen incredible pain there. She wouldn't
have the power to hurt him that badly unless he loved her.

She lay back down, glowing in her resolution and
knowing exactly what she had to do the following morning.

Her father was taken off-guard. A strategist as shrewd
as General Patton, he had slipped up. He hadn't expected
a surprise attack.

When she made her unannounced appearance in his
office the next morning, he glanced up from his highly
polished, white lacquered desk and exclaimed, "Why,
Rusty! What…what a lovely surprise."

"Good morning, Father."

"What are you doing out? Not that the reason matters.
I'm delighted to see you up and around."

"I had to see you and didn't want to wait to be worked
into your busy schedule."

He chose to ignore the note of censure in her voice
and walked around his desk with his hands outstretched
to take hers. "You're feeling much better—I can tell. Did
Mrs. Watkins offer you coffee?"

"She did, but I declined."

He regarded her casual clothes. "Apparently you're not going to your office."

"No, I'm not."

He cocked his head to one side, obviously waiting for an explanation. When none was forthcoming he asked, "Where are your crutches?"

"In my car."

"You drove here? I didn't think—"

"Yes, I drove myself. I wanted to walk in here under my own steam and stand on my own two feet."

He backed away from her and propped his hips against the edge of his desk. Casually he crossed his ankles and folded his arms over his middle. Rusty recognized the stance. It was the tactical one he assumed when he was backed into a corner but didn't want his rivals to know that he was. "I take it you read the proposal." With a smooth motion of his head, he indicated the folder she was carrying under her arm.

"I did."

"And?"

She ripped the folder in two. Tossing the remnants on the glassy surface of his desk, she said, "Lay off Cooper Landry. Drop the Rogers Gap project. Today."

He laughed at her sophomoric gesture and shrugged helplessly, spreading his arms wide in appeal. "It's a little late for that, Rusty dear. The ball has already started rolling."

"Stop it from rolling."

"I can't."

"Then you're in a real jam with these investors you collected, Father—" she leaned forward "—because I'm going to privately and publicly resist you on this. I'll have every conservationist group in the country beating down your door in protest. I don't think you want that."

"Rusty, for Heaven's sake, come to your senses," he hissed.

"I did. Sometime between midnight and 2:00 a.m., I realized that there's something much more important to me than any real-estate deal. Even more important to me than winning your approval."

"Landry?"

"Yes." Her voice rang with conviction. She was not to be swayed.

But Carlson tried. "You'd give up everything you've worked for to have him?"

"Loving Cooper doesn't take anything away from what I've done in the past or will do in the future. Love this strong can only embellish, not tear down."

"Do you realize how ridiculous you sound?"

She didn't take offense. Instead she laughed. "I guess I do. Lovers often babble nonsensically, don't they?"

"This is no laughing matter, Rusty. If you do this, it's an irreversible decision. Once you give up your position here, that's it."

"I don't think so, Father," she said, calling his bluff. "Think how bad it would be for business if you fired your most effective employee." She produced a key from the pocket of her nylon windbreaker. "To my office." She slid the key across his desk. "I'll be taking an indefinite leave of absence."

"You're making a fool of yourself."

"I made a fool of myself at Great Bear Lake. I did that for love, too." She turned on her heels and headed for the door.

"Where are you going?" Bill Carlson barked. He wasn't accustomed to someone walking out on him.

"To Rogers Gap."

"And do what?"

Rusty faced her father. She loved him. Very much. But she could no longer sacrifice her own happiness for his. With staunch conviction she said, "I'm going to do something that Jeff could never do: I'm going to have a baby."

Fourteen

~~~

Rusty stood on the cliff and breathed deeply of the cool, crisp air. She never tired of the scenery. It was constant, and yet ever changing. Today the sky was like a blue china bowl turned upside down over the earth. Snow still capped the mountain peaks against the horizon. The trees ranged in color from the blue-green of the evergreens to the delicate green of trees on the verge of spring budding.

"Aren't you cold?"

Her husband came up behind her and wrapped his arms around her. She snuggled against him. "Not now. How's the foal?"

"He's having breakfast—to his and his mother's mutual contentment."

She smiled and tilted her head to one side. He inched down the turtleneck of her sweater and kissed her beneath her ear. "How's the other new mother on the place?"

"I'm not a new mother yet." She glowed with pleasure as he ran his large hands over her swollen abdomen.

"Looks that way to me."

"You think this new figure of mine is amusing, don't you?" She frowned at him over her shoulder, but it was hard to maintain that expression when he was gazing at her with such evident love.

"I love it."

"I love you."

They kissed. "I love you, too," he whispered when he lifted his mouth off hers. Words he had found impossible to say before, now came easily to his lips. She had taught him how to love again.

"You had no choice."

"Yeah, I remember that night you showed up on my threshold looking as bedraggled as a homeless kitten in a rainstorm."

"Considering what I'd just come through I thought I looked pretty good."

"I didn't know whether to kiss you or paddle you."

"You did both."

"Yeah, but the paddling didn't come until much later."

They laughed together, but he was serious when he said, "No fooling, I couldn't believe you drove all that way alone through that kind of weather. Didn't you listen to your car radio? Didn't you hear the storm reports? You escorted in the first heavy snowstorm of the season. Every time I think about it, I shudder." He pulled her closer, crossing his hands over her breasts and nuzzling his face in her hair.

"I had to see you right then, before I lost my nerve. I would have gone through hell to get here."

"You very nearly did."

"At the time, it didn't seem so bad. Besides, I had survived a plane crash. What was a little snow?"

"Hardly a 'little snow.' And driving with your injured leg too."

She shrugged dismissively. To their delight the gesture caused her breasts to rise and fall against his hands.

Murmuring his appreciation, he covered them completely and massaged them gently, aware of the discomfort they'd been giving her lately as a result of her pregnancy.

"Tender?" he asked.

"A little."

"Want me to stop?"

"Not on your life."

Satisfied with her answer, he propped his chin on the top of her head and continued to massage her.

"I'm glad the operations on my leg have to be postponed until after the baby gets here," she said. "That is, if you don't mind looking at my unsightly scar."

"I always close my eyes when we're making love."

"I know. So do I."

"Then how do you know mine are closed?" he teased. They laughed again, because neither of them closed their eyes while they were making love; they were too busy looking at each other, looking at themselves together, and gauging each other's level of passion.

As they watched a hawk lazily circling in downward spirals, Cooper asked, "Remember what you said to me the instant I opened the door that night?"

"I said, 'You're going to let me love you, Cooper Landry, if it kills you.'"

He chuckled at the memory and his heart grew warm, as it had that night, when he thought about the courage it had taken for her to come to him and make that bizarre announcement. "What would you have done if I had slammed the door in your face?"

"But you didn't."

"Assuming I had."

She pondered that for a moment. "I'd have barged in anyway, stripped off all my clothes, pledged everlasting love and devotion, and threatened you with violence if you didn't love me back."

"That's what you did."

"Oh, yeah," she said around a giggle. "Well, I'd have just kept on doing that until you stopped refusing."

He planted his lips against her ear. "You went down on bended knee and asked me to marry you and give you a baby."

"How well your memory serves you."

"And that's not all you did while you were on your knees."

She turned in his arms and said sweetly, "I didn't hear you complaining. Or were all those garbled phrases coming out of your mouth complaints?"

He laughed, throwing back his head and releasing a genuine burst of humor—something he did frequently now. There were times when he lapsed into the moody, withdrawn man he'd been. His mind carried him back to haunting phases of his life where she couldn't go. Her reward lay in the fact that she could bring him out again. Patiently, lovingly, she was eradicating his disturbing memories and replacing them with happy ones.

Now she kissed his strong, tanned throat and said, "We'd better go in and get ready for our trip to L.A."

They made one round-trip a month to the city, during which they spent two or three days at Rusty's house. While there, they ate in fine restaurants, went to concerts and movies, shopped, and even attended an occasional social gathering. Rusty stayed in touch with her old friends, but was delighted with the new friendships Cooper and she had cultivated as a couple. When he wanted to, he could ooze charm and engage in conversation on a wide range of subjects.

Also while they were there, she handled business matters that demanded her attention. Since her marriage, she'd been promoted to vice-president in her father's real-estate company.

Cooper worked as a volunteer counselor in a veterans' therapy group. He'd initiated several self-help programs that were being emulated in other parts of the country.

Now, with their arms around each other's waist, they walked back toward the house that was nestled in a grove of pines. It overlooked a spectacular valley. Horses and cattle grazed in the mountain pastures below the timberline.

"You know," he said as they entered their glass-walled bedroom, "talking about that night you arrived has gotten me all hot and bothered." He peeled off his shirt.

"You're always hot and bothered." Rusty peeled her sweater over her head. She never wore a bra when they were at home alone.

Eyeing her enlarged breasts, he unsnapped his jeans and swaggered toward her. "And it's always your fault."

"Do you still desire me, even though I'm misshapen?" She gestured at her rounded tummy.

For an answer, he took her hand and pulled it into his open fly. She squeezed his full manhood. He groaned softly. "I desire you." Bending his knees, he kissed one of her creamy breasts. "As long as you're you, I'll love you, Rusty."

"I'm glad," she sighed. "Because, just like after the plane crash, you're stuck with me."

* * * * *